THE
MORCAI
BATTALION

DIANA PALMER

THE MORCAI BATTALION

Refreshed version of THE MORCAI BATTALION,
revised by the Author.

LUNA™

www.LUNA-Books.com

LUNA™

THE MORCAI BATTALION

ISBN-13: 978-0-373-80289-0
ISBN-10: 0-373-80289-7

This is the revised text of the work, which was first published by Manor House, Inc. in 1980 under the name Susan S. Kyle.

www.LUNA-Books.com

Printed in U.S.A.

Dear Reader,

This novel was forty-two years in the making. I'm not kidding. When I originally wrote it, there was no *Star Trek,* no *Star Wars,* no home computers, no cell phones, no women in forward positions in combat, no women at West Point or VMI, and no holographs. I was seventeen years old, living at home, and my dad, who taught electronics and was the smartest human being I ever knew, was my technical advisor.

I tried for years to sell *The Morcai Battalion.* I got rejected for having a woman in a mentally neutered military that allowed women in high command and forward combat positions. Frustrated, I took out the all-woman Amazon combat units and let Madeline Ruszel be a ship's doctor. That seemed to do the trick. I sold it, finally, and to my amazement, in 1979. The book was published in 1980 by Manor Books. The company subsequently went out of business, and all my efforts to have the book reprinted were in vain. Twenty-five years went by. I loved my original concept. The world had changed. So I thought, why not try one more time.

In 2006 LUNA Books offered me the opportunity to rewrite it, and put my original ideas back in. I was ecstatic! Thank you, Harlequin and Silhouette and LUNA Books, for giving *The Morcai Battalion* not only a second chance at life, but also for allowing me to do two sequels to it in the future. It is truly a dream come true to have this book, which was written throughout such a large part of my life, back in print and expanded and to see these characters, whom I love dearly (well, with the exception of the really bad guys,) draw the breath of life one more time. My dad would be so proud!

Keep in mind that the technology mentioned in the book did not exist at the original writing. I have tried to mix the old ideas with the new innovations and keep the feel of the published novel of 1980. I have stayed with my original research to be true to the history of the novel. In the second book of the trilogy, however, the sky's the limit!

As always, readers, I am your number one fan. Thank you for giving my only science-fiction novel a reading. It truly was a labor of love to write. Somewhere, deep in my soul, is a combat soldier who was never healthy enough to serve. Armed Forces everywhere, you have my greatest respect and gratitude for the work you do.

Susan Kyle
a.k.a. Diana Palmer

To my late father, W. O. Spaeth, a professor of science who believed in the peaceful colonization of space, and who was my technical advisor for this novel from 1963, when the first chapter was written, to 1980, when the final draft was first published.

And to my mother, Eloise Cliatt Spaeth, who didn't understand space but knew much about human nature from her nursing career, and who also advised.

And to my only sibling, my sister, Dannis Belle Spaeth Cole, who encouraged my dreams of publication and shared with me many cold nights and much discomfort with telescopes over the years as we studied space from a far more distant vantage point than we would have wished.

And to my excellent biology professors at Piedmont College, Demorest, Georgia, Rob Wainberg and Carlos Camo, who taught me incredible things about plants and animals and the chemical composition of the universe (and who were both amazed, I'm sure, that I graduated college at all). Thanks, guys!

1

Children were crying all around the chief exobiologist of the SSC starship *Bellatrix* and the woman in her green Terravegan uniform wanted to cry with them. In ten years with the Tri-Fleet's Strategic Space Command, Lieutenant Commander Madeline Ruszel had never seen such wanton slaughter.

Terramer had been a trial peace colony in the New Territory of the galaxy, populated by clones of races representing one hundred twenty federated planets. A Rojok squadron had managed to reduce it to a smoldering ball of dust in a matter of minutes. An unprovoked attack against a defenseless continent of colonists. A dream of peace gone black in the sleep of treachery. She glared at the turmoil around her. The legendary code of ethics of the Rojok field marshal, Chacon, had gone up in smoke, along with ten million colonists.

She finished the sutures in a quick cytoplasm job on a young Jebob national and gave him a reassuring smile while she checked his vital signs with the bionic mediscanner built into the creamy flesh of her wrist. The scanner, standard SSC issue, contained its own diagnostic tools, medication synthesizer and modem. Her patient's thin, blue-skinned face tried to return the smile, but even her strongest painkillers hadn't assuaged the agony of the massive radiation burns on his young body.

She stood up and eyed her medic teams. "Let's speed it up!" she called to them, brushing a long strand of auburn hair away from her sweaty temple. "I want this group of pilgrims evacuated in ten minutes!"

She avoided the pressured glares of her team. "I know, I know," she murmured, "what do you think we are, a bunch of bloody magicians?"

They were working against time trying to patch up what few survivors the shoot-and-strafe air attack had left. Human and alien children wept softly in a nightmare chorus, looking for parents they'd never see again. The children, she thought, were the worst. The radiation was most damaging to young flesh, and of a kind the Rojoks hadn't used in the early days of the warfare. It was highly resistant to conventional treatment.

She joined Dr. Strick Hahnson at the prefab communications dome that the engineering squad had assembled in minutes, and leaned wearily against the transparent hyperglas.

"We're running out of *morphadrenin,*" she told the husky blond human life-science chief. "Some of these younger ones won't make it, regardless. Strick, what in God's name did the Rojoks hope to gain by this?"

"Ask their commander-in-chief, Chacon," he replied harshly. "We've got worse problems. The comtech can't get through to HQ and I can't find Stern."

She glanced up at him. "He went scouting for the sci-archaeology group. I had hoped he'd take some ship police with him, but you know the captain. Strick, the Jaakob Spheres were on that ship, not to mention two VIP Centaurian diplomatic observers. The Rojoks may have taken more than lives here."

He nodded wearily. His blond hair was wet with sweat, and damp splotches made patterns on his green uniform. He looked worse than she felt.

"How many casualties?" he asked.

"About three hundred wounded to lift, if that's what you mean; and those are just the aliens under my jurisdiction. Human survivors number about two hundred more."

"Where are we going to put them?" he asked idly, glancing up at the gleaming orange sky where radiation danced in pale blue patterns. "What about that message, son?" he asked the young comtech in the dome.

"The interference isn't clearing, sir. I still can't get through." The boy's head lifted. "And I can't raise Captain Stern, either. He doesn't answer my commbeam."

Strick glanced down at the scowl on his slender companion's face. "We'll give him five more minutes."

Her pale green eyes swept over the carnage and the ruins of the small jem-hued shops and marble streets to the wooded area beyond. "If anything's happened to those Centaurian diplomats..." She sighed heavily. "The Council would have had a bloody war of its own holding the Holconcom back, in any case. Now, with two of their own people involved, there's no way."

"Which means we'll finally have a half chance of winning this damned war," he told her.

"Amen." She watched the medics loading casualties into the self-propelled transparent ambulifts. "Watch my boys, Strick. I'm going to find Stern."

* * *

Holt Stern strode out of the green tangle of the forest into the clearing where the main settlement had been. He brushed against a spiny moga tree and a ripple of pain shuddered down his arm. Holding it, he glanced around the camp at the neat rows of prefab medical domes where his medical specialists were concentrated.

The personnel were familiar. He knew them. But something about the maze of green uniforms worn by the Strategic Space Command disturbed him. His lapse of memory disturbed him more. It was as if his past life were gone, and only the present remained. And the throbbing in his temple was especially unpleasant.

A rustle of leaves made him freeze at the edge of the forest.

He turned to find the face that went with the husky feminine voice. Madeline Ruszel paused beside a *drekma* tree. The exobiology chief was flushed with fatigue. Beads of sweat ran down from the mass of auburn waves at her temple to the corners of her full young mouth. She frowned up at him, marring the Grecian delicacy of her face.

"Are you okay?" she asked professionally.

"Yeah. Sure. I just took a pretty hard blow on the temple. Fell over some wreckage." He glanced toward the forest and a hand went to his brow. "I found the sci-archaeo group. Their ship crashed about seventy meters away. Better send out some lifts. The Rojoks left them in pretty bad shape."

"Crashed?" Her pale eyes widened. "Stern, the Spheres?"

"I didn't take time to check," he said flatly. "The diplomatic observers are damned near dead. Better get moving before they're all gone to glory."

"On my way." She eyed him. "Stern, the observers—two of them were Centaurian, weren't they?"

He took a minute to answer. The sound of the word gave him

sudden chills. "I only saw one. Like I said, I didn't take time to check too closely. Move out, will you?"

She started to say something, but she turned suddenly and broke into a run toward her medics.

Stern strode quickly toward the comtech's hut. "Report, Mister," he said.

"Still no luck, sir," the boy replied. "Even with my boosters I can't even weed out the interference between here and HQ. There's no way to get a message home until it lets up."

Stern's eyebrows jerked. He turned his gaze to the camp, carelessly observing the medics. Sensations tugged at his memory, but they were too vague to grasp. The sight of the bodies, mutilated by massive doses of radiation, didn't affect him at all. Not even those of the children. Why should it? he thought. They were only clones. Duplicates of a dozen alien races whose originals didn't have the guts for a colonization attempt in the New Territory.

"Sickening, isn't it?" Dr. Strick Hahnson asked, ambling up at his elbow. "The last hope of a war-torn galaxy, gone down into the dust of treachery. How long did it take those ten planetary federations to agree to this? Five, ten years? It only took the damned Rojoks one solar hour to atomize it."

"Stow the poetry," Stern told him. "This is a rescue hop, not a—"

"Sir!" the comtech interrupted. "I've got a bogie! She's two AU and closing like a trambeam!"

"Configuration?" Stern asked quickly. "Is she a Rojok, Mister?"

"I can't classify her, sir." The comtech searched his readout screen. "She's making speeds I don't believe, and she scans too light to be a standard warship."

Stern sighed angrily. "Well, can't you make identification from her commbeam?"

"She isn't carrying one, sir. Her signals are too quick for my analy-banks. I'm sorry, Captain, but this one's beyond my experience. I've never read anything like her."

"Keep trying." Stern raised his eyes upward. The skies were brighter than ever with spreading blue glowing radiation. Megabeam radiation, settling on the scarred surface of the planet.

"Hurry it up!" he called to the medics. "Leave the Jebobs and Altairians for now—we'll send a relief ship back for them. Concentrate on the casualties that are ready to lift!"

He turned away from the shocked looks of the medics and back to the comtech. "What about it, Jennings?"

The young comtech shook his head. "She's positioning to assume orbit, sir."

"Beam Higgins on the *Bellatrix*. Tell him to throw up his screens and prime his main batteries. As soon as he can make a visual ID, I want it. And if she's a Rojok—" he thought for a minute "—if she's a Rojok, tell him to get the hell out of here and get the data to Lawson at HQ. Got that?"

"Yes, sir."

Stern strode out through the makeshift medical prefabs, where specialists in sweat-soaked uniforms were fighting time and the lack of supplies to save life.

"Stern!"

He whirled at the urgency in Madeline Ruszel's normally calm voice, putting a hand to his temple. The pain was back. The tall young officer slowed down from a run just in time to avoid colliding with him.

"We've got it…the sci-archaeo group," she panted. "The medtechs are bringing them in now. Stern, you'd better come with me."

"Strick," he called to Hahnson, "get your people together.

Jennings," he told the comtech, "I want an ID on that bogie the second you get it. Okay, Maddie, let's go!"

"It's the Centaurian boy," she said when they were out of earshot. "He's wearing the blue and gold colors of Alamantimichar."

Stern felt his neck hairs bristle. "The Royal Clan? My God!"

"That's not all. His sister was with him, according to the ship passenger roster, and she's missing. And so are the Jaakob Spheres. Two of the sci-archaeo scientists were subjected to mind taps. They're little more than vegetables. Two others are missing. The Centaurian boy's much worse."

His hand went to his dark, wavy hair. "There'll be hell to pay now. Those Spheres contained the DNA of every member race in the Tri-Galaxy Council. If the Rojoks have them…"

"The possibilities are endless." She stopped at one of the ambulifts. "Look at this."

Stern leaned a hand against the transparent cylinder and looked in through the blue antiseptic mist. The Centaurian boy inside looked as though someone had taken an old-fashioned straight razor to him, from head to toe. He'd been tortured.

Stern watched him curiously. He was a member of an alien race called the Cehn-Tahr from the central star system near the Algomerian Sector. First contact prompted Terravegan officials to link them with the young Alpha Centauri system near old Earth and call them Centaurians. The name stuck. That, Stern recalled, was the joke of the millennium. These aliens were an ancient race, which legend linked to Cashto, the cat god of Eridanus. Their emperor, Tnurat Alamantimichar, had formed a commando unit called the Holconcom and gone out to conquer neighboring star systems. To date, he had one hundred fifty of them under regional governors with democratic parliaments.

The alien boy seemed completely human except for the pale golden skin that peeked out from the sleeves and neck of his one-piece suit. His ears, his body, were like any human's. He had no tail or fur. But then his head turned, and Stern had to fight the urge to back away. The huge elongated eyelids opened over great black orbs that sent chills the length of his body. They weren't human eyes. They were the eyes of some human cat, slit-pupiled, unblinking and tortured with pain.

"Don't let it bother you," Madeline said gently. "They have that effect on all of us when we see them for the first time. It's the eyes."

"Cat-eyes," he murmured, but the chills still came. He wondered at his own reaction. The sight shouldn't have frightened him. He'd seen textdiscs of the race often enough.

"Not precisely," she said. "Cat-eyes don't change color. Centaurians' do. Each color stands for a separate emotion. There's blue for concern, green for amusement, gray for curiosity, brown for anger—that's a generalization, of course. It's more complicated when several emotions are at play."

"His are black," he remarked.

"That means pain and/or death. I'll explain someday. Stern, he needs medication. It's a breach of protocol that carries an automatic court-martial if I give it. I don't have a choice."

"Go ahead," he said. "I'll sit on the hot seat with you."

She smiled up at him. "Thanks."

She reached inside the ambulift and laid the bionic wrist scanner against the boy's thin chest, activating the compact unit's drug bank with her free hand. Pressing lightly, the laserdot was triggered to hammer the drug deep inside the frail chest. She withdrew her arm.

The boy's eyes dilated. *"Creshcam,"* he whispered softly. Then, all at once, the great cat-eyes closed gently and his chest went flat.

She slammed the wrist scanner back through the hatch of the ambulift and laid it against the boy's throat. An eternity of seconds went by before she straightened wearily and, glancing at Stern, shook her head.

"Captain!" the comtech sang out. "The intruder's visual! She's a Centaurian warship, and I'm getting signals from a scout about to leave her!"

"Tell Higgins to keep his distance," Stern called back. "We can't take on the Rojoks and the Centaurians at the same time. And get the ship police out here!"

"Yes, sir!"

"Now just how the hell did that Centaurian ship know what happened here," Stern murmured thoughtfully, "when we haven't even been able to get word to HQ?"

"Beats me," Madeline said wearily. "I just hope this is a congenial group of Centaurian regulars. If it isn't…"

"Go find Strick," he told her. "He's the only man we've got who can translate that cat-eyes garble. He served with them once."

"On my way."

"Jennings!"

"Yes, sir. Scout confirmed. She's on a descent course."

"SPs, line up on my flank," Stern told the ship police as they rushed into view. "*Greshams* out, on heavy tranquillizer force. Fire only at my order." He turned to the medics. "The rest of you, into the scouts and back to the ship. Move!"

The tension was electric as the taciturn men took their positions. The medics, with their charges in the ambulifts, scattered into the nearby scouts. Hurriedly they secured the hatches and began to gun the lightweight crafts up into the radiation-marked skies.

The pain in his temples subsiding now, Stern drew his *Gresham* and gripped the jeweled *emerillium* power pack tightly in his hand as the alien scout came into view overhead.

She was sleek and her burnt-copper hull drew the mingled sun and radiation onto a blemishless surface only to scatter the light in strange patterns against the ground.

With unnerving precision, her pilot set her down in the middle of the remaining prefab medical domes and ambulifts. Noiseless until now, a soft hum radiated outward from the bubble dome and suddenly died.

Madeline swept through the ship police to stand beside Stern. She was breathless, and her long hair whipped unkempt around the high collar of her uniform. "Strick's on…his way," she panted.

Stern nodded. The tension was too much for words. The responsibility was more. Centaurians were known for certain barbaric tendencies when members of their race were threatened. But this ship, he already knew, was too advanced to be part of the Centaurian regular army. It was more suited to commando missions, and if his growing suspicious proved true—

A knifelike slit appeared in the smooth hull of the scout. Suddenly nine red-uniformed Centaurians poured out of it, single-file, to converge into a tight, ultramilitary formation around it.

"Those uniforms," Madeline whispered. "My God, Stern, they're…!"

"Holconcom!" He felt chills run the length of his body at the sound of the word on his own lips. "Drop the *Greshams!*" he barked at his SPs. "They're allies!"

The Holconcom. The peacekeeping right arm of the Centaurian Dectat. A force that no military unit in the galaxy could match or best, if legends held any truth.

"Convince me," Madeline said quietly. "Just because the Centaurian government gave them absolute authority over all the services in wartime, and Lawson requested their help with investigative missions against Rojok positions, doesn't make them allies."

"Stow it," he snapped. His eyes were on a tenth alien just leaving the ship—a Centaurian in a red uniform. But this one had a single gold emblem on the high collar.

This one was taller than his comrades, and he alone wore a mustache and a beard, short, black and violently contrasting with his pale golden skin. He carried himself with the arrogance of authority, and even at the distance Stern could feel the raw power of his eyes.

The alien glanced around him carelessly, then gestured to his men. They stood at rigid attention while he strode forward, straight toward Stern. As he approached, the brown anger in his huge, elongated cat-eyes became evident and threatening under black eyebrows. He stopped just in front of the humans.

Stern presented the Holconcom officer with a rigid, military salute. The alien returned it, but without respect, then stood quietly, watching him.

"I don't speak Centaurian!" Stern said, raising his voice as if the alien were deaf rather than accustomed to a different combination of syllables. "You'll have to...!"

"I seek two survivors," the alien replied in crisply perfect, unaccented Terravegan Standard English. "A Centaurian youth and a female of our species."

Stern's muscles went taut under his uniform.

"The boy didn't make it," he replied slowly. "We found no Centaurian female."

The huge eyes began to darken even more. "Take me to the boy."

Stern was prepared for anger when they gathered around the ambulift—or he thought he was. But when the Centaurian got a close look at that frail body, with its evidence of torture, he seemed to implode.

"Maliche mazur!" he roared, and Stern could have sworn that the ground rumbled under his feet. In that one, harsh cry was a kind of grief he didn't remember ever experiencing. A grief that came without tears, but was greater than if it had.

The alien whirled on Stern, a predator looking for prey. "The other observers. Are they alive?"

"Technically," Stern replied quietly.

"You will have them in your Admiral Lawson's office ten minutes after you touch down at the Tri-Galaxy Fleet HQ on Trimerius," he told the captain. "With them, you will present yourself, your chief medic and your ship historian."

Stern started to speak, but the alien silenced him with a cold narrowing of his dark eyes. "But for now, I will know which of your medical personnel dared to lay hands on this boy!"

Madeline Ruszel's face flushed. She'd expected to catch hell for her interference, but she'd done as her code of ethics demanded. Squaring her shoulders, she stepped forward, staring up at the Centaurian officer. "I did," she said curtly. "The alternative was to do nothing to ease his suffering. I gave him a drug that made his passage easier. Nothing more. If you consider that an atrocity, sir, you are welcome to present charges against me."

"My pleasure," the alien replied icily. "Consider it done. By *Simali-char,* what manner of creatures are you humans, that you dress your women as men and send them into combat to die?"

"Barbarians," Madeline said sweetly. "Sir," she added in a drawl guaranteed to provoke him.

The alien stared at her for a long moment, during which she mentally reviewed what she knew about Centaurians to make sure they didn't eat humans.

The officer turned away. "Komak!" he called sharply.

A younger, red-uniformed Centaurian ran to his commanding officer and saluted. "Yes, Commander?"

"Take Marcon's body to the ship and have it urned." His tone was deceptively gentle. His eyes were unnerving to Madeline. "Inform Tnurat Alamantimichar and the Council of his death, and of Lyceria's capture."

"It will be done as you say."

The tall alien moved out into the throng of ambulifts. His gaze missed nothing as they wandered restlessly around the ruins. "These casualties will be lifted, of course?" he asked deliberately.

Madeline saluted, hating herself for what she was about to say. But her sense of outrage was stronger than her sense of loyalty. "Sir, Captain Stern ordered us to leave them here...."

"Yes, I did," Stern growled, glaring at her. His head throbbed suddenly. He touched his hand to it. "We don't have the space to lift them," he added tightly. "The damned Rojoks swiped the Jaakob Spheres, in addition to the carnage they did here. I have to get the surviving sci-archaeo scientists and their data banks back to HQ. These clones—" he emphasized the word as if it were dirty "—will have to wait."

The alien glared down at him. "A life is a life," he said coldly. "You will not leave these wounded behind. I will transport them myself."

"Transport them, hell!" Stern's dark eyes narrowed. "I'm in command here. This is a Terravegan Strategic Space Command rescue operation, and you don't touch those pilgrims without authorization from the Tri-Galaxy Council!"

"By *Simalichar!*" The alien's eyes dilated and darkened even more. "You have no authority here save what I allow you! The Holconcom are here by Council request."

"I don't care if the tooth fairy sent you," Stern countered hotly. "This is my operation and until I get authorization from SSC HQ, it's going to be handled my way!"

"Mister," the alien said irritably, "you are a pain in the…so you need authorization, do you?" he added. "I'll show you my authorization. Holconcom!"

Even before the sharp command died on the air, Stern found himself surrounded by nine red-uniformed Centaurians in attack formation, slightly crouching, with eyes that chilled like a fever. A soft, low growl began to rise from the unit. It made the hair on the back of Stern's neck stand up.

"This," the Centaurian officer said shortly, "is my authorization. Interfere at your own risk."

Stern palmed his *Gresham* and activated it. "Your choice," he replied.

"Hold it! Hold it!" Strick Hahnson came puffing up, stepping out of nowhere to get between the two antagonists. "Stern, put up the *Gresham,*" he said breathlessly. "You're outranked, and if you need verification for that, I can give it. I fought with this officer in the Elyrian uprising. Captain Holt Stern, this is Dtimun, commander-in-chief of the Holconcom."

Stern hesitated, but only for an instant, before he deactivated the *Gresham* and put it away. The throbbing started again in his temples.

"I know you, Strick Hahnson," Dtimun said in recognition, and extended his arm. The darkness in his eyes had paled into a warm shade of light brown.

Hahnson gripped forearms with the alien. "I know you, Dtimun. You carry your years well."

"At the moment, they lie heavily upon me. Marcon is dead. Lyceria is almost certainly a captive of the Rojoks. And your captain," he growled, eyeing Stern, "proposes the desertion of these survivors, most of whom are Jebob and Altairian nationals, allies of the Centaurian Empire. The Rojoks will most certainly come back to finish what they started here, and these wounded will be slaughtered. I will not have an interplanetary incident on my hands because of one officer's warped sense of duty. I will transport them aboard the *Morcai*." He turned to his men, who were still crouching, still faintly growling. *"Holconcom, degrom c'hamas!"*

The Holconcom stood erect at once, spread out among the ambulifts, and began to move them toward the Centaurian scout.

"Now, just hold it a minute!" Stern began.

Hahnson caught his arm and drew him quickly aside, with Madeline right beside him. She hadn't said a word, too angry to open her mouth at the treatment she'd received from the alien.

"Holt, there's been enough killing," he said gently. "Dtimun was fond of Marcon, and his temper is legend. He'll call the Holconcom down on you for little more than breathing. Let it go."

Stern sighed with frustration. His eyes went past Dtimun to the clones in the ambulifts. Something stirred inside him, remembering the alien's words. A life was a life—but, even an artificially created one? Was it entitled to the same rights as a naturally born being? For a moment, a soft compassion touched the eyes that lingered on the tortured bodies of the alien children. Then, with the returning pain in his head, it was gone.

"You read too damned many space legends, Strick," he told Hahnson. "They're just a bunch of cat-eyes to me. But all right. All right, dammit, I don't have time to argue. I've got to get my people back home before the Rojoks come back and catch us on the ground. Medics! Let's move out!"

Stern walked away.

Madeline looked up at Hahnson quietly. "He's not himself," she said. "I had to tell the Holconcom commander that he was planning to abandon these wounded. I couldn't live with myself otherwise."

He put a gentle hand on her shoulder and smiled. "It's okay, kid," he said, using the pet name that was against regulations.

She grinned up at him. "You're a nice old man."

He chuckled. "I'm only ten years older than you, hotshot," he returned.

She started to reply, but the alien commander was suddenly looking at her. The impact of his eyes was a little frightening, even to an exobiologist who specialized in Cularian medicine, to which group Centaurians belonged. She'd studied Centaurians in textdiscs in medical school. But as she was learning, textdiscs were no match for personal encounters. She found him intimidating.

Odd, the sudden pull of her mind, as if it was being examined. She shook herself. She was definitely getting fanciful, and she had work to do. She turned and went back to the ambutubes, doing what she could to sedate the most wounded.

2

The labyrinth interior of the Rojok vessel was buzzing with activity. Lyceria of Clan Alamantimichar sat quietly in her temporary quarters watching crewmen dash past the magnetized transparent cell from which there was no escape.

Her slender hand touched a dark blue bruise on the golden silk of her arm. She could control the pain, but not her rage at such rough treatment. Thoughts of her brother made the rage near unbearable. They assumed that she did not know what had been done to him. The fools did not know that the Clan of Alamantimichar were telepaths. She had felt every second of Marcon's agony. She had touched his mind at the moment of death.

She was aware of eyes staring at her, and looked up. The Rojok officer who had abducted her was grinning through the force shield. The slit eyes that peered out of that reddish-bronze face made her tremble. The shock of blond hair that fell on the Rojok's broad brow was sweaty and slick. His hair was short, denoting a lesser rank. Only high-ranking officers were allowed to wear long hair.

"You are a rare prize, daughter of Tnurat," he told her, studying her fragile beauty. "What a pity that I cannot show you to Chacon. It might mean another *mesag* mark of rank."

Her chameleon eyes made dark, angry whispers, but her composure was perfect. She rose from the contoured couch, grace personified.

"Had Chacon not ordered my capture, and the death of my brother?" she asked softly.

The Rojok laughed heartily. "Chacon knows nothing of this mission. Some think our commander-in-chief wages warfare in far too chivalrous a manner. Some have promised me his *mesag* marks for the Jaakob Spheres—and you."

"Think you that Chacon will not discover what you have done when the Holconcom come in pursuit?" she asked.

"The Holconcom?" He laughed again. "They are stories used to frighten children. But pursuers will find themselves pursued. Our forces even now are closing the distance between the planet Terramer and the Tri-Fleet battle lines. No ship can get through them now. Not even your phantom Holconcom."

Her delicate face lifted proudly. "There is one who will come to avenge the death of my brother."

"Let him try."

"Where do you now take me? To your home planet of Enmehk-mehk?"

His slit eyes narrowed. "If your arrogance persists, perhaps you will go to *Ahkmau* instead."

He was gone, and she felt the chills wander over her slender body in its silky coverings. *Ahkmau* translated in Rojok as "place of tortures." It was located on one of the three moons of Enmehkmehk, the planetary capital of the Rojok empire. It was the death camp of the Rojok tyrant Mangus Lo, and even a Centaurian could feel fear at the mention of its name. Had she been capable of shedding tears in front of these savages, she might have yielded to them. But Alamantimichar was a proud Clan, and to show weakness to an enemy was to dishonor it. She turned back to her couch. Dtimun would come. No matter the odds against him, he would come.

Back in the command chair on the SSC ship *Bellatrix's* bridge, Holt Stern forgot the carnage and the Centaurians. He had a bigger problem. Terramer was located on the edge of the Algomerian Space Sector, which the Rojoks had already claimed as captured territory. If Chacon's hunter squads were still in the area, it was going to take every ounce of his command ability to get the ship home.

"Higgins," he asked his sandy-haired first officer, "how's our fuel holding out?"

"We'll make it back, sir," Higgins said with a grin, "but we won't have enough left over to fill a java cup."

"Like I thought. Helm, is the Centaurian ship pacing us?"

The astrogator shook his head. "They were running a parallel course when we left orbit, sir, but they've disappeared. I assume they've lighted out of sensor range. Our tracker beams can't touch them."

"Sir," Jennings, the comtech, broke in, "I've got the short-range commbanks working now, and I'm getting an alien signal. Close, and on scramble."

"Ignore it," Stern said. "Rojoks use an emergency code like that to get a fix on enemy ships."

"It doesn't read like a Rojok signal, sir. There's..."

"I said, ignore it."

"Yes, sir."

He got up and flexed his shoulders while he checked the starmaps over the astrogation console in the cramped nose of the sleek starship. The headache was better now, although there seemed to be blank pieces of his life even behind the pain—pieces he didn't have time to mourn. His brow furrowed. There were no patterns to indicate an intruder, but Chacon's ships sometimes appeared like ghosts. He felt uneasy, and he'd learned to trust instinct more than machinery.

"Higgins, slow us down to quarter-light and take the ship on bearing 6.25, mark one."

"Yes, sir." Higgins gave the order to the astrogator. "Expecting trouble, Captain?"

"I'm always expecting trouble, Higgins. Steady as she goes."

"Sir," the comtech said, "that alien signal's back. It's in English this time, in the clear."

Stern sighed angrily. "Oh, hell, what's it say?"

"It's a distress call from the Vegan Paraguard ship, *Lyrae*. They're under attack from a Rojok squad and their weaponry is out."

"Location?"

"They didn't give it, sir. Shall I request…?"

"No!" He slammed down into the command chair. "Under no circumstances are you to reply to that message! Astrogator, prime the auxiliary power units. We may have to make a run for it."

"Sir?"

"Mister, if you were surrounded by a squadron of Rojok ships, and you had time for a single distress call, would you be stupid enough to omit your coordinates?"

"Not me, sir," the astrogator said, shaking his head. "Not unless I was trying to home in on a commbeam by sending it."

"Exactly. Prime those units. Jennings," he shot at the comtech, "do your sensors register any other ships in the immediate area?"

"No, sir. Just a meteor—an 'iron' judging by the density. Strange. I don't remember any on the advance scans…"

"Meteor?" He snapped a code into the console at his elbow and glanced over the up-to-date Tri-Fleet starcharts. No meteors or other celestial bodies were charted on the screen. That didn't mean a rogue asteroid or meteor couldn't be out there. Even so, he had a feel for navigation in space that many of his fellows in the Academy had envied. He knew that it was a trap.

"Throw a modifier on your scanners," he told Jennings, "and tie in the master computer for analysis. I think we've located our 'friend in distress.'"

"Yes, sir." Jennings's slender hands flew over the controls. He smiled. "Well, I'll be a—there they are, sir. Two of them, Rojok configuration. Heading toward us at two sublights, using a meteor holoscreen to mask their signals."

Stern grinned, feeling confident now. "Hold your course, astrogator. Weaponry, tie in your *emerillium* boosters and give me the best widescan spray pattern you can manage. Fire on my signal. Higgins, bring us down to half-sublight and hold."

"Aye, sir."

Stern leaned back in his chair, keeping his eyes glued to the short-range scanner screen on his console. As he watched the approach of the "meteor" he had to grudgingly admire the strategy of the Rojok captain piloting that lead ship.

The Rojok vessels drew closer by the second. Tension grew on the bridge. The crew was accustomed to these confrontations, but the effect of battle was still the same. Fear, quiet terror, dry throats were all a part of space conflicts. Retreat was impossible once combat was engaged. Where was there to go, except into cold space? Uncertainty rippled through the crew. No commander, no matter how capable, could guarantee the outcome of a battle.

The Rojoks, depending on their "meteor skin" disguise to camouflage them, were beginning to make their run. To an untrained eye, the only disturbance among the bright stars would have been a wayward little meteor feeling its way to oblivion. But Stern knew, and was ready.

"Weaponry, stand by," he called.

"Ready, sir."

"Watch your screen. Give him five seconds into the run, then lock on to him."

"Counting, sir. One…two…three…four…"

Before he could voice the final number, a violent shock wave hit the *Bellatrix* and threw it careening off course. Stern's back slammed into the arm of his chair and he fell with a racking thud to the deck as the generators that maintained the pressurized interior hit a blip. He was on his feet before the full effect of the bruising ride hit his suddenly throbbing temples.

"Grab the helm, Mister!" He hit the intercom switch. "Weaponry, post two," he called into the intership lock, "can you lock on to him?"

"Yes, sir. Got him!"

"Fire all tubes!"

The ship lurched as the condensed tubes emitting *emerillium* waves left the ship, pitching the crew against the bulkheads. Stern grabbed his chair and threw himself into it.

"Helm, divert to secondary course!" he barked.

"Leaving over, sir!"

"Weaponry, success of strike?"

"We hit one of them, sir, amidships," the weaponry officer reported. "But the others…"

"Line up your pattern and fire when ready!"

"But, sir," the officer argued over the screen, "we don't have anything left to hit them with! The hit we took blew hell out of our boosters. We're paralyzed aft!"

"Helm, can we outrun him?" Stern shot at the astrogator.

"We can try, sir, providing we have enough fuel to throw to the auxiliary units. Leaving over now."

Stern's hands bit into the soft plastiglas of the chair arms as the big ship began to lurch forward with a humming surge of power. "Come on, baby," he whispered, as if the ship were a female he could coax. "Come on."

"He's tailing us, sir," the astrogator called over his shoulder. "He's barely a parsec behind and closing. When he makes half that distance, he'll fire. And we can't make any more speed."

Speed, Stern thought furiously. Dammit, speed!

His hand went to his head, to the blinding pain that gripped him when he tried to think, to reason... He fought it. And a flash got through.

"Helm, hard right flank and slow to sublight!" he barked. "Quick, dammit!"

"Yes, sir!"

The astrogator dived for the control, and seconds later the huge ship lurched like a fish out of water. Stern ground his teeth as the braking spools were engaged, bringing the force of thirty G's down onto his chest. He could barely breathe, the pressure was so great.

The stars came blurring back into focus. The pressure eased. He pulled his aching body upright and gasped for breath. "The Rojok?" he asked quickly.

The astrogator turned with an apologetic shake of his head. "Sorry, sir. He's on to us. He slowed as we did. He's right behind us, and I can't give you enough speed to ditch him. I'm...sorry, sir."

Death. He could taste it. He could see in the faces of his crew that they, too, knew. Again, he fought the pain inside his head for a strategy, any strategy, that might spare the ship. But that, too, was a losing battle.

Wearily he looked around at the somber, set faces of the bridge crew. He sighed wearily. "If we die," he said, "we do it like men. Any argument?"

The officers and crewmen shook their heads wordlessly.

He nodded. "Turn the ship, astrogator," he said quietly.

"Course, sir?"

"Straight down the Rojok's throat," he replied, "with every ounce of speed you can manage."

"Yes, sir." The astrogator's fingers whipped the controls into position. "Ready, sir."

Stern fixed his eyes on the screen, at the oval Rojok ship hanging there in space like a fish waiting for a worm. His heart was climbing into his throat, and he felt a fear he hadn't known existed. Familiar, this feeling. As if he'd been through that narrow door once before and dreaded repetition of it. The fear simulated panic, and he had to fight the urge to get up and run.

The pain, the searing pain in his mind, grew steadily. Something alien in his brain was fighting this decision. Trying with pain to force him to countermand his own commands.

His hands gripped the arms of his chair. He remembered Madeline and Hahnson down below and tried not to think about them. He straightened with a tremendous effort. Dignity first. It was the credo of the SSC. Even in death, he had to have the dignity of his command.

Almost blind with pain, he drew in a heavy sigh. "Astrogator," he said in a gruff whisper. "Ahead full!"

The astrogator turned and met his eyes with a somber, resigned ghost of a smile. In it were admiration and honor. "Aye, sir."

* * *

The flagship *Morcai* sliced through the stars like a giant metallic blade, her massive engines making far less noise than her first officer. Komak's usual high spirits did as much for the weary bridge crew as the promise of shore leave. Only the *Morcai's* stoic commander seemed to be unaffected by it.

Dtimun, sitting in his spoollike command chair, listened only half-heartedly. His mind was a galaxy away, on Enmehkmehk, home planet of the Rojok Dynasty. It was there that Chacon would surely take his captive—to *Ahkmau,* the infamous death camp on one of its moons where political prisoners were kept. The thought of Lyceria in such a place was torture, even to a career soldier's trained mind.

"ETA Trimerius?" he asked the helmsman.

"Two mekkam, Commander," was the reply.

Komak joined the older Centaurian, and the laughing green light left his eyes. They grew blue with concern. "Your eyes speak for you," he told Dtimun, careful lest the others hear him. "I regret Lyceria's capture. I know that the commander's heart was soft for her."

"My heart is soft for no one." Dtimun's darkened eyes belied the words. His gaze went to the main viewscreen. "*Maliche,* I could make more speed in a crippled scout! Are your gravs malfunctioning, helmsman?"

The pilot glanced at him. "I have not fired them, Commander," he said, and his eyes went to Komak.

"I assumed," Komak told the commander, "that you would wish a lesser speed to keep the Earth ship under surveillance. Should it encounter a Rojok patrol, its defense systems would render it incapable of a counterattack. Human ship designers make no allowance for stabilizing BEK gyros and reflectors such as ours."

Dtimun glared at the younger Centaurian. "I will not play parent to an inferior shipload of aliens. I have no more love for humans than does the Rojok tyrant Mangus Lo, or his field marshal, Chacon."

"Were it our race that Mangus Lo persecuted in his death camps," Komak said quietly, "instead of the humans, I think your sympathies might find more interest in them."

"By *Simalichar,* you try my patience!" Dtimun stood up. His chameleon eyes faded from a concerned blue to a questioning gray. "What merit can there be in a race whose entire history is preoccupied with pride in cruelty and contempt for life?"

Komak's eyes went green with mischief. "I had not known that the commander's library included textdiscs on human history."

Dtimun ignored him.

Komak studied the older alien with respectful eyes. In a society where Clan was life itself, the commander wore no Clan insignia and claimed no allegiances. He was as mysterious as he was feared and respected by his men. In his years of commanding the Holconcom, no challenge to his authority had ever been given. Not even by the emperor, whom Dtimun treated with utter disdain. His ongoing feud with old Tnurat Alamantimichar, head of the Dectat, was legendary in the space services. No one knew what had started it. No one dared ask. But Komak knew things about him that the other crewmen didn't. Dtimun was aware that Komak's odd outbursts of insight had a basis in fact. It had been disconcerting when he realized that Komak knew more about him than he'd anticipated. As he thought about it, Dtimun glared at Komak.

"Commander," the comtech called out, "the Earth ship has disengaged her lightsteds and is slowing to a crawl. I show two Rojok destroyers trailing her."

Dtimun turned his angry eyes from Komak to the viewscreen at his semicircle console. The Rojoks were already firing when he engaged the video. The Earth ship hung as if dead in space, offering no resistance as salvo after salvo connected with her hull and sent her reeling to and fro. Then, with the suddenness of a cosmic storm, she turned slowly and began to pick up speed as she began a run that would take her on a collision course with the lead Rojok vessel.

"Is that black-eyed captain of theirs a madman?" Dtimun growled. "What use can this strategy serve? Komak, check the energy scanner."

Komak's hands flew over the scanner switches on the command console. "His weaponry is useless," he reported. "His fuel output reads less than one-quarter capacity and his repulsers are almost gone. I estimate two more hits will finish him."

Dtimun watched the sleek starship bear down on the Rojok, so quickly that the enemy ship couldn't possibly get out of the way in time. "I understand his motive," he said. "A laudable last resort, but a hollow victory. Helmsman, hard about and prime main batteries!"

"Aye, sir."

Dtimun dropped into the command chair with his long fingers barely touching the master weaponry control panel. It was going to require precision timing, this maneuver. If he fired too soon, the second Rojok vessel would have time to destroy the Earth ship. If he fired too late, the spray pattern would destroy both ships.

The *Morcai* began to bear down on the Rojoks like a flash of light, and the stars around her seemed to be speeding in the opposite direction in her wake.

"I register a scan," Komak said quickly. "The Rojok has spotted us."

Dtimun's fingers tensed on the firing switch. "If he changes course," he said tightly, "I may cost the human his ship. Helmsman, take me in on a deflect pattern, close range. Time will allow me only one shot. I want the best I can manage."

"Yes, Commander. Leaving over now on deflect course. Engines ahead, full-drive."

Dtimun focused his huge eyes on the screen. His long fingers curled around the firing switch. Out in space, the Rojok grew like a suddenly inflated balloon, filling the viewscreen.

Holt Stern sat quietly in his chair, watching the Rojok flash toward the *Bellatrix,* with a deceptive numbness in his chest. The bridge already had the feel of a morgue as each crew member spent his last seconds in stonelike aloneness, untouching, unspeaking. Stern clenched his teeth to hold back the fear. At least, he thought ironically, the headache would die with him. And then, the Rojok ship filled the viewscreen...

The Rojok came screaming in toward the *Bellatrix.* There was a final surge of power as Higgins ordered the astrogator to throw the throttle wide-open. Then, quite suddenly, a ball of green mist enveloped the enemy ship.

It took Stern precious seconds to realize what was happening. In a mind yielded to death, thought came slowly.

"Full about!" he barked at the astrogator, praying the man would recover fast enough to make the maneuver. A split second's delay, and the *Bellatrix* would go up in atoms along with the Rojok.

"Aye, sir!" The astrogator's thin, trembling hands seemed to hit the switches in slow motion.

Stern felt the huge starship vibrate like a running heart with the sudden braking. She bolted under the pressure, as if torn apart between time and speed. Then, with a recovery that was nothing short of miraculous, she began to turn and inch away from the doomed Rojok ship. In seconds that were centuries to her crew, she pulled away with a rippling burst of speed just as the Rojok ship exploded in silent fireworks out in the eternal night. The shock wave that came in her wake was enough to rattle the scanners on the bridge.

"God!" Stern breathed in mingled relief and gratitude.

"Sir, we've got the megatrons back in working order, now," Higgins said quickly. "Not nearly up to par, but I think we've got enough charge to hit the other Rojok."

"Lock on target and fire at will!" Stern told him.

"On target, Captain. Megas away!"

Stern watched the blue bolts fly into the second Rojok with boyish excitement. The resulting explosion was no less enjoyable than the first had been, and the colorful display produced nothing more than a light jar to the *Bellatrix*. Stern leaned back in his chair with a long, shuddering sigh.

"Good work, Higgins," he told his exec. His eyes went to the astrogator and fished for a name, and was surprised when he couldn't find it. "What's your name, son?" he asked.

The astrogator gaped at him. "Why…it's Crandall, sir."

Stern nodded. "Crandall. Good man."

"We're lucky you spotted the first attack in time," Higgins said with a grin at his commanding officer. "If you hadn't, we'd be atoms by now."

"Speaking of attacks," Stern said, leaning forward, "where did that one come from?"

"Had to be the Centaurian," Higgins replied. "But he's…"

"Interspace comm coming in, sir," the comtech broke in.

"Throw it over here, Jennings. Higgins, get me a damage report."

"Yes, sir."

Stern switched on the viewscreen, to be met with a pair of slightly amused pale green cat-eyes. "You present an interesting case for your race, Captain," Dtimun said over the screen. "I had not credited it with such ingenuity. Status of your vessel?"

"Higgins?" Stern asked.

Higgins's thin face seemed to grow longer. "Sir, we took a hit amidships. Damage control reports thirty injuries and fifty-five dead, including our Amazon unit," he added, noting the specialized female attack squad that was regulation aboard all SSC vessels. Females served in combat, as well as in support units. Many former members of Amazon squads, like Madeline Ruszel, were now officers. A good many were assigned to SSC ships like the *Bellatrix,* although Stern had no female bridge crew on this particular mission due to rotation and R & R.

The Amazon units were the most well-known, the most respected of the SSC's forward units. They were known even by outworlders like the misogynist Centaurians. Madeline Ruszel had started out in an Amazon unit before she felt an inexplicable urge to practice medicine and petitioned for the right to be sent to medical school. She had a soft spot for the Amazons, especially for the unit that served aboard the *Bellatrix*. Its commanding officer had gone through training with Madeline.

"Damn!" Stern cursed. Madeline was going to take the news hard. "All of them?"

"Yes, sir," Higgins replied. "It gets worse. Our backup fuel units were destroyed, we have three crushed bulkheads, and our primary engine batteries are dead. We've also got grav holes that we have no means of plugging. We're leaking atmosphere at a lethal rate. Unless that Centaurian ship has a repair deck, we're...well, we're finished, sir."

Stern stared at him blankly. "In other words," he said quietly, "we're a dead ship." He sighed and turned back to Dtimun's image on the viewscreen. "Nice try, Commander, but you might as well have let the Rojoks take us out. We'd need two weeks in a shipyard just to begin repairs."

"If you expect to find one this deep in captured territory, I withdraw my former statement regarding your ingenuity," Dtimun replied. "Prepare for ship-to-ship lock. I'm evacuating your crew and complement to the *Morcai*."

"With all due respect," Stern protested, "you could just as easily throw a towbeam on us and…"

"Such a rescue operation is beyond the capability of my vessel," Dtimun replied. "Considering our normal cruising speed, your ship would be ripped in two by the pressure. You have your orders." The screen went blank.

Stern glanced around the somber bridge crew. Their faces were mildly accusing. He almost understood the feeling. The *Bellatrix* had been home for six years, and her deck had a familiar feel. But what could he do with such a damaged vessel except scuttle her?

"Higgins," he said, rising, "order abandon ship and tell the medics to start loading their patients into the port escape hatches. Prepare for ship-to-ship lock."

"Aye, aye, Captain," Higgins replied halfheartedly.

"Something on your mind, Higgins?" Stern asked.

The executive officer eyed him quietly. "Just one thing, sir. We're damaged, sure, but couldn't we call for help?"

Stern felt sick. "We'd be a sitting duck, with Rojoks everywhere and no weapons. Dream on, son."

"Yes, sir. I guess you're right. I just hate giving up our ship."

He watched his exec as he walked away, with growing resentment. For the first time he could remember, he felt a vague distaste for the entire crew.

3

The darkness had already fallen on Enmehkmehk when Lyceria was taken from the Rojok ship with her head solidly encased in an opaque helmet. Except for the bonds on her slender wrists, she might have passed for a female Rojok soldier in the thin copper armor she wore.

She knew better than to make an outcry. Her captors had warned her of the consequences. She followed them meekly, gracefully, through the gemstone streets, past the glowing multidome architecture that housed the barracks of Enmehkmehk's largest military base. *Maliche,* she thought, surely they wouldn't imprison her in a common soldier's barracks! She was a member of the Royal Clan. It would be an outrage that would reverberate all the way home to Memcache, the home planet of the Centaurian Empire and the emperor, her father, himself! No power in space would save Mangus Lo from the Holconcom if she were harmed.

But it seemed that the Rojoks had no fear of her people, because the barracks were, indeed, her destination. She was taken into a small circular building adjacent to the main complex and thrown unceremoniously into a small compartment. A heavy door was lowered, and she found herself in complete darkness.

Her huge eyes dilated to let in the faint light, and she had her first look at her new surroundings.

There was nothing in the room except for a small synthesizer on the wall. But she could see two panels near it that would account for a retractable couch and toilet facilities. The floor under her was crystalline and cold, but it was spongy, too, and it broke her fall so that she didn't even feel bruised. Perhaps its function was to absorb force, as well as sound. The walls seemed made of the same amber glowing crystal.

Her hands were still tied. Groggily she pulled her aching body up and walked cautiously to the synthesizer. Leaning against the cool wall, she touched the button to the left of the oval housing with her chin. A contoured couch inched its way out of the curved wall and spread onto the floor. She dropped down onto it, noting that it was made of the same shock-absorbing material as the floor and walls. She worked at her bonds. They were tight, but perhaps they could be loosened with some careful meditation.

Her slender body relaxed on the soft couch. Her eyes closed. She drew inside herself, seeking the strength she would need for the task at hand. Slowly, gently, she focused her mind on the bonds. Concentrating, gently concentrating, she saw them loosen and fall to the soft material under them. Fall, she thought. Fall. Fall!

Her hands were suddenly free. She stood up gracefully, rubbing her sore wrists. Her hands reached up to the thick helmet still on her head. She wrenched it off and tossed it angrily against the wall.

In the dim light, a pale green colored the pupils of her large, elongated eyes. The door was next. Only a little more concentration, and...

Before she could finish the thought, the door shot up and two Rojok soldiers tramped into the compartment. One of them grabbed her roughly and held her down, while the other jammed a tiny cylinder against the bare flesh of her arm. There was a stabbing pain, followed by numbness.

"What…have you done?" she demanded, breathless.

"You will soon know," one of them said, grinning down at her with pale slit eyes in a copper-colored face.

She felt a wave of nausea. Then the room began to grow dark around her. She pitched forward, her legs turning to jelly beneath her. The couch rising up to meet her was the last thing she saw.

Komak was busily directing the humans to their berths when Stern walked through the ship-to-ship elevator tube onto the main deck of the *Morcai*. It was noticeably colder and there was a smell to it that, while not unpleasant, was definitely alien.

Stern hadn't expected the space he found. Twelve men could walk abreast in the corridor without touching shoulders. The bulkheads were curved and glowed with soft, white light. Centaurians dressed in the familiar red uniform trotted noiselessly past with a military precision and routine that was fascinating to watch.

"I know you, Captainholtstern!" Komak said in greeting, running the human's name together as was his custom, because he had scant knowledge of human address protocol. His green eyes twinkled as he approximated an SSC salute. "As you see, I have studied your Terravegan protocols!"

Stern threw him a salute, too tired and angry to react well to the younger man's banter. "Request permission to come aboard, sir," he said formally.

The young alien's eyes faded to a somber, questioning blue as he stared unnervingly at Stern. "Excuse me, is there some significance among your people to this question?" he asked politely.

Stern relaxed his military posture with a frown. "It's military tradition in our branch of the space services to ask permission to board another ship," he explained. "Like the salute, it's a custom held over from seafaring days on ancient Earth, the home world of the Terravegan colonies. I'm a Terravegan," he added when the alien looked puzzled.

"We do not salute one another," Komak replied. "Only the commander is accorded such respect." The boy's eyes went suddenly green with mischief. "He has forbidden us to salute even the emperor, Tnurat Alamantimichar. I think it has caused the head of Clan Alamantimichar much discomfort at ceremonial occasions, which is one of the few things that cause the commander's eyes to laugh."

"I know another one," Stern said resentfully, remembering the other alien's amusement at the loss of Stern's ship.

"Where can I set up my surgery?" Dr. Madeline Ruszel interrupted. She was flushed and furious. She'd just come aboard, heading a team of medics guiding ambulifts, and her drawn face showed not only the strain of the rushed evacuation, but of the loss of the Amazon unit, as well. "I've got people dying over here!"

"Follow me," Komak told her at once. He led the medics into what appeared to be a mess hall, with Stern bringing up the rear. The ambulifts were quickly loaded onto the long, oval tables against the bulkheads while Madeline supervised the placing and energized the sterilization units on the cylinders. The young alien watched her with odd interest. Perhaps, she thought, it was her red hair that intrigued him. She was the only member of Stern's crew with hair that color.

"Stern, I need *morphadrenin*," she called over her shoulder. "Every gram I can lay hands on. And if the C.O. can spare some qualified help, I'd be in his debt."

Stern glanced at Komak. "How about it?"

"The commander's contempt for medics is second only to that which he holds for our emperor," the alien replied somberly. "We carry no complement of medics aboard. But I will inform the commander of the need for additional medical stores. Shall you come with me, Captainholtstern?" he asked, apparently fascinated by Madeline. Odd, he looked at her as if he knew her, somehow...

"Lay on, McDuff," Stern agreed with a grin at Madeline.

"My name is not McDuff," Komak said, puzzled. "It is Komak, of the Clan Maltiche. You have heard of it, of course," he added with faint arrogance.

"Oh, yeah," Stern quipped. "It ranks along with the great Clans of Jones and Smith back home."

"Jones and...?" Komak faltered.

"Never mind," Stern said impatiently. "Let's go. Maddie, I'll see what I can do about your supplies," he called over his shoulder as she went quickly back to work.

Komak started off at a fast trot. Stern increased his pace to keep up with the long legs of the Centaurian. "What's the rush?" Stern asked. "Everybody on this ship seems to be on his way to battle stations all the time."

"It is routine aboard the *Morcai,*" Komak informed him. "All personnel are required to run from post to post. Elevator tubes are strictly outlawed for crew use, as well," he added, bounding onto a ladder that led to the upper deck.

"Uh-huh." Stern got brief glimpses inside the various sectors they passed as they climbed access ladders up three decks. Nothing looked familiar. There was alien script on the walls, unreadable and unpronounceable, denoting departments. The temperature was at least ten degrees cooler than the *Bellatrix.* The alien, spicy smell of the corridors was overpowering. And the icy looks the human got from passing members of the Holconcom were uncomfortable. Stern began to feel like an invading disease. If his reception as an ally officer was this cool and resented, his people could expect even less. Madeline, of all his crew, was going to feel the pressure keenly, since the Centaurian empire did not allow females aboard its warships. He hoped the trip back to the Tri-Galaxy Fleet base on Trimerius would be quick.

Stern was winded by the time they got to the command deck of the enormous vessel. The oval, high-domed bridge made the *Bellatrix*'s bridge look cramped and primitive by comparison. Above his head, a second bridge circled the main sector like a smooth, white balcony. And both bridges seemed to be perfectly coordinated, as well as efficiently manned. The ten crewmen on the lower level maintained their posts with a silence that would have been impossible for a human crew.

Dtimun, noticing the approach of the human, rose from his spool-like command chair and joined Komak and Stern beside the communications banks. Stern saluted unconsciously, but Dtimun waved it aside without returning it.

"Your people are evacuated?" he asked formally.

"Every one," Stern replied. "What about the *Bellatrix?*"

"Your ship?" Dtimun nodded at a crewman against the opposite bulkhead. A viewscreen was activated which covered the width and length of half the command sector. The *Bellatrix* hung there in black space like a charm suspended by a chain. A flash of bluish-green light shot out from the *Morcai*'s copper hull and enveloped the sleek starcruiser. Then, there was a violent red explosion that came and passed without a sound. Only empty space was left.

"We leave no vessel behind where the enemy might salvage tech," Komak explained.

Stern's eyebrow jerked carelessly. "She was a good ship," he said quietly, and wondered why he didn't feel a sense of loss for his command vessel.

Komak drew to attention and jerked his head in a salute. "Commander, Dr.Madelineruszel," he continued, running her names together again, "has requested supplies of *morphadrenin* and medical assistance. I informed her that we carry no medics, but…"

"Dr. who?" Dtimun asked, frowning slightly.

"The female with hair like sunfire," Komak explained. "She is a medic among the humans. I have given her the mess hall on deck four for her surgery. Dr. Hahnson has the supply sector on deck four. The other crewmen of the *Bellatrix* await assignment. I did not know where to place them."

"*Maliche,* can no one function without using my brain?" the alien exploded with darkening eyes. "Ascertain their specialties and place them in the appropriate departments!"

"The *morphadrenin?*" Komak persisted, apparently not put off by his superior's bad humor.

Dtimun actually seemed to flush with anger. "I carry on my person nothing save the communicator ring you see on my forefinger," he told the younger alien. "I am not a walking ordnance store! Show the mutinous female where the synthesizer is located and acquaint her with its use!"

"Yes, Commander."

"And make the humans aware that they must not come in contact with the *kelekoms,*" he added at once. "They carry unknown bacteria that might harm the machines."

Stern's eyes almost popped. "Bacteria…"

"The *kelekoms* are our, how do you say, supercomputers," Komak explained at once. "They are living, self-repairing biological entities, and they are extremely sensitive to alien bacteria. If they become ill, they do not work."

Stern blinked, only half understanding what he was being told. This technology was far in advance of anything the Tri-Fleet had.

"Tell Hahnson I will expect him to keep his medics in line, and out of the way of my crew," Dtimun told Stern.

The comment almost flew by Stern. He frowned. "Hahnson?"

"He is chief of your medical staff, is he not?" Dtimun replied.

"No, sir," Stern told him. "Dr. Ruszel is."

Dtimun stared at him blankly. "The female? A female commands your medics?"

Stern cleared his throat. "Sir, I do understand that Centaurian social structure is far different from our own. We don't differentiate between male and female in our military. We're mentally neutered to the degree that 'relationships' between enlisted personnel are impossible. Even if they weren't, it's the only death penalty left on our books."

"Your military is mad," Dtimun said flatly. "Women have no place in combat."

"If you tell that to Madeline Ruszel, make sure you have a running head start," Stern murmured, tongue-in-cheek. "She started out as a member of our Amazon Commandos. In fact, she captained a squad of them."

Dtimun shook his head in disbelief. "How many other females do you have in your complement?"

"We had thirty-six, but our entire Amazon unit was wiped out during the Rojok encounter," Stern said quietly. "Madeline's taking it hard. She went through training with the unit's commander."

"Which does not answer my question," Dtimun shot back.

"We have one female in our crew, sir—Dr. Ruszel."

"She is quite lovely," Komak said.

Dtimun's eyes darkened and he glared at the younger alien. "You have your orders. Obey them!"

"Yes, Commander." Komak saluted and turned. His eyes gave a green laugh as they met Stern's. "Is his great affection for me not obvious?" he teased. "He…"

"*Domcan h'ab leche!*" Dtimun thundered in Centaurian.

"Yes, Commander!" Komak disappeared down the escape ladder, but his eyes were still laughing when he left the bridge.

Dtimun turned to Stern. "Come with me."

Stern followed the tall alien into what appeared to be a briefing room of some sort. It was bare except for an oval desk and a smattering of chairs secured to the deck. Apparently the Centaurians also had trouble with occasional gravity failures. They were an infrequent but annoying nuisance on SSC ships.

Dtimun perched himself on the edge of the desk and folded his arms over his broad chest as he studied Stern. "The nearest route to Trimerius," he began, "will still require five solar days' travel. During that time, certain things will be expected of you and your men."

"Such as?" Stern asked.

"The majority of the Holconcom were reared in a clonery." He waited for the shock to leave Stern's face before he continued. "They have never known touch, save in battle. I know little of humans, but it is said that you are a physical race. Take care that none of you lay hands on the Holconcom, either in sport or anger. To do so could easily provoke a massacre. Second, I expect no interference from your personnel in the routine of this vessel. Conversation will be held strictly to military necessity. Nor will I tolerate idle wandering in the corridors. While aboard this ship, your men will adhere to its disciplines. All personnel will run from post to post, and the first man I catch using a ship's elevator tube will be brigged."

"May I ask what the elevator tubes are for?" Stern asked with growing irritation.

"For transport of casualties, Captain, and heavy equipment." He glanced at a viewscreen on the desk and his huge eyes darkened to a somber, angry blue-gray. His fist slammed at a switch on the console. "Degas, your lightsteds are at one-half capacity. Explain!"

The alien was speaking in his own tongue, but the machine simultaneously translated Centaurian into Terravegan Standard to Stern's amazement. Perhaps the briefing room was constructed to allow conversation between alien races of different tongues.

"If you please, Commander, I had just started to contact you," the Centaurian officer said quickly. "My *tramaks* register a fleet of Rojok vessels closing in from several *deshcam* away in all directions, all sending out force nets to mesh the distance between them!"

"Well, Mister?" Dtimun demanded, eyeing his comtech over the viewscreen.

The Centaurian officer met those accusing eyes levelly. "We are cut off from Trimerius, Commander," he said matter-of-factly. "The Rojok fleet is attempting to press us into their advance lines. Once that is accomplished..."

Dtimun nodded. "Yes," he said, cutting the officer off midsentence.

The thought of capture by the Rojoks was oddly satisfying to Stern. He caught himself before a smile flared on his face, and wondered at the unfamiliar feelings that had begun to race through his mind; alien, traitorous feelings that frightened him. Strange, he thought, how those feelings had suddenly and completely replaced his earlier headaches. He hadn't been the same since they lifted from the Peace Planet.

"Tekar, can you beam a message through that net?" Dtimun asked his comtech on the bridge.

Another alien face came into view on the screen. "No, Commander," came the reply. "Our strongest megabeams cannot pierce the molecular density of the barrier."

Before Dtimun had time for another question, Madeline Ruszel came storming into the briefing room, her flowing auburn hair sweaty in spite of the cool atmosphere, her green eyes blazing. Stern ground his teeth together and waited for the explosion.

"I've got people dying down there!" she raged at Dtimun without preamble, bracing her legs as if preparing for a hurricane. "I can't resupply any *morphadrenin* because your damned synthesizer absorbed some bacteria from my fingers when I touched it, and it's sick. Sick! What the hell kind of machines are you using on this bloody space-going whale? And that's not all! My life monitors are malfunctioning from some kind of magnetic interference, and I...!"

"*Baatashe!*" the alien thundered, staring down the furious exobiologist with angry brown eyes that silenced her immediately, to Stern's amusement. "By *Simalichar,* hold your tongue before I have you spaced! If you have a request to make, make it in understandable tones and not in the language of a *hashheem* from a pleasure dome!"

Her mouth opened slightly, and her green eyes dilated. But she regained her composure at once and stood her ground. "All right, sir," she said, emphasizing the "sir." "I need access to a working synthesizer because my *morphadrenin* is exhausted and my patients cannot withstand delicate invasive surgery without it. I also need a mute-screen to mask the magnetic interference that's disrupting my life monitors. Because this," she added, indicating the bionic panel in the creamy skin of her wrist under the sleeve of her green uniform, "can't be five places at once to read vitals. Furthermore, my medics are going into their thirty-second straight standard hour without sleep or rest, and two of them have already collapsed on me. In short, sir, if this ship doesn't make Trimerius within one solar day on the outside, we're going to lose every bloody alien casualty we're transporting and maybe the humans in Hahnson's medical complement as well!"

"We cannot make Trimerius in one solar day," Dtimun said in a deceptively gentle tone, "nor one solar month, nor one solar millennium. Because, Madam, we are gradually being surrounded by a fleet of Rojok vessels and we are cut off from Tri-Fleet Headquarters."

"Surrounded?" she echoed numbly.

"Yes. Surrounded." The Centaurian sighed angrily, as if the prospect of impotence was beyond acceptance or even belief. "No one ship, even this one, could penetrate the force net of the Rojok fleet and survive. They now seem intent on capture rather than destruction or they would already have fired on us. And that," he said in a chillingly soft voice, "I will not permit, even if it means destroying the *Morcai* myself."

Stern glanced at the Centaurian, puzzled. "Why so much flurry over one lone ship?" he asked pointedly. "They have the Jaakob Spheres and the Centaurian princess. What's left?"

The alien ignored the question. He turned back to the comm unit and addressed his navigator. "Degas, how many ships are they throwing against us?" he asked the comtech.

"I read two hundred, Commander, traveling at half sublight speed."

"*Maliche,* they are confident!" Dtimun growled.

"The casualties can't take another battle," Madeline said tightly. "And I didn't save them just to have you blow them up, *sir.* It isn't their bloody war. There must be one aid station we can reach before—"

"What we have reached at the moment, Madam," the Centaurian interrupted abruptly, "is the limit of my patience." His eyes were enough to silence her. He turned slowly to the comm unit again. "Degas, can we make Benaski Port?" he asked, naming a notorious way station on the outskirts of the civilized galaxy.

"If we reduce our weaponry capability and divert all power to the engines," the Centaurian navigator replied. "It is the only neutral port within reach."

"Then throw your lightsteds and make for it at maximum light."

"Yes, Commander."

Dtimun turned back to Madeline, his eyes calmer but still tinged with brown anger. "I will have Komak supply another synthesizer, which you will not touch. They respond readily to speech, even Terravegan speech, because of the translators we employ in all comm units aboard. I gather that your knowledge of bionic tech is as limited as your knowledge of proper female behavior."

"Proper...?" Madeline just gaped at him.

"Our science has been long capable of producing self-sustaining, self-perpetuating machines. Living machines, if you will," he continued unabashed. "They are extremely sensitive to alien bacteria, a fact which Komak was sent to impart to you. Apparently he was too late."

Her green eyes narrowed. She was struggling with an urge to knock him on his superior rear end.

His eyebrows arched, and his eyes became threatening at once.

Madeline blinked. It was coincidence, surely, that anger. "What a pity," she said with mock softness, "that your science couldn't also provide a means of inoculating the machines against alien bacteria."

Dtimun let that insult fall unnoticed. "Until your people were taken aboard, no humans had ever set foot aboard the *Morcai*. Such preventions were unnecessary. We have had to make modifications to our language banks to accommodate you. There was no time to attend the machines."

"What about more medtechs?" she persisted.

"I suggest that you make arrangements with Hanhson to acquire some of his." He held up his hand when she started to protest. "I am aware that your specialty is Cularian medicine, and his is Terravegan, but surely some medical expertise is preferable to none at all. That problem rests with you. Benaski Port is still three days away at our present speed. You must accommodate the delay."

"Perhaps some of the wounded will last that long," she said tightly. "By your leave, *sir,*" she added with a salute.

"One thing more, Madam."

She turned, the question only in her resentful eyes.

"The next time you step onto my bridge," he said quietly, "tread lightly. Your disregard for military routine could easily grant you a place in history textdiscs as the first human female ever spaced aboard a Centaurian warship. Am I understood?"

Her teeth ground together. But all she said was, "Yes, sir."

The alien watched her leave the bridge with a ramrod stiffness in his posture. Then he turned to Stern. "See to your men, Mister. Word has already reached me of unrest among them, even in the small time since you came aboard. No incidents of violence can be tolerated."

"For that," Stern told him, "you will need a miracle. Sir."

He saluted and followed Madeline's trail off the bridge. For that one, brief instant, he felt almost like his old self.

Mangus Lo, the Rojok dictator, sat at his many-hued stone desk in the *palcenon* and drank in the news his chief advisor had just provided.

"Is it true?" he asked with a malicious smile. "The Holconcom vessel has fallen into the trap? *Cleemaah!* We have him!"

"But, Excellence, the trap is not yet sprung," the tall, slender Rojok advisor protested gently.

"A mere detail. Chacon knows nothing of what has been done?" he asked quickly, searching the younger man's eyes.

"No, Excellence," he replied. "I instructed the soldiers in secret, as you ordered."

The dwarfed, middle-aged Rojok nodded in something like relief. "He is my ablest commander," he said, "yet his distaste for my methods is a hindrance. The terror must be maintained!" He slammed the polished stone desk with both fists and his eyes gleamed almost transparently. "Compassion is the death of the cause! Why does he oppose me? Does he not know that I could have him killed with a word?"

"If your Excellence will permit me," the advisor said, "he has become something of a legend among our people. To have him killed would be to welcome revolt."

"Silence!" Mangus Lo eyed the advisor with a piercing, deadly fury. "You, too, are expendable! You are all expendable!"

"Excellence, I did not mean…!" he began quickly.

The dictator waved him off. He stood up slowly, dragging his withered, useless leg as he moved, eyeing the advisor for any sign of contempt—a sign which, if he saw it, would cost the ambitious diplomat his life.

"The trap will shut," Mangus Lo said. He gazed out the oval window at the small, white moon over his towering winter palace on Enmehk-mehk. *Ahkmau* was there, his notorious place of tortures. In his mind, he could see the smoke rising from the sonic ovens. He did so enjoy watching the annihilation of his enemies. He smiled. "I will have Dtimun. And, with him, I will have the power to bring the Tri-Galaxy Federation and the Centaurian Empire itself to their knees!"

"I…do not understand," the advisor ventured.

He whirled on the younger Rojok. "You are a diplomat! You are not expected to understand, only to obey!" he screamed. "One word more and I will have you sent to the ovens!"

The advisor paled. He stood rigidly, unmoving, unspeaking.

Mangus Lo smiled at his companion's terror. He turned back to the window, his eyes glowing with a strange, mad fire. "It is ironic," he mused, "that only I know Dtimun's worth. When I have him, I have the universe in my hands. The universe!"

Holt Stern called his officers together in a briefing room near the improvised medical stations and delivered Dtimun's ultimatum. The reaction was predictably unfavorable.

"Like being captive on a slaver," a weaponry officer grumbled.

"Aye, and it's not even our fault," Declan Muldoon, the aging engineer, agreed with a harsh glance at Stern.

"If there's any fault," Stern said loudly, "it's the Rojoks'. Whether we like it or not, we're stuck here for the next three solar days and we'll make the best of it. I want our boys kept in line. Do it with words if possible, brig them if you have to. I don't want any trouble on our side."

There were irritated looks all around. Stern could feel their eyes measuring him, and the unfamiliar hostility infuriated him.

"You shudna let that cat-eyed terror yank us off the *Bellatrix* and blow her up," Muldoon said reproachfully. "We could have got her to port."

Stern glared at the Irishman, then at each man in turn. "The past is dead, gentlemen. I'm in command here, and you'll follow orders or I'll brig the lot of you. Is that clear?"

Muldoon lowered his mutinous eyes, but his face only grew redder.

"I've had reports of grumbling and even threats being overheard," he told them. "If you've got a problem, you tell me, and I'll handle it. Who's first?"

Higgins stood up. "Sir, before I became your exec, I was trained to be an astrogator, and they've assigned me to the weapons deck. I'm not complaining, maybe there's no room for another astrogator in their navigation sector, but I'm getting a lot of static and hard looks from the Centaurian execs. I don't know their technology, and no one will explain it to me."

"I'll see what I can do." Stern looked around. "Anyone else?"

"Yes, sir." Jennings, the comtech, rose. "The communications exec's got me polishing the consoles wearing space gear. He says I'm a walking bacteria bank and he won't let me touch his precious equipment unless I'm properly attired. I started toward the *kelekom* unit but he stopped me outside the door. He said something about me giving his *kelekoms* germs. Sir, what the hell kind of cyberbionics do they use to run this crazy ship?"

A brief skirl of laughter passed through the crew and they relaxed a little. Stern remained rigid. "They use living machines," he said, "highly vulnerable to our bacteria. Do what they tell you."

Madeline Ruszel stood up. "Dr. Hahnson and I are currently practicing medicine," she said, "in a glorified storage room and what seems to be a mess hall," she added with a wince. "The Centaurians are still trying to use the mess hall and storage facilities with our sterile fields in operation and surgery being performed."

"I'll take care of the problem," Stern assured her.

Muldoon stared at the dark-eyed captain. "Sure, and what'll you do about them cat-eyes struttin' around like they was kings and making one big joke out of us? One of those SOBs threw a damplegraft at me and made noises like a mugwort when I fell trying to catch it. I canna press two hundred pounds of metal! I almost threw a punch at the..."

"Keep your hands off the Centaurians," Stern told him. "That goes for the rest of you, as well. If you mix it up with the aliens, it'll be your necks and I don't have the authority to countermand the commander's orders. All I could do is wave at you when he kicked you out the airlock. It's his ship."

"Thanks to you," an anonymous voice muttered.

Stern ignored it. "If that's all?" He waited, but only a sullen, resentful silence met his ears. "All right. Dismissed."

Madeline was the last of the *Bellatrix* department heads to leave the compartment. She turned at the door. "You made a mistake, Stern," she said.

"What kind of mistake?"

"Telling the men you wouldn't back them up. It does nothing for morale, and theirs is just about shot. They're being bullied by the Centaurians. You've as much as said you won't stop it."

"Why lie?" he asked blankly.

Her eyes narrowed. "What's the matter with you? I've never known you to back away from a fight, even when you were outmatched!"

"Maybe I'm tired," he said coldly, resenting the words.

"Maybe you'd better pull yourself together before you get the bloody lot of us killed," she snapped back. She turned and left without another word.

Stern glowered after her. She irritated him. They all did. The humans were suddenly as distasteful to him as the aliens.

He shook his head as if to clear it. Other thoughts were shaping themselves in his mind. It would be soon, now. He had duties to perform, a mission to accomplish. Let the humans whine while they could. A slow, alien smile touched his lips.

The massive Tri-Galaxy Council chambers had the feel of an eons-old tomb. Tri-Fleet Admiral Jeffrye Lawson, a Terravegan native, sat numb and rigid in his solitary chair, unmoving in the maelstrom of motion around him.

The gray-haired old warhorse eyed the diplomats with quiet contempt. The stoic neutrality of the majority here in the costly war was responsible for casualty lists that left him sleepless and haggard. Idealists, the lot, he thought bitterly. Establishing "Peace Planets" like the colony on Terramer while the Rojoks were building better ships and bigger armies and sending hunter squads to terrorize the New Territory by killing colonists. The neutral solar systems didn't even have the guts to send representatives of their various governments to Terramer, at that; they'd sent clones. In this universe, clones had no social status whatsoever, despite the best efforts of activists. They were property, at the mercy of governments that had no mercy.

Above the heads of the member delegates, Lokar, the Jebob chairman of the Council, stood quietly at his raised podium. In his thin, blue-skinned hands he held the small communidisc that had heralded an emergency session in the middle of Trimerius's night.

Around Lawson, diplomats in various state of national dress were hurrying into their seats around the circular chamber. In seconds, all eyes were on Lokar's long face.

"As you were told," Lokar began in a gently accented voice, translated by the prompter into an uncountable number of languages and dialects that fed directly into each member's implanted receiver, "the communication I hold is from the Imperial Dectat of Centauria—the seat of the one hundred twenty planet empire of Tnurat Alamantimichar."

Lawson grimaced and moved restlessly in his chair, waiting for the patient old Jebob to continue in the sudden death hush of the assembly. Just the mention of Tnurat's name was enough to cause panic.

"I will activate the message." Lokar laid the disc on the dais and touched it with his sonar ring.

Tnurat Alamantimichar's deep, powerful voice filled the chamber. No image came with it. Only high military and political leaders had ever seen him. The emperor's reputation for privacy was legend, like his military. "At 1600 hours Terravegan standard time this day," he began, "the Rojok federation decimated Terramer. Among the dead is my son, Marcon. My daughter, Lyceria, is presumed to be a captive of the Rojoks. This Council," he said accusingly, "guaranteed the safety of my children as diplomatic observers on Terramer. The guarantee was worthless. The Holconcom, after rescuing one of your Tri-Fleet ships from attack, was cut off behind enemy lines and communication discontinued. Before contact was lost, I was informed that the Jaakob Spheres were also in Rojok hands."

There were murmurs among the councilmen. Lawson cursed under his breath. It was a disaster. The Spheres gave the Rojoks the key to the DNA of every Tri-Fleet member race. With them, the Rojoks could engineer viruses to target each specific race. But, even worse, there was one tiny strand of DNA which encoded the history and military capability of each one, as well. These secrets were not even shared with outworlders. Old Lokar had persuaded the Tri-Galaxy Federation members to include that secret in the Jaakob Spheres, guaranteeing their safety. They had been carried aboard the diplomatic observers' ship for safekeeping. What a joke! Safekeeping, indeed.

"I demand," Tnurat continued, "that the Council retaliate for this atrocity. If such retaliation is not forthcoming, the Dectat will act in a declaration of war on the neutral member planets of the Council. I allowed the limited use of my Holconcom as forward scout support for the Tri-Galaxy Fleet in response to a plea from your Admiral Lawson, after the latest Rojok incursion into Tri-Fleet territory. Now I ask, no, I demand, that the Council, including the neutral worlds, send armed units to support my government's troops in a declaration of war on the Rojok tyrant Mangus Lo. The alternative is that you will fight not only the Rojok, but the Centaurian Empire, as well. The vanguard of our military is the Holconcom," he added in a soft threat. "Some of you may remember how they put down revolutions in our planetary space. And how they deal with enemies. The choice is yours. Help me rescue my daughter and stop Mangus Lo's aggression, or face the consequences. I will expect a reply within one standard hour."

A long, heavy silence fell over the room. Lawson watched idealism die in the eyes of the diplomats, giving way to what was undeniably fear.

The Terravegan ambassador stood up. "May I speak?" he asked Lokar.

"You may. I present the human ambassador from the Terravegan colonies, Giles Mourjey."

"Honorable Chairman, members of the Council," Mourjey began, his eyes sweeping among the male and female delegates of the Tri-Galaxy Council, one of whom was an imposing Centaurian female named Karimasa. "The only force standing against the Rojok invasion of the New Territory has been the Royal Legion of Terravega, with some small assistance from the Altairian and Jebob militaries. I think it goes without saying that the human regiments of the Tri-Fleet have made the larger sacrifice of men and women. You may also have heard of *Ahkmau,* the Rojok death camp, where two million human soldiers have been systematically tortured to death in Mangus Lo's insane lust for galactic conquest. With all due respect, delegates, while you were pursing the idealism of interracial harmony with your clones on Terramer, the Royal Legion of Terravega's Strategic Space Command was pursuing a different goal. It was enforcing the only war vote of any member planetary systems in this Council, standing against a bloodthirsty dictator who's already enslaved two planetary systems that declared neutrality. The humans have been decimated by Rojok attacks in the New Territory!"

A dark green, slender delegate stood up quickly. "What he says is not true," the delegate, a Vegan colonial, growled. "The Meg-Vegan High Council also issued a war vote and our Guards even now fight with the humans."

"Yes, indeed, Ambassador," Mourjey replied, "in rec halls on bases all over the three civilized galaxies, they fight *with* us. But on the battle lines, they turn around and run!"

The Vegan turned dusky under his green skin, but he didn't deny the charge. Instead he sat down, smoldering.

Mourjey faced the Council. "Delegates, the human colonies are getting damned tired of fighting this unholy war virtually alone. If it's peace you want, if you hope to retain your own planetary systems, you'll have to crawl out of your holes and fight for them! If you'd rather not involve yourselves in the danger, then by all means, go home and learn to speak Rojok. That is, if the Rojoks don't take the New Territory before you have the time, and throw the lot of us into Mangus Lo's sonic ovens!" He sat down.

Lawson swung around and got to his feet. "He's right," he said. "I've tried to tell you delegates that the conflict can't rock on like this. I've only got five hundred thousand men left in the Strategic Space Command of my Royal Legion, out of the five million I started with. We've lost ships, we've lost supply transports, we're even now patching comm units into neutral ships because we're losing outposts by the day. I need help, or the Rojoks are going to grab the solar systems in the New Territory. If they do that, its mineral resources and colonization possibilities and water resources and fertile farming plains are going to be dead to us. Our overflow populations and dwindling energy and food stores will send some of us into oblivion as a race, and the Rojoks won't have to fire a single shot to accomplish our demise."

"You might also remember the Spheres that were captured by the Rojoks," Mourjey broke in. "If the Rojoks have them, they hold the key to the complete obliteration of every member race of the Council. The military information alone which they contain will guarantee our defeat. I'm sure some of you remember slavery?"

The Rigellian delegate pursed his yellow lips. "Some of us also remember the Great Galaxy War," he said quietly. "Another like it and some of us would be obliterated regardless."

"Freedom has a price," Lawson said philosophically. "But fighting Rojoks isn't your only option now. You have a choice between fighting the Rojoks or fighting the Rojoks and the Centaurian Empire as well. Would any of you care to match the cream of your military forces against the Holconcom?"

There was a long silence, interspersed with urgent whispers. Council members glanced at each other in obvious apprehension.

Lokar spoke for them. "Some of us have also suffered the penalty for provoking the Holconcom, and remember it well. Nor do I harbor concern for the Holconcom ship, which has been cut off by the Rojok vessels," he added with an amused glance at the Centaurian delegate, whose fine lips pulled into a very human smile. "My sympathy, rather, is for the Rojoks. We will call a vote."

Lawson saluted Lokar and left the chamber. He knew when he left what the outcome would be. He only regretted that it had taken so many lives, and Tnurat Alamantimichar's threat, to open the eyes of those diplomatic moles. So many human lives, so many atrocities…

Then he remembered the reference to the Holconcom rescue operation. He permitted himself a tiny smile. The *Bellatrix*. It had to be. And Captain Holt Stern and his crew were alive after all. But for how long? Humans and Holconcom together, in a confined space, under pressure. The Holconcom would slaughter them with little provocation. They knew nothing of humans. Only Dtimun had any real experience of them, and he was notorious for his dislike of the entire species. His heart sank. Perhaps it would have been more merciful for the humans if a Rojok blast had claimed the *Bellatrix* with all aboard!

The harsh sound of Rojok voices brought Lyceria back to consciousness. Waves of vertigo wound through her head as she tried to sit up on the bed. She peered through the dim light toward the door. Behind it, a flood of Rojok voices rushed in at her. Three voices; one obliging and placating, one defensive, one harsh and threatening.

The autodoor zipped up. One lone Rojok entered the small cubicle. He walked with authority. He was tall, reddish-skinned, hard-muscled. His long shock of blond hair was neatly trimmed, flowing down over the high collar of his black, long-sleeved uniform jacket. His slacks followed powerful legs down into heavy black boots. His slit-eyes peered at her from a lean, stern face that showed no emotion. His sleeves displayed a pattern of *mesag* marks that denoted high rank, as did the long hair, which only officers were permitted to wear. He had faint scars on his face, and lines around his eyes. He was a warrior.

Lyceria stood up, only a little intimidated, preparing herself for whatever was to come. "Am I now to be taken to *Ahkmau?*" she asked.

A flicker of shock touched the alien face. The Rojok's eyes narrowed and his jaw tautened proudly. "It is not the custom of the Rojok," he said in perfect Centaurian accents, "to condemn royalty to the death camps."

"No?" A tiny smile touched her full lips. "I was told that if I did not comport myself as expected, I would be placed there."

The Rojok glared toward the door where the other two aliens stiffened, quickly saluted and moved back a safe distance. In different circumstances, the action would have been amusing to Lyceria.

When he looked back at her, his eyes were still narrow with fury. "No more threats will be made against you. You have my word."

"It is said," she replied, "that the word of a Rojok is as the wind."

"Is it also said of the word of Chacon?"

Her eyes flashed brown at the Rojok as she recognized him from textdiscs. Here was no ordinary soldier. This was the most powerful field marshal of the Rojok army, the most famous of them all.

"You!" She stepped forward, momentarily forgetting the required dignity of her station. "Murderer of women and children! Torturer of boys!"

A muscle in his cheek flinched. "The attack on Terramer was perpetrated without my knowledge," he stated flatly. "As was the murder of your brother. Those responsible will be punished."

"And what punishment will return my brother to me, Commander Chacon?" she asked bitterly. "Tell me that."

"I cannot undo what was done. Atrocities are frequently committed in the name of war, by all soldiers." His eyes softened slightly. "Come. You will be provided more suitable quarters."

"In your prison, no doubt."

He watched her quietly, with eyes as deft as a hunter's aim. "Your bitterness is understandable. But bitterness is an acid. Beware, lest it eat you alive."

"Grief is not shared with outworlders," she told him.

"Not among Rojoks." He stood aside to let her pass. "Have you eaten?"

"I care for nothing," she replied. Inside, her ribs felt near collapse from the three-day fast.

"You will eat," he said, "or you will be fed forcibly. Do you understand? I will not allow you to commit suicide."

"Allow?" She looked at him defiantly, with brown anger coloring her pupils. "And do you think to dictate to me?"

He smiled. A thin, self-confident smile that was disconcerting. "Until the war is over, at least. You are a political prisoner. As such, you will tolerate my 'dictates.'"

"And the consequences?" she chided. "Shall you send me to *Ahkmau?*"

"If you continue to oppose me, you may be sent to my harem," he warned mockingly.

Had she known how, she would have blushed. A mingling of color touched her eyes, and she hid them from him. Dtimun would teach this Rojok *choapha* manners. Among other lessons the Holconcom would provide.

* * *

Stern was still nursing hostility when he went into the mess hall with Madeline and Hahnson two "days" later. The tension in the room was so thick it could have been filleted.

The compartment was filled to capacity, with humans and Centaurians sitting uncomfortably integrated at the long tables. The close quarters bred tension.

The ship was still running from the oncoming net of Rojok ships, which it had managed to avoid with amazing tactical skill. Stern was beginning to believe the C.O.'s reputation for eluding superior forces. Apparently there was some sort of technology in use that was able to broadcast false ion trails to lead the Rojok ships astray. How long that would continue to work was anyone's guess. Meanwhile, hope was growing that the vessel would make neutral Benaski Port in time.

The situation aboard the *Morcai,* however, was growing desperate. In the past twenty-four standard hours, disaster had been averted by seconds on every deck. The mixture of aliens and humans grew more explosive by the minute. Thanks to the translators, the humans understood enough Centaurian to realize that they were being chided, denigrated and insulted with every other breath. The Holconcom were eloquent about their distaste for having to share quarters with those they thought of as inferior beings. They abused the humans for being unable to meet the same physical challenges as the Centaurians. They chided them for their lack of stamina. The humans, on the other hand, knew that the Centaurians were clones, and treated them with contempt. Among human colonies, clones had no status, no rights, and were frequently kept in cooling tanks in suspended animation and used as spare parts for their originals.

Some of the Centaurians had to move out of their quarters to accommodate the unexpected guests aboard their vessel. The humans got in the way of routine. They didn't understand Centaurian discipline, they didn't follow the protocols, and they acted as if they owned the ship. Stern made no attempt to smooth things over. Hahnson had, but his misgivings grew when he noticed how careless Stern's attitude was to the growing danger. He'd mentioned it to Komak, who frowned and commented that perhaps a word to Dtimun would be wise. The exec offered to speak to his commanding officer for Hahnson, and not mention it to Holt Stern. Hahnson dreaded having Stern find out that he'd gone behind his back. But something was different about his captain; something radical. He looked around him at the integrated mess hall and wondered how anyone could think combining the groups a good idea. The Centaurians had never known physical contact with other races except in war, and these humans knew nothing of how they fought on a battlefield. Hahnson had known humans to have nervous breakdowns just from seeing the Holconcom fight. Stern had never seen them in combat. Perhaps that helped explain his odd lack of concern for his men.

Madeline was watching a group of Centaurians and humans at another table with growing concern. The "accidental" elbowing by the humans was all too conspicuous, and the chiding tones were unmistakable despite the language barrier that even the rudimentary translators were working valiantly to correct.

"He might have left us segregated," Madeline said angrily. "This forced integration is going to cause a riot before we ever reach Benaski Port."

"Forced?" Hahnson eyed her. "Did Dtimun give orders to integrate at mess? I can't believe he'd risk it." He frowned as he studied the other diners. "This could result in a slaughter. Are you sure it was the C.O.?"

Madeline scowled. "Well, no. But if not him, then, who...?"

"I integrated our ship's complement with the Centaurians," Stern said carelessly. "They'll have to learn to get along one way or the other, and the sooner the better."

"Are you nuts?" Hahnson exclaimed. "Don't you know what's going to happen if one of our men lays hands on one of the Holconcom?"

"The Holconcom will sit there and take it, of course," Stern replied smugly. "You yourself," he added to Hahnson, "told me that the commander threatened to kill the first one of his men who fought back if there were any confrontations."

"The commander still doesn't realize just how physical humans are," Hahnson protested. "I'm the only one he's spent much time around, and we never came to blows!"

"Try the green jell," Stern said casually, lifting a spoonful to his lips. "It tastes like anything you imagine it to be. It's ingenious."

"Holt…"

Hahnson never finished the sentence. Before he could, an ominous clatter of hyperplastic hitting the deck cut him off. A brief, stunned silence followed the commotion.

A *Bellatrix* crewman shot to his feet, glaring down at a Holconcom noncom beside him. "That's it, you damned cat-eyes!" he roared, red in the face. "I've taken all the insults and all the sarcasm I'm goin' to take from you!"

The Holconcom pointedly ignored the outburst and kept eating.

Confident now, the human grew bolder. "No guts," he spat at the alien. "You guys are all talk. Come on, stand up and let's see if you bleed!"

Hahnson gaped at the crewman. He knew the man. It was one of the engineers, Declan Muldoon, and he was one of the most levelheaded humans he'd ever known. It wasn't like Muldoon to actually start a fight.

Just as Hahnson started to relay that opinion to his colleagues, Muldoon laid a heavy hand on the Centaurian he was baiting and, deftly turning him, threw a heavy-handed right cross to the alien's jaw.

The Holconcom sat and stared at the human, unmoved by the blow, which would have felled any crewman at Stern's table.

"Tough guy, huh?" Muldoon persisted, grinning. "Try this on for size!" He threw another punch, putting everything he had into it. The Holconcom absorbed it as easily as he had the first. But his eyes began to dilate. As he turned toward the human, Madeline saw the elongated cat-eyes slowly turn brown.

"Stern, do something while there's still time," Madeline said quickly.

But the *Bellatrix*'s captain only sat watching the byplay with oddly blank, dark eyes.

Suddenly a low, soft growl began to grow in the silence that followed the human engineer's next deliberate blow. The sound built on itself, like a low roar that quickly took on the ferocity of a jungle cat's warning cry. It exploded abruptly in a high-pitched inhuman scream that froze Stern's heart in his chest with a terror that bordered on panic. The blank look left his eyes as his jaw dropped. He'd never heard such a nightmarish sound in his life, even in combat.

"My God!" Hahnson whispered. "The *decaliphe!*"

Before the soft words died on the air, the Holconcom regular was on his feet. He began to crouch, his eyes darker by the second, his hands slowly assuming the shape of a cat's open paw. They flexed. Beneath the tips of the fingers, steel claws began to extend in gleaming sharp points. It was a form of bionic engineering that none of the humans had yet seen.

Madeline pushed Stern, but he didn't react. He was frozen in place by the low growl that built again in the Centaurian's throat.

Madeline grabbed for Stern's *Gresham* and fired it at point-blank range, into the back of the Holconcom, with the setting on maximum burn. It should have killed the alien. It should have dropped him to his knees at least. It did neither. She fired again, cursing under her breath, with the same result.

"What in the seven netherworlds...!" Madeline exclaimed huskily.

The Holconcom group had risen in unison. They were standing, watching the other Holconcom who crouched in front of Muldoon.

Hahnson got to his feet. "Twenty *Greshams* wouldn't stop him now!" he told Madeline. "He gave the *decaliphe*—the death cry. Only Dtimun can bring him down! Hold the other men back, no matter what the Holconcom do, if you can. I'll get the C.O."

He was out the door at a dead run. Madeline moved forward with the *Gresham* leveled, ignoring Stern, who still sat as if in a trance.

"Hold it!" Madeline barked at two human noncoms who were in the process of rising from their seats. "Move and I'll drop both of you," she added, her green eyes backing up the threat. They sat down.

But Lieutenant Higgins, the *Bellatrix*'s exec, rose from his chair despite the threat of Madeline's *Gresham*. Across from her, the Holconcom regular was moving with a catlike stalking gait toward Muldoon, who had by now realized his peril and had begun to back away, his face mirroring his fear.

"He'll kill Muldoon, if we don't do something," Higgins pleaded huskily. "He's my friend. If we could just get Muldoon out of here...! You don't know what they'll do if the alien actually attacks Muldoon." He nodded toward the Holconcom. "You haven't seen them fight. I have." He swallowed, hard. "There won't be enough of Muldoon left to bury, and then they'll go for the other humans in a solid mass. They can't help it, Doctor, it's the way they fight...!"

Another sharp, catlike cry from the Holconcom interrupted him.

The hairs on the back of Madeline's neck stood up, but she held her ground. She had, after all, been an officer in the Amazon regiment, long before she became a doctor. "Move toward him again,"

Madeline told Higgins, "and he'll have company. It's Hahnson's show.
He knows what he's doing."

The rest of the Holconcom were still standing, and when the
humans began to stand, as well, the Centaurians' eyes began to grow
darker and the pupils dilate.

Hurry, Strick, she thought silently. She wasn't certain what the
outcome would be, but she was inclined to believe Higgins. She'd
heard things about the way the Holconcom fought, as a unit. None
of the Amazons had ever seen them in combat or been liaisoned
with them. The Centaurians had no female military, due to their obviously backward culture, she thought wickedly. But she had a
feeling that if any of the humans made a move toward Muldoon,
the Holconcom would mass and there would be a massacre. Higgins
meant well, but his interference could bring about the very situation he feared.

Muldoon was looking paler by the minute, but he stood firm. "Go
ahead. Kill me. Or try to kill me," he taunted the Holconcom.

"Shut up, Muldoon!" Madeline called to him, in a tone that
demanded obedience.

He gave her an odd look. One of the other humans turned to the
Centaurian next to him and put up his fists. There were more growls.
The Holconcom began to merge into a mass of red uniforms.

God, Madeline thought in anguish. There was nothing else she
could do. If Hahnson didn't hurry...!

She heard the autodoor opening behind her with relief, and moved
her eyes to it.

But it wasn't the C.O. It was Hahnson, grimacing. "Komak's going
after him," he told her.

"Think we have time?" she wondered with black humor, taking her
eyes off Muldoon for an instant.

It was enough. Higgins sprang into action. He went for the Holconcom bracing Muldoon and clipped him at the knees.

Incredibly the Holconcom was like a solidly rooted tree. He didn't move an inch. But his hand did. He caught Muldoon by the throat with one hand, flung the human away and slammed him to the deck, where he lay still, unmoving. Then he turned toward Higgins.

"Oh, God!" Madeline ground out when she saw the Centaurian's eyes. They were black. Pitch-black. As black as death. She'd never seen that color, but she'd read about it...

She fired the Gresham, again and again and again, but the *emerillium* propelled plasma spray simply bounced off. She could hardly believe her eyes. Then, just as the Holconcom reached Higgins, there was a sound behind her.

"Mashcon!" The single word had the ring of steel hitting rock. It froze the humans in their stances, like action figures. It muted the building growls of the other Holconcom.

All eyes turned toward the doorway. Dtimun was standing just inside it, with Komak at his side. The alien's eyes, as black as those of his Holconcom, looked and held on those of the Centaurian who had Muldoon in his grasp.

The soldier's eyes suddenly calmed. The black death was gone from them, to be replaced by a color that Madeline's whirling mind couldn't classify. His face abruptly contorted, and he screamed— something unheard of in the ranks of the Holconcom.

The scream died. He stood there, facing his commanding officer with a fear so complete it seemed to radiate from him and touch every Centaurian in the mess hall.

"You were warned," Dtimun said, very quietly, "of the consequences of conflict. You have seen the power of the Holconcom. Now see the power of their commander."

He moved forward so quickly that he was a blur in the eyes of the humans. He had the Centaurian by the neck in a heartbeat. A split second later, his hand flexed and the alien flew completely across the mess hall, over the heads of the Centaurians and the humans, with lightning speed. The offending Centaurian hit the Plexiglas wall and bounced off onto the floor, to lie still with his huge eyes open, with his mouth open, as well. He arched, once, and then lay unmoving, like Muldoon.

Madeline swallowed hard. She was a doctor. Before that, she'd been an elite warrior. But in all her battles, she'd never seen anything like the commander in action. She'd never have believed that any humanoid could move that fast until she'd seen it. Beside her, she felt Hahnson's arm tense like a coiled spring.

Dtimun's black eyes calmed into a somber blue. He straightened regally, with barely noticeable effort, and turned to the others. His expression was so fierce that Higgins actually backed up. "There will be no further incidents," he said quietly. "Or the perpetrators will answer to me. Am I understood?"

The entire complement of the mess hall stood at rigid attention, including the Holconcom.

"Who integrated the mess?" the alien added abruptly, and turned to Komak.

"Not I," Komak replied.

"I did," Stern said, finding his voice at last.

Dtimun moved toward him without seeming to move at all. He was a head taller than Stern. He stared down at the human with barely concealed rage. "Once, I would have killed you for such an infraction. Your rank in the Tri-Fleet prevents me from such discipline. However," he added with cold eyes, "it will not spare your subordinate." He whirled and shot an order in Centaurian. Two Holconcom went to the downed human, Muldoon, and dragged him to his feet. He was conscious, wide-eyed and visibly terrified.

"Captain Stern!" Muldoon called piteously. "Help me!"

Stern's mind was a nexus of conflicting emotions. He stared at Muldoon blankly as he realized what he'd done, and what the consequences could have been. He couldn't believe he'd put his men at risk like this!

"What will you do with him?" Stern asked the Holconcom commander.

Dtimun didn't reply. He turned back to his officers. "Prepare him." He glanced at Stern. "All officers will go immediately to the green section airlock," he added. "Video monitors will be activated for the crew, so that they may watch, as well."

He made a gesture with one lean hand, which prompted the Holconcom with Muldoon to act immediately, almost carrying a protesting Muldoon out of the canteen. The man's sobs could be heard like echoes of fear.

Madeline gasped aloud. "You can't mean to space him!" she exclaimed. "There are protocols…!"

Dtimun didn't answer her. He looked straight at Stern. "Ask your captain the penalty for inciting intermilitary conflict in time of war." He turned and followed his officers and Muldoon, expecting obedience.

The humans gave Stern shocked, angry looks as they filed by, too shaken by what they'd seen to risk the commander's temper.

"Stern, for God's sake, do something!" Madeline raged.

"It's too late," Hahnson said for him, his face set in hard lines. "No power in the galaxy will stop Dtimun when he thinks he's right. Damn it, Stern! You've cost us one of our best engineers!"

He filed out behind the other humans. Madeline hesitated, but only for an instant. She was shocked at Stern's unnatural behavior, at his instigation of the conflict. She turned her eyes forward and followed Hahnson.

Stern watched them go with wide, blank eyes. He was puzzled and vaguely frightened by his actions, but he couldn't seem to stop doing insane things. Perhaps his concussion had prompted it. Regardless of the reason, Muldoon was about to be spaced, and Stern couldn't do a thing to stop it. Not a single damned thing.

5

By the time Stern got to the airlock station, Muldoon was standing inside the closing doors. Dtimun's third officer, a tall Centaurian named Btnu, was at the wall with his hand on a switch.

Madeline started to protest, but Hahnson kicked her boot. Hard. She swallowed her rage and glared at Stern instead.

Dtimun turned and looked straight at the human crewmen as he gave the order to Btnu. Inside the airlock, Muldoon was pounding at the transparent screen, yelling, his face red and swollen. He looked frantic.

Idly, Stern thought how out of character it was for Muldoon, who was one of the bravest engineers he'd ever served with, to behave in such a manner. He'd seen the Irishman beaten bloody and still struggling to his feet to give back the punches. He wasn't the sort of soldier to beg and plead.

While he was thinking it, Btnu threw the switch and Muldoon was suddenly floating in space.

There was a muttered curse from beside him as the Irishman tumbled over and over and slowly became a speck in the deep black of star-sprinkled space.

"This is what you can expect if there are ever additional incidents of this sort," Dtimun said in a deadly, soft tone as he turned to face the humans. "We are at war. Aboard this ship, we fight Rojoks, not fellow crewmen—even reluctant ones! Remember what you have just seen. Never forget it!" He glared at them. "Dismissed!"

The humans grouped together like defiant, belligerent insurgents and left the deck. The Holconcom showed no emotion whatsoever. They saluted their commander and followed out behind the humans.

Madeline's fists were clenched at her sides. She said nothing, but her eyes spoke for her. She'd almost run out of vicious names to call him, mentally, when he suddenly turned on his heel and glared at her.

Dtimun abruptly walked to her side and stopped with his hands linked behind his back. His posture was threatening enough, without the dark anger of his elongated eyes. "I have no qualms about spacing women," he pointed out, in deep tones without a trace of an accent. "Interfere again and I will prove it. You have duties, Doctor, none of which pertain to command of this vessel. Attend to them!"

She swallowed, her teeth clenched so hard that she thought they might break, and snapped the hateful alien a salute before she turned with perfect posture and marched off the deck.

Hahnson grimaced as he saw Stern's expression, but he said nothing. He saluted and joined Madeline outside.

Dtimun's expression never wavered when he looked at Stern. "The Holconcom fight as a unit," he said. "If I had not intervened, you and your entire crew would be dead. Explain your behavior."

Stern frowned. His hand went to his head. There was a terrible pain, a shattering pain. He could hardly bear it.

The alien's eyes turned blue. He cocked his head. "This pain," he said, "is it from the concussion?"

It didn't occur to Stern to wonder how the alien knew he was in pain. He could barely think. "Pain," he gritted. "So...much...pain...!"

He dropped to the deck, unconscious.

When he came to, he was in the makeshift human sick bay and Hahnson was bending over him, a concerned expression on his broad face as he checked Stern's head with a small device that read through tissue and blood and bone.

"Will I live?" Stern husked.

"You may not want to, considering how much trouble you're in," Hahnson told him quietly.

"The commander was out of line, too," Madeline muttered, standing just to the side of Hahnson. "I'm saving up infractions. When we port at HQ, I'm bringing him up on charges."

Hahnson gave her a tongue-in-cheek glance. "Pay your burial fees first."

"I'm not afraid of him," she said curtly. But she didn't push the issue. "How is he?" she asked Hahnson.

"No major damage that I can see," Hahnson said absently, checking his scanners. "But there are some minor deviations in the endorphin levels, and there's some foreign substance that I can't even identify."

"I have some memory loss," Stern admitted at last. He winced. "And headaches that aren't even describable."

"Maybe the deviations are responsible," Madeline interjected.

"That doesn't explain them," Hahnson replied. He handed Madeline a copy of his readings. "You're better at exobiology than I am. Run those through your diagnostic computer, will you? Perhaps you can find something that my scanners can't read."

"My degrees are all in Cularian medicine," she pointed out. "That's Rojok and Altairian and Centaurian genetics."

"There are some similarities to Rojok cell structure," Hahnson said surprisingly.

Stern sat up too quickly, grabbed his head and groaned.

"Just lie back down, if you please," Hahnson said, easing him onto the medical scanner array. "I'm not accusing you of being a Rojok spy. I said there were similarities, that's all. You might have picked up some cellular residue left behind by the Rojoks when they attacked the colony. This equipment is sensitive enough to detect week-old skin cells."

"Oh," Stern murmured.

Madeline peered into the computer built into the examination array and frowned. She exchanged a glance with Hahnson that Stern didn't see.

Hahnson read it very well. He patted Stern on the shoulder. "You just lie there and rest for a few minutes. I'm going to walk Madeline through the sensor workup. Okay?"

"Okay." He opened his eyes and looked up at his comrades of many years with a worried frown. "What's wrong with me?" he asked abruptly. "I let that cat-eyed terror blow up the *Bellatrix* without a protest. I let him space Muldoon. On Terramer, I was willing to sacrifice the Jebobs and Altairians. What the hell am I turning into?" he asked in anguish. "Why can't I remember anything before we left the Peace Planet? Why didn't I rush that cat-eyed terror when he spaced Muldoon?" He groaned, holding his head. "The pain...is terrible. I can't...function...like this!"

"We'll find the answers, Holt," Madeline said quietly. "I promise."

He drew in an unsteady breath. "Muldoon's gone. It's my fault."

"It's his," Hahnson corrected shortly. "He could have gotten us all killed. If you'd ever seen the Holconcom fight, you wouldn't be apologizing." He shivered faintly. "It's not a sight you ever forget."

"Enough philosophy," Madeline told Hahnson. "Let's go."

They stopped just at the door to Madeline's makeshift sick bay. She looked around at the antiseptically clean corridor and at the walls. "Think they have AVBDs out here?" she wondered softly, using the abbreviation for audio-visual biodetectors.

"I'm not sure we'd know if we were being watched. Their biotech is centuries ahead of ours. They have living, breathing machines called *kelekoms,* that work as a connected bank of high-level super-computers. There are only four aboard the *Morcai,* and the opera-tors are joined to them for life. The *kelekoms* actually feel. They're biological entities, from a world of beings who lead noncorporeal lives bound to technology."

She grimaced, only half listening. The corridor was too cool to be comfortable. Like Stern and Hahnson, she was a Terravegan national. The human colony was subtropical, with lavish pink and black sand beaches and incredibly lush flora. She missed it from time to time, although most of her life had been spent in the military, from the age of three when she entered a cadet training center. She was one of the few military officers who knew one of her biologi-cal parents. Her father was Colonel Clinton Ruszel, a Paraguard officer in the Tri-Fleet. He'd kept tabs on her all the long years, and there was a sort of affection between them, despite the mandatory mental neutering of the military that made it difficult to maintain any sort of emotional ties. Ideally she shouldn't have been able to feel any sort of familial affection. Certainly it was designed to prevent sexual attraction between the coed military, and it worked. Very few tried to have the required mental neutering reversed.

Fraternization was the only offense left on the books that carried the death penalty.

"You're worried," Hahnson noted.

She nodded, looking at the scanner in her hand. "These are more than just discarded Rojok cells. There's a genetic structure here that I've never seen, except in clones."

"You don't think Holt is a clone, surely?" he laughed.

She didn't smile. "He was missing for a long time, Strick," she reminded him. "We know that the Rojoks are experimenting with instant cloning."

"Like they're going to have it on a remote planet in the middle of nowhere," he scoffed. "They were after the Jaakob Spheres, they weren't cloning people."

"If they were," she persisted, "think how devastating it could be to our war effort. Suppose you could clone a military officer or a high official, program him to do what you wanted and then replace his original. If you'd downloaded his memories, his education, as well, the clone would be virtually undetectable. We've been working on such tech for the past five standard years, and we're on the verge of a breakthrough. What if the Rojoks already have it? They experiment with all sorts of biotech at *Ahkmau*, their notorious prison camp on Enmehkmehk's moon. They could develop this before we can, since they are not restricted by ethics as we are."

"Stern had a concussion," Strick said gently. "That explains the headache and the behavioral anomalies."

"Does it?" she replied. "Then why didn't he save Muldoon?"

"He'd have been spaced alongside him."

"That wouldn't have stopped the Stern we both know," she pointed out. "Remember when Lawson had Danny Bean arrested for a murder that Stern could prove he didn't commit? We actually broke

Danny out of maximum security in the brig. Stern knew it would mean a reprimand on his permanent record. He did it anyway."

Hahnson nodded slowly. "Well, concussion has been responsible for some very odd behavior," he said, clinging to his theory.

She moved a step closer, wary of passersby who might overhear her. "I think his brain has been altered," she persisted. "Remember that brain scan I ran on him just after we came on board this ship? I found an abnormality in the neurotransmitters. His norepinephrine levels have been chemically altered, and there are anomalies in the neurons, as well. The bone scan detected an altered cell structure we can't duplicate. Not only that," she added wearily, "the biorhythm scan was indecisive. His pattern was run less than a month ago—standard procedure—and charted. I compared the new one with it. The change is too radical to be explained away by concussion. Someone's been experimenting on Stern. I think."

Hahnson blew wind through his lips. "God, what a mouthful! All that evidence, Maddie, and you only *think* his brain's been tampered with?"

"I can't deny that the concussion could be responsible for some of the readings. Theoretically it could have affected the outcome of a brain profile, I suppose." She sighed. "And you're right about those stray Rojok cells. They could have contaminated his cell structure if he was exposed to residual traces of them."

"Theoretically black holes could be harnessed for time-drive systems if they'd stop gobbling up our scientific expeditions," he countered. "Well, what do you want to do about it?"

"Watch him closely until we get to Benaski Port. What else can we do?"

He cocked his head. "We could talk this over with Dtimun, you know."

Both auburn eyebrows went up. "With that strutting, black-

browed, inhuman son of a…" she began, her voice gaining power
with each word.

"Maddie!" Hahnson cautioned hastily, his eyes intent over her
left shoulder.

Slowly she turned to meet a gaze as black and dangerous as a
hungry *galot*'s. The raw power in those dilated cat eyes could have
backed down a group of mutineers. Madeline's eyelids flickered as
if the impact of his glare had actually been physical.

"Finish the description, Madam," the *Morcai*'s towering commander said, his gentle tone far more threatening than pure rage.

Madeline swallowed. Hard. "C…Centaurian, sir," she said, hating
the tremor in her voice, hating the fear, hating *him,* and her eyes told
him so. She was a combat veteran, a leader of elite troops, but this
creature was more than her match.

"Tread softly, warwoman," he told her with a cold bite in his
words. "As I have said, I have no compunction about spacing a human
female." He made the adjective sound like a disease, but his eyes dared
her to challenge him. "What was it, Madam, that the two of you were
considering to discuss with me?"

Hahnson cleared his throat. "Commander, it was the matter of our
patients," he hedged, thinking fast. "Time is getting precious. Is there
some chance that we can make it to Benaski Port before the Rojok
ships close in on us?"

The Centaurian's eyes became a cold, solemn blue. "A chance," he
agreed finally.

Hahnson's eyes narrowed as he studied the alien. "When we served
together, you were legendary for pulling rabbits out of hats, theoretically speaking. Why is it so difficult for you to find a way around
our pursuers?"

The alien's eyes burned brown as he glared down at Hahnson. "Do not try friendship too far with me, Hahnson," he said coldly. "My capacity for it, as you well know, is limited. Both of you, back to your posts. I expect your patients to survive until we reach port."

"Another matter I haven't had time to discuss with you," Madeline told the alien commander. "What about cloning Muldoon? We have the tech…"

"No," he said flatly.

She was shocked. "But, sir, the copy would have the same capabilities…"

"No," he repeated. His eyes dared her to continue the argument. "My personnel will attend to his urning. And to the recloning of my officer."

"Are we still being followed?" Hahnson asked abruptly.

"More closely by the parsec," Dtimun replied.

"Do you have any ETA on Benaski?" Madeline added cheekily as the alien walked away. But no answer trailed back.

"You're tempting fate," Hahnson told her. "He isn't himself. Something's wrong."

"What is he made of?" she asked suddenly. "You saw what he did to his own man in the mess hall, Strick. It was beyond even the means of a combat-trained Holconcom. And why are the Rojoks throwing so many warships against one lone vessel, even a Holconcom ship? What's aboard that Chacon wants so badly?"

"I honestly don't know," he replied. "But if we can't get Stern back to himself, we may very well find ourselves in another bloodbath before we reach a neutral port."

"I could have cloned Muldoon," she muttered.

"And he could have been an outcast, especially in our own society," Hahnson replied curtly. "Would you really wish that on him? Yes, he had great knowledge of space engineering, but it would be insane to bring him back into a life worse than hell."

"I suppose you're right," she said heavily. "I'll miss him, though. Well, I'm going to go synthesize some more *morphadrenin* for my patients. Poor devils," she said, thinking about the horror the refugees had endured. "Only clones, but they bleed and think and feel and cry just like us. And they can't even vote, Strick, or marry or hold public office. They can't serve in the military. They have no legal rights at all. They're walking spare parts in our culture. I must have been insane to propose that for Muldoon."

"Stop," Hahnson said as they turned back down the corridor. "Don't tell me, tell the Council. I feel the same way. Now, get to it, old girl, before the man on the bridge decides to take a bite out of you."

"Let him. I'd give him hives," she muttered.

"He has changed over the years," Hahnson said as they jogged toward their respective makeshift sick bays. "The Dtimun I used to know would have stood you up in the brig with novapens leveled at your nose until you apologized. Strange."

"Double-check my readings on Stern, will you?" she added.

"Will do. Maybe," he added, tongue-in-cheek, "the ship's scanners caught a cold and it blurred their vision."

"A remark like that," she called over her shoulder, "could get you inoculated for diseases they haven't even discovered yet!"

On a screen halfway through the ship, a pair of elongated dark blue eyes was watching a plasma screen. On it, a redheaded woman in uniform was walking back to her makeshift sick bay. He touched the screen and the image faded. Seconds later, he was in the corridor.

Madeline had gone over the cell structure twice, with the same disquieting results.

She leaned forward, with her hands spread on the microanalyzer stand, frowning.

"It doesn't make sense," she murmured to herself.

"Perhaps it does."

She jumped at the deep voice behind her and whirled, her green eyes wide. Dtimun stood there, unsmiling, his eyes a deep violet-blue as he looked at her. "You do have AVBDs in the corridors," she said quietly, grinding her teeth inwardly as she recalled some of the things she'd said about Stern.

He nodded. "Although we rarely use them," he told her. "The *kelekoms* can 'see' for us, even there."

"*Kelekoms*..."

"Our living machines. What you call computers."

She averted her eyes to her patients. Her mind, occupied for so many minutes on her lack of basic medical stores, began to work rapidly. Hahnson's admiration for the alien had caught her attention. She'd been grossly unfair in her judgment, but Muldoon's spacing had blinded her to the situation they were in. Dtimun had saved them when the *Bellatrix* had been threatened. He could easily have let the Rojoks slaughter them and escaped on the *Morcai* unscathed. But he hadn't.

She was just beginning to see things that emotion had blinded her to, earlier. Dtimun's quick action had stopped a massacre. Even she had to admit that Muldoon had precipitated the near disastrous conflict in the mess hall. But when she considered the spacing that had made her so angry, she saw more than she had at first. Something didn't quite make sense about the public execution of the Centaurian officer, and of the *Bellatrix*'s chief engineer...

She turned to Dtimun and studied his strong, golden-skinned face. The fact that he'd refused to let her clone Muldoon, especially given the Centaurian respect for the procedure, had gnawed at her brain since their earlier conversation. Was there some other reason that he'd denied permission to clone the *Bellatrix*'s beloved eldest engineer? Some…stranger reason?

"You killed Muldoon." It was more a question than a statement, now that her sharp mind was working properly again. She'd also had time to note some anomalies in the fight in the canteen and the spacing she'd witnessed.

Not one iota of expression escaped Dtimun's control. "An example was necessary to avert a massacre."

She searched his eyes. "I don't remember ever reading that a Holconcom officer screamed, even when he faced death at the hands of his C.O. Not only that, Muldoon also screamed," she said suddenly, as the event ran again through her mind.

One dark eyebrow lifted.

"I've served with him for six years aboard the *Bellatrix*. We've been in combat together. Muldoon has never screamed in his life," she explained.

"Perhaps he had never faced certain death in a controlled environment," Dtimun suggested.

"He was acting," she persisted.

The other eyebrow joined the raised one.

"Besides," she added, the argument solving itself, "his face never changed color or showed any reaction to the vacuum of space. Odd, isn't it?" she added musingly. "Not something even a first-year med student would miss, if she was watching carefully. I must have been really distracted not to notice that."

His eyes faded from a royal-blue to an amused, soft green, only a few shades lighter than her own. But he said nothing.

"You're not going to tell me anything, are you, sir?" she asked.

"I will tell you not to offer these strange observations to your crewmates."

She searched his eyes. "Very well." She felt odd. As if she and the alien were sharing secrets. More than secrets. He'd infuriated her, made her angry, insulted her, threatened her with the discipline of the military. None of that had fazed her. Now he made her uneasy, but not in any way she'd ever felt before.

"You told Hahnson that you found something in the scans of Stern's brain," he changed the subject.

She grimaced. She didn't want to confess it to an outsider. Hahnson would never make public his knowledge of Stern's condition without real need. This alien was different. She was apprehensive about what he might do if she told him the whole truth. "I've served with Stern and Hahnson for ten years," she pointed out, "ever since I gave up combat command and obtained my medical degree."

"And you feel loyalty to your captain. Is that not against regulations?"

The question was unexpected. Her eyes were troubled. "It is. I was an SSC Amazon Commando from the time I was nine, until my eighteenth year. When I left, I held the rank of captain," she told him. "I never understood, either, why I left, or what led me to medicine. Even SSC HQ questioned the choice. It was inexplicable, even to me."

"Sometimes," he said in an oddly soft tone, "our destinies shape us, rather than the reverse."

"Perhaps." She turned back to the sensors. "Do you understand the basics of viral transmutation?"

He nodded. "We do not perform medical research, since even the most basic tampering with DNA in nonclones carries the death penalty in my culture. But we are privy to the experiments of your government with genetic alteration. Viruses are nonliving organisms which achieve the extreme of evolutionary specialization for parasitism."

"Very good, Commander," she said, impressed. "Well, Rojok scientists have found a method in which it is possible to engineer a virus and introduce it into a human body to activate certain behaviors, which would be abnormal under ordinary conditions."

He folded his arms over his broad chest. "You speak of biogenetic engineering."

She nodded. "It only takes a second to introduce the virus. It doesn't even require injection. It can be placed in the nostril." She hesitated. "Stern was missing for several hours. When he came back, his behavior was, to put it mildly, odd."

"Hahnson said the same thing."

"Yes. We're both concerned. In fact," she added, facing him, "Stern himself is concerned. He doesn't understand why he didn't inter-fere when you allegedly spaced Muldoon."

He cocked an eyebrow. "I suggest you omit the adverb if you repeat this conversation."

"Allegedly means it isn't proven." She smiled.

He didn't react. "I want you and Hahnson to watch Stern closely," he told her. "I have a—"he sought the right word "—feeling that there may be more to this than an erratic personality change."

"You think the Rojoks may have gotten to him?"

He nodded. "Anything is possible. Stern would be a valuable tool in the hands of Rojok spies."

There was a loud moan, coming from the back of the mess hall where Madeline had several critical cases in ambutubes. She moved quickly to peer inside the torpedo-shaped Plexiglas case. Inside was a blue-skinned Altairian boy, a clone, crying out in pain. His culture was notorious for its stoicism. The pain, she thought as she opened the case, must have been monstrous. She'd been giving him opiates since he'd been brought aboard. The pain hadn't dimin-ished very much.

She reached in with her wrist bank of precious opiates and started to laserdot one into his primary thoracic vein once more.

The commander's arm came out and blocked the move.

"He's in pain," she began to protest.

Before she got the last word out, Dtimun bent over the boy. He touched him gently on the forehead and closed his eyes. Only a second later, the child looked up at him with royal-blue eyes and smiled.

"*Degrak mogkrom,*" the child said.

Dtimun actually smiled. "*Toshwa,*" he replied in the same tongue.

The little boy's eyes closed. He went to sleep.

Dtimun stood erect, visibly affected by the action. He caught himself and stood erect.

"Sir, are you ill?" she asked.

"I am not," he denied.

"What did you do?" she persisted. "I've given him every opiate I possess, but nothing has completely contained the pain."

He looked down at her with curious, pale blue eyes. "I convinced his mind to forget the pain," he said simply. "It is a technique we employ with our own military. You may have noticed that we carry no medical complement."

"But what if someone is critically injured?"

He didn't reply at once. "We have methods of treatment that are somewhat advanced," he said at last.

She wanted to press the issue, but Komak appeared in the doorway, his eyes a twinkling green. "Strickhahnson wishes to borrow a *fledelwongmatzel,*" he said with a nicely imitated human grin.

Madeline's eyes bulged. It was a very naughty word.

"*Nos hac malcache!*" Dtimun shot at him.

The irrepressible alien didn't react to the harsh tone. "It is Terravegan," he explained to his superior officer. "It means..."

"Never you mind what it means!" Madeline said shortly. "If you'll excuse me, sir, Hahnson needs his mouth washed out with soap." She saluted and marched out the door.

"It is a curse of some magnitude," Komak elaborated. "The human physician also threw a large object at a tech who questioned his orders."

Dtimun chuckled, a trait he'd picked up from humans over the years. "He has improved with age. When we knew each other many years ago, he threw the techs themselves."

"These humans, they are fascinating, are they not?"

"They are volatile and unpredictable," Dtimun replied. "Stern must be carefully observed, at all times. There is something…"

Komak nodded. "I, too, feel it," he said, the humor going into eclipse. His elongated eyes narrowed and grew dark blue. "There is a Rojok pulse here."

Dtimun moved a step closer. "You must never speak of such intuitions in front of the others," he said firmly. "Much less reveal that you feel them."

Komak sighed. "We keep so many secrets," he said.

"To reveal them would be catastrophic," Dtimun replied. "Especially for you."

"I live and die at your command," he said with a smart fist to heart salute. He grinned.

"One day," Dtimun threatened, "I will make soup with your bones."

"You will become the first cannibal of your Clan, and my ghost will avenge me," he shot back.

Dtimun's eyes burned dark brown.

Komak held up both hands, palms out. "I know, we never speak of Clans. Forgive me. I shall return to duty immediately. I would make very bad soup."

The boy saluted again and ran for his life.

Dtimun moved back to the ambutube that contained the young Altairian. The boy's eyes opened. Dtimun placed his hand over the boy's heart and stared into his eyes with a deep blue gaze. After a minute he nodded. The child smiled faintly and once again went to sleep.

On his way back to the bridge, the C.O. stopped in the *kelekom* sector. One of the operators, the current supervisor, gave him a worried look.

"The *kelekoms* have been following the Rojok pursuit," the operator told him. "The Rojoks have modified their sensors to detect our faint heat signature. They have turned and are approaching."

Dtimun drew in a long breath. "Who commands the pursuing fleet? Is it Chacon?"

The operator shook his head sadly. "It is one of their most fanatical captains," he replied. "The *kelekoms* infer that our capture would mean *Ahkmau* almost immediately."

"Keep me informed," Dtimun replied quietly, and left them. As he started down the long corridor, he felt a sudden, stark pain in the center of his breastbone, between his two hearts. He stopped, caught his breath and managed to regain his composure before approaching crewmen saw any weakness in his posture. So it was beginning now, a year too soon. And at the worst possible time. He must speak to Komak quickly, in order that the chain of command would be intact if the worst happened...

Admiral Jeffrey Lawson was downing a quick cup of java while he waited for the first report from Terramer. His lined face showed the effects of only an hour's sleep. He was impatient for news; for confirmation that it had been Holt Stern's crew that the Holconcom had rescued.

He got up and paced the dim confines of his office. His mind still balked at the idea that Chacon had led the merciless attack. The wily Rojok commander-in-chief's code of honor in battle was legendary. An attack on a defenseless colony of clones was hardly in keeping with that reputation. Mangus Lo would be capable of such an atrocity, but would Chacon submit to an order that conflicted with his code of ethics? Lawson shook his head. Perhaps the patrol he'd sent to Terramer could provide some answers.

"Sir!"

The sound of his adjutant's voice froze him in thought.

"Yes, lad?" He activated the automatic door and strode quickly into the outer office. "Any word?"

"Yes, sir." The automatic comtech translated the message as it began to come in on the intersystem scanner. "The scouts report fatal magnabeam radiation blanketing the planet now. All the casualties seem to have been removed. The patrol's just beginning to search the area. Sir, they have found one thing in the wreckage of the sci-archaeo ship—carefully hidden inside a bulkhead."

"Well, what it is, boy?" Lawson demanded when the younger man hesitated and grimaced.

"A body, sir," he said reluctantly.

"Only one?" Lawson's brows drew together. "Can they give us an ID?"

The adjutant sighed and lifted his eyes to Lawson's. "Yes, sir. The officer in charge knew the victim personally. Positive ID. The body, sir...it was Captain Holt Stern."

6

Hahnson's scowl was the darkest Madeline Ruszel had ever seen on his face. He was alone in his office, beyond the closed and sound-proofed hyperglas door behind which Holt Stern lay in an ambutube.

"You've been corrupting Centaurians," she told Hahnson.

He shrugged. "Only Komak. We could call it improving his education in Terravegan slang," he replied. He folded his arms across his chest, his expression worried. "Look at this, Maddie."

She moved to his side and looked at the diagnostic screen. In seconds she was scowling, as well.

"That's what I was afraid of," she said quietly. "I ran the same scans and came to the same conclusion. Stern," she added, meeting his eyes, "is definitely not himself."

He nodded.

"You aren't trying to pacify me, are you?" she queried, used to arguments from her colleague. "I haven't gone space-happy."

"I know that," he said. "I matched his bioscans from a month ago to these new ones and got the same result you did. The change is too radical to be natural. Someone has altered Stern's mental patterns."

"Yes," she agreed, lowering her voice. "Does he know, do you think?"

He nodded. "Let's say, he suspects. It's an amazing alteration, too," he agreed reluctantly. "There are no definite signs of tampering except for the rogue cells and the bioscan patterns. If we'd been less detailed physicians, we'd never even have suspected. He seems perfectly normal most of the time."

Madeline glanced at him and wanted, so badly, to tell him what she suspected about Muldoon. But she didn't dare. Now that she knew the *Morcai* carried AVBDs, she couldn't risk it.

"Strick, you don't think he's a clone?" she asked suddenly, and felt such a sense of loss that her eyes almost watered.

He gnawed on his lower lip. His broad shoulders moved uncomfortably. "I don't know."

"You suspect something," she persisted.

He drew in a painful breath. "It wouldn't serve Rojok purposes to leave the original alive if they deliberately replaced Stern. But we have no proof of that, remember? It may be just what it seems—a strange pattern due to a head injury."

She folded her arms tightly across her chest. There was a deep, throbbing pain in her very soul. "The three of us have been together for so long—" Her voice broke. If she hadn't been so involved in the theory, she might have realized that it was rare for her to feel such a burst of emotion. "We'll have to watch him closely until we get to Benaski Port," she added. "If we're still convinced by then that he's showing signs of brain pattern alteration or brain damage," she said heavily, "I'm going to have to file a Section 10-010 with the portmaster."

"That could cost Stern his command," he reminded her.

"Don't you think I know that?" she asked with tortured, pale eyes. "Strick, he dragged me out of a moga swamp and carried me two miles to an aid station on Signus Four. He could have left me there to die, and no military tribunal in the galaxy would have charged him for it. But he didn't. He's my friend," she added simply.

"He's mine, too." He looked drawn. He glanced down at her with concern. "I've been relegated to medicine because the emotion suppression didn't work on me. It was the only way I could stay in the SSC. But you were a combat officer."

She realized what he was saying. Her green eyes lifted to his. "Apparently the emotion drain didn't completely work on me, either, Strick." She smiled faintly. "I don't share that tidbit at HQ, and you mustn't, either. I'm still an Amazon reservist. I don't want to lose my status."

"You know me better than that." He studied her curiously. "How did you get past the scans? And why didn't the drugs work on you?"

She leaned closer. "My dad is Lieutenant Colonel Clinton Ruszel of the SSC Paraguards, Royal Legion of Earth," she reminded him. "He took an unusual interest in how his donation to the sperm bank was being used. I'm his only progeny, and I understand that he was having me watched almost from birth. I think he may have had something to do with the drugs' lack of effectiveness. Even when I served with the Amazon squad, I had problems." She looked up at him. "You know Dad, don't you?"

He nodded. "I fought with your father and Dtimun in the Great Galaxy War," he reminded her. "He and Dtimun were even closer than the commander and I are, and that's saying something. Our temporary C.O. hates most humans."

She nodded. "Dad mentioned having served with the Centaurian divisions, but he didn't mention the C.O. by name." She frowned. "I wonder why?"

Several sectors away, a pair of laughing, green elongated eyes stared down at a remote vidscreen with real humor.

She shrugged off the question. "I'm going to miss Muldoon. He was a pain in the butt, but he was a hell of an engineer."

Hahnson had graduated best in his class at the Tri-Fleet Medical University. He gave her a steady look. "Muldoon never screamed in his life, you know," he said pleasantly.

"Don't!" She grimaced, looking all around. "He'll think I told you!"

A pair of amused green Centaurian eyes behind a monitor disputed that.

He cleared his throat. "Yes. Well, we won't discuss it outside this room. But just between us, I never believed the spacing to begin with. Or, for that matter, the way he dealt with his officer in the mess hall. The Holconcom never scream, either, you know."

She gave him a curious look.

"I told you that I served with Dtimun in the Great Galaxy War," he reminded her. "The officer I knew was above such methods to control crewmen." He smiled. "He and Chacon were cut from the same cloth."

"I wouldn't agree at the moment," she said on a sigh. "Chacon has lost his mind if he ordered that shoot and strafe on Terramer."

"Chacon wouldn't do it in a blind fit of rage," Hahnson said firmly. "It was the Rojok emperor, Mangus Lo, or I'm a wimbat."

"You do look a little like a wimbat, Strick," she mused. "Especially when you haven't slept in forty-eight hours."

"Watch it, or I'll tell Stern you set him up with that Mervician shape-shifter the last time we were at Benaski Port."

She held up a hand. "Okay, okay, I withdraw the comment. But you carried the vidchip about her to him for me."

"One slip in a brilliant career." He chuckled.

She smiled at the memory. "We've had good times, even though we're not supposed to be allowed to feel camaraderie."

He glanced at her. "Outcasts, all of us," he agreed. "But Stern has never been the same since he lost Mary."

Her smile faded. "He still carries that blue ribbon around with him everywhere," she said. She frowned. "I wonder if we might use that memory…"

"…and ask him about it?" he wondered. "What if he's lost it somewhere?"

She cleared her throat, unzipped her sleeve pocket and produced the ribbon. "He gave me this bit of it on Montclair Colony two months ago," she reminded him. "I saved him from a nasty *chova* bite and shot a bat creature that went for the blood."

"I had it the last time, when I pulled him out of the moga swamp with a broken leg."

She fingered the ribbon gently. "Mary was wearing the main part of it that Stern kept when she died," she whispered, feeling the pain. Mary had been a colleague of hers and Strick's, a brilliant surgeon.

"Holt always thought of it as a medal," he replied. "Because she saved two children from certain death by throwing herself in front of the captured *Gresham* handgun when the Rojok fired it." He shook his head. "I thought we'd have to bury Stern with her. He wasn't the same for months. The neutering didn't work well on Stern, either."

"But not like he is now," Madeline said, putting the ribbon back in its place. "I think we should show him the ribbon."

"So do I. But not today. We don't want him to become suspicious. And if he has been altered for some dark purpose, where does our allegiance lie?" he added. "Can't you imagine the damage he could do when we reach Tri-Fleet HQ? He's done enough aboard this ship in one day. Not to mention," he added heavily, "that we're still being followed by a Rojok fleet that seems bent on our capture."

She grimaced. "I know."

"You don't like Dtimun," he said out of the blue. "But he's an honorable man. He's legendary, in his use of tactics and his courage. He——"

"He brings out my stubborn side," Madeline interrupted. "But I respect him." She smiled. "He's a lot like my father. He doesn't back down. I like that."

The unseen pair of green eyes twinkled even more.

"Be careful how you talk about him when you think he isn't listening," Hahnson chuckled. "There are things you don't know."

"I don't discuss people except with you and Holt." She felt sad. "I don't want to think about him being altered, being a stranger. I don't want to——!" Her voice broke and tears threatened.

He caught her arm, firmly, and shook it. "Watch it!" he said shortly. "You're having too many of these episodes lately. It will be noticed. You could be thrown out of the service for any display of emotion, you know that. Even your father couldn't save you."

She swallowed, and then swallowed again. She drew in a steadying breath. "I don't understand it. Emotion is drugged out of us the minute we enter the military. It's chemically erased. I took all the required drugs when I first enlisted!"

"In one percent of subjects," he reminded her blandly, "the process reverses itself spontaneously."

She hadn't remembered that. She looked absolutely horrified. "Do you think that could have happened to me?" she asked, lowering her voice.

"I think it's very possible," he said.

She laughed humorlessly. "Maybe I'm a clone."

"Bite your tongue," he uttered. "You'd be sent to an organ supply house on the spot."

"Yes," she sighed. "In our society, clones are nothing but spare part banks. The Centaurians may be prehistoric in their attitudes toward genetic engineering in their main population, but they treat the clones of the Holconcom with great dignity and respect. We treat them as disposable organic donors."

The remote eyes narrowed and darkened with anger.

"Maybe that will change someday," Strick said gently, "when people realize that they're sentient beings. They deserve better treatment from a so-called civilized society."

"They do." She sighed. "But none of this solves the problem of Stern."

"Dtimun already suspects that there's something wrong with Holt," he told her. "Whether or not we discuss this with him, he'll be watching."

Her eyes widened suddenly and she started looking around the room like a fugitive from justice.

Hahnson turned away. "We'd better get back to our patients. Stern isn't going anywhere for the moment. Let's keep watch and hope for the best."

She turned and followed him. "I guess you're right." She locked her hands behind her as she walked. "I wanted your opinion on one of my Jebob patients..."

Stern felt the pain slowly begin to ease. His head was throbbing, but he could manage. He sat up, grimacing when it briefly increased the discomfort. He didn't know himself anymore. He had memories of his distant past, but the recent part of it was blurry and incomprehensible. His mind was still a blank, but the memory of Muldoon's horrible fate intruded and left him weak.

"My mind's going, isn't it, Strick?" he asked the husky medic, who was finishing up a test.

Hahnson spared him a glance and a grin while he turned off his scanners. "No more than mine," he said. "Relax, Holt. It's only a minor irregularity in the bios, after all. Probably due to that bump on the head you got on Terramer. You'll be yourself in no time."

"Sure," he said, unconvincingly. He sat up on the table and shook his head. "Funny," he said with a hollow chuckle, "I think Muldoon was one of my engineering officers for years, but I don't remember anything about him."

"Memory lapse. Understandable."

"Is it, Strick?" He eyed his friend. "Or have I really changed so much in a few days that my own men don't know me?"

Hahnson laid a heavy hand on his shoulder. "I know you. Cut out the questions."

He sighed wearily. "The C.O. How did he kill that Holconcom so easily?"

"Let's just say," he replied, choosing his words carefully, "that he has an uncommon gift of both strength and mental abilities. I don't know if the gift isn't more curse than blessing."

"Who is he?"

"Who knows?" Hahnson shrugged. "His Clan is as secret as his private life. I served with him for two years, and it might as well have been two days for all I learned. Even Komak doesn't know him well, and he's Dtimun's executive officer and his friend."

"Somebody wants that cat-eyed terror pretty bad," Stern remarked, "to throw a whole fleet of ships against a single Centaurian ship." He frowned. "Fleet of ships..." He sat up quickly and clasped his head because of the sudden pain. "Are they still following us?"

"As far as I know, yes," Hahnson said worriedly. "Nobody's talking about it right now."

Stern scowled, rubbing his eyes. "How do I know that they're after the C.O. and not the ship?" he asked blankly. "How can I know that?"

It was a question his friend couldn't answer. He grimaced. "Let the C.O. worry about pursuers. I'm only concerned with getting you back on your feet."

Stern gave him an appraising look. "How do you propose to do that?"

Hahnson picked up a laserdot syringe and showed it to him. "A mind stimulator," he said. "It targets memory."

For some reason Stern was reluctant to let the medicine be injected. He pushed it away. "Let's…let's wait a day or two, until I feel stronger. Can we do that?" It was imperative that he retain his clarity of thought. Something very important was about to happen.

"We can wait," Hahnson agreed. But he wondered what was going on behind Stern's black eyes. He was going to have to talk to Madeline, and quickly.

Madeline was making final adjustments to a programming bank as she finished the delicate genetic mending of an Altairian's torn thigh muscle. She shot an amused glance at two Centaurian engineers who were watching her with open curiosity.

"This process isn't totally unknown to you, is it?" she asked, puzzled by their continuing watchfulness.

The younger of the two struggled for the Terravegan Standard verbs to express himself in Madeline's language. "We—how is it said?—will never have seen a female in military uniform, Dr.Madelineruszel," he explained, giving her two names a typical Centaurian compounding. "Or a female trained as you are to perform medical procedures."

Abandoning the complicated operation for an instant, she gaped at them. "Never? Well, what do your females do?" she exclaimed.

The shorter of the two shrugged. "Some, the most gifted, create offspring, and rear them. Others compose great works of music, or write poetry, or make paintings. Still others involve themselves in political occupations or manage industries essential to our culture. None go to war," he added. "It is considered to be a threat to the continuity of our race, that if our females risk themselves in war, they would contribute to our own extinction as a race."

She blinked, astonished.

"In a time long past," the taller one added, "it is said that many of our females were great warriors. The old emperor, Tnurat Alamantimichar, came from a strict culture which denied women any place in public life. Only in recent years has their position in politics and business been modified."

"There were riots," the shorter one said abruptly.

Madeline hid a smile. No wonder, she thought. She studied them curiously. "The Holconcom are clones, aren't they?"

They nodded. "All of us have our roots in cloneries, where our donors were chosen from the best mental and physical specimens in our culture. We know little of civilian life, however."

"Neither do I," she confessed. "Among my people, there is no distinction between male, female, and *berdache*—our three genders."

"Three genders?" the older Centaurian asked, surprised.

She nodded. "The *berdache* mates within its own gender, but has the rights and privileges of the other two genders. Equality is our most precious right. Our soldiers come from breeders."

"But you must have clones, also?"

She grimaced. "Yes. We have clones." She gave them a sympathetic glance. "But our society is less enlightened than yours in this one area. Civilians and military alike treat clones badly."

The tall one gave a green laugh with his huge eyes. "Only our Holconcom is made up completely of clones, save for our commander. The emperor has been known to order a public *escareem*, a trial, for civilians who dare to patronize us. We have full equality under our law."

She smiled, privately curious about why Dtimun was himself not a clone. "A shame that we don't all have it."

"The Holconcom have never been mixed with other facets of our military, not even with the nonclones of the regular divisions, whose strength is vaguely comparable to our own. Brawling is strictly forbidden because of our physical superiority to other soldiers. It is the one reason we will not be able to mix with the humans for very long, I think. Your people are a physical race. They will try to test us, as we have already seen happen with tragic results."

"Tragic, indeed," she mused quietly.

There were other words for it, as well, she thought later, when she ran up on a scathing disagreement between two of the *Bellatrix*'s complement.

"...tell you, we're going to be slaughtered," one of them muttered. "A whole damned fleet of Rojoks ships is closing in on us, and our captain won't even fight for us!"

"You got that right," his companion agreed darkly. "Stern won't fight for us, and these cat-eyes won't lift a finger to help us. Inhuman alien devils, I think...!"

"You'd better think about your jobs and spend less time griping," Madeline said shortly, glaring at them. "Or I'll have both of you thrown in the brig. Is that clear?"

They snapped her a salute. "Yes, sir," they chorused.

"We can't fight the Rojoks and each other at the same time," she reminded them.

"That black-hearted alien killed Muldoon!" one of them said shortly. "Let the Rojoks have them!"

"We're all on the same ship," she returned curtly. "If the Centaurians die, so do we."

They didn't have a comeback for that. She was about to add to the statement when the audio kicked in.

"Dr. Ruszel, sick bay, stat!"

She turned and took off at a trot, closing her mind to some insulting remarks her shipmates were muttering behind her. She only hoped that if it came to a fight, the humans would resolve themselves to the situation.

Mentally she cursed the size of the ship and the lack of suitable facilities for use as a sick bay. Sixty critical patients of all races, stuffed into one medium-size mess hall. Strick's facilities were even smaller and he had a like number of severely injured patients. The ambulatory were confined to two other storage units aboard ship, where they spent their time caring for the children with minor injuries. No spare ambutubes. No medical stores except what an alien synthesizer could imitate. Overworked personnel, a hostile ship's company, and one exobiology chief to cope with clones of half a dozen alien cultures. Why, in the name of the seventh nebula, didn't this Holconcom warship carry a medical unit? Was it conceit or pure apathy? The audio paged her once more, and she ran faster.

"The trap," Mangus Lo shot at his tall advisor before the younger Rojok could enter the private chamber. "How does it progress?"

"All is well, your Excellency," the advisor said smugly. "The Centaurian vessel is making for Benaski Port, but our ships are slowly closing in on it. It is only a matter of time."

"Good. Good." The crippled little dictator made a net of his six fingers and watched them, hypnotized. "The Spheres, have our scientists made any progress in deciphering them?"

"There...there is a problem. The Council of the Tri-Fleet took precautions against just such an eventuality," the advisor stated nervously. "The Spheres have been recorded in a Terravegan dialect which is completely unknown to our people. It is taking a great deal of time to even begin to translate them."

"We have no time!" The dictator glared at the younger alien. "Already I have word that the Tri-Galaxy Council has issued a war vote against us! Within a handful of time periods, we will find ourselves fighting a multitude of races besides the humans! We must have the genetic codes of those races so that we can infiltrate them as we have already infiltrated the humans!"

"I have already said as much to our scientific staff," the other alien returned. "Also, when we capture the Holconcom ship, we will obtain clones of additional races which can be used for study in our experimental station at *Ahkmau*."

"Clones will be of doubtful use," Mangus Lo growled. "Clones are genetically altered in most cases for the duty they are created to perform. A screen is used, as well, to prevent tampering with the basic DNA." He smiled coldly. "You see, I am not so stupid as you assume!"

"Your Excellence, I did not mean to insinuate...!"

"Shut up." The dictator's eyes narrowed even more. "The Centaurian princess. Why have you not brought her to me?"

The advisor cleared his throat. "At this point, your Excellence, we are not absolutely certain that she was taken along with the Spheres.

The officer who told me of her capture has suffered an unfortunate amount of brain damage which might account for some fabrication. None of his men have reported seeing a Centaurian female aboard any of our vessels."

"What?" The dictator came out of his seat like a striking serpent, his dusky complexion gone scarlet in anger. "You promised me that she was captive. You lied!"

The young alien paled. "Please, your Excellence, I imparted only the information I was given. If it was incorrect...!"

"Have your officer sent to *Ahkmau,* at once!"

"Yes, at once!"

Mangus Lo's eyes narrowed. "And have your men search for the Centaurian princess. My instinct tells me that there is a plot underway. I will have the truth."

"It will be done immediately!"

"And..."

"Yes, Excellence?"

"Send Commander Chacon to me."

"At once! At once, your Excellence!" he echoed, his face drawn, his eyes brimming with terror. "By your leave...!"

Madeline's senior medtech was waiting for her at the doorway of the makeshift exo sick bay, apprehension in his whole look.

"The last of the Altairian patients," he said, not wasting words, following her to the ambutube that contained a small, blue-skinned girl with huge amber eyes. They were tortured, wet with tears of pain, looking up at her through the antiseptic green mist. She laid her wrist scanner over the small chest and engaged the nanodrive. Seconds later, the readings told a sad story.

"Myocardial infarction," she muttered. "A massive one. Debucarbonal, stat!"

"There isn't any, Doctor," the medtech replied sadly. "The last of it went to the girl's mother, before she died."

"They'll all die," she murmured furiously, "unless we reach Benaski Port soon. All right, get me some of the Vegan touch-serum."

"Gone," he returned. "All of it, for the Cereboan child."

"Well, how about…never mind, there's no time. Get me the cardiovac!"

He handed it to her. She worked at the child's thin chest with the pacer, trying desperately to stabilize the erratic heartbeat which was so faint as to be undetectable except with the scanner. But the pulse only increased. The child's chest jerked, and a sharp cry passed her blue lips before she went unconscious.

"Defib!" she shot at her medic. "Get me a unit, stat!"

"Sir, there's only one left and Hahnson has it…"

"Steal it! Beg, borrow. But get it!"

"On my way," he said, rushing out.

She slammed the cardiovac onto the child's chest and energized it again and again, feeling the uselessness of the action even as she took it. She was sweating with the effort, despite the maintained sixty-three degree Fahrenheit temperature in the compartment. Perspiration drained down her flushed face into her eyes, her mouth. Watching the child tortured her. The little girl's face was twisted with pain, her skin ashen and drenched in cold sweat. Death was a sigh away. Never once did it occur to Madeline that this was a clone. She worked desperately to save the child.

Involuntarily she remembered Dtimun saving the little Jebob boy with nothing more than his touch. She wished that she had such a gift…!

A sound behind her brought relief. "Did you get the damned thing?" she shot over her shoulder. "Bring it here!"

But the face that moved into view had serene blue cat-eyes. "We will discuss your language presently," Dtimun said calmly. "But for the moment, tell me the child's condition."

"If I don't get a defib unit in twenty seconds," she ground out, "her condition is going to be dead! What the hell kind of ship doesn't have a medical department and even the most basic medical supplies…!"

While she cursed, he touched the child's chest with long, golden-skinned fingers. The little girl took a sudden breath, let it out and her eyes opened, wide with surprise and delight. She smiled.

Dtimun smiled back.

Madeline snapped out of her trance long enough to check the little girl with the scanner. Her heart was perfect.

The door zipped up and the disheveled medtech ran in with the portable defibrillator in his hand. "I got it!" he panted victoriously.

"Take it back," she murmured absently, her eyes still on the child.

"Back!" he exclaimed, his mouth open. "But I had to throw a punch at Hahnson's medtech to get it…!"

"I'll recommend you for a medal, too," she agreed, glancing at him. "Give it back."

He left, shaking his head.

Madeline stared at Dtimun with unconcealed curiosity. "That's twice you've saved a patient for me, without drugs. How? Mental healing? Empathy?"

"Of a kind," he said.

"Could you be a little more specific, sir?" she prompted. "I mean, I feel as if I'm practicing medicine with flint-knapped stone tools at the moment."

He turned and looked down at her. "I would call that," he said, "an apt comparison."

7

Madeline barely heard the insult. She was paying attention to the relaxed breathing of the little girl in the ambutube, still amazed at the Centaurian's mental abilities.

"Her heart was damaged by shrapnel," she said. "Now it's whole again."

"Some few members of the Holconcom have healing abilities," he replied quietly. "The basis of which we do not share with outworlders," he added. He glanced down at her solemnly. "And which you will not discuss with your shipmates, save for Hahnson."

Curious, she thought. It was as if he knew that she'd discussed him with her fellow medic. "Of course," she replied. She drew in a long breath. "Well, thank you. Again."

He folded his arms over his chest. "I said that we would discuss your language," he continued. "A female does not use such words. It is a breech of custom for a female to curse and brawl and act as a warrior."

"Sorry, sir, I forgot that your women are still living in the Dark Ages."

His eyes widened, dark blue with curiosity. "Dark Ages?"

"Your sexes are unequal," she explained. "Among Terravegans, all genders are treated equally in the military. We're mentally neutered. I don't have the slightest idea of how a female is expected to behave in a male-dominated society. I've never even seen a breeder."

"Breeder?"

"Women chosen for specialized childbearing, outside the in vitro government baby mills. It's difficult to explain."

The alien studied the woman in the green uniform—the long auburn hair, the pale complexion with a tiny row of freckles just across her nose, the long-lashed green eyes. He shook his head. "To make a woman into a poor replica of a man while she retains the beauty of her gender is an abomination," he said finally. "Your society is mad."

Beauty? Unused to the kind of scrutiny she was being subjected to by those elongaged, alien eyes, she felt a strange tensing of her muscles. She turned away from him, suddenly breathless. "Yes, well, if you'll excuse me, sir?" She went back to her patient, and she didn't look at him again.

The mess hall that Madeline was using for a sick bay was one of the smallest compartments on the ship. Two Centaurian technicians passed by it in deep conversation about the growing tension between the human and alien crew members. Their guttural tongue was like a ripple of wind and song in its high and low tones, its odd nasalized consonants. Although they couldn't know it, the language had an uncanny similarity to the tongues of nomadic dwellers on the ancient planet that spawned the Terravegan society.

Whatever words existed in that musical pattern of sound must have been more interesting than a human mind could grasp. Because the Cen-

taurians never saw a soft shadow pass along the programming computers that ringed the engine room, or a white-skinned hand reaching for
the panel which controlled one segment of the memory banks.

And before they noticed, much later, that one master unit was just
slightly out of sync, the shadow had long since disappeared. So stealthy
was it that even the alert *kelekoms* in the classified sector of the ship
weren't disturbed by the tiny, faint change of rhythm in the engines.

Holt Stern pressed his back hard against the bulkhead in the
deserted food processing sector, his face an agony of conflicting
emotions. He understood, finally, what was expected of him. He had
no option, and perhaps it was a small price to pay for an end to the
violent headaches that had plagued him from Terramer. But something
deep inside him ached. A tiny bubble of guilt and regret blew up in
his brain and he wanted to tell someone, anyone, that he was...sorry.

They wanted the commander. So he had to make sure they could
take the Holconcom ship. First the slight adjustment of the ships
engines. Then a sudden death to divert the crew. Afterward, a new
clone to assist him when the Rojoks closed in. He hated himself for
what he was doing, but he couldn't stop himself. He was programmed, somehow, for these tasks. His meddling would mean the
death camps for Madeline and Strick and the other humans; and the
alien crew, of course. The Centaurians would be no sacrifice, he told
himself, they were warriors. They expected death. But, oh, God, this
kind of death...!

Madeline's face was there, in front of his eyes, already haunting
him. *Why* was this treachery necessary? What had been done to him
that brought about such changes in his personality?

He held up his hands and looked at them, turned them over,
studied them. He was Stern. There were lapses in his memory

pathways, but he was Stern, and he was human, and he belonged to the Tri-Fleet. Why was he doing this? Who were *they*—how did he suddenly know what he had to do, and why hadn't he refused to do it? Why couldn't he refuse?

"God!" he cried huskily, his hands crushing at his temples. "Who am I? Who am I?"

But no answer came. The moment of weakness began to pass. He straightened with a hard, heavy sigh. There was work to be done, and quickly. And, fight it mentally as hard as he might, his feet turned him to the passageway and carried him relentlessly down it. A voice in the back of his mind told him, too, that from now on he must do his damnedest to convince his comrades that he was back to normal. He *was* normal. What had possessed him to make him think otherwise? He was having fantasies about betraying his crewmates, but surely they were only fantasies. No doubt they were caused by the concussion. His nostrils extended in distaste as he passed by a group of humans, but he controlled a grimace and grinned at them instead. He was playing a part. He had to play it well. It wasn't so hard after all.

Madeline was eagerly trading insults with Hahnson when Stern joined them in the mess hall.

"Hi, gang," he said cheerfully, flashing a convincing smile in their direction as he flopped into a chair and ordered a steaming cup of horrible-tasting imitation java from the small oval synthesizer. "You two look like prospective Vegan organ donors at the Emergency Surgical Sector," he remarked. "You'll trip over your lower lips in a minute."

"Stern!" Madeline exclaimed. "You're back to normal!"

His eyebrows went up over dancing ebony eyes. "I don't think I've ever been accused of that. But the headaches are gone, and I'm beginning to get my memory back."

"I told you it was the blow to the head," Hahnson told Madeline with a smug look.

"Remind me to recommend you for promotion, Doctor," she replied. "Not on my staff, of course, but..."

"How come," Stern asked Hahnson, "you're older than she is, but she outranks you?"

Hahnson shrugged. "Easy. She's two centimeters taller than I am."

Stern sipped his java with a chuckle. It was easier to fool humans than he'd thought.

Lyceria found the quarters Chacon had provided for her more to her taste than the rude dungeon. But captivity was slowly draining her spirit. And for some reason of his own, Chacon had allowed no one near her save himself. The loneliness had an almost tangible feel. It was as consuming as her fear of *Ahkmau*.

She touched the sleek fabric of the dress he brought her on his last visit. It was more comfortable than the Rojok armor she'd been required to wear in the beginning of her captivity, and infinitely more lovely. Its pale golden color shimmered in a delicate variety of patterns as the chemicals imbedded in its composition reacted to the heat of her body. The colorful gift had pleased her, although she was careful not to let the pleasure show.

A footstep at the door made her heart shudder. She stood like a fragile statue, a study in feline grace, as she began to rise.

Chacon moved into the room and stopped, his slit eyes drawn like electromagnets to the portrait she made. The silence was long and unbroken except for the soft whisper of the door sliding down again.

"You flatter the dress," he said.

She lowered her eyes before he could read the warm brown shades that touched them. "You flatter me."

She felt his gaze cling to her even as he spoke. "I bring unpleasant news. I had thought your capture was the doing of one of my men—whom I saw punished for the act. But it was more. Mangus Lo himself ordered the death of your young brother, and your capture. The knowledge was carefully concealed from me, until now."

She raised her face and met his level gaze with eyes the pale gray shade that denoted curiosity. Behind the question was a fear that she dared not show. "Why? Why?" she asked.

"I do not know. The only information I was able to obtain was that it had something to do with another goal—the capture of the Hol-concom commander. Even now, I fear that goal is being accomplished. And I know all too well what treatment will be given my old enemy."

"There speaks compassion in your voice," she said, surprised.

"A warrior can hold respect for even an enemy who warrants it. But now my concern is for you. It is only a matter of time until Mangus Lo learns where you are being kept. The threat of *Ahkmau* has loosened many a tongue, and my confidants are not immune."

She barely heard him. Capture Dtimun? *Maliche,* they might as easily paint cloud pictures on the wind. But if Mangus Lo by some dark power accomplished that end—her hands trembled involuntarily.

Her wide, graceful eyes wore the blue color of deep concern. She looked into his. "You cannot protect me further without jeopardizing your own life. This, by custom, I cannot allow. I do not fear death."

"Nor I," he replied with a tiny smile. "Madam, I cannot condone the murder of a female. It is a breech of my own honor. I will take you to a place of safety."

"There are no places of safety," she said gently. "They exist only in the mind."

"There is one which even Mangus Lo would not think to search. My harem."

A faint pink tinge washed over her pale, golden complexion. "I should prefer *Ahkmau,*" she said proudly.

An expression came and went in the glittering depth of his slit eyes, but his expression remained untouched. "I mean you no insult. I offer you the only protection I am capable of giving, and it is good only so long as Mangus Lo does not guess my involvement. Will you trust me?"

"Trust carries with it an awesome responsibility, Commander Chacon," she said. Her eyes studied his face, dusky, masculine, rugged with the years of combat and command. There was no softening there, no weakness that could be perceived. She sensed a deep sadness, a loneliness, however, that had no echo in his expression. She weighed the legend against the man—and found a balance. "I...will trust you," she said after a minute. She felt an odd sensation from him, although his expression never wavered. "But why will you risk so much for an enemy of your people?"

He smiled, a slow, quiet smile that was almost affectionate. "If you must have a reason, call it repayment of a debt. Perhaps the next time you see the Holconcom commander, you may ask him to explain. Will you come?"

She followed after him, surprised at her own acquiescence. She must be cautious, she reminded herself, she must not be so ready to trust him. Whatever else he was, he was also the enemy. And she was Alamantimichar. Chacon surely knew that he could ask any ransom for her return, and Tnurat would tender it. An ambitious soldier possessed of such a captive could name his own price. She wondered what Chacon's would be.

Another solar day had gone by, and it brought a new tragedy. Madeline and Hahnson were discussing a missing crew member with Stern.

"It's Merrick," Stern said. "He wasn't at roll call, and I can't find him." He didn't add that he'd had another of several peculiar black-outs just minutes before. The medics were already suspicious of him. He wasn't going to let himself in for more questions and tests. Surely it was just a minor result of the concussion. He might even remember where he'd been eventually.

"Merrick." Madeline sighed. "He's been one of the most uncooperative of the crew since we've been on board."

"It will get him in big trouble if he pushes any of the Centaurians," Hahnson added.

He was about to add something else, but he stopped when Komak appeared beside them so silently that none of them noticed him until he spoke.

"Dr. Strickhahnson," he addressed Strick, "please come with me quickly. There has been an…accident. Perhaps you should come, as well," he told the other two.

Hahnson glanced curiously at his companions and started down the long passageway with them past other members of both crews.

Komak stopped at a sector marked only by a strange Centaurian scrawl and cautiously motioned the humans inside. Madeline stopped just inside the doorway for an instant before she joined her comrades.

While Hahnson knelt beside the blond human casualty on the floor, Madeline dropped to one knee across from him. "Merrick, you fool," she muttered under her breath.

"What happened to him?" Stern asked curiously.

Hahnson was examining the crewman. "His neck's broken," he said at once. "Crushed would be a better adjective. The cervical vertebrae are literally shattered. A damned neat job of it, too. Quick and efficient. I doubt he knew what hit him."

"Who?" Madeline asked curtly.

"The human was strong," Komak broke in. His eyes wore a

solemn blue shade. "And such ability is rare in humans. I think it must have been one of the Holconcom. I have sent word to the commander."

"God!" Madeline exclaimed, rising. "I thought the trouble was over!"

"Only suppressed," Stern guessed quietly. "At least we know why he was missing from roll call," he added.

"I overheard him in the corridor a day ago, muttering about the Centaurians and how he hated them. I wonder if he provoked one," she replied.

"I cannot believe," Komak said, "that any of the Holconcom would dare disobey a direct order from the commander. It has never been done."

"Indeed," Dtimun said unexpectedly behind them.

They whirled at the curt tones, and Madeline wondered once again at the amazing ability of the Centaurians to move noiselessly. Dtimun eyed the dead human with angry, dark eyes.

He shot a question to Komak in Centaurian. The reply was equally unintelligible to the humans.

Dtimun's towering form turned to Hahnson with a grace that was purely feline. "The manner of death is positive?"

"I'm afraid so," Hahnson said. "This couldn't have been done by a human hand—and the finger marks indicate that it was one hand, not two. It had to be one of the Holconcom."

"Impossible!" Dtimun gave the word the ring of rock hitting steel.

"You can't be everywhere, Commander," Stern told him, feeling a strange urge from somewhere to argue. He stuck his hands on his hips and glared at the alien. "One demonstration doesn't convince two warring ships' companies, especially if the majority of one of them—the human one—didn't even see it. Your men may be physically superior to us, but they're a hell of a long shot from perfect."

Madeline flashed a conspiratorial glance toward Hahnson; a glance that said, "He's back to normal." Hahnson winked.

Dtimun's black eyebrows met over his elegant nose. "My compliments to your physician on your recovery," he told Stern. "Now, before I brig you, what provocation would one of my Holconcom have for killing this human against orders?"

"Merrick had a temper," Stern said. "Your men saw what you did to the Holconcom officer in the mess. No sane officer or enlisted man is going to admit to an offense that carries the death penalty. Merrick could have pushed him too far. Ask them," he added, nodding toward the other humans.

Dtimun considered that for a few seconds. "You have much to learn," he said finally. "About the Holconcom. And about me." He turned to Hahnson. "Have the human cloned. I will seek out the assassin."

"You don't have a medical section, so where are we supposed to do the cloning, sir?" Madeline asked the commander, buoyed by Stern's sudden strength. "Why couldn't it wait until we reach Benaski Port? Assuming that we ever reach it at the speed we're going," she added.

"Madam," Dtimun replied with flashes of angry brown lightning in his elongated eyes, "your concern is healing, not command of this vessel. Am I understood?"

Her temporary truce with him, since he'd healed two of her patients, expired under the whip of his temper. She stiffened. "Yes, sir!"

With a final, narrow glance at the body on the clean deck, he strode out of the compartment.

"You risk much," Komak told Madeline gently. "I have never known the commander to be so lenient. Beware lest you find a sleeping *galot* with your prodding. He is not himself."

"There's a lot of that going around lately," Hahnson said innocently, with a grin at Stern.

Stern actually flushed. Without a word, he turned and marched out into the corridor. Hahnson sighed. "Well, I'll go get a levigurney to transport Merrick," he said. "We can do the cloning in the *kelekom* section, can't we, Komak?"

"Yes."

Madeline started to go after Hahnson, but Komak stepped in front of her and prevented it. She looked at him curiously.

"There has been sabotage," he told her very softly, so that his voice didn't carry to personnel who were going to and fro on the deck. "We will not reach Benaski Port, I think. Soon, the Rojok fleet will have us encircled."

"You should be telling this to Stern," she began.

"No." His eyes were a solemn blue. "You must ally yourself with me, if we are to survive the coming aggression. Your captain has a cold darkness about him that permeates. I know little of humans, but he makes my hair bristle. I do not trust him."

Her lips opened to protest, but she couldn't. She grimaced.

"Nor do you trust him," Komak said suddenly, nodding when her expression became one of guilt. "One of our *kelekoms* has observed a shadow moving in the engine compartment. Adjustments were made and not discovered in time. The ship has slowed. In the time it will take to correct the adjustments, we will be captured."

Everything she'd ever heard about *Ahkmau* rippled with terrifying clarity through her mind. "What can we do?" she asked. Not once did it occur to her to ask why this young Holconcom trusted her, a human, more than his own people.

"Keep a close watch on your captain," he replied. "Come to me if you see behavior or actions that puzzle you."

"You said the commander wasn't himself," she said quietly.

He drew in a long, harsh breath. "You specialize in Cularian medicine."

"Yes."

"This includes physiology of Centaurians."

Her lips parted on a quick breath. "Well…yes."

"Your skills may become more precious than you realize." He held up a hand when she started to question him. "All will become clear, in time." He looked down at Merrick. "But make sure that during the cloning process, no one has access to this man. Especially," he added coldly, "Holtstern."

Madeline wanted desperately to talk to Hahnson about what Komak had told her, but she didn't dare. She accompanied the human medical chief down to the *kelekom* unit, where the four operators sat in front of their glowing consoles.

She was less than useless with human cloning, which was strictly Hahnson's area of expertise. But she kept a watchful eye around her while her colleague initiated the burst of genetic information to the protoplasm that constituted the heart of the cloning technology.

One of the *kelekom* operators was watching her curiously.

She glanced at him and smiled. "Living machines," she said softly, her eyes quiet and intent on the glowing console in front of him. "They're legendary, even among humans. You must feel very privileged here."

"We do," he replied in thickly accented Standard language. "We are bonded to our companions—we do not refer to them as machines," he added gently.

She flushed. "Sorry."

"You have little understanding of our culture, we know this and do not take offense. You may approach, if you like," he added unexpectedly.

With a quick breath, she moved forward only two steps. "We know about the effect alien bacteria has on them," she explained. "I don't want to endanger your…companion."

There were sounds like muffled human laughter. "We have taken the necessary steps for immunization," the *kelekom* operator assured her.

"We know that you occasionally have to leave the ship, when you go on scouts," she said. "But how do you lift so enormous a unit?"

With a wave of his hand, the *kelekom* began to glow. Seconds later, an oval panel, still glowing, detached itself and adhered effortlessly to the uniform front of the Holconcom, just at the sternum.

Madeline gasped. "That's amazing!"

"It is, even to us," he replied.

"Can you really see light-years ahead through them?"

"Yes. They have many capabilities which would seem quite fantastic to outworlders," he replied. "They are capable of independent thought and, when necessary, action. Each operator is bonded to his companion for life. We have an agreement with their race, centuries old, which assures us of liaison with four of the more adventurous of their leaders. They live among us and in return, we send units of our finest Holconcom to live among them and provide protection to them from their own enemies."

"Have they been studied?" she asked.

He chuckled. "One does not study them. One is studied by them."

She laughed.

"Ready," Hahnson said behind her.

She thanked the *kelekom* operator and his companion for their time and went back to join Hahnson.

"Initiating resequence," he said, waving his hand over the control unit.

Just as he did, there was a sudden dimming of wall light and a surge in the engines.

"What was that?" Madeline asked uneasily.

Hahnson looked at the controls. There was a slight fluctuation in the numbers, but the unit kept working. He relaxed. "Must have been a power surge," he said. "Nothing to worry about. It's okay."

"Thank goodness," she replied, relaxing.

Farther along the corridor, Holt Stern eased out of the engine compartment, where a small fire in a disposal unit had momentarily diverted the engineers. He was smiling.

Another solar day passed. The accelerated growth potential of Hahnson's makeshift cloning chamber, which the Holconcom had perfected from stolen Rojok technology, had already produced an exact copy of Merrick. A single cell from the original contained not only the blueprint for his physical restructuring, but his collected lifetime memories, as well. The technique, for all its sophistication, was only a century old. Cloning dated back to old Earth, in the Sol system, but stolen Rojok technology had refined it to a method of almost immediate replacement of soldiers killed in action. The ability to clone memory, as well, had given the technology a perfect place in war. No training was necessary when the clone emerged from his artificial womb; he forgot nothing between his death and resurrection.

But sadly, Merrick reawakened with his old prejudices intact, as well as an unexpected magnification of physical strength. It was the same magnification that Madeline and Hahnson had found in their respective physioscans of Stern.

Merrick moved out of the *kelekom* unit in his old uniform and went right up to a small complement of Holconcom security officers before Hahnson or Madeline could stop him.

"You damned cat-eyes, which one of you killed me?" he demanded, loudly enough that a small passing group of humans could hear him, as well. "Butchering us, you devils! How many of us have to die before we reach a neutral port and get off this space-going cat park?"

"Merrick!" Madeline snapped, but he ignored her.

"He's a clone, who gives a damn what he thinks?" a human close by asked sarcastically.

"Well, he's right, just the same," another human interjected. "I want off this ship. I want to die fighting Rojoks, not wait for these cat-eyes to pick us off one by one!"

One of the Holconcom moved forward, and his eyes grew dark brown. "You are inferior," he shot at the human. "You are weak and cowardly. You will run, not fight, when we go into combat. You will all die!"

"Not damned likely!" a human called. "Not if we get you first!"

"Yeah," someone else echoed, and the humans moved forward.

"You beg for death, human!" the lead Holconcom said. "We are superior!"

As he moved, so did the rest of his small group, encircling the humans. A strange, low, deadly growl began to penetrate the murmured anger of the humans, who were feeling at their duty belts for *Greshams* they didn't have anymore. The commander had confiscated them soon after the combination of the *Bellatrix* crew with his own.

"For God's sake, not again!" Madeline said harshly, provoked into action. She stepped boldly between the Holconcom and Merrick.

"Butt out, Doc!" Merrick told her, and literally shoved her aside.

It was a mistake. Madeline had commanded a unit of Amazons, and she was far and away more dangerous than Merrick. She whirled, landed a kick at his temple and sent him flying into the nearby bulkhead, her auburn hair whipping around her pale face like a halo.

The Holconcom watched, agape. None of them had ever seen a female fight. She dived at Merrick and the aliens actually froze in place, fascinated, as she taught the belligerent clone a lesson in humility.

Someone was taking bets. In a matter of seconds, she had the clone on the deck, facedown, with her boot securely pinning his neck. Two of the Holconcom were actually grinning. Merrick muttered curses.

"You're breaking my back!" he growled.

"Not to worry, I can fix it. I'm a doctor," she reminded him with cold humor.

She looked around for some way to tie Merrick up. But before she could get her bearings, the intercommunications network exploded and diverted everyone's attention with the angry whine of general quarters.

Forgetting the confrontation, humans and Holconcom alike reacted to their military conditioning and peeled off toward their battle stations.

Madeline twisted Merrick's forearm painfully and gave him to Hahnson with a grin as she ran for her own sector. Merrick was going on report the minute they reached an SSC base, she promised herself. She shook her right hand, feeling a tear in the skin. She was probably going to be in trouble with Dtimun for brawling, as well. But right now, her only concern was her patients.

"All execs and department heads to the main briefing room," the intercom blared, alternating between Centaurian and Standard. "All execs and department heads to the main briefing room, on the double!"

She did an abrupt about-face, and met Hahnson, minus Merrick, as she made a jump up on the interdeck access ladder. "Damn Merrick!" she growled. "Wait until we get back to Trimerius!"

"Cloning carries its own punishment," Hahnson reminded her. "Merrick will end up in a medical supply unit as spare parts."

She felt momentarily sick at her own behavior. "Strick..."

"No time. Move it!" he said as they reached the top of the access ladder that ended on the main flight deck at operations.

He jogged into the briefing room with Madeline at his heels. It surged with pent-up energy as Dtimun took his place at the head of the glowing, oblong table and called the group to order.

"We are surrounded," he said coldly, without mincing words. "The Rojoks have just meshed us in force nets which our depleted *emerillium* banks are unable to blast away. Our only hope now is to sabotage the ship."

"Commander!" Komak exclaimed, as if in disbelief.

The older alien looked straight at him, with black eyes. Jet-black. Madeline searched desperately in her memory for the meaning of that color. Black...death!

"You cannot!" Komak raged.

Dtimun glared at him, seeming to flinch as he whirled to face the younger Holconcom. *"Debles 'ha mechmal?"* he growled furiously, and he shivered suddenly.

"Camache..." Komak began uncertainly.

Even as the guttural word fell on the sudden silence, the Holconcom commander fell, as well, crumbling onto the deck in front of his shocked officers.

Around the compartment, the Centaurian faces registered something like disbelief. Only Komak moved, dropping quickly beside his fallen leader, his long-fingered hand searching for a pulse.

Before he could speak, a shudder went through the deck, a metallic shudder followed by the sound of an explosion somewhere nearby in the corridor.

8

Madeline moved forward and knelt beside Komak while two of the other execs ran into the corridor to look for the cause of the disturbance.

Komak made an expression which, in a human, would have been a grimace. *"Dylete,"* he murmured to Madeline.

She laid her wrist scanner against the commander's unmoving chest. "Yes, it is," she confirmed tautly.

"You are familiar with it?" Komak exclaimed.

"My specialization is in Cularian medicine, which includes Centaurian physiology. *Dylete* is the time of half-life," she said professionally, deaf to the speculative whispers around the table from both races as she kept her eyes on the wrist unit readings, "when the changeover from the first heart to the second occurs. Studies have confirmed that over fifty percent of your people would die without medical intervention if there are complications." She frowned. "But I understood that it only happened past the Centaurian half-life period. The commander is so young..."

"The commander," he corrected her, "is eighty-seven of your years old."

She caught her breath, because the unconscious alien could have passed for a human in his early thirties, as far as appearance went.

"It is time," he told her. "The very worst time. You must tend him," he added. "I will do what I can to save the ship."

As he got to his feet, Madeline motioned to Hahnson, who'd just come back into the compartment along with Holt Stern, looking grim. "Strick, get me two medics and all the *digammonalin* you can synthesize. I'm going to inject him with the last of my *epenefadrenin* and pray that it will put one last surge of life into the old heart and delay the *dylete*." As she spoke, she was programming the wrist unit's micro drug bank to synthesize the tiny amount of medicine that was left from her treatment of the Terramer refugees. She felt the laserdot hammer the dose directly into the older of Dtimun's two hearts. The new one, fully grown and vibrant, had not yet been stimulated into action. The curious configuration of the cardiovascular system in Cularian species had fascinated the first Terravegan exobiologists who encountered it. The body grew one heart, which performed until a new one was grown in tandem. As the new heart began to function, the old one decreased in size and was absorbed back into the tissue of the cardiac muscle. New blood vessels emerged, attached to the older ones and gradually replaced them, as well. It was a process unknown among humanoid types in the Tri-Galaxy. Nor had medical science progressed enough to explain or duplicate the process.

"Will he die?" Holt Stern asked suddenly, dropping down beside Madeline.

"Wishful thinking?" she murmured with an unfamiliar bitterness in her tone. She was remembering Dtimun smiling at her two small patients, the ones he'd saved with nothing more than the power of his mind.

"As a matter of fact…" Stern began coldly.

"Look!" Hahnson interrupted, nodding toward the alien's broad chest. "It's working!"

Slowly, so slowly, the muscles in that powerful torso began to vibrate as the lungs responded to the medicine. Madeline scanned his pulse. It was weak and erratic, but it was a living pulse. Her heart warmed.

"Keep him alive," Komak told her, sounding for all the world like Dtimun himself. "At least until I can find time to talk with him."

"He can't hear you," Madeline protested. "It's only a pulse. He's in a mild coma…"

"He will hear me, when he has to," Komak said quietly. He stood up and faced the other officers. "Decisions must now be made, while there is still time. The last explosion was the reserve engine bank being destroyed. We have only our primary lightsteds and enough power to the main weapons to sustain a short engagement."

How could he have known that? Madeline wondered absently while she worked on stabilizing her patient.

"I have broadcast a distress call on scramble through a tiny distortion in the force nets," Komak continued. "It may or may not reach the Imperial Dectat in time. We have, therefore, two options—to draw the Rojoks in and attack them from a set position, or use what speed we have left and attempt to run."

"Either way will be suicide," Stern said calmly. "You can't reach Benaski Port, your path is cut off. You can't sit still or they'll blow you out of space. If you try to run, they'll flank you and destroy your engines. Face it. We're dead in space."

Komak's eyes darkened visibly as they scanned the human's impassive face. "Our weaponry units still function, Captainholtstern," he said coolly. "And they are superior to the weaponry of the Rojok vessels. So long as they function, we are not without hope, even though we are outnumbered."

"So long as they function," Stern agreed with an enigmatic smile that chilled Madeline to the bone.

"I must study the starmaps before I make a final decision," Komak told the others. "For now, secure for battle and prepare for any eventuality."

"There isn't much hope, is there?" Madeline asked.

Komak's eyes gave a flash of pure green mischief. "Dr. Madeline-ruszel, do you know from which legend the *Morcai* takes its name?" She shook her head. Komak continued, "The Morcai were a warrior race known for their courage in the face of impossible odds. As the story goes, a hundred of them once warred against the extinct Crucerian Warlords with their legions of lightships—and won. There are no absolutes. Anything is possible."

"But not everything is probable," Stern interrupted.

Komak only glanced at him, but the sudden dark anger in his eyes spoke. "To your stations," he said. "Dismissed."

"I can't do it!" Madeline told Komak with fire in her pale green eyes. "I simply can't perform surgery on him, Komak. I don't have any actual experience in Cularian surgery. If the *dylete* itself doesn't kill him, I surely will!"

"He has resources which I cannot explain to you," Komak replied. It was an hour since the commander had fallen, and the two of them were alone with Dtimun in Madeline's makeshift sick bay. "If he is restored to health, even these odds will not affect his ability to save us. Without his help, we cannot avoid capture. I am inexperienced at the helm, for all the commander's tutoring. I do not delude myself that I am his equal as a strategist. I know two theories of combat, attack and retreat. I cannot retreat, so I must attack. And without his help," he added, nodding toward the alien in the ambutube, "I have little hope of victory. He is more than my commanding officer, Madelineruszel," he added solemnly, sadly. "I wish...that I could explain this to you. I do not dare."

She drew in a long breath. "I'm amazed that he's lasted this long," she said. "By all logic, he should be dead."

He hesitated. "I could be spaced for telling you this," he said slowly. "But it may allow you to save his life. Look." He reached into the ambutube and touched his hand to the commander's hairline. He pressed his thumbnail into the flesh and extracted a tiny, pulsing dot of energy.

She gasped. *"Microcyborgs!"* she exclaimed. "I've studied them theoretically, of course, in premed at the academy, but I've never actually seen one before. They're like your *kelekoms,* aren't they? Sentient technology, with amazing abilities that they share with a bonded companion."

"Yes. They were created by old Tnurat Alamantimichar's scientists, almost two centuries ago, from clones of the *kelekoms.* They are not only sentient, they lengthen life spans, enhance intellect and magnify strength and latent psychic abilities to an almost magical degree. We all have them, we of the Holconcom," Komak told her. "However, the commander carries more than the rest of us. It gives him superior strength. There is also the question of his mental abilities, which are exceptional, even for a Holconcom, and of which you must never speak."

She was curious, but she forced herself not to ask any more questions. "I give you my word," she said formally. She frowned. "Then, the microcyborgs are keeping him alive."

He nodded.

She narrowed her eyes. "Can you get the other Holconcom to give up one microcyborg each?" she asked, thinking quickly.

His eyes widened. "I...yes!" he burst out, delighted. "I am certain that I can!"

She smiled, feeling optimistic for the first time. "They just might make the difference. I know it's a breach of ethics for you to admit that they even exist—the technology is outlawed in the Tri-Fleet, as I'm sure you already know. But the extra units will keep him alive, for the time being."

"I will obtain the units. Then you must operate," he said quickly. "I cannot let him fall into Mangus Lo's hands. His capture would provide the Rojoks with means to overcome the entire Centaurian Empire. It is imperative that he live—or die—free."

"What is he?" she asked abruptly. "Why does Mangus Lo want him so badly?"

"It is a secret matter," he replied sadly. "I cannot speak of it. If we do not avert capture, I must kill him. It is that important."

She ground her teeth. It was a horrible responsibility. She wavered. After all, she was far more qualified than Hahnson to perform the procedure, and she had the knowledge. It would be no more risky to interfere with the *dylete* than to let the process continue naturally and possibly cost the commander his life. She kept seeing the face of the tiny Altairian boy whom Dtimun had saved...

"All right," she said. "I'll...try."

"Good."

"Komak, alternatively we might place him in a stasis tube," she said quickly. "I saw at least three of them in the sector near the *kelekom* unit. One was in use..."

"You did not interfere with it?" he asked abruptly, frowning.

"Of course not!" She hesitated. "Why?"

He averted his eyes and stood erect. "I must manage the technology while we have time. I must also conceal the *kelekoms* in case we are boarded. I will return shortly."

She stayed with Dtimun, her eyes curious on the rapid eye movement. Was he dreaming? Did Centaurians dream? And just what was in that stasis tube that Komak didn't want her to see? Why was Dtimun so important that Mangus Lo would send an entire fleet to get him? So many questions, she thought, and so few answers. There was also Stern's odd behavior during the commander's collapse, which she didn't understand. She hoped Hahnson was keeping a close eye on their captain. She didn't dare allow herself to think about Dtimun dying. It was curiously painful, and she had more than enough problems as it was.

Komak, true to his word, returned in minutes with a small tube of glowing microcyborgs. Madeline quickly implanted them just under his hairline, noting that his pulse and breathing regulated even more as they pulsed and began to entwine themselves in the neurons of his brain.

"If we can just outrun the Rojoks," she began.

The whole ship rocked. Komak stood up and his eyes went an opaque-blue. *"Maliche!"* he burst out, his head jerking as if he saw something unthinkable. "Madelineruszel," he said at once, even as he started out of the sector, "gather all the instruments you would require for emergency surgery and conceal them in your boot. Hurry. We have no time left!"

"What in the seven netherworlds...?" she faltered.

But he broke into a run and went through the hatch before she could get the question out. Even as he left, a red alert sounded shipwide. It didn't take a military expert to guess that the Rojoks were closing in. But Komak had known before. How?

With cool efficiency, even through her apprehension, she quickly gathered her instruments and put them in a protective pouch, securing them in the high-topped boot on the unconscious figure in the ambutube. She might be searched. She was hoping that the commander would not be. There was one other thing she could do, with enough time, and that was strip every mark of rank from Dtimun's uniform, which she did, pulling the rank mark and the insignia of command from his high collar and throwing them into a nearby disassembler unit.

As an afterthought, gritting her teeth, she used a sonic wand to remove the commander's short, neat beard. Many of the Holconcom wore mustaches, so she left that. When he was back on his feet, he'd court-martial her for removing his facial hair. The short beard was as much a symbol of his rank as the embryo-shaped motif on his uniform. What a good thing, she thought, that Centaurians had that golden-hued skin that didn't tan, so the quick shave wasn't going to be noticeable to an outworlder. The skin under the beard was the same soft gold as the rest of his skin. Once more, she found herself studying him, amazed at his similarity to a human, right down to his ears and fingernails. Except for the golden skin and elongated eyes, no one could have distinguished him from a human.

A sickening wave of fear washed over her as she felt the ship suddenly shudder and buckle, slinging her headlong to the deck. A second later, she heard the explosion as it reverberated throughout the ship. The Rojoks surely had them. They were stopped dead. The engines no longer hummed under her feet, as they did continually when the ship was in motion. The attack was already underway, and she knew with horrible certainty what the outcome would be. In her mind, she could see the classified holophotos depicting the open, waiting doors of Mangus Lo's sonic ovens on *Ahkmau*...

* * *

Komak took the bridge access ladder at a dead run, and seconds later he was secure in the spool-like bridge command console. His solemn blue eyes took in the situation at a glance as he studied the defense computer screen.

"Helm, how much speed can you give me?" he asked in Centaurian.

"None," came the astonished reply. "Somehow, our engines are completely offline."

Komak said a word in his own dialect, which caused the astrogator to raise an eyebrow. "Weaponry," he snapped. "Set your timers, prepare to…"

"Impossible, sir," the weaponry officer apologized. "We cannot self-destruct. The *emerillium* power units are fused. Useless."

The young Centaurian sat there quietly, his huge eyes swinging around the bridge, watching the others of his race in a static, brief silence. Never in the history of the Holconcom had a Centaurian Holconcom commander been made prisoner of any other race. Now, that proud tradition was about to be broken, and on his watch. His jaw clenched with futile anger.

He knew, however. Quite suddenly, he knew how the ship had been sabotaged, and by whom. "Find the human captain Holtstern," he told his chief security officer in rapid-fire Centaurian, "and the cloned Merrick. No quarter. You understand?" he added grimly.

"I understand," the security chief nodded and trotted off toward the access ladder.

Komak's hands clenched on the arms of the console. At least Stern would not live to boast of his treachery. He kept brooding on the fact that no Holconcom commander had ever been captured in battle. It was unthinkable. That must be prevented, at all cost. He only regretted that there was no way to destroy the ship in time. That would have been the best solution to this monumental tragedy.

He stood up. There was one last duty, which only he could perform. He would allow no other soldier near the commander. This, he thought furiously, had not been part of the design at all. His sketchy knowledge of these days, this incident, did not include the death of the commander...

"Sir," the astrogator asked quietly, "what do you wish of us?"

"Courage," Komak replied. "And patience. If we cannot die as a unit, there is little logic in half measures. Let us show the Rojoks that Holconcom will not be subjugated by fear, as are other races. Let the Holconcom set an example of bravery that will be remembered as the valiant Morcai are remembered."

"The commander would wish this, also," the astrogator replied, with a green smile in his eyes.

"Yes," Komak told the bridge crew as he turned away, with death and anguish in his dark eyes. "The commander would wish it."

"They will demand surrender," the astrogator reminded him.

"They will have to board us to obtain it. I will not yield the colors." He turned again toward the access ladder. "Should you require me before they come, I will be in the makeshift exobiology sector of Dr. Madelineruszel."

As he ran there, once down the access ladder, he wondered about the paradox he was about to create, and if he would vanish in a haze...

Madeline Ruszel was checking the rest of her shaken charges when Komak entered the sector. His eyes, dark with pain, fixed on the ambutube containing Dtimun's powerful body.

"What's going on?" she asked.

"We are surrounded and about to be subjected to capture," Komak told her. "However, your captain and the clone he managed to repro-gram will not live to see it. They cost us the engines and our weaponry. My security chief is searching for them now."

Cold chills ran down her spine. She knew the answer even as she asked the question. "What will they do? What will happen to Stern and Merrick?"

Komak met her gaze levelly, and there was no compassion, no concern, *nothing* in his elongated cat-eyes. "They will be killed," he said simply.

She hesitated. "Please," she said gently. "You don't know Stern, the way he was before this happened. He was one of the finest command-ers in our service…!"

"So was my commander, Madam," he replied quietly. "I cannot allow him to be captured." His hand went to the panel that would open the ambutube.

"Komak, what are you doing?"

"What I must. I have no more options. You have no idea what a medically weak Centaurian could suffer under Mangus Lo's execu-tioners, the treatment he would endure on *Ahkmau*."

"There are always options!" she argued, moving to the ambutube.

He drew in a harsh breath. "You do not understand!"

It occurred to her that he hadn't yet identified his commander with the still figure in the stasis unit. Nor could she. "You can't hurt this crewman!" she raged. "Not when I've gone to such lengths to try to save him!"

"You have no idea of the pain it gives me to even contemplate it," he ground out. He glanced into the ambutube and hesitated. His eyes flickered when he saw the changes she'd made to the commander's appearance. "*Maliche!* What have you done to him?"

"What do you mean?" she asked deliberately, because even now

Rojoks might be aboard, watching the remote audiovisual units, searching for Dtimun. "I haven't done anything to this crewman." She emphasized the last word. She moved between Komak and the ambutube. "This poor, sick Holconcom crewman," she continued deliberately, "has only had too much synthe-ale and is sleeping it off. You can't kill a man for dereliction of duty, now, can you?" she persisted doggedly. "Your commander is already dead, but this soldier might live...!"

Komak hesitated, his eyes gone blue with surprise, as he registered what she'd just said. It was only for a second, but it was already too late....

Admiral Jeffrye Lawson stared blankly at the small pile of personal effects that his adjutant had dumped on the highly polished moga wood block his desk had been carefully carved from.

"What a hell of a legacy to leave behind," he murmured to Ambassador Giles Mourjey, who was receiving a last-minute briefing on the state of the war effort before his long journey back to Terravega.

Mourjey studied the meager leavings. "Indeed. Two mems," he noted, touching the small, silvery coins, "an ID disc, assignment disc, a ring watch, and...a piece of blue ribbon?"

Lawson frowned. "Part of a piece of blue ribbon. I wonder where the rest of it is?"

"Does it have some significance?"

Lawson smiled. "Stern carried it everywhere. The men used to rib him about being sentimental, because it had belonged to a woman he knew. He always kept the main piece, but he and his bridge crew used to pass part of it around like a medal, for valor under fire."

"His service record was exemplary," the ambassador said.

Lawson nodded, his silver hair glistening in the soft glow of the ceiling. "He was one of the finest officers in the SCC fleet. And this had to happen…" He sighed wearily. "Sometimes this damned job gets to me. The casualty figures are more than numbers when you have to send condolence holos to families all over the galaxies."

"Did Stern have a family?"

Lawson shook his head. "He was from one of the baby mills. One of the few without a known parent." He touched the remnant of blue ribbon. "Madeline Ruszel and Strick Hahnson were the next best thing to his 'family.' Doctors, both of them—two of the best. I'll bet they took it hard. God, if anything happens to Ruszel I'll have the whole damned Paraguard on my neck. Her father is Lieutenant Colonel Clinton Ruszel. Remember him? Old Blood and Mud? He still commands a wing of the Paraguard Commandoes and, despite the regulations against any sort of emotional bonds, he'd fight a herd of *galots* for his daughter. I hope she and Hahnson survive the Holconcom. What am I saying?" he asked, wiping his steamy brow with his hand. "I hope the Holconcom ship survives. They've not been heard from since they rescued the crew of the *Bellatrix*."

"What are the chances of getting a rescue force together to go after them?" Mourjey asked.

"One in a billion," Lawson said flatly. He started pacing the room. "I'm just now massing troops for an all-out offensive in the Algomerian sector, and munitions and food stores are holding me up. We're having to import them from the Vegan colonies, and the Rojoks are having a field day shooting the transport freighters out of space."

"The Holconcom commander, Dtimun, is supposed to be something of a legend," Mourjey said with a smile. "I understand the Council once awarded him its highest honor, the Legion of Valor. They say he threw it in Lokar's face and walked out."

"That's so," Lawson chuckled, remembering. "I was just a cadet at the time, but I recall the ceremony. Dtimun has a temper that's as legendary as his abilities as a strategist. He'll get through the Rojok trap. I'd bet everything I own on him."

"He's older than you, isn't he?"

Lawson nodded, smiling. "He's in his eighties, although he could pass for much, much younger. His men would follow him out an airlock, and he has a sense of humor that sits oddly on that stoic reputation of his as a fighter. I've never known a commander like him. Pity we can't shanghai the Holconcom into the Tri-Fleet. We'd be invincible. But old Tnurat Alamantimichar hates humans."

Mourjey watched the light fading outside the Tri-D window with a long sigh at the swirl of candy colors on the horizon. There was such beauty out there, and humanoids eternally seemed to prefer blood to sunsets.

"You're not listening," Lawson chided. "I said, how soon can I get that armored cavalry division your government promised me?"

"I'll check and let you know. Jeffrye, I should have stayed at home and become a writer of poetry," he said as he clasped forearms with the older man. "I find no glory in war."

"Nor do I, Giles," Lawson agreed. His gaze fell involuntarily to the small length of blue velvet ribbon on his desk. "God, nor do I!"

Holt Stern and the clone, Merrick, stood sweating with apprehension in the tiny storage cubicle as the security squad passed right by them without stopping to check it. The armed guards were everywhere, and it had taken all the cunning he could manage to save the pair of them. But if those damned Rojok raiders didn't board the *Morcai* pretty soon, it would be beyond his ingenuity to escape detection. He knew instinctively that he'd be shot on sight. He only wished he knew if Dtimun was still alive. It was important that the cat-eyed terror was captured in one piece. He'd collapsed, but he knew Madeline would soon revive him. She was very skilled. It had to be on Dtimun's orders that security was looking for Stern and Merrick. Or did it? What if Dtimun was dead? There'd be hell to pay. Komak didn't like or trust him. Yes, it could be Komak who had a search party out looking for him. The younger Centaurian would make a tireless, relentless enemy, especially if Dtimun died.

He flexed his aching shoulders. Soon. Soon, it would be all over. The Rojoks would take the ship to *Ahkmau,* and it would all be over. And he and the clone would be...where? Rewarded? Confined? That thought had never occurred to him before. And again he could see Madeline Ruszel's face in front of him. *Maddie!* He cried silently, involuntarily. *Forgive me!*

He felt Merrick's clone watching him, and he wiped the anguish from his face. This would never do. He would have to control these strange surges of emotion. His eyes closed as he hoped fervently for an end to the waiting.

In the makeshift exobiology sector, Madeline Ruszel's fingers closed on a *Gresham* that was lying beside her on a computer console. She had to be quick and accurate. Komak was debating his next move, and she saw in his eyes that he had made it. His hand went to the controls on the ambutube. Another instant and the tube would open. Komak's merciless hand would close on Dtimun's neck. It would be too late. She didn't want to hurt Komak, whom she liked, but it was stun him or lose the commander. Remembering the children who would be dead but for Dtimun's intervention, she knew she couldn't let Komak commit murder, not even to save the alien from Rojok hands.

"Komak," she began, clasping her fingers around the weapon.

He glanced her way.

Before she could fire, there was a muffled commotion in the corridor. Suddenly five uniformed Rojoks burst into the sector with raised *chasats*. The first blue blast took Komak to his knees. The second felled him, stunned him unconscious. Misunderstanding the *Gresham* Madeline was holding as a threat to them, the Rojoks fired on her, as well. One blast was enough to carry her down, unconscious, beside Komak. Stepping over the two unconscious officers, the Rojoks moved toward the Centaurian in the ambutube, their slit eyes emotionless, their weapons still raised.

9

"We have him, we have him!" Mangus Lo laughed, raising his arms over his head as he leaned back in his silver throne. "I could wish for no brighter news to begin the day. He is being taken to *Ahkmau,* surely?"

"Yes, your Excellence," the Rojok officer reported, but he was sweating.

"Good. I will send my personal emissary to bring him back here!"

There was a hesitation. "There is a...very small problem."

"Small problem? What small problem?"

The officer swallowed. Hard. "He has, temporarily, only temporarily, managed to secrete himself somewhere aboard the ship."

"And?" came the impatient reply.

"We are searching his ship, of course," the younger Rojok said quickly. "It is only a matter of time until he is discovered."

Mangus Lo's dusky face became duskier. "How can the ship's commander hide, even aboard his own vessel?"

The younger alien was becoming more and more agitated. "Through our monitoring, we learned that he had reached the *dylete*," the alien confessed heavily. "There is a very, very slight possibility..."

"What? What!" the older Rojok demanded, furious.

"That the Holconcom commander died and his corpse was launched into space," came the miserable reply. "We are not certain, of course, and we will continue to investigate. But it is a possibility."

"Dead? Dead!" Mangus Lo sat down heavily again on his throne. He had waited for so much time, plotted, consorted even with the enemy to make sure that the Holconcom was commanded to the Peace Planet after the Rojok attack. It was all a means to an end, to capture Dtimun. And now a disease—no, not even a disease—had put an end to his life and robbed Mangus Lo of his most valuable prize. He breathed more roughly with each second. The eyes he finally turned to his officer were murderous.

"Then you will have ships search with every possible technology for his corpse, in the area of space where you think he was expelled from the ship!" Mangus Lo demanded.

"But it will take forever...!"

"No matter if it does," Mangus Lo bit off. He leaned forward. "As for the rest of his miserable command, all of it is to be taken to *Ahkmau*. One by one the crew is to be interrogated, in the sonic ovens if necessary. Some one of them will eventually give you the truth of the commander's final hours and the location of his body. I can have him cloned, even if he is dead!"

"Yes, your Excellency!"

"But first I must have the corpse." His eyes narrowed. "Kill them all if you have to. But find what is left of the Holconcom commander!"

"It will be done!" the officer promised. He saluted and left the throne room. He was glad that he hadn't mentioned the addition of the humans to the Centaurian crew, or the fact that Dtimun might still be alive. It would be more comfortable for all Rojok military if Mangus Lo was convinced of Dtimun's death. And it would save this officer's life and career.

Holt Stern was still recovering his composure when the Rojok troop carrier left its orbit around Enmehkmehk, the home planet of Mangus Lo's tyranny, and moved rapidly into orbit around the first of Enmehkmehk's three moons. *Ahkmau,* the notorious death camp of the Rojok Empire, was located there. It was a site so secure that its borders had never been breached. The newest and most formidable of the Rojok military's secret shield technology kept the camp of horrors safe from attack from any outworld raids.

The Rojok officer had just told Stern that he'd been cloned on Terramer to infiltrate the *Bellatrix* and, later, the *Morcai.* Stern was devastated at the news. The officer seemed to find his shock amusing. Stern had a purpose to serve, the officer continued. It was time he repaid the kindness of his Rojok comrades for his new life. Some life, Stern thought to himself, seeing his career vanish in front of his eyes as the realization that he was a clone hit home.

Komak's security guards had been within a whisper of killing Stern and his cloned associate, Merrick, when the Rojok soldiers in the corridor swept through and rescued them. Stern was astonished that the enemy aliens didn't even attempt to fire at him or Merrick. They knew who Stern was and treated him well. But Stern felt uneasy just the same, and he had an attack of nerves that was completely new to him.

Ignoring his silent companion, he watched out the starboard porthole as *Ahkmau* came slowly into view on the horizon. The whole hemisphere of the moon where the notorious death camp was located was a sprawling red desert that contained no speck of life. What little atmosphere and water that might have existed here eons ago was long gone. The Rojoks had made the moon habitable by converting its desert into a highly sophisticated complex of encapsulated prisoner of war camps. Each pressurized command dome contained a self-supporting community of prisoners and guards. Stern lost count of the individual prisoner cell-domes. They dotted the endless swirling landscape like blisters on red flesh.

"Impressive, is it not?" a Rojok security officer asked Stern. "Each of those confinement domes has the capability to house at least twenty-five prisoners, and we have a thousand in this complex."

"Not very many…" Stern began.

"They are temporary housing only, of course," the officer continued, as if Stern had never spoken. "The prisoners are useful only while they contain information, which we require of them. Afterward, they are placed in the sonic ovens." He waved a hand toward the complex. "We must, of course, import stores of hydrogen and oxygen to replicate water, but it is recycled from wastewater and, of course, the normal excretory functions of the prisoners for reuse. In emergencies we can resupply with transport ships."

"Efficient," Stern said stiffly.

"We are quite efficient," the Rojok agreed. "The prisoners are fed a specialized chemical diet, which reduces the amount of solid sewage to be recycled. Most are disposed of and their biological attributes harvested, but the healthiest and strongest are conserved for our labor pool, to manufacture goods to further our war effort. The five large domes contain industries that produce the metal framework and the power supply for our *chasats*. They also manufacture engine parts for our ships, with minerals mined from the surrounding area by our robotic machinery."

"How many workers?" Stern asked, curious.

"It varies," he replied. "We dislike the idea of keeping workers for any great length of time, so we purge the population at intervals and replenish it from new prisoners. Some races are more adept at the fine work than others. The Centaurians," he added smugly, "are quite strong and resilient. If we can tame them, they will be of great use to us in the construction sector, programming our constructdroids."

"Centaurians do not make good slaves," Stern said, wondering how he knew. "And these are Holconcom, not regulars."

"We know of the Holconcom. Their reputation in battle is exaggerated, we are certain of it. And the Holconcom is inferior, made up of clones only," the Rojok said with contempt. "I think we shall have no trouble with them."

"How do you control the population?"

The Rojok shrugged. "It is a matter of chemistry. There are rewards for good work and punishments for failure to cooperate or laziness. We simply start removing body parts until rebellion is over, then we replicate the missing parts and reattach them." He laughed. "It is a very painful process, which is demonstrated in front of all the prisoners. Cooperation is usually immediate." He noted Stern's involuntary shiver. "However, we treat the water which is provided through replicators in the domes. We use a special form of chemicals which induce euphoria and inhibit hostility. It works quite well."

"What happens if someone escapes?" Stern asked with a flicker of hope.

"That has never happened," the officer said indifferently. "No one has ever escaped from *Ahkmau*."

Yet, Stern wanted to say. No one has escaped *yet*. The smug look on the Rojok's dusky-skinned face made his fists itch to hit out. Despite the indoctrination that had submerged the human part of him, he felt a quivering ache in his mind to know freedom. To think as he pleased. To think freely. Even the idea of captivity was abhorrent to him. There must be some spark of the original Holt Stern left in him, in this copy of all that was the former captain of the SSC ship *Bellatrix*. Deep inside, he ached to be the genuine article. And knew he never could be. He thought of the torment to come, and his mind went rapidly to Madeline and Hahnson. As he pictured them being tortured, he felt sick to his soul. They would die screaming, and he'd put them there.

"You seem restless, comrade," the Rojok remarked, eyeing him closely. "Something troubles you?"

"Yeah," Stern said, making a show of wiggling his black boot. "My foot's gone to sleep."

The Rojok shuttle ships graved down toward the dome that held the hangars and smaller transports. The bubble rippled open like a transparent mouth to receive them as they left the command ship in orbit. Once inside, the ripple became a steady, visible barrier to flight. The Rojoks had obviously perfected their liquid shield technology since the early days of mechanical hangar doors. Only the far-flung Tarmerian dynasty had such technology. It didn't take much reasoning to conclude that one of their scientists had been tortured into revealing its secrets. The sci-archaeo group that had been observing the colony on Terramer must have been brought here, along with the Jaakob Spheres, which contained the knowledge of a hundred worlds. Their scientific breakthroughs would be used with glee by the Rojok Empire to extend its borders. And it didn't end there. Stern shuddered when he realized what his crew would know of Tri-Fleet battle groups and unit deployments, and what they would endure before inevitably telling the Rojoks every single secret they knew.

The ship's terminal access bubbled open and a cylindrical corridor appeared that led into the main hangar, where smaller ground-based transports were waiting for the crew. Stern noted that the men weren't being segregated.

"Why are you putting the Centaurians in with the humans?" he asked his companion.

The Rojok scoffed, "The combination will spare us the logistics of dispatching so many of the crew," he said simply. "It is known to us that the Holconcom are always segregated from other units, even of their own race, because they are cloned to be both aggressive and physically superior to other humanoids. If they are touched by an enemy, they kill without hesitation. They will kill many of the humans, I think, before we get around to interrogating them."

It was true. Stern felt even sicker. He searched the crowds of uniforms, but he couldn't pick out either Madeline or Strick. He wouldn't get to say goodbye. He felt a lancing pain. By now, they'd know that he'd sold them out. He'd delivered them into the terror of *Ahkmau*. They would die, by his hand...!

"You surely feel no remorse," the Rojok said suspiciously, reading his expression. "You were cloned to be loyal only to Mangus Lo."

"As I am," he said, turning to follow the officer away from the transports. "I was looking for someone."

"For the commander of the Holconcom?" The officer laughed. "You will not find him. We received word from a contact in the *palcenon* that the Holconcom commander died aboard ship and was consigned to space. Mangus Lo even now has search vessels looking for his body."

So the commander was that important, that even his body was valuable to the Rojok dictator. Interesting. He wondered why. He had to steel himself not to ask questions or send any more worried looks behind him. He felt an odd sadness at the loss of the Centaurian leader who had saved his ship and crew from what he would have deemed certain death at the hands of the Rojoks. No one knew that the situation had been created as a ploy to get the humans—and Stern—aboard Dtimun's vessel so that it could be sabotaged and delivered up whole to the Rojoks. Dtimun hadn't known that, though. He'd been saving a fellow space combatant. It was a noble act. It made Stern feel even worse, remembering. He drew in a quiet breath and walked out of the hangar.

Madeline Ruszel stepped through the airlock behind Strick Hahnson, her eyes searching the gray, military atmosphere of the hangar with restless apprehension. A former captain of the Amazon squads didn't panic. But she knew more about *Ahkmau* than most of the other captives around her, because she'd once treated a victim of Rojok interrogation techniques. The victim had come from a battlefield, not the notorious Rojok death camp, but she'd lost sleep over his mutilation. They'd cut off his hands and feet while questioning him, one centimeter at a time while he screamed and gave up everything he knew. If he hadn't been rescued by a SSC covert ops team, the Rojoks would have regrown the missing parts, reattached them and started the process all over again until they were certain he was empty of all useful intel. Not the most barbaric of the Tri-Fleet battle groups would even contemplate such a method of interrogation.

The formidable guard stations surrounded the blisters of the cells. They were three-level caricatures of modern architecture, gray-hulled and roughly finished, as though they'd been built carelessly and in a rush. They lined the entire outer perimeter of the complex and doubtless contained weapons to neutralize any prisoner who tried to escape.

The inner circle was a scramble of small, individual domes that looked as though they could accommodate up to twenty humans. They were interspersed with smaller domes that must have been guard stations. The minidomes had a privacy screen that circled them about one-third of the way from the bottom. The rest was transparent, allowing the guards to see every movement that went on inside. It was daylight now, and a reddish light burned through the heavy hyperglas dome over the entire complex of minidomes. Probably at night, Madeline thought uneasily, the prison spheres were bathed in artificial light. She had a mental image of how the hundreds of blister cells would look in the darkness. If they were solar powered, they might glow in the darkness, like jewels on the sand from an orbiting ship's vantage point. If the Rojoks had any humanity, there would be some sort of ultraviolet shielding that acted automatically to filter out dangerous light. But she doubted it.

The atmosphere inside the complex had a strange odor, she noticed, as she and Hahnson and several other humans were marched toward the center ring of spheres. An odor that was musky, sweet and heavy and strangely dry. It was hot, too. Hotter than summer in the shade. She wondered what temperature the Rojoks would consider cold?

She wondered, too, what had happened to Dtimun, and to the four *kelekom* operators—and to the *kelekoms* themselves, those sentient beings with such fantastic psychic abilities. Komak had said he was making arrangements for their concealment. She hadn't had time to ask how. Did the Rojoks know about them? Or did they, like most Tri-Fleet military people, think they were just some ancient legend? Of the *Bellatrix* crew, only Madeline had actually seen a *kelekom*. She hoped they would survive. They were so few.

Dtimun might be dead by now. And what of Komak? And Stern? She hated the idea that Stern had sold them out. She'd had to tell

Hahnson. It was the final proof that their old captain was truly dead. The real Stern would have chewed through hullplates to get them out of captivity. They were deep in Rojok space. No rescue would be possible. It made the future grim.

The majority of the prisoners they met on the way to the cells were thin and their expressions were blank. Apparently there were shifts of captives, because these were being led out of one of the domes. There were about fifteen of them, emaciated and forlorn. Once, Madeline met the eyes of a dark-haired young captive Altairian soldier. They had the look of ancient tombs—a sad, cold darkness that was as empty as space. Dead.

They weren't all soldiers in this camp, either. As she watched, a small blur of blue skin shot between the small domes, to be brought up short, suddenly, in front of Madeline's group of prisoners.

The boy was Altairian, about the age of the clone she and Dtimun had managed to save aboard the *Morcai*. His huge, hunted eyes bulged as he looked, terrified, from one Rojok soldier to another. His gray prison utility suit hung from his thin body. There was a nervous, desperate trembling in his long, tapered arms and legs, in the thin tentacle fingers that moved like leaves in a strong wind. Beads of sweat dribbled down his long face as he panted for breath, like a small furbearer being chased by a *galot,* one of the legendary Centaurian feral jungle cats, which were said to contain a genetic link to the evolved race.

The Rojok guard in the lead made a sound that would have passed for laughter in a human. His six-fingered hand went out toward the boy, and Madeline almost smiled herself, already seeing that alien hand tousling the silvery mat of hair on the child's head. It was such a natural thing to do. Most soldiers, of all races, had a weakness for children. She was still nursing the smile when she realized that the

Rojok's hand had moved slightly, and was now holding the child's head aloft. The crumpled, small torso lay bleeding on the absorbent hypoturf that covered the sand in the dome, the neck neatly sliced through by a cutting beam from a small *chasat* that Madeline hadn't even seen concealed in the guard's hand.

"Oh, God," she whispered. For the first time in her life, she knew the taste of terror. Even her military background had not prepared her for the sight of an unforgivable atrocity.

With utter contempt, the Rojok tossed the child's head into a nearby collection tube and led on toward the individual prison cells.

Madeline and Hahnson were two of the first to be called, from a list in one of the Rojoks' hands. The guard produced a sonic pen and, leveling it at the nearest dome, produced a two-foot slit in the circumference—just enough to let the humans inside through it.

Madeline, Hahnson, Engineering officer Lieutenant Commander Latham Higgins, Astrogator Ole Crandall, Communications Specialist Hugh Jennings, Komak and three other vaguely familiar Centaurian officers, plus one ailing Holconcom being borne in by his comrades, were rudely forced into the cell. The slit opening was immediately fused and the humans and the Centaurians stood facing each other like athletic teams looking for weaknesses.

"Well, Komak," Hahnson said with a weary grin, "do you think we can survive each other while we work on a printout of our conditions for surrender for the Rojoks?"

Komak's huge eyes made a green smile for the human. "After what Madelineruszel has accomplished," he said, meeting her curious gaze, "that might be made possible."

"I don't understand," Hahnson replied, growing more curious as he watched the play of eyes.

"Have you not noticed our poor fallen comrade, Strickhahnson?"

he asked, dropping to one knee beside the unconscious red-uniformed Centaurian.

"By God!" Hahnson broke out after a brief scrutiny of the bedraggled, shaven alien on the hypoturf floor of the cell. The beard was gone, giving him a totally strange appearance. He looked much younger, even though the thin mustache remained, and some of his usual authority was missing because the great eyes were closed. But it was, despite the lack of insignia on his uniform, most definitely the commander of the Holconcom lying there.

"You really should have brigged this crewman, Komak," Madeline said matter-of-factly with a look that belied her casual remarks. "Getting sauced in the middle of general quarters! But he'll sleep it off, I guess. I'll give him an injection to bring him around."

Desperately she hoped the others around her would get the message. Most certainly, the cell was linked to an AVBD at the guard cell. One word, one look, could cost the commander his life. And while the Centaurians would never betray him, she wasn't dead sure about the other three humans in their cell, especially after Dtimun had publicly spaced Muldoon. The Irishman had many friends among the crew.

Higgins stared at the unconscious alien for a minute, then at Madeline. "Damned slacker," he muttered derisively. "He ought to be ashamed of himself!"

"I'm sure he'll admit the error of his ways when he comes around," Astrogator Crandall said with a grin, following Higgins's lead. "And if he does it again, sir, we'll hang him up on the wall and shoot Greshams at him."

"Not a bad idea, Komak, but he's your officer," Higgins said to the alien, shaking his head. "Bad lapse of discipline on your part."

The young Centaurian's eyes flashed green for an instant.

Madeline had to stifle a smile. It was what she'd hoped for; the confinement turned the warring humans and Centaurians of the *Morcai*'s crew into just crewmates facing an ordeal. They couldn't fight the Rojoks and each other. The humans had decided, without a word being spoken, that they would protect the commander of the Holconcom. *The enemy of my enemy,* she quoted silently, *is my friend.*

"Indeed," Komak replied. "Perhaps we may rehabilitate him, though, Strickhahnson."

A long look passed between them. "It's going to take a miracle to accomplish that, I fear," he said quietly.

"Byclearius of Domageddon said that miracles are the by-product of stubborn faith," Madeline told them with a weary smile. "And I always did like a good fight."

"What a splendid opportunity you have for one at the moment," Hahnson replied. "How about giving our friend here something to help dry him out?"

"It would be a step in the right direction, wouldn't it?" she asked, dropping down beside the Holconcom commander. She activated her wrist scanner. "How about checking that synthesizer on the bulkhead to see what kind of supply banks it has?"

"I'll bet you it won't give us the time in Standard," Hahnson said dubiously as he studied the compact but aging old supply computer. "It looks like a holdover from the Great Galaxy War."

Komak knelt on the other side of his commander, looking across the massive chest at Madeline. "You may require assistance. However," he added with a level look, "it may be more feasible to wait for a more opportune time to...dry out...our companion. So long as he is...comfortable."

Madeline studied the impassive golden-hued face, the solemnity in the young alien's gracefully elongated eyes. Odd, how human

Komak could seem at times. His skin was lighter than the rich gold of the commander's complexion, and his eyes had an odd shape. She blinked. She must be stressed out to question his background when it was well-known that the Centaurian emperor Tnurat Alamantimichar had put to death every single member of his race—and there were only a very few—who crossed racial lines to mate. Komak stared at her and frowned, then blinked. He started to speak but abruptly averted his eyes, almost as if he'd sensed her odd thoughts.

She lowered her gaze to the rise and fall of Dtimun's chest and read her wrist scanner. She nodded slowly. He was stable, for the moment. "He's just dead drunk," she murmured. "There's nothing worrying about his condition."

"Then, whenever it pleases you, we may consider reviving him," Komak said.

"We can hold him down for you, if you need help," Higgins said with a wide grin. "Crandall and I are old hands at handling unruly drunks. We've been picking each other off barroom floors for years."

"I know," Madeline replied, tongue-in-cheek. "I've been doing it with you for years, too."

They both laughed.

"Excuse me?" Komak asked, listening intently.

"She was a captain in the Amazon Division," Higgins told the alien. "We used to get in brawls regularly with the Second ParaWing Division. You might not believe it to look at her, but the doc here can press her own weight *and* heave an adversary right out through a hyperglas wall when she's in the mood."

Komak's eyes flashed green. "It cannot be so!"

She shrugged. "I couldn't let the guy sideline Higgins," she pointed out. "He's too good an exec."

"Thanks, Doc," Higgins chuckled.

"Your military allows you—allows females—to fight, physically fight, with male soldiers?" Komak found this idea incomprehensible.

"It doesn't exactly allow it," she replied. "But our military authorities see no difference between us, genderwise. We're mentally neutered, Komak," she added. "There's no sexual fraternization among space soldiers. It's the only death penalty left on the books."

"Not that we need a law for it," Hahnson added easily. "We don't feel physical attraction to each other. It's the price we pay for military service."

"When you are discharged, then?" Komak asked, as if he was really curious.

"We aren't," Madeline told him. "We serve until we're too old to be useful, then we're transferred to the rimscouts or to interstellar medical units like the *Freespirit,* which crosses battle lines in war to treat combatants."

"You will never be permitted to mate and breed?" Komak asked, horrified.

Madeline and Hahnson gave him a blank look. "They have state breeders for that," she answered for both of them, "genetically selected and used as base pairs for population revitalization. Some are used to create clones, which are used for..." She grimaced. "Forgive me, Komak, but they're used in our society as spare parts. Clones have no political or military status in the Tri-Fleet. They're hardware."

Komak actually paled. "Barbaric!"

"Considering the reverence clones inspire in your society," Hahnson said to the alien, "I can understand your distaste. We don't like the way clones are treated, either, but it would require a revolution to stop it." He shrugged. "Nobody wants to repeat the mistakes of the Great Galaxy War. Our entire society was almost destroyed by the very clones we created to protect our cities."

"There are some bad memories connected with our participation in that conflict," Madeline conceded. She looked at Komak with sadness. "Not that I was old enough to participate in it," she added. "My father fought the Rojoks, along with the Holconcom. In fact, I remember seeing your C.O. back then," she recalled. "He saved my life. Funny, I'd forgotten that." She pretended a look of utter sadness. "I'm so sorry he died aboard the *Morcai,* Komak. It will be devastating for your crew when they hear it."

"So it will," Komak agreed, keeping the green amusement in his eyes hidden.

"At any rate," Higgins remarked, eyeing the unconscious alien on the floor, "all of us will be pleased to do anything we can to help rehabilitate your comrade here. Not that he deserves help, the sot. Drunk on duty, can you imagine? If we get him back home, he'll be court-martialed for sure."

Komak was watching him. "Someday, I would be interested to hear your rationale," he said quietly, and they were both remembering Muldoon's resigned face as he went out the airlock on Dtimun's order.

Higgins only nodded. "It might surprise you, sir," he replied quietly.

"We've been avoiding it, but we might as well know now. What are they going to do to us, Komak?" she asked.

"We are not given the status of political prisoners," the young alien replied somberly. "We are Tri-Fleet and Holconcom personnel, with information, which would be invaluable to the Rojok war effort. I need not tell you, Madelineruszel and Strickhahnson, how that information is usually extracted. I know that you have seen battle casualties from the Rojok sector."

Higgins and Crandall frowned, because they didn't know. Madeline ignored their curious looks. She wasn't about to share the information. They were going to need their nerve.

But remembering the Altairian boy who'd been beheaded on the way to this cell, she shuddered involuntarily. If it came to that, her wrist scanner was equipped with a potent poison sac, which she could utilize in milliseconds if necessary. Her medical knowledge of Cularian physiology and pharmacology would give the Rojoks a great advantage over the Centaurians. She couldn't afford to let the enemy have access to it.

Also, if the torment became too unbearable, the poison would give her a way out. But the commander, Strick, the others… Was it fair to take the easy way out and leave them to bear the agony of this place without the small mercy that a physician could dispense? Ethics, she thought angrily. Damn ethics and damn integrity. What good were they in a hellhole like this, where it was every soldier for himself? On the other hand, she'd just seen a form of nobility she hadn't expected in Higgins and Crandall, who were willing to keep their silence to protect an alien who'd cold-bloodedly spaced their comrade Muldoon. *The enemy of my enemy,* she thought again, ironically, *is my friend.*

She started to speak when movement caught her eye. She turned. A Rojok officer—one of high rank, considering the *mesag* marks on the sleeve of his red uniform—was moving toward their cell, with an armed escort. Madeline and the others got to their feet as he approached.

The Rojok officer stopped at the control panel on the outside of the dome and just stood there, his arms folded across his chest, studying the occupants of the cell as if they were caged animals.

"Komak of Maltiche," the Rojok said finally, in perfect Standard, the amalgamated language used throughout the galaxies between races who couldn't speak each other's tongues, his gaze going to the young Centaurian at the head of the imprisoned group. "You are the *Morcai*'s exec?"

"I am," Komak replied with a quiet arrogance that made the Rojok stiffen.

The Rojok's slit eyes narrowed even more. "We have carefully searched the complement of the *Morcai,*" the alien officer said quietly in a tone that was chilling. "We also have ships searching the sector where your ship was captured. We have failed to find any trace of your commander or his corpse."

"Indeed?" Komak asked indifferently.

"Where is he?" the Rojok continued. "And consider carefully your reply," he added with a cold, arrogant smile. "Because if you do not produce him, we will torture every single member of the *Morcai*'s crew, one by one, until we find him!"

10

Madeline felt her heart sink to her stomach. Torture. They would torture the entire crew in order to find Dtimun. Was it worth the risk, to protect an alien who might die naturally in the next few hours? A sudden, unfamiliar anguish stabbed her at the thought of that proud alien dead.

But she didn't have to consider her answer, because it was impossible for her, ethically, to turn Dtimun over to these murderous dogs. Given a choice, she'd take torture and hope to God that she wouldn't break under it. She glanced at her crewmates and saw the same resolve in them.

"The commander is dead," Komak repeated.

"Untrue," the Rojok replied with equal firmness. "We found no record of his death in your ship's log—neither was there any evidence of a recent urning aboard the vessel. It is Centaurian law that a commander of flagship rank is to be urned ceremonially," he added, airing his knowledge of their culture.

"There was such a cloning less than two solar days ago," Komak said evenly, "and we did not note it in the log, as we were under alien attack. That is also our protocol. The urn has been concealed. You will not find it." He studied the enemy. "We also cloned two crewmen…"

"You cloned one," the alien corrected smugly. "And he was reprogrammed by our operative, who was cloned from a member of the human crew, which answered the distress call on Terramer."

Madeline and Hahnson exchanged horrified glances. They meant Stern! He hadn't been mentally altered—he was dead! Holt Stern was dead!

"It is no use insinuating that your commander was an altered clone," the alien continued in a monotone. "I will ask you one last time. Where is Commander Dtimun?"

Komak raised his head. "Dead."

"A lie! And we will uncover the truth if it requires the systematic torture of every one of your crew! Even now, an emissary from Mangus Lo's *palcenon* is on his way to us to take Commander Dtimun back to our imperial Excellence. It is unthinkable to keep the emperor waiting!"

"Gee, fella, we're sorry," Madeline said with mock sincerity. "It's okay with us if you want to take the C.O. to Mangus Lo. Isn't it, guys?" she asked her comrades.

"Sure," Hahnson said with a shrug. "I don't mind."

"Me, neither," Higgins seconded. "Hell, sir, you can take him sand-swimming for all I care."

The Rojok seemed to burn purple under his dusky complexion at the insolent treatment he was getting from these inferior humans. "You will not be impertinent!" he sputtered.

"Impertinent?" Madeline frowned. "Say, is that anything like being hungry? I just remembered, I didn't get time for mess before you people took over our ship."

"You will tell me what I want to know!" the Rojok officer fairly screamed. "I will have you all tortured!"

"Whatever he has in mind," Lieutenant Higgins said lightly, "can't be much worse than having to listen to him rave. How about some java, Dr. Hahnson?"

"Fine!" Hahnson said.

"I could use some coffee, myself," Madeline agreed pleasantly.

The humans turned their backs on the interrogator and moved to the ancient synthesizer on the bulkhead of the dome.

The Centaurians in the cell with Madeline and the others stood grouped together, watching with puzzled blue-gray eyes, as if the whole incident was Greek to them.

The Rojok officer let loose a stream of what sounded like curses, gathered his official pride and his escort and stomped away toward the HQ complex.

"Excuse me," one of the young Holconcom soldiers asked, moving to stand beside Madeline while the other humans conversed, "I do not understand how you can treat imprisonment here so lightly. Are you not afraid, you humans?"

"Afraid?" Madeline laughed softly. "I'm terrified. I can't remember a time in my career when I could taste and smell fear the way I can right now. But whatever I feel, I'm an officer in the Strategic Space Command—one of the Royal Legion of Terravega. And I'm doing nothing that might disgrace this uniform. That includes keeping my fears to myself, if I have to chew my tongue off. The Rojoks may kill me, but they won't break me."

The young alien cocked his head in confusion, but there was a soft spray of light green laughter in his color-changing eyes. "As a race, I find you completely unintelligible."

"That goes double for me, about yours," she replied. She smiled. "I'm Lieutenant Commander Madeline Ruszel, formerly captain of the Amazon Terravega Brigade, now chief exobiologist and medical chief of staff aboard the SSC *Bellatrix.*" She hesitated. "The former SSC ship *Bellatrix,*" she added sadly.

"We regret the loss of your ship," the alien replied formally. "I am Abemon, engineering executive officer of the *Morcai,*" he added.

"A pleasure to meet you," she replied, smiling. "I'm sorry we won't have the opportunity to serve together."

"As am I," he replied with green, smiling eyes. "Among us there was a saying, that the urn had not been constructed, which could hold our commander."

"I wish that had been the case," she replied, both of them wary of listening Rojok ears. She turned to the unconscious alien on the floor. "Well, I'd better see what I can do for our inebriated crewman. Excuse me."

She dropped down beside Dtimun and activated her wrist scanner, hiding her arm from view in case the Rojok AVBD was aimed in her direction. If they didn't know about the scanner, which was her own original piece of high tech, they couldn't take it away from her.

The readings she got from the alien were erratic, but he was holding his own so far. She gave his chest a quick laserdot injection of *morphadrenin* from her hastily concocted supply aboard ship and watched the reaction on the scanners. It wasn't encouraging. For some reason, Dtimun's second heart wasn't even trying to accept the load from the burned-out old one. If something wasn't done to help it initiate function, the Centaurian would die.

Hahnson, noting the worried expression on his colleague's face, moved to her side.

"How is he?" he asked in Old High Martian, a subdialect of ancient Terravegan that the Rojoks wouldn't have the means to decipher. It was the tongue of the Jaakob Spheres, and only a half dozen humans even spoke it. Madeline and Hahnson had found it on a library computer while they were in basic training and used it, with Stern, as a secret code. It had come in handy on missions, when they were among possible spies. Now Stern was the spy. It hurt to know that.

Madeline watched the commander's chest rise and fall, her eyes drawn involuntarily to the hard lines of his golden-skinned face, the jutting brow, the stubborn jaw, the closed elegance of his elongated eyes with thick, black lashes. He was very attractive, even to a human female, although it shocked her that she was thinking such thoughts. She clamped down on them at once.

"He's dying," she told Hahnson.

"Can you operate?" he continued in Old High Martian, his voice low and covered by the din of conversation among the humans.

"I've got some instruments," she confided. "But even though I'm familiar with Cularian humanoid physiology, I'm not a specialist in its pharmacology. If the commander isn't a clone, like the rest of the unit, it means using a different technique altogether, due to some... slight modifications in his cell structure. My wrist scanner doesn't have the resources of my medicomp aboard ship. And although I do know the technique used to interfere with the half-life, I've never performed it. If the *dylete* doesn't kill him, I probably will."

Komak knelt beside them, his dark eyes warm with affection as they dropped to the commander, then solemn blue as he lifted them to Madeline's face.

"Can you operate?" Komak repeated Hahnson's question, and also in Old High Martian.

They both gaped at him.

His eyes made a green smile for them. "The commander insists that we speak all alien tongues in case the Holconcom conquers a new race."

"Pure arrogance," Madeline said with twinkling eyes. "There are a hundred alien races with about a thousand dialects."

"And we speak them all," he returned with a muffled laugh. He sobered. "Can you interfere with the *dylete?*"

"Hahnson and I were discussing that," she replied. "The problem is, it's in direct violation of the Malcopian Articles of War to perform surgery on a species of which the surgeon has no experience. Further, it's also a violation of Centaurian protocol, isn't it, Komak?" she added. "No female may perform medically on a Centaurian male. That's why the commander was going to put me on report, because I tried to treat the Centaurian prince on Terramer." She shook her head. "If I save him, he can bring me up on charges before the Military Tribunal and end my career."

"Then, you will not operate?" Komak replied.

Her eyes widened. "Are you kidding? If I save him, I get to throw it up to him for the rest of my life! Of course I'm going to operate!"

Komak made a sound like laughter.

"But there is still the cultural thing," she pointed out.

"It is true that there is an ancient taboo, which still holds my people in bondage," Komak replied. "And which only the old emperor has the power to outlaw. I cannot tell you why this is so important," he added quietly. "But it is imperative that you act, for the sake not only of the commander, but of your own species, as well. More is at stake than I dare tell you."

"You wouldn't be exaggerating a little?" she probed.

"I cannot force you to act," he replied. "I can only tell you that if the commander lives, we all live. Without him, what was done to the Altairian child when we arrived here will be play compared to what will be done to these soldiers—and to the clones of the civilians from Terramer who lie wounded in their ambutubes. Nor will the Jaakob Spheres be recovered before the Rojoks have the opportunity to decode them."

She closed her eyes, picturing the dangers vividly. "I wasn't going to refuse, anyway," she assured him.

"Saving life is…" Komak began.

"…an obligation, not a kindness," she finished for him, and knew that he was remembering, as she did, the words spoken in the commander's deep, gruff voice.

"When do we begin?" Hahnson asked.

"As soon as it's dark. It's going to be touch and go every step of the way," she reminded them. "At the very best, under these primitive conditions, it's going to be a four-hour job, and we'll probably have to dodge Rojok sentries every step of the way. If we're caught," she said, looking from one face to the other, "it means instant access to their sonic ovens. Are you both still willing to assist?"

Komak shrugged. "They will kill us anyway. And I will not give up the commander now, Madelineruszel, after you have gone to such lengths to keep him alive." His green eyes twinkled. "He will owe his life to the three of us," he added with glee. "I shall never let him forget!"

Madeline laughed in spite of herself. "Good for you. Strick?"

He glanced at the commander. "Remind me to tell you about a run-in I had with a terrorist group during the Great Galaxy War— and how a Centaurian Holconcom officer saved my life."

She smiled, understanding what he was telling her. "There's just one other little problem," she added, sitting back on her haunches to glance warily toward the bustling complex outside the dome. "They know the commander is either in an urn somewhere, or concealed among the crew. They're not stupid. They want him very badly. What that officer said about the two clones—I've got an idea that they had an operative on the ship all the way from Terramer. One of them may be able to recognize the commander—even disguised."

Komak's eyes darkened. "It is something over which we have no control, Madelineruszel," he said. "We must, therefore, accept whatever comes. *Karamesh,*" he added with a green smile in his eyes when her eyebrows lifted. "It is an unwritten destiny that sweeps us along on paths not of our making or choosing."

"We call it fate," she replied with a smile. "We'll worry about the problem when we have to. For the moment, I need to start carefully synthesizing some additional equipment. We'll hope the place isn't too illuminated at night, and that these ancient synthesizers don't have monitors the way ours do. Considering their age, I doubt it." She hesitated. "The commander won't last until morning," she added, "even with the boosters."

"Boosters?" Hahnson asked.

"Never mind, Strick, that's between Komak and me," she added. "We've got one more problem, too. We're going to need some help diverting the guards' attention. Komak, we'll have to rely on your men for that. I don't know if we can count on any human cooperation from the other cells, knowing how they felt about Muldoon being spaced," she said flatly. "Higgins and Crandall and Jennings were close to us, because they're officers." She nodded toward the humans at the other side of the dome, working the synthesizer. "It won't be the same with human crewmen who see the Holconcom as enemies."

"I understand," Komak replied. "We will assure that our crewmen say nothing of what is happening to the commander to the humans."

He stood up, watching the dull, sluggish movements of the other Holconcom in adjacent cells as they slumped without the microcyborgs that had given them such an edge of strength.

Madeline followed his gaze and grimaced. She knew that the Rojoks would have looked for the microcyborgs and removed them before celling the Holconcom.

"They didn't check him for…boosters?" she asked Komak, indicating Dtimun.

Hahnson gave her a patient look. "I know what the boosters are. I served with the Holconcom in the Great Galaxy War."

She grimaced. "Sorry. Anyway, they didn't check him?"

Komak smiled. "I informed them that another officer had already removed his units and mine. I was very convincing."

She gave him a disbelieving look. She was about to say that only a telepath could have influenced a suspicious Rojok in that manner, but she didn't say it. She turned away before a flash of green touched Komak's eyes.

Higgins came back from the synthesizer with a small cellular cup of java from which he sipped. "Nice of them to integrate us like this," he muttered.

"Even Rojoks like to be entertained," Madeline remarked. "They're expecting a floor show. And they're about to get one," she added.

In a nearby cell, a human officer and a member of the Holconcom were already slugging it out. Without his microcyborgs, the Holconcom was only a little stronger than the human, and it was a well-matched struggle. Others in that cell were grouped around the pair, watching, weighing, considering. Madeline turned away.

"It won't be so amusing once the Rojoks realize that no massacre is going to ensue," Hahnson muttered.

"We can't fight the Rojoks and each other," Madeline growled.

"Divide and conquer. They don't care if we kill each other, only that we'll try to. Damned Rojoks."

"We'll get out of here," Hahnson promised. "Wait and see."

"Strick, did you see where they put Stern?" she asked, mentioning their cloned comrade reluctantly. "You know that he sabotaged the ship. Just before we were captured, Komak ordered him shot, along with the cloned Merrick."

"Komak had no choice," he defended the somber alien. "You know that. If you'd been in command, you'd have done the same. Recriminations won't change anything. We have to assume that Stern's been eliminated. What matters now is that we have to watch each other's backs and try to find a way out of here. Or in the words of Napoleon Bonaparte of ancient Earth, when facing adversity, Audacity, audacity, audacity!"

"Thank you for that stimulating lecture on comparative philosophy, Dr. Hahnson, honey, and how do you feel about bees?" she returned with a hint of her old sarcasm. "Let's do what we can for old pain-in-the-pockets over here, and then we'll discuss terms for letting the Rojoks surrender to us."

He grinned. "I'm with you!"

Mangus Lo wheeled as his commander-in-chief, Chacon, entered the throne room. Mangus Lo was almost toppling over in his fury.

"Your men have let the Holconcom commander escape!" the little madman raged at Chacon. "I will have you publicly dismembered!"

The towering Rojok field marshal folded his arms calmly over his chest, the spray of *mesag* marks on his sleeves gleaming gold against his black uniform. "I have let whom escape?" he asked politely, as if he were speaking to a child.

"Dtimun! You have let the Holconcom commander escape! You

fool," Mangus Lo whispered fiercely, leaning forward to hiss the words at his military commander, his puffy face seeming to bulge with his discontent. "With him as our prisoner, we could conquer the galaxy! He is worth an army, a division, a planet! His power... *cleemaah!* And you have let him escape!"

"I was not aware," Chacon replied gently, "that the Holconcom commander was our prisoner."

"Of course he is a prisoner! We have the *Morcai* and its complement and a shipload of humans and the Jaakob Spheres, as well! Do you not read your own intelligence reports?"

Chacon seemed to stiffen. His slit eyes were piercing and hot as they met Mangus Lo's. "I was not informed of this capture. May I ask why?"

Mangus Lo looked momentarily disconcerted, as if he suddenly realized that he had given away too much. He paused, thought for a moment, then focused his attention on a bright globe of nightflies fluttering in stasis webs on his desk. "We have our reasons," he said finally. "What of the Centaurian princess?" he added craftily.

But Chacon was a hunter, and he recognized traps. "Centaurian princess?" he asked with a scowl. "Your Excellence has deprived me of much information, it seems. Either I am in command of the military, or I am not. Shall I take my resignation to the people?"

"No, no, there is no need for that!" Mangus Lo exclaimed quickly, almost in panic. It was a well-known fact that Chacon was held in higher esteem than himself. He couldn't risk a showdown, not just now. "You have not been deprived of any information. I was only ascertaining that it was...correct...before concerning you with it!"

"What of the Holconcom commander?" Chacon asked.

Mangus Lo dropped into the chair behind his desk. He toyed with the globe of nightflies, watching them burn like tiny blue fires in the soft pink shimmer of the stasis webs. "They have lost him, the fools!

He was aboard the *Morcai* when it was taken, I am certain of it. But when the complement was transported to *Ahkmau,* he disappeared."

"You had the Holconcom sent to *Ahkmau?*" Chacon exploded. "But it is a camp for political prisoners, not military…!"

"It is a camp for my enemies, whoever they may be!" Mangus Lo shot back, his eyes wide and threatening. "Even you may be sent to *Ahkmau,* my commander! The terror must be maintained! Without it, we will lose everything!"

"With it, we will lose everything!" Chacon countered. "Honor, integrity…"

"Our people are starving," Mangus Lo growled. "Will integrity and honor fill their empty stomachs? Will it undo the pollution that makes our fields dead and lifeless? Will it strengthen our economy enough that the poor will no longer have to choose between energy for their homes or food? Will it provide jobs for the unemployed? You idealists make me sick! My way is forcing a path for us into the New Territory. It is creating jobs in the military and the various death camps, and the munitions industries. It is giving us the opportunity to spread our mushrooming population onto new worlds. It is putting life back into a dead economy. Will your honor and integrity do that, Commander Chacon?"

Chacon stared at the small maniac with something like pity in his dark, quiet eyes under their shock of blond hair. "Honor and integrity will not do that," he conceded. "But," he added, "neither will they ask the sacrifice of a million lives a year in a camp already notorious for its depravity."

"Depravity!" Mangus Lo's face almost purpled. "It is not depravity to eliminate inferior races and enemies of the state! Will you argue that the humans are equal to us? Or the Altairians? *Cleemaah,* let it be known across the galaxy that what opposes us is horribly destroyed. I have said before, Commander, that the terror must be maintained! It is our banner of victory!"

"It is our symbol of disgrace," Chacon argued, his eyes cold and raw with emotion.

"And have you hopes of liberating it, Commander?" Mangus Lo spat. "Forget them! If you so much as set foot on *Ahkmau,* I will have you imprisoned there! Do you understand?"

"I understand," Chacon said icily. "By your leave…Excellence." And he made of the one word an insult.

One day, Mangus Lo promised himself as he watched that stiff-backed soldier withdraw, he would eliminate the field marshal. He would have to. He could not tolerate a soldier whose popularity was double his own. Chacon was dangerous.

Holt Stern's head jerked back when the Rojok officer's merciless six-fingered hand connected with it.

"You lie!" the Rojok growled furiously. "You must know the Holconcom commander's whereabouts!"

"How could I?" Stern returned, his blood churning fury in his veins. "The damned exec of the *Morcai* ordered the two of us shot before your men even boarded the ship! All I know is that Dtimun was critically ill and they said he would die. That's it. Period!"

The Rojok glared at him, but Stern didn't back down an inch. He compressed his lips stubbornly as he stared up at the alien with narrowed, dark eyes.

"You are of no further use to us," the Rojok said finally, "unless you learn cooperation. We will allow your former comrades to convince you."

"Better them than you, buster." Stern grinned, and gave way to a strange impulse to pat the Rojok's dusty cheek.

"Get him out of here!" the offended officer yelled to a subordinate.

Stern chuckled as he followed the guard out into the complex. It was as if all the conditioning, all the programming, was beginning to lose its potency. He wondered vaguely what the original, the *real* Holt Stern was like. Perhaps someday he'd find out.

Madeline had just gathered the last of her improvised necessary surgical tools, juryrigged unknowingly by the synthesizer, when Hahnson caught her attention.

"Remember when we were wondering about what happened to Stern's body?" he asked.

"Yes," she said slowly, giving him a puzzled look.

"Here it comes."

"What!"

She joined the husky surgeon at the front of the dome, and watched, shocked, as Holt Stern was marched toward the cell in front of an armed Rojok sentry.

"What the hell is this?" she wondered softly. "An infiltration? Do they think we're stupid enough to trust him?"

"He may not be here to infiltrate," he said in Old High Martian. "He knows what the 'old man' looks like. He may be here to point the proverbial finger for his new buddies."

"Oh, my God," she whispered in a husky prayer. "Not now. Not when we're so close!"

The cell opened wide enough to accommodate Stern, and he was pushed through it by the Rojok. The cell closed. The guard watched as Stern straightened. He looked around the cell slowly until his eyes lit on Dtimun's unconscious form.

His eyebrows arched. "Well, well," he chuckled. "What have we here? Isn't this just like a family reunion?"

He glanced toward Madeline and Strick Hahnson, who were standing mutely like statues, their eyes glaring at him with pure hatred.

Madeline couldn't decide between going for Stern or praying.

Higgins and Crandall and Jennings flanked the doctors, glaring at the newcomer. Komak and Btnu joined them, their eyes burning a solemn blue before they slowly darkened to brown anger.

"No welcome?" Stern exclaimed. "No hugs?"

"Let me find my scalpel and I'll give you a really warm welcome," Madeline began.

Stern's jaw dropped. "What the hell is wrong with you people?" he burst out. "Don't you recognize me?"

The silence was rudely broken by Higgins, his fair complexion gone red with fury as he moved toward Stern. "You ungodly traitor," he breathed furiously as his fist drew back.

Stern's hand shot out like lightning, inhumanly strong, almost breaking the bone as he grasped it. "I pulled you out of that burning freighter on Megus, boy…don't make me regret it," he said harshly, idly wondering at the memory and what reservoir of experience it had sprung from.

Higgins gaped at him, his brows drawing together as he stepped back. "Sir, you…couldn't possibly remember that," he faltered. "The medics had to remove a portion of your brain when the bulkhead collapsed on you afterward. They said…there was no way you'd ever remember what happened!"

"You'd be amazed at what I remember," he said quietly, and his dark eyes went straight to Madeline.

She met that level gaze squarely, frowning, not sure what was happening here. "You sold us out," she accused. "A Rojok officer told us you'd been cloned from our captain, Holt Stern."

He shrugged. "Like I had a choice," he muttered. His eyes

narrowed. "If you keep glaring at me like that, I'm taking back the blue ribbon."

"There's no way in hell you could remember that," Madeline began.

He pulled a tiny remnant of it from his pocket and displayed it. "We split it on the last successful mission, as I recall?"

Madeline was still unconvinced and uneasy. Especially when Stern's gaze went back to Dtimun.

He moved toward the alien and shook his head. "Why's old Fred still flaked out like that?" he asked casually. "Is he drunk again? And on duty? My God, why doesn't somebody report him before he causes an interplanetary incident on one of these binges? Komak, you're slipping, to let one of your crewmen slip up like this!"

11

Madeline recovered quickly from the unexpected help from Stern. "We can't sober him up," she added.

"Alcohol affects my race differently than yours," Komak volunteered. "It takes much longer for the effects to abate."

"Tough," Stern said. He glanced toward the Rojok, who was still watching. "We're going to need every crewman sober when the Rojoks surrender."

The Rojok guard made a sound like contemptuous laughter, sealed the cell and continued on his way.

Madeline took a deep breath. It had been close.

"Why did you not betray us?" Komak asked Stern in Old High Martian, his eyes still an angry brown but slowly mingling with flecks of blue curiosity.

"Pure cussedness," Stern replied with a grin. "The Rojoks threw a few punches at me and demanded to know where the commander was. Nobody does that to me. I clammed up, and here I am. Sorry your boys missed, back on the ship?"

Komak eyed the human in a silence more eloquent than words.

"You don't trust me, do you?" Stern persisted, and the gleam of laughter left his eyes. "I can't say that I blame you. If one of my command staff had done to me what I've done to you, I'd share the sentiment. You all know what I am now, don't you?" he added slowly, looking around him at the somber humans.

"A Rojok operative," Komak spoke for them, "programmed and probably genetically altered so that your strength and sensory capabilities would equal those of a Holconcom."

"A genetically altered clone," Stern corrected, and his lightning glance didn't miss the looks of anger mingled with sadness on the faces of Strick Hahnson and Madeline Ruszel. "My...original...was killed on Terramer. They told me. They told me what I was. Strange, I seem to have most of the original's memories. I don't...feel...like a clone, however clones feel. But," he added with a glimmer of bitterness, "ability doesn't lie, and mine is far superior to any human's. If it's any consolation to those who knew the original, I had no choice about my actions. They were programmed into me at the instant of duplication. In all honesty, I don't know how I managed to throw off the programming just now—or whether it may be the Rojoks' way of giving me enough rope to hang us all."

"Your honesty is to your credit," Komak said warily. "For the safety of the ship's complement, I should dispose of you now, Holtstern."

"I don't think you can," Stern replied quietly, leaning back against the firm dome wall of the cell with his arms folded. "Oh, you're welcome to try. But they replaced the calcium in my bones with a synthetic material stronger than *zenokite*—they won't break. All my senses are magnified, as well. I can even hear the sentries talking through the walls. I can sense radiation and body heat, and my sight is twice as good as yours, Komak. I make a formidable adversary, physically. And my improved mental capabilities would rival yours, as well, from an intellectual standpoint. I don't possess psychokinesis or telepathy, but I'm not sure if that's part of the programming, or if I just haven't learned to use them yet."

Madeline Ruszel moved slightly between the two officers, her solemn face as smooth as a rain-wet leaf. "Fighting won't solve anything. We've got to see about him," she told them, gesturing toward Dtimun. "They want him, we've got him, and if they find out, he's dead. We're all dead."

Stern glanced around the cell, his eyes narrowing on the ancient synthesizer. "Have any of you consumed anything out of that monstrosity?" he asked, nodding toward it.

"Sure," Hahnson told him. "Why?"

"How much, how long ago and how many of you?" Stern asked quickly, his dark eyes concerned.

"Higgins and I had a cup of java about an hour ago," Hahnson said easily, grinning as he pointed at the engineer of the now-destroyed *Bellatrix*. "I don't guess anyone else has had the inclination yet. We're kind of new to the joint, Holt, old boy."

"Do you want to leave here, Strick?" Stern asked the husky physician.

"Leave?" Hahnson burst out. "In God's name, what for? We've got free meals, a roof over our heads and we're out of the war for the duration. We're even going to be assigned to technical work, not hard labor. So who the hell wants to leave?"

Madeline looked at her colleague as if he'd taken off his nose and waved it at her. Komak only stared, his great cat-eyes the soft gray of curiosity at first, and then suddenly they darkened into deep blue certainty.

"A drug?" he said, turning to Stern.

"A very potent drug," Stern said calmly, "which attacks the neu-rotransmitters and increases the norepinephrine production—mag-nifying the subject's ability to perceive pleasure." He glanced at Madeline. "Tell him."

"We…use such a drug," she faltered, her glance sweeping Hahnson's dreamy expression, "in the treatment of incurable organic paranoid schizophrenia—the cases that are violent and don't respond to genetic therapy. In ancient times, such aberrations were confined to prisons. Later, subjects were treated with mood-altering drugs, but those were only effective if taken daily. Now, we can induce a state of permanent serenity with a single dose. Apparently the Rojoks have modified the drugs to induce euphoria."

"There's another drug," Stern told her, "that produces exactly the opposite reaction. One of many minor tortures they use to extract information, or as a medical research tool on alien races. They use sensory deprivation and subsonics, as well. The drug is the best, though. It's cheap, in large supply and readily available. Just the thing for an inflated economy if you can't afford the really expensive form of torture…"

"This is no time for cheap humor," Madeline told him. "What do we do?"

"Don't drink anything or eat anything out of that synthesizer for a start," Stern told them.

"Just how long do you think we'll last without water in this hellish heat?" Madeline asked irritably. She was already brushing at sweat on her flushed brow. "There's no coolant in these ventilators. Deliber-ate, I suppose."

"I don't suppose anybody thought to bring along a few Milish Cones?" Stern mused.

Madeline turned and looked, hard, at Komak.

The alien's eyes turned green. He produced two of the pocket water synthesizers out of a pocket in his uniform.

"Smart," Madeline said with smiling praise.

"Good for you," Stern added. "Share it covertly with the others. If the guards see it…well, you know."

"We waste time," Komak said after a minute, his great eyes going to the complex beyond the domed cell. Darkness was finally coming on the horizon beyond the jagged magenta peaks of the mountain chain that ringed the desert complex. The interior of the great pressure dome, which contained all the cells, began to give off a faint reddish glow. So did their own small cell.

"Will we have daylight equivalent in here, do you think?" Madeline asked the somber alien.

"I think not. No more than you see at the dome's zenith." Komak turned to Stern. "We propose to interfere surgically with the *dylete*. If you cannot assist, will you at least agree not to betray us to the Rojoks?"

"That depends on my conditioning," Stern said truthfully, "not on my inclination. We both know that."

"Then go sit in a corner and count your toes, old man," Madeline said, giving him a wan smile. "Better yet, count the sentries."

"No problem." Stern's gaze was drawn to the slender, hard-muscled Centaurian who was lying unconscious in his technician's uniform, on the padded covering under the dome's softly glowing reddish light. "Now that the drugs have been dispensed, and most of the prisoners have consumed them, they're not expecting trouble. I doubt there will be more than one or two patrols all night."

"The Holconcom," Madeline asked Komak. "Will the drug work on them?"

Stern grimaced. "I don't know how to tell you this. The Rojoks removed their microcyborgs."

Komak's eyes flashed a dangerous brown. "Barbarians!" he exclaimed. "The Holconcom wear them from infancy. It will be, for them, the equivalent of broken bones!" He looked at Madeline. "I still have mine, however."

Her eyebrows arched. "Where?"

He gave her his best approximation of an indignant look.

"Never mind," she said quickly. "I've also secreted quite a number in our comrade," she added, meaning Dtimun. "If we can get out of here, I'm fairly certain that the *kelekoms* can replicate more."

Komak looked uncomfortable. "Madelineruszel, outworlders are not permitted to know such things about the *kelekoms*."

She held up both hands. "Forget I said a word. The *kelekoms*...?"

Komak closed his eyes, opened them again and smiled. "The Rojoks believe their very existence is a myth."

"Lucky for us," Madeline agreed. She sighed heavily. "Look, I managed to secure a cyberscalpel and a medisynthe. I have a bank of drugs and a miniaturized lab in my wrist array. The Rojoks won't know about it— that's classified tech. But Komak, I don't have any graduate experience in Cularian surgery. The physiology, yes. Even some of the pharmacology. But I'm not experienced in this sort of surgery."

"You are his only hope," Komak said simply.

She grimaced. "The operation itself is what kills most Centaurians who can't overcome the *dylete* naturally. The first heart is forced into stasis while the second is stimulated with a high current cardiogenerator. Two out of three times, the current itself is enough to cause fatal heart failure. Not that I believe in the use of cardiogenerators. I'd rather take my chance with old-fashioned open-heart surgery. I can do that blindfolded."

"I know. I've seen you perform it on the battlefield," Stern interjected.

"On humans," she agreed. "But Centaurians differ drastically in such basics as temperature, blood pressure, pulse, even respiration, all of which have to be carefully balanced in surgery. We won't even go into the matter of anesthesia, which is more dangerous even than the surgery."

"So, you can't do it?" Stern asked carefully, and without looking at her.

"I never said that!" she returned defensively. Her brow knitted. "The Roard-Nielson method. That might work," she murmured, thinking aloud. "Vegan surgeons have used it successfully for years, and they share some striking similarities of Centaurian physiology. Yes. It just might work. But I'll need a blood donor. Even my minilab can't supply the amount I'll need for surgery."

"Will I do?" Stern volunteered.

"A Centaurian blood donor," she specified.

"My blood is of excellent quality," Komak told her with a faint green-eyed smile. "It will cause our comrade to be indebted to me for the rest of his life, if I share it with him. I will never let him forget, in fact!"

Madeline managed a smile of her own. "I hope you can outrun him."

"When do we begin?" the alien asked.

"As soon as it's completely dark," she replied. Her eyes were worried. "But we may need diversions from time to time, to keep the guards from checking us too closely. Even weakened, the Holconcom would help us if they could. The humans..." She grimaced. "They're probably all drugged anyway. I doubt they'd do anything to help the officer who spaced Muldoon."

"It would take something more potent than pleasure," Stern agreed. "A cause. A holy grail. We're damned short on miracles, Ladybones. But we can try."

Her green eyes wandered over his hard, swarthy face, the crisp, curling dark hair. So familiar. So unfamiliar. "You're very like him, you know," she told Stern's doppelgänger.

He grinned. "We had the same father," he said, tongue-in-cheek.

While they were talking, Komak had moved to the cell facing the complex's entrance. He stood there, his cat-eyes wide and deep blue. He caught the attention of a Holconcom junior officer in a nearby cell and began to make odd hand movements. The other alien apparently understood them. He nodded, turned and spoke to his comrades in the cell. They spread out and began using hand signals to other cells.

"At a guess," Madeline told Stern, "he's trying to warn the Holconcom about the synthesizers."

"Good idea. I know enough Elyrian sign language to warn our own shipmates. If it's in time for any of them," he added darkly. He went to join Komak, passing along the news in a language that humans would understand. Some of the occupants of the other cells were lounging on the floor apathetically. But a few gathered at the front of their cells and watched. Madeline noticed a lot of elbowing from the humans aimed at their Centaurian cell mates—because they hadn't been segregated. Her heart fell. It didn't auger well for their imprisonment if the two ships' complements were going to fight each other. It would make any escape attempt impossible.

"What the hell are you people doing?" Strick Hahnson growled suddenly. "I told you, we don't need to escape!"

Madeline glanced at Komak. The alien nodded his understanding. She activated her wrist scanner's drug banks and, before Hahnson could move, she jetted the laserdot at his broad chest. Whirling, she repeated the action with Higgins, who was sitting beside the doctor. Two drugged officers melted into fleshy heaps on the padded floor and lay still, eyes closed, surreal smiles clinging to their faces even in oblivion.

"This is a derivative of what the Rojoks are using in the synthesizers," she growled, glaring from Hahnson and Higgins to the rest of the humans in the cell, who were lying complacently on the padded floor, smiling blankly. "Like one endless pleasant dream," she muttered. "What a way to control the masses. Cheap and effective. I wonder how long it takes their version to wear off?"

"Undoubtedly it does, at some point," Komak agreed. "But I imagine the effects are cumulative, Madelineruszel. I communicated to my men that the synthesizer produced a drug that hampered free thought. However, it is unlikely that they have been desperate enough to sample the fluid banks. We can go long periods without water."

"We can't," Stern told him. "But I got through to one cell of our shipmates, and they're passing the message on—to your Holconcom, as well, just in case, Komak. I gave our men a cause, too."

Komak actually frowned. "Camaashe?" he queried in his guttural language.

"Never mind," Stern said smugly. "Just do what you have to. I've got the men in my unit organized. They'll help divert the sentries, too, if they have to."

"That isn't likely," Madeline said quietly, "after what the C.O. did to Muldoon."

"You might be surprised at the comradeship a common enemy will provoke," Stern told her. "We're all in this together, you know, Centaurian and human alike."

Madeline was studying him curiously. "You sound just like Holt Stern," she said solemnly. "Are you sure you're a clone?"

He grinned. "Now that you mention it…"

"I must trust you, Holtstern, clone or not," Komak said with a flash of solemn blue eyes. "Trust is an awesome responsibility when so many lives are at stake."

"I won't let you down intentionally, Komak," Stern promised.

"Then I can ask no more than that. We begin at first dark," the alien replied.

"I like the way you said, 'we,'" Madeline told Komak with a smile. "I never like to operate without an assistant, particularly when he can double as a blood donor. You and the crewman share the same blood type and group, and I've already rigged a Galason Tube."

"If I share my blood with him, Madelineruszel, will I be transfused with his bad temper, as well as his blood cells?" Komak asked with a flash of smiling green eyes.

"I'll remember to ask him when he comes out of the *dylete*," Madeline replied.

"When you ask him," Komak groaned, "remember to include a plea to spare my life and my career."

"Never mind the worrying," Stern intervened. "With Maddie for a doctor, he's got the best. He'll make it."

"I hope we all will," she replied quietly. "I hope we'll all make it out of here."

Enmehkmehk's other two moons, rising like fireballs in the distance, looked vaguely like smears of blood…

Lyceria felt the touch of apprehension with a vague urge to conceal it, to ignore it. But she knew deep in her mind that trouble was coming this day. It was an instinct as old as her Clan, as familiar as the colors of her moods. Before the day was out, her life would change.

She wondered at the absence of Chacon. Lithe, colorfully garbed Rojok women lounged in the spacious harem with her, divinely pampered and unconcerned with the world outside these flowering walls. Education was forbidden to them, as was any contact with worlds outside their own. None of them spoke Centaurian. They seemed to find the confinement pleasing. Lyceria found it distasteful. Her educated mind rebelled at the idea of such seclusion from life.

The Rojok commander had been conspicuous by his absence since bringing her here, although Lyceria, who spoke Rojok, heard from the other women that he was still in residence. She also heard, with puzzlement, that he paid no visits to the harem. The women were pampered, of course, but they had no duties to perform and were curious as to why. It seemed that the Rojok soldier maintained them out of protocol alone. They had belonged to his brother, who was killed in battle early in the conflict. He kept them out of family obligation only.

Why was he ignoring her? It irritated her like the thousand nagging bites of a millekat. It angered her. Although, just perhaps, he was even now negotiating with the old emperor for her return to the Centaurian Empire. Perhaps...

The sudden, unannounced entrance of a squad of Rojok soldiers cut into her thoughts. They came to surround her, like a living net. With drawn *chasats,* they forced her out of the luxurious confines of the harem into the corridor.

The apprehension that she had felt now became understandable. Because, minutes later, she was standing in the imperial throne room of the Rojok *palcenon* itself, facing a dwarfed, slit-eyed little madman who ruled an empire gone equally mad.

"I suspected as much," Mangus Lo said, his gaze sliding contemptuously up and down the lithe figure of his captive. "Commander Chacon was too casual when he assured me that he knew nothing of your capture. It is unfortunate that he begins to lie to his emperor. Now I can no longer overlook his behavior. I must deal with it. He is far too dangerous to remain alive. But the people love him too much for a public trial and execution." He stilled. "He will be of much more use to me as a dead hero. The people can still love him, not knowing what a traitor he truly was. I will build a monument to him, I think," he added thoughtfully. "Yes." He nodded, seeing blankly into a fantasy future. "I will build a monument."

"You cannot mean to kill Chacon?" The words slid from her mouth before she could prevent them, the thought chilling her.

Mangus Lo's eyebrows went up in sincere astonishment. "You, a Centaurian, are concerned for the life of an enemy soldier who has killed many of your people?"

"The commander is much respected among all alien races," she hedged proudly, "even by his enemies. He is…an honorable antagonist."

"Honor and integrity," Mangus Lo spat, whirling to drag his useless leg along with him as he made his way back to his throne. Behind the throne, an elaborate red wall tapestry ran down the jeweled walls like blood.

"Guard!" he called, slumping down in his throne.

A uniformed Rojok appeared and saluted.

"Take her to *Ahkmau* at once," Mangus Lo said with a satisfied smile, noting Lyceria's sudden loss of color with pleasure. "And give orders to my commandant there to make certain she is…interrogated…before she goes to the ovens."

She felt herself tremble at the sentence, but none of the terror she was feeling made its way into her solemn blue eyes or her proud carriage. She only stared at the emperor.

"And send Mekkar to me," Mangus Lo added. "I have an interesting assignment for my court executioner."

"Yes, your Excellence," the guard saluted. He prodded Lyceria with a *chasat* toward the great arched exit way from the sprawling throne room.

* * *

It seemed like years to Holt Stern before the two suns of Enmehk-mehk finally set on the horizon. The combination of the red super-giant and the blue-white dwarf produced a stunningly beautiful nightfall. A dark band running through the supergiant like a ring seemed to link it to the tiny jewel-blue companion in swirls of fire as the suns touched the highly defined jagged mountains on the horizon. It was, Stern thought, a strange touch of beauty in a night-marish setting.

Ahkmau, located on one of three moons, rotated around the planet, but in such a manner that it had both day and night.

As darkness finally fell, Madeline and Komak made their way in-conspicuously to Dtimun's side, while the other occupants of the cell, except for Hahnson and Higgins, who were still unconscious, took up apparently careless positions in the cramped confines—positions that deliberately hid the commander's unconscious body from probing Rojok eyes.

"Everybody on the alert," Madeline told the others in Old High Martian. She linked Komak to the Holconcom commander with the Galason Tube. She activated her cyberscalpel and the miniature au-tomated sterilization units combined within it. "I can't make promises, but I'm going to give it my best shot."

She took the cyberscalpel in hand, and Stern saw her eyes close for an instant. Then she bent and began to pierce the sterile field over the alien's bare, hair-roughened, golden-skinned chest...

The silence in the cell at that instant was so ominous that Stern could hear the sound of his own strained breathing. Time dragged, passing in lazy drifts that were almost tangible.

Watching Madeline and Komak fight to save the alien commander, Stern had to bite back a grin at the utter futility of it all. Even if they managed to save Dtimun, it was a waste of time. The Rojoks had briefed him well. Gain their confidence, they told him, tell them just enough to make them trust you. Then open your ears wide and listen.

He'd listened, all right, and he had plenty to report. Their first action when he told them about Dtimun would be to take the alien to the interrogation sector. He frowned. Why did that thought bother him? Something Dtimun had said, back on Terramer, when Stern had made a remark about leaving the clones behind—"A life is a life, is it not?"—kept repeating in his mind. He recalled without wanting to that the Centaurians, of all races, elevated their clones to the same position as natural members of their race. There were laws against prejudice. So unlike Terravega, where a clone was only a living bank of spare organs for its original...

Unwillingly his eyes swept the quiet, dimly lit cell, and fell on the unconscious Centaurian. Madeline might have been talking to him for all the indication she gave of performing life-saving surgery. Komak seemed to be sacked out at the tall alien's side, idly listening to conversation. It looked so innocent: why should the guards suspect anything? The humans and Centaurians were supposed to be drinking the drugged water from the synthesizer, weren't they? Why should there be any problems?

Except that Stern had warned them not to drink the water, and that hadn't been part of the Rojoks' plan. He wasn't supposed to tell them about the water. But he had. He'd told them things about this camp that the Rojok commander-in-chief, Chacon, didn't even know.

Above and beyond that, he'd organized the humans in the *Morcai* complement. From his memory, he'd dredged a tiny mystery and dangled the solution tantalizingly in front of the other humans—most of whom wanted that answer as much as they wanted to know why Komak had ordered one Centaurian in every domed cell to pretend to be unconscious. I'll tell you about the blue velvet ribbon I carry, Stern had promised the humans in his crew. It was an old secret, much discussed among the crew. And it was cause enough to make them fight the drug, to refuse further nourishment from the synthesizers. Because every crewman who served on the *Bellatrix* knew about the blue velvet ribbon that Stern carried, and wondered why.

Stern wondered himself, about his involvement with this crew. He was a clone. That stood out more than anything else he'd been told about himself. He…was…a…clone. A shudder of anguish washed over his mind. Clones, he remembered, were less than people to the human populations of all the Tri-Fleet member worlds. Less than animals. They were different, so they were either feared or hated because of that difference, minute though it was. He wanted to scream that he was human despite the difference of his entrance into life. Not some monstrous caricature of humanity, like a cyberdroid. He was human!

He could feel the stares of the other humans in the cell. Hahnson and Higgins were just beginning to come out of their drug-induced euphoria, and with sanity came the realization that the original captain of the *Bellatrix* was dead. It was in their eyes—all the grief and pain. The disgust. He was a thief, the looks said. He'd stolen Stern's face and voice and body.

Was it going to be like this from now on? the man behind Holt Stern's face wondered bitterly. Will I ever be allowed to live in peace?

His eyes went back to Dtimun. If the alien could be saved, he could get Madeline and Hahnson and the rest of the *Bellatrix*'s crew out of this hellhole. He could protect them from Mangus Lo's sonic ovens. Knowing that, knowing his friends would die if the alien did, could he turn informer again and live with himself?

The conditioning he'd been given was growing steadily weaker as

Stern's memories grew stronger. Memories hammered in his brain. Bits and pieces of another time, another life. Sounds and smells and faces. He sighed wearily, his gaze going outward, toward the other domed cells where hundreds of humans and Centaurians and Altairians and Vegans and even Rojoks with unpopular political views were waiting to die. Waiting in a drug-besotted stupor that was paradise itself for the sudden, inevitable drop into hell when the captives outlived their usefulness to the Rojok state.

It was ironic, he thought, that he and Madeline had been Dtimun's coldest enemies from the first confrontation. And now, here they were, risking everything to save him...

A loud, steady tread of booted feet reached his ultrasensitive ears, bringing him back to the present. He looked up to see a Rojok prison patrol marching straight toward their cell!

12

"Guards coming!" Stern barked in a loud whisper at Madeline.

She stopped at once. "Over here, Komak. Quick!" she breathed.

She had Dtimun, Komak's arm and her small array of tools under the thin, ragged thermoblanket in a flash. Hurriedly arranging the tattered tan blanket over an equally ragged part of the floor pallet, she stretched out beside Dtimun, tucking her hand against his broad chest under the cover to hide the faint bloodstains. The cyberscalpel was constructed of a miniaturized laser so efficient that bleeding was almost nonexistent in surgeries, as the instrument cauterized as it incised. But inevitably when working through bone under such primitive operating conditions, some slight bleeding could occur.

As she motioned, Stern threw himself down at her side and feigned sleep. Let the guard think they were huddled together for warmth, she thought. Perhaps they wouldn't consider it too odd to find two Centaurians and two humans in such physical proximity. Jaws would fall anywhere in the SSC at such a sight.

Stern could almost feel the eyes of the Rojok guards on the occupants of the domed cell as they paused outside it to study the occupants. So could Madeline. She closed her eyes tightly and prayed that none of the other prisoners would betray them; especially Stern. She still didn't quite trust him. At her side, she felt Komak's powerful body tensing, as well.

Stern felt the sweat beading on his swarthy forehead. If Madeline had been in a crucial stage when interrupted, the Holconcom commander could be dying even now while the arrogant guards pointed to the human/alien group on the floor and laughed. Apparently they did find the arrangement unusual and amusing. He felt a surge of rage as he considered what was going to happen to all of them, if they didn't find a way to escape. Damn the Rojoks, he thought furiously, and damn *Ahkmau!*

Madeline was counting her own heartbeats and monitoring Dtimun's with her hand buried in the thick black hair over the golden skin of his bare chest. She was mentally neutered for military service, so of course she felt nothing sensual from the contact. Except that her own heart skipped and she felt an odd warmth in the pit of her stomach. Fear, she told herself. It was only fear. It was impossible for her to be attracted to any male, especially this arrogant, strutting Centaurian son of a...

There was an odd smothered laugh from Komak; almost as if he read her thoughts. That was ridiculous and only highlighted the extent of her silent hysteria, because it was a known fact that Centaurians weren't telepathic.

Just as she was considering drastic action, the guards spoke to each other again, laughed again and slowly started away from the cell to patrol further. She spoke just enough Rojok to understand one phrase—something about the drugs working unusually well, so that the Centaurians didn't find the repulsive humans bad company.

She counted the seconds until they were out of sight and earshot. "Barbarians," she muttered in Old High Martian, which was the only language they dared use among themselves now. "That was just too damned close. I'd only finished sealing what passes for his damaged left ventricle in the new heart! Stern, better check and make sure they're really gone," she added.

He got carefully to his feet, leaving the other three in their positions on the pallet. The other prisoners in their cell, including Hahnson and Higgins, were awake now and aware of something odd in the positioning of their cell mates. They darted quick, apprehensive glances toward the makeshift surgical suite nearby, then at Stern. It seemed to surprise them that he hadn't alerted the guards.

It surprised him, too, because that's what his conditioning dictated that he should have done. But for some vague, barely discernible reason, he simply couldn't. He felt a sensation of belonging among these people. It was new, and precious and fragile. He wasn't about to risk it for those bloodthirsty mental defectives who ran this place.

He took up his position near the synthesizer, looking out into the compound again, his eyes growing slowly accustomed to the reddish glow of the cell block in the darkness. Above the main dome, in the night sky where the clearly outlined jagged mountain peaks met the sky itself, a dark red band from the long-set two suns swept across the stars. In its beauty, it was as alien as the Centaurians in the cell with Stern, and his human comrades.

Something made his skin tingle, and he turned his head to meet the glowing eyes of a Holconcom officer in a nearby cell. He shivered involuntarily. The alien's eyes were like a cat's in the dark, glowing a surreal green. Most humans reacted similarly to their first sight of it.

He realized after a minute that the alien was watching him, reading his face, in what precious light there was in the dome. Two other Holconcom joined him, also watching.

"We're under observation," Stern murmured.

"By the Holconcom?" Komak asked in a strangely weak tone.

"Yes."

"They will help, if they can," the alien sighed. "But most of the other cells are too far away to know what we are attempting."

Stern pursed his lips. He began signaling to the humans, a quick and staccato sentence that said only, "We're trying to save the C.O." The humans understood. They gave the message to the Centaurians. They nodded and turned, gesturing to other cells, mindful of the guards.

"Back on ancient Earth," Stern murmured, "they'd call that the jungle telegraph."

"Excuse me?" Komak asked.

"They're passing it along."

Komak's chest rose and fell slowly. "They would do anything for the commander. As I would. But your human comrades…"

"They'll do anything to find out about the…secret I promised them," Stern said.

"Without their microcyborgs, they're not much more powerful than the humans," Madeline murmured while she worked. "It will give them points in common while we need them."

"A likely summation," Komak agreed.

Stern turned toward him, frowning. "Komak, do you think…" He stopped and grabbed his head. Amazingly, he saw a rolling montage of pictures running through his mind, alien and strange. Frightening beasts who fought like *galots,* the Centaurian jungle cats, tearing and ripping their prey; a woman, a beautiful Centaurian woman, weeping. Warriors slashing at their arms with sharp implements. Then, as the pictures merged, there were others; the Commander, but years younger, on a desert planet, riding a huge furry *yomuth;* a young alien woman in silks lying dead, blood around her. Then there was an old Centaurian yelling, the Holconcom filing into the *Morcai* at a Centaurian spaceport. There were flashes of Madeline, not as she was now, but older and more beautiful, wearing elegant robes, and her belly faintly distended…

"No!"

The sudden command from Komak, the brown threat in his eyes, brought Stern back to the present. He blinked, drawing in a long breath. "What the hell…!" he burst out.

Komak stared at him, narrowed his eyes, pinned him with them. Seconds later, Stern couldn't remember anything he'd seen. He blinked. "Boy, do I need a brain scan," he said aloud.

"Shut up and get me another small sterile towel out of that damned synthesizer," Madeline muttered, working. "This cyberscalpel isn't fully charged. God, I hope it doesn't fail!"

"Bite your tongue," Stern said.

He got the towel and gave it to her, his eyes alert to any new threats. He watched Madeline, noted that she was sweating wetly. He could hear her ragged breathing. She, like the rest of them, was stressed almost to breaking point. She was a good battlefield surgeon, but she'd been mostly administrative in recent years. The strain was telling on her.

Hahnson was snoring. He'd almost come to earlier, now he'd relapsed. Pity, Stern thought, the surgeon could have been a lot of help to her.

"Can I do anything to help?" Stern asked.

"If you're offering, get back to the ship and fetch my emergency kit…"

"Anything I can do in here," Stern corrected.

"Sure. Grab one of those sponges and get this sweat out of my eyes, will you?" she asked, breathing raggedly.

He picked up a worn, orange-red sponge and soaked off the beads of perspiration on her forehead. "How's it coming?"

"Barbaric conditions," she muttered. "No oxygen ampules, anesthetic or even another bank of *morphadrenin*. No nanobytes, endomorphins, no cell regenerators…" She stopped, shaking her head. "If it weren't for the scattering of microcyborgs I concealed under his scalp before we were captured, I'd already have killed him. How he's enduring this without adequate anesthetic is fascinating. It's almost as if he can control pain itself, even unconscious." She leaned back to flex her shoulders. "I must have had my brain baked when I agreed to this half-gassed piece of idiocy."

"Don't give up now, Ladybones," he replied. "Think what fun we can have throwing this up to him when he recovers. It might even spare us a court-martial when we escape." He grinned, and when his dark eyes sparkled like that, he was just like the old Stern.

Her eyes went back to Dtimun's chest, barely visible in the automatic light from the retractors she was using to keep his rib cage open. Incredible, she thought, that even with all its advances, heart surgery still demanded this ancient butchery of opening the ribs to access the heart. It was more controlled in sick bay with robotic operators, of course, and pain screens overlaid with the other tech that controlled breathing and blood pressure. "We both know that I never quit," she murmured to Stern. "Okay. I've sealed the damaged artery in the new heart, along with the damaged nerve receptors that were impeding changeover. But I'll have to do the changeover manually. That means I have to transfer the load from the failing heart to the new one, but the second heart is unusually weak, and the old one is damaged beyond my present ability to repair." She tossed her sweaty hair out of her eyes. "Once that's done, if the regenerated heart can be strengthened, I have to regress the old heart back into tissue." She shook her head. "This is a job for a specialist, Stern. I'm doing my best, but the transfer may kill him if I can't stimulate the action of the new heart in time. This is what kills most of them, you know," she told him with somber eyes. "They don't allow medical intervention in their own culture." She hesitated. "Now there's a cheerful thought. If I save him, I'll be court-martialed. Maybe the Rojoks will save my career by killing me here."

"Stop that," Stern said firmly. "You're just tired. Don't think past this minute. Go to work. Repair the commander so that he can get us the hell out of here!"

Her eyebrows arched. She grinned. "Nice motivation," she nodded. "I'll recommend you for promotion."

That really was a joke, considering that clones had no status in the Tri-Fleet. But he didn't say it aloud. He laid down the sponge and went back to his vigil at the outside of the dome.

The guards came into view on patrol again, and Stern stiffened. His eyes drifted to the cell nearest him, where several of the Holconcom seemed to be waiting...

As the guards came close, a quarrel suddenly broke out in that nearby cell, loud and threatening even through the Plexiglas.

The two guards spared the conflict only a glance, unimpressed. They continued straight for the cell where Madeline was trying to save the alien commander.

"Watch it!" Stern hissed to Madeline. "They're coming straight for us!"

"I can't," she bit off, her face contorting as her hands flew with the instruments inside the open chest. "If I don't finish this suture, he's dead!"

Stern's heart froze like water thrown on dry ice. The guards were moving quickly toward the cell, and there was no hope that they wouldn't see what was happening this time. No hope at all. Desperate, Stern looked for a way, any way, to divert them. If only he had a *Gresham;* even a novapen! God, they couldn't do this, they couldn't!

Suddenly a loud, nerve-scraping wail broke the silence in the compound. The guards whirled, wild-eyed, and broke into a run toward the nearby cell where three Holconcom were starting their attack on the humans in the cell with them. It looked, on the surface anyway, as if a massacre was taking place. Those wails, like the sound an angry cat made, were nightmarish. The humans in Stern's cell tensed and looked hunted as they heard it, as they saw the slow, graceful, deadly motion of the Centaurians nearby.

Stern didn't know if prayers got answered or not, but he was grateful for the intervention, whatever the cause of it. "We've only got a few seconds before they come back," he called to Madeline. "Make them count!"

"Stand back and watch me," she said tersely.

The Rojoks had opened the cell now and they were taking two Holconcom and three bruised humans out of it.

"You will cause less trouble in our interrogation sector, I think," one of the burly Rojok guards sneered at the prisoners, "and be of more use to our cause. The first fifty of your complement to be interrogated have been sent to the ovens already. You should have made better use of the synthesizers. The ovens would not have been so appealing that you became eager to test them, had you consumed more water."

"We cherish freedom above all," one of the Holconcom prisoners spat at the guard. "Freedom, Rojok. It is more potent than all your neurotranquilizers, more precious than all your pleasure drugs!"

"You tell him, buddy," one of the bruised humans seconded as he moved to stand beside the Centaurian and glare hellishly at the two Rojoks.

The Centaurians and the humans straightened proudly into a tight, military line. They turned in one body and marched off toward the mysterious interrogation sector, their backs as straight as geometric lines, humans and Centaurians together. If Stern had any doubts about the brawl being staged, they were now erased.

A wild, booming cheer broke out in the cell complex for the departing prisoners in a queer combination of Terravegan Standard and Centaurian. The uproar grew and spread, from one cell to the other, so that the Plexiglas walls couldn't contain the sound. It burst out like a crude song into chants of "Freedom! Freedom!" that twined into a deep, strong chorus in many voices. It didn't begin to die down until the five prisoners were completely out of sight. Seconds later, the complex was deathly quiet.

Suddenly every eye in the complex seemed to be on the cell that held Dtimun, and Stern could taste the tension. Those soldiers knew what was going on. But even the humans were now involved in the life and death struggle of the alien commander. The Rojoks' vicious tactics had only served to create a bond of fellowship.

Stern turned to Madeline. "How's it going?"

"Another couple of turns and a stitch… Finished!" She hunched her shoulders with a weary groan. Mending torn blood vessels was something best done under proper conditions, and with greater tech than she possessed. But it wasn't a bad job, she told herself as she tidied up the sutures and prepared to stimulate the second heart.

"I'm ready for the hard part," she told him. "Stern, it's going to take all three of us to handle this."

He slid across the floor to her side. "Okay. What do I do?"

"Assist." She handed him the small, heavy cardioprobe. "Komak, are you still with us?"

"Yes, Madelineruszel," he said.

"Okay. Get your hand as close to that pressure point as you can without actually touching it. Good." She leaned forward. "I'm going to force the old heart into cardiac arrest. When that happens, he'll jump. I'm going to count on you to put him out as soon as you see the first sign of reflex action. If you don't act in time," she added, very somberly, "you can make up a suitable eulogy for Stern and me, because the shock will produce a fight-reflex in the commander's brain and Stern and I will be dead very fast. When we make it to that point, Stern, if we survive it, I'll need you to apply the cardioprobe to the second heart on the count of odd numbers while I massage the heart muscle manually. Got that?"

He nodded. "How about sterilization, since you aren't using the laserscalpel?"

"I've already laid down a field with the retractors," she replied. "Let me emphasize this—no matter what happens, come Rojok patrols, quasabeams, or fusion tissue bombs, don't lose your concentration for an instant. Once we start, it's a total commitment. One second of hesitation and the commander is so much raw meat."

"So are the rest of us," Stern added.

She nodded. "All right. Let's go." She leaned forward toward the blood-rimmed opening in Dtimun's muscular chest, and looked at Komak. "Ready?"

"I...am ready," the boy said weakly, and Stern hoped he was stronger than he sounded. Madeline had tapped his veins already for quite a large amount of blood, transfused as she worked.

Madeline's slender, capable hands disappeared into the cavity, straddling the smallest of the alien's two slick-tissued hearts, one very tiny, the other twice as large as the first. She began to massage the tissue. "Stern, ready?"

"Yes."

"Go on even numbers with the stimulator. Okay. One, *two*..." She applied pressure, made a turn and a hard jerk, and Dtimun sat straight up with open, black eyes. Black, in a Centaurian's eyes, were the color of certain death. A faint, deep, menacing growl grew in his throat.

"Komak!" Madeline cried.

There was no answer, and the commander's eyes turned, riveted to Madeline's face. The growl grew more deadly.

"Komak!" she called again.

But there was no answer. Komak was unconscious.

"Stern!" she called to him. "Get around behind the commander! Find the pressure point between the second and third cervical vertebrae and pinch it, hard! Hurry!"

He moved faster than he could ever remember moving before. Catching the alien's thrashing head, he dug his fingers in at the neck and held on for all he was worth. Even as he applied the pressure, he was aware that no normal human would have been strong enough to temporarily paralyze the nerve. For seconds that seemed like hours he was afraid it wasn't going to work at all. Around them, Madeline's instruments were doing a shimmy on the pallet as the commander fought Stern's hold. Concentrating all his strength, Stern pressed harder. In a human, compressing the carotid artery would produce the same result, but Centaurian physiology was very different. Stern groaned. If any guards were within sight of the cell now, and they looked this way...!

His heart froze as the sound of running footsteps echoed in the complex. Oh, God, he thought, even as he felt Dtimun's body relax, it's too late, it's all over, they'll see!

But there came with the footsteps the familiar sound of growls and curses and human voices yelling. And then came the sound of quasabeams from *chasats,* humming like angry bees in the semidarkness. Afterward was silence. Silence unbroken except for the shuffle of marching feet and hoarsely yelled threats. Again, that chant of "Freedom! Freedom!" And then, again, silence. How many lives this time, Stern wondered? How many more lives would be lost to pay for this one life in Madeline's hands?

"Will you listen to me!" Madeline snapped at him. "Pay attention, Holt! We've only got seconds to force the changeover before the lack of circulation does irreparable damage to his brain! Its structure is so radically different from our own... God, I hope the sutures I made will hold! We can't lose him now!"

Stern rolled away from Dtimun and back to his original position, cardioprobe in hand. He didn't have time to be relieved, only to act. He thrust the instrument, cold and heavy, down onto the motionless second heart while Madeline counted off the pulses.

"All right, go again, use the stimulator on the even numbers, ready? One, *two,* three, *four,* five, *six,* seven, *eight,*" she droned, massaging on the odd numbers. "That's good, that's very good, Stern, nine, *ten...*"

His mind felt numb as her voice continued the count, and he worked only by reflex, mechanically, efficiently. A life is a life, he thought. A life is a life is a life, and even if he lives, how the hell are we going to get hundreds of our people out of here?

"It's working!" Madeline said suddenly, sitting up straight, her face flushed but beaming, at peace for the first time since the ordeal had begun. "It's beating on its own! That's enough, Stern, you can stop now. We did it."

He leaned back and slumped, letting the words register. Around him, he heard the enthusiastic murmur of their cell mates as they, too, heard the news.

"I'll induce regression on the tissues of the old heart," she droned, "and then it's just a matter of knitting back the bones and nerves and blood vessels and muscles."

"Three hundred years ago," Stern reminded her, "he'd be in a body bag, if I remember old Earth terminology."

She smiled. "Yes, he would." She went to work. "When I've finished, I'll bring Komak back around." She began closing, her eyes intent on her task. The cyberscalpel was very small to perform such a profound task, but it worked quickly and efficiently. The process was so seamless that Stern unconsciously marveled at the beauty of it. "I wonder what happened out there when we were at the critical point?" she wondered apprehensively.

"I'll see if I can find out." He eased up to the front of the dome, noting an absence of guards, and caught the attention of one of the humans in a nearby cell. Using the Elyrian sign language, he asked quickly for the outcome of the diversion.

The human's solemn face was a study in impotent rage as he flashed his hands in answer to Stern's question. "Simulated riot to divert Rojok guards," the human "told" the *Bellatrix*'s skipper. "Guards quasabeamed prisoners inside cell with *chasats*. Five dead, four badly wounded and carried off to interrogation. We did our best." It wasn't possible to send curses with the hand signals, but Stern could read them in the crewman's face. Damn the Rojoks!

Solemnly he sent out a signal of his own about the commander of the *Morcai*. The impact on the prisoners as his contact relayed it to his mates in the cell was staggering. Broad smiles broke out like rashes among the humans—the *humans*—in the cell! The Centaurians' huge eyes made green laughter so vividly that it was visible in the semidarkness from several meters' distance.

Stern could hardly believe the sight of humans and Holconcom talking to each other jubilantly, much less the sight of gold-skinned hands clasping white ones as the message was relayed from cell to cell by humans and Holconcom alike. Something seemed to uncurl inside Stern, like a spring wound too tight suddenly letting go. All the aching indecision and confusion passed from him in one long, rustling sigh. His eyes closed as he leaned wearily against the cool Plexiglas, giving in to a feeling of luxurious calm, a paradox if ever there was one.

"I'm home, Maddie," he said quietly. "I've broken their hold. I'm home, at last."

"What are you muttering about over there?" Madeline asked. "Did you find out what happened?"

"Five dead, four wounded. This has been an expensive operation," he told her with a tired smile. "But I think it was worth it. They're shaking hands."

"They?" she asked, puzzled.

"The humans and the Centaurians."

She paused as she worked on Komak to gape at him.

"They're shaking hands," she said slowly. "Why?"

"They've made peace," he explained. "Apparently being imprisoned together has done something all the commander's threats couldn't."

She lowered her wrist scanner to Komak's chest. Odd, one of those readings would indicate human DNA. That, of course, was absurd. Her scanner, under so much pressure, was probably prone to glitches. "Confinement does strange things to people," she agreed.

"How long before he comes out of it?" Stern asked, nodding at Dtimun.

"Minutes. Hours. Days." She helped him shove the used bloody sponges into the disposal unit before they could be spotted by any passing guards. She activated the hyperclean function on her instruments and stuck them in her boot. You never knew…

"Will he live?" Stern persisted worriedly.

"That's out of my experience," she said quietly. "That he lived through the procedure is a miracle in itself. That particular surgical technique was theoretical, none of the Terravegan surgeons ever having performed it on a living Cularian subject. It was a gamble."

"Every breath we take is that," he replied. He studied her flushed face, her flyaway auburn hair curling in the sweltering humidity. "If he lives," he added, glancing at Dtimun, "we've got something for the men to hold on to. Saving the C.O. It's like a catchy tune that caught on in the sensorama."

"Love the underdog, and all that?" she mused. "We humans still love a loser, Stern." She pursed her lips. "Are you really going to tell them about the blue velvet ribbon? You wouldn't, would you?"

Both his dark eyebrows went up and he grinned. "Keep the C.O. alive and I may be able to find a way around the whole truth."

Madeline, stretching wearily, managed to bring Komak around. "It would be like giving away the color of Lawson's Skivvies," she said to herself. "Or spraying morph gas into the Tri-Galaxy Council chambers."

"That was a lie. I only threatened to do it. I had to stop Lawson from transferring you back to Terravega," Stern chuckled.

Suddenly her eyes came up and met his and there was shock in her expression. "Stern?" she whispered.

"Yes," he replied. "I think it's really me. Or what's left of me. Trust me, Maddie," he added with solemn dark eyes.

A long time seemed to pass before she finally nodded, a swift, curt jerk of her head before she programmed her wrist scanner for a drug to spear consciousness back into Komak's stirring, but still limp, body.

Lyceria let the Rojok guards lead her from the sand skimmer onto the gray hypoturf. In the dirty tan uniform they had given her, she looked little different from the other prisoners in the compound, except for her huge, unblinking eyes—eyes that rigidly held a solemn, calm royal-blue color while inside her the terror was screaming.

"Well, where do we put this one?" one of the guards growled in harsh Rojok. "They are being sent to us more rapidly than the sonic ovens can dispose of them! We must either build more efficient ovens or find other, better ways of mass execution."

The other nodded. "It is so. The cells grow more cramped. The latest additions are being held for mind sensings, are they not, since the Holconcom commander has not been found among them."

"Yes," the guard muttered. "It is an unforgivable burden on my men, having to turn extra duty to guard them. Not to mention the expense of pumping the pleasure drugs into them, and the extra strain on our water and sewage facilities. Then, there is the annoyance of feeding them..."

"They do not seem tranquillized, the humans and the Centaurians," the other remarked, puzzled. "I noticed as I came in, they were jubilant, not quiescent as they should have been in their pleasure."

His companion shrugged. "I cannot chart the effectiveness of the drugs on each individual prisoner and race, when I have eleven thousand prisoners in this complex alone. The emperor sets me an impossible task, and expects perfection without adequate funding!"

"I thought the camp was operated by recycling," the newcomer queried.

The older guard shook his head. "The prison wavelength rumored that inmates were eating their dead comrades. We had carefully treated the recycled prisoners, but in the end we had to return to the more expensive chemical diet. It was…unfortunate."

Lyceria shuddered in her mind at the calm discussion of such barbarism. For so long, she had dreaded even the thought of this monstrous place. Her mind had trembled at the sound of it, as if her fingers had touched death every time she heard the name *Ahkmau*. It was, she knew now, the certainty that her destiny was entwined with this place. It was a premonition of many years. She had always known it, felt it, as if she had looked into this life from still another life and seen what would be.

"For now," the Rojok guard said, "you may place her in with the Holconcom prisoners in the *greeshmah* sector."

As she started to sigh with relief, the other Rojok interrupted.

"That will not be agreeable. This one was sent by the emperor himself." He moved uncomfortably. "It was his wish," he added, "that she be treated to the full capabilities of *Ahkmau*."

The guard looked bored. "As you wish." He checked a compudisc in his six-fingered hand. "There is a sense-cell free on the upper level. I will have the technician bathe her with subsonics for a day or so before she is placed in total sensory deprivation. The shock of transition," he added with a meaningful, cold smile, "is enough to rip even a Centaurian's mind apart. It was used today on five of the Holconcom prisoners. They got down on their knees and begged for death. Interesting, is it not, when the Holconcom is rumored to be the terror of the Tri-Fleet vanguard." He laughed.

Lyceria stiffened. Her heart had lifted with hope when she heard that the Holconcom commander was still missing. Now, it fell heavily in her chest. If the Holconcom could succumb to torture, Dtimun must truly be dead. His will, as much as the secretive technology of the microcyborgs, kept the Holconcom strong. It came to her uncomfortably that the microcyborgs must have been removed by the guards. She closed her eyes with a shudder. Poor soldiers, to have their great strength ripped from them in such a place...

Never had she felt such hopelessness. She bowed her head and let them march her away to the cold, gray Plexiglas building that would soon become her tomb.

13

Three days had passed. One by one, two by two, the Holconcom of the *Morcai* and the humans of the *Bellatrix* had been taken away by armed guards, never to be seen again. As the numbers began to dwindle, the Rojoks became more determined in their search for Dtimun. They began to look for the Holconcom soldier that the humans had carried into the cell block, claiming he was inebriated. The emperor was making terrible threats. He was not convinced that the commander of the Holconcom was dead, and ordered that every single crewman be tortured until someone told the truth.

In the cell with the *Morcai* and *Bellatrix* execs, Dtimun still lay unconscious on his pallet. Despite Madeline's frequent checks and attempts to revive him, he never moved. His pulse, however, was strong and regular, his Centaurian blood pressure normal. He was breathing regularly and without effort. But he wasn't moving.

Despite the surgery and all their sacrifices and their hopes, he lay like the dead. Madeline grew more depressed.

Strick Hahnson, who was now free of the effects of the Rojok drugs, conferred with her, but neither could think of a technique that might restore Dtimun to consciousness. Nor did Komak have any hope to add.

"If something doesn't happen, and soon," Strick said quietly, "there won't be any of us left to salvage from this red death. They took another thirty of our people away to the interrogation sector this morning. It's hell."

"Tell me about it," Stern growled, hitting his fist against the Plexiglas dome. "My God, how do you think I feel? Those are my people they're stuffing into those damned ovens, Strick. I trained those men. I know every one of them by sight and name. Here I stand while they go out there to stare hell in the face. And I put them there!"

Hahnson moved closer. "The Rojoks put them here," he corrected. "The Rojoks, Holt."

"He's right, you know," Madeline seconded.

"Recriminations will not help now," Komak said, adding his voice to the others as he faced the humans. "We must find a way to get the men out of here. It appears that we must do it without the commander, since we can spare no more time to see if his condition improves or worsens. Perhaps..."

Before he could finish the thought, the Rojok officer who was in charge of this sprawling complex marched toward their cell with deliberation in every step, and Stern knew why he'd come.

"You," he said, indicating Stern as guards suddenly flanked the slit entrance the sprung magnalock had created. "Come."

Stern stood his ground, folding both arms across his chest. "No," he said stubbornly.

The Rojok officer's eyes narrowed, if possible, even more. "You have no choice," he told Stern. "It is part of the programming. You cannot refuse."

"The hell I can't," Stern replied coolly, although the effort the refusal was costing him was evident in his strained expression. "It's going to take more than those two lizard-faces to get me out of this cell."

"If you do not come now," the officer warned, "you will be interrogated with the others. You will die with them."

Remembering the Holconcom officers marching proudly to the ovens, the humans standing at attention while they were mowed down by *chasats,* the pain and agony in the faces of his men while man after man was taken off to the interrogation section—his body straightened suddenly as rigid as steelex. "I belong to the *Morcai* Battalion, Mister," he said in his best military tone. "I win with it, or I die with it. But I will not, *ever,* surrender!"

Something in his carriage, in his voice, in the strength of will in his tone, carried to the others in the nearby cells. None of them knew yet that he was a clone, but they knew he was a fellow prisoner and that was enough. Like blood calling to blood, it made them move to the front of the domes, their eyes watchful, angry. And, man by man, slowly, very softly, the hundreds of humans and Centaurians who had been forced together on the *Morcai* to this place of tortures, began to chant. The sound of it grew like a prayer in intensity, stronger and louder and deeper and prouder until it made a roar of emotion loud enough to shake the pillars of the gigantic dome itself. "Free-dom! Free-dom! *Free-dom!*"

Stern raised his fist and chanted with them.

The dusky-skinned Rojok shut the door to the cell again, and with a red-hot glare of hatred at Stern, who was smiling, he whirled on his heel and marched his soldiers out of sight, with the chanting war cry dogging every step he took.

"That," Madeline remarked seconds later, "was a damned stupid thing to do."

Stern grinned. "Would you rather I'd gone with him and spilled my guts?"

Hahnson chuckled steadily. "Threw them a curve, didn't you?" he asked. "That wasn't in the plan, apparently. You were planted here as a spy, weren't you?"

"Dead-on, my friend," Stern replied quietly. "For the moment, anyway, I seem to have thrown off the Rojok influence on my mind."

"With a vengeance." Hahnson grinned at Komak. "How do you like the unit's new name—The *Morcai* Battalion?"

"Our numbers do make a Battalion as Centaurians reckon it, Strick-hahnson," Komak agreed, "and we were together as a unit on the *Morcai,* so the name does suit. However, the commander's reaction to it may be more…emotional…than mine," Komak added with a flash of laughing green eyes. "He—how is it said?—finds humans distasteful."

"He leaves a bad taste in my mouth, too," Madeline retorted, smiling at Komak's puzzled expression. Colloquial expressions were lost on aliens. Her eyes went to the commander's lithe form on the covered floor. "I really am going to expect a knighthood for this, you know," she said, tongue-in-cheek. "Furthermore, I expect to throw it up to the commander for the rest of my life that his hearts belong to me—every time I see him, that is, which I hope is only over an interstellar vidscreen every fifty years or so."

"When you throw it up to him," Stern told her, "please make sure that I'm in the next solar system. As your skipper, he'll hold me responsible. I'll be lucky if I get off with less than eighty years of forced labor when he runs through my court-martials."

Komak frowned. "Holtstern, why should you be court-martialed?"

Stern looked weary. "How's treason for a start? Followed by aiding and abetting the enemy, attempted murder…"

Komak shook his head, an oddly human movement not common to Centaurians. "I will not allow you to be court-martialed," he said quietly. From his imposing height, he seemed as formidable as the commander had been. His eyes mirrored blue solemnity. "Without your cooperation, the commander would be dead. And the trap of the Rojok would have been sprung, even had you not been with us. *Karamesh,*" he added with a soft green smile in his eyes. "It means, in your tongue, fate," he translated.

The living shadow of Holt Stern smiled at the *Morcai's* exec, oblivious to the glances of the other occupants of the cell. "Do you think you could save up that speech," he asked Komak, "and recite it quickly to the commander when he comes out of the coma—you know, just before he snaps my neck?"

"Oh, I will certainly try, Holtstern," Komak agreed readily, and the green laughter danced in his eyes.

There was no laughter in Chacon's slit eyes when he heard his aide's urgent, whispered message. The look on his taut, dusky face caused the young officer to take a quick step backward.

"When was she taken?" he snapped, and his eyes took on a glitter that was all too familiar to the younger Rojok.

"Two days ago, my agents told me," the aide said uneasily. "I would stake my life that it was not one of your personal guards who betrayed her, Commander."

"So would I, Lieumek," Chacon agreed coldly. "The emperor's spies are legion, and there are loose tongues in any harem."

"He has summoned Mekkar," the young Rojok added nervously.

Chacon's thin-lipped mouth tugged upward in a half smile. "He thinks I will allow myself to be assassinated? By the hour, he grows more *groshmot*. It is no less than I expected. He has always been unpredictable, and his obsession with the Centaurian Holconcom commander has no logic in it." He locked his hands behind him and stared sightlessly at the vidscreen of his flagship, where a colorful array of distant nebulae and suns stained the black velvet of space. "Lock in a course for *Ahkmau*."

"*Ahkmau?*" Lieumek gasped. "You are as mad as Mangus Lo! It would be suicide…and even if not…think of your career!"

Chacon turned and looked down at the younger alien. The raw power in those dark slit eyes was part of the warrior's legend, and it was no less potent now than on the battlefield. The young Rojok saluted smartly.

Chacon watched him march away in a silence that was broken only by the mighty hum of the ship's engines. *Ahkmau*. Lyceria, in that place of nightmares! A jewel flung into mud. A Silesian butterfly with its gossamer wings ripped. His tormented eyes closed. He was a warrior, used to combat and death and the horror of the battlefield. He should not have had this reaction to the news. One female was much as another, and he had never felt the need to be bound to one for life. His career was all he lived for. It had been demanding. There had never been the thought of a home other than the deck of his flagship. There was nothing so unusual, after all, about this Centaurian princess. She was expendable. She meant nothing to him, nothing at all…

He waved his hand over the vidscreen control and brought up the helmsman on the bridge. "Throw the lightsteds and give me all speed!" he growled to the officer, in a razor-sharp tone that brought a dozen startled pairs of eyes toward the helmsman's screen.

* * *

The death camp was literally crawling with guards, searching, prodding. Stern watched them in a creeping silence that ended abruptly when the camp commandant came back with death in his whole look late in the afternoon.

"It has been decided," he told Stern and Komak, "that since interrogation has not produced the Holconcom commander, that a public execution might loosen tongues. There is much…affection…among the human element for Dr. Hahnson. He will, therefore, be the first victim. You may save his life by telling me which of the remaining Holconcom in the internment camp is Commander Dtimun. I have no more time to waste on examinations. Over forty-five have already been conducted with no results and I tire of subterfuge and silence!"

While he was speaking, six Rojok guards armed with *chasats* entered the cell, thrust the other occupants aside and dragged Hahnson out of it. The action was so rapid that none of the cell's complement even had time to react until it was too late. Stern and Komak made a grab for the struggling victim, only to be *chasated* at stun setting and crumpling to the floor before the Rojoks left the cell.

"Fools!" the commandant growled contemptuously. "Resistance will accomplish nothing here. Tell me what I need to know and I will spare the surgeon. You are humans. The Holconcom commander means nothing to you. Save your comrade. Speak."

"You can't kill him!" Madeline Ruszel yelled furiously. "It's in violation of the Malcopian Articles of War!"

"We do not recognize them here," the commandant said haughtily. "Compassion is for weaker races than ours. Take him away," he ordered the guards.

"Let him go, you damned sand lizards!" Higgins broke out, leaping toward the dome.

"Strick!" Stern whispered, his fists taut at his side.

Impotent, helpless, he watched them frog-march Hahnson away to a hastily prepared transparent torture cell in the center of the domed complex. It was elevated, visible to the entire camp, and equipped with sound amplification. The latter fact became immediately apparent when Hahnson was slung into it, by the one vibrating word that passed his lips—the last that ever would.

"Malenchar!" he yelled in Centaurian, at the top of his lungs. A second later, the multisonic transmitters were turned on. The next sound was a scream so tortured, so piercing, it turned Stern's feet to jelly under him.

"Oh, my God," Stern groaned, his fists hammering impotently at the flexible strength of the transparent dome that held him prisoner. "Oh, sweet God, not Strick!"

Beside him, Madeline Ruszel stood reciting curses like whispered rosaries as she watched, and knew better than the rest just how potent Hahnson's agony really was.

"Will it kill him quick, at least, just tell me that!" Stern asked her, his eyes riveted to Hahnson's shuddering body.

She was a professional. But Strick, like Stern, was an old, old friend and comrade of many battles. "The...uh...the unit," she said, struggling to keep her voice calm, "has a...a self-repairing mechanism. It injects modified stem cells enclosed in nanobots into his...his body. The nanobots repair the disrupted cells instantly, so that it can...can burn them up and heal them and start all over again. He will, eventually, die," she choked. "But not for a...long time."

Both Stern's fists hit the dome at the same time. "I've got to stop it somehow," Stern husked, hating the Rojoks, hating the camp, hating himself for his programming that had brought them all, that had brought Strick, to this hell. His insides felt empty. "I've got to stop it!"

In his mind, he was seeing a husky blond soldier at Tri-Fleet HQ, years before Mangus Lo rose to power, years before there was *Ahkmau*.

"They call this unit the Strategic Space Command," Strick Hahnson had told the new Lieutenant J.G., Holt Stern, as the two of them boarded the Royal Legion of Terravega ship *Bellatrix*. "Brand-spanking-new outfit, this. The elite of the space services. They said they needed a few good spacers, and I'm just about the best there is, so I knew they'd want me," Hahnson had added with a grin. "Name's Strick Hahnson, Doctor of Interstellar Medicine, homo sapiens division."

Stern had grinned, too, at the other's dry sense of humor, and locked forearms with him. "Holt Stern. I figured they could use some good pilots to go along with the troops, and they don't come any better than me. I fly by the seat of my pants."

"So do I, occasionally," Hahnson had laughed, "depending on how many drinks I've had when I start throwing challenges at rival crewmen."

It had been a beginning. From rescue hops to scientific observation jumps, he and Hahnson and a budding medical legend named Dr. Madeline Ruszel, the only Cularian specialist in the fleet, had protected each other against Rojoks, terrorists, wildlife and other rival crewmen for almost ten years. In all that time, he'd never once had cause to regret his friendship with either one of them. Despite the SSC's rigid policy of mentally neutering coed personnel in the military, the three had formed into something like a family. It was a close-knit, caring family, any one of whom would gladly have died for the other two.

Stern owed his life to Hahnson a dozen times over. Now he was standing helplessly in a cell on a red dustball of a moon, watching his friend die by inches. And there wasn't a damned thing he could do about it. On top of that, he had to live with the knowledge that it was his fault. His fault.

Something wet misted his eyes, made a path down one lean, darkly tanned cheek. He tasted salt in the corner of his parched mouth.

Beside him, he heard a broken sob in a woman's voice. Beyond the cell, he could see Strick Hahnson's face contort into something so hideous that it was barely human. And still the screams came, piercing through the agonized silence of the cell complex as every crewman of the *Morcai* and the *Bellatrix* watched, and every ear listened.

"Now will you tell me?" the Rojok officer demanded of the imprisoned soldiers. "Will you say where is the *Morcai*'s commander? Each of you who remains silent is guilty of this officer's torture! Unless you speak, each of you must bear the guilt of his painful death!"

Holt Stern's tall frame shuddered with rage. "Don't you buy it!" he yelled in Terravegan Standard, loud enough that his voice penetrated the cell dome, its speaker enhanced so that the occupants could tell the Rojoks what they wanted to know the minute their spirits broke. It was backfiring on the Rojok commandant, as Stern used the opportunity to keep the men quiet. "Hahnson wouldn't sacrifice even one life to save his own, and you know it! If you talk, the Rojoks win!"

The humans, who all knew Hahnson, gazed toward Stern for a minute and then began to speak to each other in huddles.

"It is as he says," Komak said suddenly, his loud voice, in Centaurian, echoing behind Stern. "Hahnson gave the war cry of the Holconcom—*Malenchar!* Our honor demands that we not betray his sacrifice!" He turned to the Rojok commandant, standing confused at the dome. "You will find no traitors in the ranks of the *Morcai* Battalion, Rojok! We live or die together. We will not, ever, surrender!" It was an echo of Stern's own speech, almost verbatim.

The Holconcom made odd sounds in their throats as they turned, angrily, to face the Rojok commandant of the camp. Weak from self-enforced hunger, from lack of water to escape the Rojoks' drug, torn and ragged and weary, still they fought back in the only way left to them.

"Free-dom," they began to chant in Terravegan, deliberately drowning out Hahnson's agonized screams. "Free-dom! Free-dom! *Free-dom!*"

The humans quickly joined in the chant, gathering with the Centaurians at the part of their cells that faced the platform where Hahnson was shivering with pain. *"Free-dom!"* they chanted in unison. They stood at attention, defiant and proud, daring the Rojoks to come and get them.

Stern felt a pride that overwhelmed him. "By God, that's doing it!" he whispered hoarsely, his eyes never leaving Hahnson. "They're drowning him out. Now maybe the Rojoks will get tired of hearing us and put an end to it. Oh, God, maybe they'll let him die now. Maybe they'll let him die!"

Madeline was less hopeful. Tears ran helplessly down her face, but her green eyes blazed up like living flames. "The inhuman sons of bitches," she bit off coldly. "If we ever get out of here, that commandant is mine. I'll filet him like a Tiranian goldfish!"

"I'll lend you a knife," Stern gritted.

Higgins came up beside Stern and hesitatingly laid a hand on his shoulder, very gently. "We all liked Dr. Hahnson, sir," he said unsteadily.

Stern drew a deep breath and managed a wan smile for his sandy-haired exec. "Thanks, son."

"Sir?"

"Yes, Higgins?"

The young first officer of the *Bellatrix* drew himself up proudly. "I don't give a damn whether you're a clone or not," he said abruptly. "I'll follow you straight to hell if you want to go there, sir," he added with a pale grin.

Stern couldn't manage an answer. There was one hell of a lump in his throat. He nodded his gratitude, turning his tortured gaze back to the cell suspended above the panorama of domes.

"You will not talk!" the Rojok commander growled, as the chant continued. His thin lips twisted into a demoniacal smile. "So you choose to condemn your comrade to death. Very well. Then watch what your refusal has caused. See what you have condemned this poor human to!"

Every eye snapped to Hahnson's cell. The chanting stopped as the Rojok commandant gave a signal to his underling. At the sign, the Rojok began, slowly, deliberately, to hack away at Hahnson's sensitive hands with a *chasat*. A half an inch at a time, he sliced away flesh and tendon and nerve and bone as the husky doctor screamed and screamed and screamed, writhing in agony, kept conscious by the damned alien machine as the *chasat* whined.

"Damn you!" Stern yelled hoarsely, tears of impotent, unbearable rage streaming down his face. "Damn you to hell and back again! I'll kill you!"

"His hands," Madeline ground out. "Dear God, not his hands!" She beat her fists against the dome, as Stern had done earlier. "You cowards!" she raged at the Rojoks. "You cowards!"

Inside the cell, Hahnson was still conscious, his screams hoarse now, as the damned nanobots repaired damaged cells so the disruptors could begin again to rip him apart.

Madeline hit the cell wall one last time, her eyes drowned in tears. With a husky sob, she began to pray aloud, the last resort of the doomed. They were light-years away from the Tri-Fleet. No SSC commander would be reckless enough for a suicide mission like the rescue of the *Bellatrix*'s crew. The Holconcom were indispensable to the defense of their homeworld, but no one knew where the crew of the *Morcai* was. She wondered if the old Centaurian emperor would even believe it, if someone told him his crack, elite troops had been captured and tortured.

Her eyes drained tears of absolute anguish. As Hahnson's voice rose to a nerve-shattering peak of agony, there was a sudden murmur of Rojok voices, followed by quick, frantic activity.

Frowning, Madeline strained to see what was going on. Several Rojoks were moving toward the platform where Hahnson was being held. Even as she turned to ask Stern who it might be, a voice as commanding as Dtimun's rose above the murmurs. It had the ring of steel hitting rock.

14

"Cleemaah!"

The clear, piercing authority in that harsh Rojok command spread a silence like that of decaying tombs over the complex. The humans and Centaurians, diverted, stopped raging about Hahnson. The Rojok commandant, recognizing the other Rojok, turned white and ran, *ran,* to the platform where the newcomer was standing beside Hahnson's cell. The guard who had been conducting the torture suddenly stood at rigid attention with the blood-spattered *chasat* still clenched in his hand. The camp commandant and his two other guards hastily followed suit.

Stunned at the Rojoks' unexpected timidity, Stern and Madeline watched a tall, powerfully built Rojok soldier, with many slashes of *mesag* marks on the sleeves of his black uniform, signal to his bodyguard. He was abruptly flanked by six of the burliest, most military-looking Rojok soldiers Madeline had ever seen. The raw power of the newcomer was evident even in his posture, as though he commanded by his presence alone. His long, straight blond hair gleamed like pure honey in the glaring reddish light of the other two moons, burning like the slit eyes that seemed to glitter even at a distance as they took in the evidence of the prison commandant's handiwork.

"Most honorable visitor," the flustered, flushed Rojok commandant began in a nervous, respectful tone.

Before he could finish the sentence, and without a single word, the towering newcomer pulled a *chasat* from his belt and cut the officer in half with it. Mercilessly, with a savage contempt, his highly polished black knee-high boot lobbed the dead man out of his way. Before the guard who had been torturing Hahnson could react, the same muscular officer had whirled and, in a single graceful motion, separated the murderous guard from his head.

A guttural flow of Rojok followed the snap executions. The tall Rojok gestured toward the cell imperiously. It was opened and Hahnson's handless, bleeding body was lifted, *gently* lifted, and carried out of it by two members of the newcomer's bodyguard.

"By the ten plagues," the tall Rojok cursed at the two remaining compound guards on the platform who were staring at him with dawning horror, "I will have your heads for this! Lieumek, have these barbarians thrown into their own sonic ovens! Both of them, now!"

Not one of the guards made a single protest. Nor did the bodyguards. The tall Rojok waited until the order was carried out, standing like a statue as his slit eyes scanned the cells, the dehydrated bodies, the undernourished prisoners crammed together without so much as a blanket.

Another flow of orders followed the first flurry, and Madeline caught something about bringing in fresh water and food and blankets, and gathering medical personnel from among the prisoners to treat the survivors—the rest was urgent, but too fast for her to translate, even with her meager store of Rojok verbs. She could hardly believe her ears.

"What the hell is going on?" Stern asked for all of them, shocked at the staggering pace of unlikely events. "Who is that Rojok?"

"Excuse me," Komak apologized quietly. "I thought you would have recognized him from battle vids. He is Chacon. He commands the Rojok fleet."

Chacon! Stern and Madeline exchanged puzzled glances as they watched Rojok medics scattering among the cells to seek out prisoners with any medical experience to help treat the sick and injured. They saw the individual cells being given rations of water and food— quite obviously from the field marshal's own stores. Madeline began to believe the legend of the Rojok commander whose code of ethics had earned him the respect of the worst of his enemies. He had been known to halt a successful attack long enough to let medics evacuate the dead and wounded of the vanquished. He had never fired on a medical transport.

"Why is he here, though, Komak?" Madeline asked the tall alien beside her. "We're the enemy, and this camp is Mangus Lo's pride and joy. Surely he isn't acting under orders?"

"Hardly," Komak returned curtly. "Although, it is possible that the Rojok emperor sent him here to identify the commander," he added uncomfortably. "He alone of all the Rojoks will know the Holconcom commander on sight."

"Well, that's lovely," Madeline said shortly. She ran a hand through her sweaty, dirty auburn hair. "After all we've gone through to try to save him. And then to lose Strick..." She swallowed, hard, and turned away, ashamed of letting her tears be obvious. She cleared her throat as she stared through the dome at the flurry of activity. Bodies dressed in red Holconcom uniforms and green Strategic Space

Command uniforms were pulled from the sonic ovens while the prisoners watched. "What a waste of lives!" she bit off.

"Madelineruszel, look!" The Centaurian she called "Abe" burst out suddenly from the commander's side.

She whirled, her eyes widening at the sight. Dtimun was stirring. There was eye movement. His breathing, though a little quick, was regular and steady. "What's that old saying, Stern, that good can come of the worst evil? Praise the fleet, look!"

Dtimun's head began to move slowly, back and forth on the pallet. She dropped down beside him and before she considered the wisdom of the move, her hand went down to check the big artery at his throat.

But even as her fingertips touched his golden skin, his big, golden-skinned hand whipped out like a quasabeam and snared her wrist. Pain lines cut into her complexion and she groaned.

"Maddie!" Stern called out, moving quickly toward her.

"Stay back!" she whispered huskily, drowning in pain. "Don't move. Whatever happens, don't interfere!"

"Komak, can't you do something?" Stern growled.

"I am sorry, no," the younger Centaurian replied sadly, his tall body tense and restless. "I do not think he will kill her—but even though he alone of the Holconcom is not a clone, he is as unused to touch without combat as the rest of us. If we rush him, he will certainly snap her neck. We can only wait."

Dtimun's eyes dilated until blackness filled them. His lean face tautened. *"Quy nom holconcom!"* he growled huskily at the human in his grasp.

Komak paled. *"Maliche!"* he swore softly. "Madelineruszel, repeat what I tell you, with the exact inflection," he called to her. *"Bacum... tocache. Bacum...tocache!"*

Madeline struggled to breathe. The words were like ancient native dialects, with high tones and low tones and glottal stops. The pain was slowing her thought processes. She pulled against his hold with both hands as she tried to repeat the rising and falling tones.

"What are you telling her?" Stern asked urgently. "What's happening?"

"See his eyes, Holtstern!" Komak ground out, watching as the commander began to rise from the padded floor into a sitting position, his hand loosening its grip on her wrist—only to curl suddenly around her throat. "He thinks she is an enemy soldier. He will kill her!" Ignoring Stern's sudden pallor, he repeated the words again to Madeline, who had garbled them. "Say the words! Quickly!"

Her mouth opened, but the commander's grip on the softness of her throat was too secure. The words formed only on her lips as they began to go numb from the lack of oxygen. She must try. She must try, to live. *"T…tocache!"* Madeline husked through her tortured vocal chords as the commander's hand tightened.

"No, Madelineruszel!" Komak said in something like horror, if a Centaurian Holconcom could feel horror. *"Bacum tocache!"* he emphasized the first word.

But, unbelievably, the word softened her captor. The alien's eyes lost their murderous black color all at once and became suddenly a quiet, curious, soft shade of brown as they searched Madeline's flushed face.

"I remember, little one," he said strangely. "You bite."

Her eyes widened incredulously. Surely, she thought, she was delirious from lack of oxygen and hearing things.

Dtimun released her abruptly and stretched his taut muscles, drawing up a long leg so that he could lean his forehead against his knee. Weak, but alert, his huge, elongated eyes swept the compound and the realization was suddenly there in eyes colored dark brown in anger.

"Ahkmau!" he snapped, his furious gaze going directly to Komak, who winced. "In the history of the Holconcom, no one of us has ever been taken prisoner in battle! Why did you not blow up the ship?" he demanded hotly. "And, failing that, why did you not kill me, knowing what could happen if I fell victim to the Rojok madman?"

Komak seemed to pale under his golden complexion. "The *Morcai's emerillium* drive units were fused," he said simply. "We could not ignite them. And I did try to take your life..."

Madeline glared at him. Dtimun only stared relentlessly at Komak, his eyes hard and unblinking as he waited for the answer.

"It is," Komak said, moving uncomfortably, "very difficult to explain. First, I tried to...dispose of you aboard the *Morcai*. Madelineruszel delayed me until the Rojoks dropped us both with *chasats*. You were barely alive when we were brought here. I thought, forgive me Madelineruszel, that surgical intervention under these conditions would hasten your demise. So I urged Madelineruszel to interfere with the *dylete*." He looked embarrassed. "You did not die after all. She saved you, under impossible conditions and with the barest minimum of surgical tools." He smiled apologetically. *"Karamesh,"* he added. "Fate. As I already believed, it was not your destiny to meet your end here."

"My God," Madeline breathed, shaking her head. "I never suspected why you were so keen for me to operate," she said, addressing Komak, who only smiled again. Her gaze went to Dtimun. "Well, that ought to brighten an otherwise dreary day for you, sir. You can bring me up on charges before the military tribunal on two counts of dereliction of duty, including breaking a Centaurian cultural taboo and defying the Malcopian Articles of War. My court-martial should be quite colorful," she added pleasantly.

"You'll enjoy mine, too," Stern assured him, folding his arms across his chest. He grinned. "Not to mention the spacing that's sure to follow the court-martial. I'm a clone of the original SSC Captain Holt Stern, genetically altered by the Rojoks as an infiltrator. I was responsible for sabotaging the ship so that it could be captured. I'm the reason we're all here together in this Rojok hell."

The cat-eyes studied Stern for a moment, and the human felt strange, probing sensations in his mind. Dtimun's gaze shifted to Madeline, then to Komak, and his expression went bland as if he now understood everything.

Dtimun carelessly raised an eyebrow as he turned to Lieutenant Higgins, who was watching the byplay uneasily. "Higgins, have you nothing to confess?" he asked with a flash of green eyes. "This seems to be the time."

"Well, sir," Higgins complied with a shy grin, "before I actually confessed to anything, I'd have to have some assurance that it wouldn't be used against me when we get out of this place. After we process all the Rojok prisoners we take, that is."

The arrogant statement brought another flash of green to Dtimun's eyes. "Humans," he said. "How does Lawson bear it?" He looked around the cell at Crandall and "Abe" and Jennings and the others. They were thin and weary and subdued, and there were new lines in the female medic's face. "Where is Hahnson?" he asked abruptly. "Is he in another cell?"

"He...they used multisonics on him," Madeline said softly, her eyes glued to the floor of the cell as she fought for composure. "After the Rojok commandant of this place tortured him to make the men tell where you were, they...the Rojok...he was slicing away Strick's hands. His mind was already...and they...Chacon stopped it, but it was too late, you see. It was..." Despite her best efforts to stem them, tears made silver tracks down her flushed cheeks. "Nobody said a word," she defended the men, raising her face proudly to the commander's eyes. "Not a word, human or Holconcom! And Komak told the Rojoks that the *Morcai* Battalion stood by its own, human or Centaurian. A lot of the men died for you, Commander. To keep the Rojoks from finding you. And we did that. All of us, we did that."

"*Maliche,* why?" the alien asked in astonishment.

"Because it isn't our way in the SSC to let any member of our unit be used as blackmail to force information. It's a thing called honor." She shrugged. "Besides, Komak said that if anyone could get us out of here, it would be you. We had to give you the chance to live, so other lives were sacrificed. Can you get the men out?"

"Madam," he said with a heavy sigh, "I will get them out if I have to chew through the hyperglas. But what is meant by the *Morcai* Battalion? I was not aware that I commanded such a group," he added wryly.

"You do now," Stern told him. "About four hundred of them are human, too. How's that for good fortune?" he added with a grin and a touch of the original officer's impertinence.

A stream of guttural Centaurian passed the commander's lips, and Stern had the feeling he was fortunate to lack a translation.

"You mentioned that Chacon was here," Dtimun said as he rose to his feet a little unsteadily. "Is he still?"

"I think so," Stern replied. "He was going through the place with scanners looking for somebody and he was in a red temper. He had two of the guards sent to the ovens the minute he got here. And he killed the two Rojoks who tortured Hahnson personally. One was the camp commandant."

"Rojok death camps are notorious for their use of mind-altering drugs," the commander began.

"Yes, we found out the hard way," Stern told him. "We were given synthesizers preprogrammed to add pleasure drugs to anything we drank or ate from them. Nobody's been near that synthesizer for water since we found out. I'm not going to risk it now, either, although my damned throat's parched. We've been using these," he added, showing the alien a tiny hydrotox pills. "Madeline had a few of them left in her drug banks, but we're running out. Komak had two Milish Cones. God, the other poor devils in this place haven't even had that!"

Dtimun digested that in silence. He seemed preoccupied, and not just a little weak from his brush with the hereafter, Stern thought.

"Was Chacon searching the camp for me?" Dtimun asked.

"It is probable," Komak replied, his eyes a troubled blue-gray. "The Rojoks had standing orders that you were to be taken to Mangus Lo the instant you were located."

Madeline wondered absently how Komak had come by that information, when nothing had been mentioned in her hearing about it.

A green smile colored the Holconcom commander's eyes. "I can think of nothing that would give me greater pleasure."

"You must not kill him," Komak warned. "The Council would space you for it. Whatever the provocation, as the head of a government he has the right to trial and the Tri-Galaxy Council has the right to exact payment for his crimes."

"That conclave of gaggling old women?" the commander burst out, his eyes brown with anger. "They will not even agree to make proper war on the Rojok. Only a few governments have sent troops to the intersystem force."

"It's not because Admiral Lawson hasn't tried," Stern reminded him with a grin.

"Lawson is one man. And by now, certainly he has old Tnurat to contend with, as well. The Centaurian emperor has no patience with weakness and bureaucracy—even less than Lawson. And his temper is meaner," the Centaurian added.

"Even if Lawson could get a war vote," Stern added, "it wouldn't do us much good, would it? Most of the member planets can't even get along in peacetime. We've been segregated into planetary units ever since the war started, and there's no coordination among the few fleets that were sent to fight for us. Only a unanimous war vote would change that, and too many pacifist governments won't sign such a treaty."

"Indeed," Dtimun said. "If a war vote came today, it would be many of your months before Lawson could organize the divisions and supply them for deep space. To mount an offensive in space is a great deal more difficult logistically than to deploy troops on solid ground."

"What's going on outside?" Madeline interrupted from the front of the dome. She'd been only half listening to the discussion behind her. There was a growing force of Rojok guards moving toward the entrance to the huge complex.

"They mass for action, unless I miss my guess," Dtimun said calculatingly. "And I am not sufficiently recovered to fight," he said. "Nor are my Holconcom," he added with a pointed look toward Madeline.

She knew that he meant the Holconcom had their microcyborgs removed. A number of them were implanted under the commander's scalp.

As she thought it, he scowled and his hand went to his thick black hair. He gave her an odd look.

She actually flushed. He couldn't have read her mind, of course. It was only coincidence.

But his next statement belied any coincidence. "They must be transferred without explanation," he said abruptly, looking straight at her. "There are enough for most of the Holconcom, though they will necessarily fight at lesser strength through dilution."

"I can do the transfer," she replied. "If you can get us out of here."

He nodded. The others stared at them uncomprehending, all except Komak, who smiled. The microcyborgs were powerful. They would lend the commander stellar physical abilities as long as his body harbored them, but only two were designated to each of his unit. They were the size of pinheads, but their incredible abilities were known to only a few souls in the galaxy. Madeline was one. Komak understood without being told that she had shared that knowledge with no one.

"The Holconcom are as vulnerable as the humans," the commander continued. "And all are weak and depleted physically since they have been avoiding the synthesizers."

"We've got to do something quick," Stern interrupted, watching the Rojoks. "I sense trouble."

"I agree," Komak added, studying the enemy aliens. "I sense one faction building to confront another."

Dtimun's eyes searched the Rojoks as one company of them began to loosely form the ancient phalanx. In the distance, the planet's twin suns were looming closer to the horizon, bringing again the red haze of sunset to the horizon.

"One of the groups is going to be Chacon's, I imagine," Stern said.

Even as he spoke, the Rojok field marshal moved into view at the head of the phalanx. He shot an order to the men there and suddenly turned, commanding even across the space of the complex in his height and the arrogant self-confidence of his stride. He began to walk between the rows of domes. His slit eyes carefully searched each one as he passed it, two of his personal bodyguard flanking him as the others stood at attention.

"We'll hide you," Madeline said quickly.

"You will not," Dtimun replied somberly. "If Chacon wishes to find me, by *Simalichar,* I will let him!"

"But, Commander, you can't let him arrest you...!" she protested.

"In all probability," he reasoned with her, in solemn tones, "you have rearranged my inner organs in such disorder that I will likely die anyway. What have I to lose?"

She gaped at him, her mind clouding as she read the laughing green of his eyes and tried to understand how he could succumb to humor at a time like this.

"If Chacon finds the commander," Stern explained with exaggerated patience, "he'll have to open the cell to take him out, won't he? And if he does, we'll jump him. With Chacon as a hostage, they'll give us the place!"

"Well, gee whiz, what a simply super idea!" Madeline said in mock astonishment. She glowered. "You think Chacon's going to march into the cell alone, without armed guards?"

"We could ask him if he'd oblige us," he said reasonably.

She threw up her hands.

"*Bataashe!*" Dtimun shot at them suddenly, his body tensing as the Rojok warlord moved toward them, searching each domed cell that he passed.

But he stopped suddenly at the entrance of Dtimun's cell and stood there, tall and imposing, as proud as any emperor, just staring at the Holconcom commander. His reddish-skinned face was expressionless, his long, blond hair falling, wet from sweat, onto his forehead and into his slit eyes. Stern felt the power in their narrow gaze as if it had the power to burn.

"I find you in a strange place, Dtimun of Centauria," Chacon said. "Legend has it that no Holconcom has ever been taken prisoner in battle."

"Until now, that was true," Dtimun replied.

Chacon nodded. His gaze swept over the other prisoners in

Dtimun's cell. His thin lips turned up into a kind of smile. "Which is worse, I wonder, the confinement here or the constant company of the humans?" he asked the Centaurian. "I seem to remember that you nursed a violent distaste for them."

"How could he," Madeline interrupted, "when he's never eaten one of us?"

"Yet," Dtimun said with a narrow glare in her direction.

Chacon chuckled. "This one would be too spicy for your palate, I think." He stared at Madeline. "Dr. Ruszel, I presume?"

He knew her? "Why…why, yes, sir," she faltered, her eyes wide with surprise.

"The human in the multisonic cell," Chacon explained, all the humor suddenly gone out of him. "He said to tell you that he didn't deserve the blue velvet ribbon this time." The Rojok frowned. "It makes no sense at all, this message he asked me to give you."

Madeline swallowed hard and stood as tall as she could. "It makes all the sense in the three galaxies, sir," she said with a glance at Stern, who nodded solemnly. "Thank you," she added huskily. "And thank you for…putting an end to the torture."

Chacon stared back at her, his eyes kindling with anger. "No soldier deserves such a death," he said curtly. "Even war demands some rough thread of honor, if only to remind us that it is all that separates us from savagery." His eyes swept to Dtimun. "I must take you to Mangus Lo. As I once allowed you to take me to the *Pyrecrete* on Thesalfohn. You remember?"

Dtimun's eyes went gray with thoughtfulness, and suddenly burst with colors, the predominant flash of which was green. His gaze went to Stern and Komak. He read accurately the coiled alertness in them, felt the tension of muscles waiting to spring.

"I will go with you," he told Chacon at once. Then he added, quickly, "Watch these two beside me. They will attack if they can."

Komak and Stern stiffened, their eyes incredulous as they met the Holconcom commander's. Something flashed in his, a passage of information that registered also in Komak's eyes.

Komak straightened. "We will not interfere. My word as a Holconcom."

Stern's mouth flew open. "What the hell...?"

"You can't just let him take you away!" Madeline burst out. "Not after all the time and effort and sacrifice of lives...!"

"Do not interfere," Komak shot at her.

"I'm not interfering!" she muttered, her lips set. "But I'm not going to stand here and watch my greatest medical achievement walk off to the sonic ovens...!"

"Bring her, too," Chacon said curtly as his guards graved the cell doorway open. "We have no time for verbal combat."

"Maddie, no!" Stern cried, diving for the guard.

Komak caught him with one long, efficient arm and held him, struggling and cursing, until the cell closed once more. Stern fought the younger alien for all he was worth, but he couldn't match Komak's steely strength. First Strick, now Maddie. It was beyond bearing!

"Damn you, let...me...go!" Stern roared, and with an inhuman burst of strength, he actually broke the Holconcom's hold and stood facing him with dilated eyes, his body crouched to attack.

"No outworlder," Komak said blankly, "has ever escaped me!"

"There's always a first time," Stern replied harshly. "They'll do to her what they did to Hahnson, damn you! I ought to kill you, Komak!"

"You are welcome to make the attempt," Komak replied. "But it would be less a waste of time to let the force of life sweep you along instead of trying so hard to swim against the current."

"I am not in the mood for any damned Centaurian philosophy!" Stern raged.

"Stern, let it go," Madeline called to him, standing tall and proud between two Rojok bodyguards, her auburn hair gleaming like red honey in the light of the two moons as they hung low on the flat horizon. "I'm not afraid of these two-legged lizards," she said in a coldly, steady tone. "Just get the others out of here, Holt." And it was the first time since their escape from the Peace Planet that she'd used his first name. "Just do that, and it will have been worth it all. Okay?"

His fists clenched impotently. His eyes were dark, full of death and anguish. "You got it, Ladybones," he said very quietly.

Chacon, who had been watching the byplay as intently as Dtimun, nodded. "Loyalty. I have noticed it often in this particular humanoid sect. Even torture does nothing to weaken it."

"On the contrary," Dtimun replied, "I think it strengthens it. Lead on, Rojok. I will show you how a Holconcom faces the ovens."

Madeline straightened. "And I'll show you the human equivalent," she added, not to be outdone as she marched away beside Dtimun, surrounded by guards. "Give 'em hell, boys!" she yelled to the SSC officers and men in the cells.

Cheers went up from the prisoners as the small group disappeared from sight. And it wasn't just the humans cheering.

15

"Why?" Stern asked Komak, the fury still in him as the other humans moved to his side in the cramped cell.

"Trust me," Komak said, not oblivious to the confrontation in the making as the other Holconcom surged around him. The female medic was beloved by the human element. They would not understand why Komak had stopped Stern from preventing her removal from the cell.

"You ask a hell of a lot," Stern said flatly, and saw Higgins nod beside him.

"I know," Komak told him with a soft green smile in his eyes. "I have a—how is it said?—feeling of affection for the fire-haired female. I do not think that I could stand by and watch her go to her death. Knowing that, will you now trust me, even though I cannot provide evidence to support my actions?"

Stern scowled. His eyes measured the Holconcom officer and he knew, suddenly, that one word from him would decide between the forged comradeship of the prison and a life or death struggle in this small cell. One word could have the humans and the Holconcom in a minor bloodbath. And some residue of the Rojok programming wondered what the outcome would be…

Madeline and Dtimun were taken quickly out of the cell complex into the Rojok flagship, its bulging saucer design comparable to the *Morcai,* except that this ship was at least twenty degrees hotter. Apparently the Rojoks were much like their exothermic reptile ancestors in their inability to produce heat internally.

Chacon led them into a compartment near the engine room, and, dismissing his select bodyguard, magnalocked himself in the small area with them. A touch of his graceful six-fingered hand cut off communications completely, a move Dtimun's sharp eyes didn't miss.

"*Maliche,* you tempt me!" Dtimun said shortly, his tall body tensing, the muscles rippling in his arms, his legs. "What manner of trickery is this? And what purpose does it serve?"

"Call it repayment of a debt, Centaurian," the Rojok officer said quietly. "You saved my life on Thesalfohn." He straightened. "I have Lyceria."

Dtimun seemed to explode. Without the appearance of movement, he had the Rojok by the throat and black death dilated in his eyes.

"Look into my mind, Dtimun," Chacon said steadily, no trace of fear in his slit eyes. "See the truth for yourself."

Madeline watched the byplay with fascination. These two didn't act like enemies.

"Where is she?" The Centaurian's grip tightened visibly.

"Two cubicles away, her mind in darkness that may become permanent if you do not listen to me!" Chacon growled, his fingers grasping Dtimun's wrist firmly, forcing the hand away from his throat. "Mangus Lo had her brought here from my harem and subjected to sensory deprivation…"

"Your harem?" Even as he spoke, his hand grasped the Rojok's throat a second time.

Chacon slapped it away and actually hit the Centaurian, sharply, across his broad chest. "*Islamesche,* will you listen to me, you hardheaded first cousin to a *shazemech?*" he thundered at Dtimun, his slit eyes like beams of black radiation. "Her sanity depends on you! I had her taken to my harem because it was the one place I thought Mangus Lo might not look for her, not because I used her as a warrior uses a *pazheen!* Now will you hear me?"

Dtimun seemed to relax, but only slightly. "*Mashcon shelach,*" he said quietly.

"She was placed in a sensory deprivation booth," Chacon continued, his eyes burning at the memory. "Her mind, in rebellion, has withdrawn into a shell. If it is not brought back into the light, and soon, she will remain so for her lifetime. You and Dr. Ruszel, between you, must find a manner of returning her to reality. You are her only hope, and there is little time. My presence here is against explicit orders. Mangus Lo will know it very soon and send his bodyguard to intercept me."

Madeline was puzzled at the reason a Rojok commander would risk his life for a Centaurian captive, but she didn't have time to ponder it. "Is she aware of her surroundings at all?" Madeline asked professionally. "Does she respond to verbal stimuli?"

"She has not spoken since I brought her from the chamber," Chacon said quietly. "She only stares into space with eyes that see nothing. Nor does she move."

"With an injection," Madeline told him, "there's a possibility that

I can stimulate the neurons in her brain to activity. But it would take neuroprobing by a psychtech to reach her mind and coax it back. I haven't the credentials or the training for that."

"That is why I have brought Dtimun," Chacon said mysteriously.

The two aliens exchanged a look that Madeline couldn't decipher.

"I would know what your reason is for taking such a risk as this," Dtimun told the Rojok. "And you must realize how great a risk it is. Inevitably there will be a confrontation, especially if you have defied Mangus Lo to come here. He will have his spies watching."

"The confrontation forms as we speak," Chacon replied. "As to my reason, I have never been known to tear wings from starflies, Centaurian," he added. "This camp makes me want to retch. Until I came here myself, against the emperor's orders, I had no idea of its depravity. We were told that it was a camp for political prisoners and that the gossip by outworlders was only propaganda."

Madeline frowned. "Sir, you've never been here?" she asked Chacon.

"It was forbidden by military protocol," he said. "I see why, now. War is one thing—I can see rare glimpses of nobility even in its horror. But this place is an affront to sanity. It should be reduced to atoms and a Tri-D projector left in its place to flaunt forever the fruits of appeasement. You know of what I speak," he added.

"Yes," Dtimun agreed. "The Tri-Galaxy Council has a history of appeasement and pacifism."

"One of your senators knows of this place," Chacon said, surprising his companions. "And he has said nothing to his colleagues about it. Money has changed hands. You understand?"

"Who?" Dtimun asked, making a laser of the word.

Chacon shook his head. "I know nothing of his appearance or position, only that he is a senator and has links to our empire. A doctor has helped him. Not this one," he said, with a faintly pleasant glance at

Madeline. "A psychologist. But we have no time for discussions of genocide. I am a soldier, not a diplomat. Mangus Lo's insanity is no less than that of your Tri-Galaxy Council, which permits him to commit genocide with mild protests and no military action to speak of."

Dtimun only nodded. "The bureaucrats of the Council decided long ago to deny the New Territory to nonmember worlds, a decision which surely forced your people to war, since your politics and those of the Council will never mix. However, at the moment my concern goes no further than the daughter of Tnurat Alamantimichar—and my *Morcai* Battalion."

Madeline smothered a grin at that last sentence. The Holconcom commander who first, and reluctantly, brought humans aboard his ship in what seemed lifetimes ago, would never have made such a statement.

"I will have the princess brought here," Chacon said, moving to the bulkhead, which concealed a private discalator. He stepped inside. "I will return shortly. You will not be disturbed."

Madeline and the *Morcai*'s commander were left alone to study each other quietly, warily, with eyes free to discover, to explore, out of sight of other eyes.

"You have no fear of the Rojok commander," Dtimun said.

She nodded. "When he first got here," she said, "an aide to the Rojok commandant of this place was…slicing off Hahnson's fingers. He'd already used multisonics on him and the screams…" She drew a breath. "Anyway, it was just one more unbearable torture, and his hands…you know, they mean everything to a surgeon…and the Rojok was just slicing them away! Chacon didn't bother with accusations or explanations. He whipped out his *chasat* and cut down the camp commandant who ordered the torture, along with the guard who'd been doing the torture." A tiny, bitter smile touched her full mouth. "He cared. He cared that a soldier was being tortured, and he didn't stop to see what race the victim belonged to or whether or not he was an ally. Compassion is such a rare virtue, Commander," she added. "My father—he's a mean-tempered colonel in the Para-guard—says that it's the death of an army and shouldn't be tolerated. But a few of us escape the indoctrination."

"Your father is Colonel Clinton Ruszel, is he not?" Dtimun asked her, and a green smile touched his eyes at the astonishment in her face.

"Why…yes!" she stammered.

"You were only four years old when your father and I rescued you and two hundred other Tri-Fleet children from terrorists on Mal-gomar. I doubt you remember the incident, but I remember you vividly, Madam. I picked you out of a cremeceton bush, and the in-stant you were free of the thorns, you sank your teeth into my forearm." He pulled back his sleeve and showed her the tiny scar buried in the dark hairs of his golden-skinned flesh. "I promised Clinton that day that I would repay the injury when you were older."

"What did he say?" she asked curiously.

"That you would likely die of blood poisoning from biting me," he told her, with a green smile in his eyes. "Now," he said, the smile fading to blue concern, "tell me about Stern. All of it."

And she did, every bit of it, ending with the cloned human's attempt to unite the prisoners, save Hahnson, and to help her save Dtimun. "He'll be persecuted, you know," she said defeatedly. "They'll never trust him. They'll say he's just a clone and give him over to the rimscouts, and they might as well lob his head off as assign him there. Clones are people, too. They should have rights, just as we do. But in my society," she added curtly, "it isn't like that. Clones are property. Stern's clone…is all I have left, now. Stern and Hahnson are both dead…" She turned away, ashamed of the emotion that was betraying itself in her face, her voice.

"And the emperor's young son, along with them," Dtimun said quietly. "War demands many sacrifices, Madam, none of them pleasant."

Before she could reply, the bulkhead opened and Chacon stepped through it, the lithe form of the Centaurian princess clasped close in his strong arms, cradled like some exquisite treasure against his broad chest.

And like a puzzle suddenly putting itself together, Madeline knew why the Rojok field marshal had risked so much to come here. It hadn't been to free the prisoners. It had been to find and rescue Lyceria.

Why, she thought incredulously, *he loves her!*

"Obviously, Madam," Dtimun said aloud, but absently, as if he'd forgotten himself in the emotion of the moment.

But Madeline flushed to her toes as the truth sank in. The Holconcom commander had read her mind. Those two words had linked her to a secret that probably no other officer knew, not in the civilized worlds. It was a tremendous responsibility, that knowledge. But as she watched him stare at the princess, she wondered if he even knew that he'd given himself away.

Chacon laid the princess gently on a velvety couch against one bulkhead and stood back. Madeline moved to the young woman's side, using the wrist scanner as a neurosensor to ascertain the damage. Even as she worked, she marveled at the princess's feline beauty. She was like a graceful work of art chiseled from golden stone.

"Well?" Dtimun asked impatiently, glancing at Madeline.

"Sorry," she murmured as she injected the motionless body with a neurostimulant and stood erect. "She's very beautiful," she explained with a self-conscious smile.

Dtimun looked at her and she felt odd tinglings in her body, as if it had been stroked. *As are you,* she imagined she heard in her mind. She must be imagining things!

She cleared her throat. "If you probe her mind, very gently," she told Dtimun, "and coax her consciousness back with the barest suggestion of reality, there's a chance. Her mind is damaged, but not beyond repair. The thing is to make her want to live. But you have to be patient."

He nodded, slowly, his eyes probing hers until she lowered her gaze. He sat down beside Lyceria on the low couch. He smiled. "A hunter learns patience in infancy, Madam," he told the female physician. "In all things," he added deliberately, with a taunting green smile in his eyes.

She blushed, again astonished that he could provoke such a response.

Dtimun closed his eyes and Chacon scowled as he stood riveted to the spot, waiting, waiting...

"Commander Chacon!" came a sudden shout from the other side of the bulkhead. "Commander, the emperor's flagship is throwing its antigravs in orbit, in preparation for a landing. Our agents think he and his personal bodyguard have come with Mekkar to take you!"

"Later," Chacon murmured, his eyes fixed on Lyceria. "Later, Lieumek. I have no time for war now."

Madeline studied the Rojok in silence. And wondered if there was so much difference in their races after all.

Stern watched Komak in a silence that grew unbearable before he finally relaxed his threatening stance with a harsh sigh.

"I have to trust you," he said finally, and with a grin. "It's a little too late for anything else, now."

Higgins was watching something in the distance with curious eyes. "Sir, what's going on over there?" he asked.

Stern and Komak joined him at the front of the domed cell. While they watched, two shiploads of Rojoks, red-uniformed, gained entry at the front of the massive domed complex, silhouetted against the darkening sky with its band of dark red bathed in dying sunset.

"Mangus Lo's personal guard," Komak said uneasily. "Here to kill Chacon, unless I miss my guess. The Rojok commander, by coming here to rescue the Centaurian princess, has condemned himself to death."

"Rescue the princess...!" Stern gaped at him. "Is she *here?*"

"Of course. Why do you think he took the commander and Ruszel if not to mend her from *Ahkmau*'s tortures?" Komak asked calmly.

"But how do you know?" Stern demanded.

Komak looked uneasy. His eyes averted to the new complement of Rojoks entering the camp. "It was known to us that the Rojok emperor had her," he said. "We thought she would be brought here."

"But that doesn't explain," Stern persisted.

"Later, Stern," Komak replied. "We have problems enough."

"You're sure that's why the Rojok commander took them? He isn't going to stick them in a sonic oven?"

Komak shook his head. "I assure you, that was not his intention."

"Then she'll be all right," Stern said with a heavy sigh. "Thank God. And we'll be all right, too."

"Think so, sir?" Higgins asked uncomfortably, nodding toward the complex's entrance, where two full companies of red-clad Rojok elite guardsmen were just entering the darkened complex.

Darkness. Darkness everywhere, and behind the wall it was safe and warm. Coldness outside, a numb coldness that was deadly. She must not leave the wall. She dared not!

But...a voice was calling. Remembered and beloved, a voice was calling to her from the darkness. She wanted to go and find it. But the cold, the cold...!

Again and again, the slow, deep voice whispered, and like a silver shadow, it touched her. She ventured to the very edge of the wall and stood, trembling, listening. Again it came, coaxing, beckoning to her...

"I am afraid," she thought to it. "Afraid!"

"You cannot stay behind the wall forever," it whispered to her mind.

"I can. I can! It is safe here, and warm, and nothing can harm me."

"That is existence, not life. We were not meant to stay in the womb. Without conflict, there is stagnation. Without agony, there is no ecstasy. Come out."

Tears were in the soft voice now. "I do not wish to be born again!" she thought. "I am safe. Oh, let me stay here!"

"And do what?"

"And...simply stay here. I need do nothing."

"What will you accomplish, by doing nothing?"

"You...confuse me. Go away!"

"No."

"Please!"

"You will miss the sunlight, the touch of *canolithe* on the *celamas*. You will miss the smell of green things, the soft cut of the wind on your face. You will miss life."

"I will not be hurt here," she protested. "You offer me pain!"

"Pain, and pleasure. After the cut, the kiss of healing." There was a pause. "The Rojok is here."

A reaction! Her mind burst with color. "He? The bad-tempered one?"

"The one who took you to his harem."

"Yes, to save me from Mangus Lo. And he never touched me..." A pause. "Chacon? He is here?"

"Yes. He risked everything to find you, to save you."

Another burst of color. "He was kind to me. Kind, even when I cursed him. When I told him that I would prefer *Ahkmau* to his harem, I saw him flinch. I...he makes silver ripples, in my mind."

"He waits. Come out and see."

"For him, I would walk into *Ahkmau* again. Are you ashamed of me, *becamon tare?*"

"You will never call me that in the presence of others!" he flashed at her.

"Oh, do not be angry with me," she pleaded. "I promise."

"Come, then."

"Perhaps I will. For the bad-tempered one. And for you."

Lyceria's great cat-eyes opened suddenly, to the amazement of the two spectators, who had heard none of the exchange between the two Centaurians.

Her gaze, blue and soft, went first to Madeline, who was nearest, and then to Chacon, who stood like stone, watching, worried.

While Chacon looked long and deeply into the Centaurian woman's soft, blue eyes, Dtimun moved to the synthesizer on the wall and calmly ordered a *chasat* from it.

He took the weapon, turned and leveled it at Chacon. "And now," he said, "you will move in front of us into the complex and I will free my command."

Madeline winced. It had been a truce. But she considered the price her comrades had already paid, she couldn't voice her opposition.

"Is this an example of Centaurian integrity?" Chacon asked proudly.

"An example of necessity," Dtimun replied. "This is war and I am a soldier. My primary duty is to free my men."

"With a single *chasat?*" Chacon probed. "Once, you would not have needed a weapon, I think."

An odd look passed between the two aliens. "So. This explains why Mangus Lo would risk a fleet on my capture."

"I told him nothing!" Chacon retorted, eyes blazing.

Lyceria moved gracefully forward. She stared at the Rojok for a long moment. "He speaks truth," she told Dtimun.

The tall Centaurian's body relaxed, but only a millimeter. "I must use the tools I have to procure our release. A *chasat* is more visible than other...inducements," he added enigmatically.

"But he saved my life," Lyceria interjected.

"And if I had the choice, I would spare his," Dtimun replied solemnly. "Let us go."

The four no sooner left the Rojok ship and moved out into the dark complex than the newly arrived red-clad Rojok force was sighted, entering at the gates, only to be met by an equal force of Chacon's personal bodyguard in its black uniform.

"What the...!" Madeline exclaimed.

"The Rojok emperor's personal elite, are they not?" Dtimun asked the Rojok field marshal, his great eyes narrowing, darkening. "Because of Lyceria, Rojok?"

Chacon laughed shortly. "Because I dared to oppose this insanity, and to his face."

Without hesitation, Dtimun flipped the *chasat* and handed it to Chacon. "I would have made a Holconcom of you, under other circumstances."

"And I, a *mecmec* of you," Chacon replied with dignity. "*Karamesh,* is that not what you Centaurians call it? *T'cleemech,* Dtimun of Centauria," he said, extending an arm.

"*T'cleemech,* Chacon."

"Now go, quickly, while this contest of forces plays itself out," Chacon told them. "With luck, you may effect the rescue after all, and lacking a high-level hostage."

The Rojok's eyes went one last time to the Centaurian princess, whose anguish was plain in her beautiful dark blue eyes. He smiled gently at her before he turned with the *chasat* close at his side to join his men, who were massing at the gate of the complex.

Unbelievably a sob broke from the lips of the Centaurian princess.

"Bataashe!" Dtimun growled fiercely, his eyes silencing the alien woman. "Remember who you are!"

Wordlessly she bowed her head in deference to his authority, while Madeline looked on with pure shock. She was certain that no other military commander in the Tri-Galaxy would dare speak to a member of the Royal Family like that.

"Will he escape, do you think?" Madeline asked, to break the tension, as she jogged along beside the two gracefully moving Centaurians.

"Chacon is an able commander," Dtimun replied, "and his personal guard is formidable in the field. He commands a loyalty not evident in Mangus Lo's bodyguard."

"Those guards in the black uniforms," Madeline muttered, watching them mass in the distance where Chacon had disappeared, "look formidable."

"Wait until we release our men," Dtimun replied, "and you will see a formidable force, Madam. The Rojoks will regret what they have done to us, I promise you."

And, she thought impishly, they would certainly give Chacon and his men a fighting chance to escape, as well.

"An interesting proposition, is it not?" Dtimun said aloud, glancing at her with a flicker of green in his eyes. She blushed for the second time in a single day, aware also of dancing green lights in the Centaurian princess's soft eyes.

As soon as they reached the dimly lit cell that contained Stern and the others, Dtimun used his fist to jam the mechanism and pop the hyperglas open like a ripe melon.

"Time is precious," he told the officers inside. "Come with me."

"I wouldn't miss this for a thousand mems and two months' liberty!" Stern chuckled maliciously.

"Nor would I," Komak agreed, relieved to see the two comrades and his commander reappear in such good health.

"He is here!" Lyceria said suddenly, in a harsh tone. "Mangus Lo. He is here!"

"Where?" Dtimun demanded.

She turned around slowly, stopped and indicated the newly arrived Rojok ship. "There! He waits for his bodyguard to bring Chacon to him, so that he can be killed!" Her eyes, wide and fearful, sought Dtimun's.

"He will not kill the field marshal," Dtimun said quietly.

"We're going to make a try for Mangus Lo, aren't we, sir?" Stern asked with a grin.

Dtimun shot him a glance from eyes that glowed green in the darkness. "A try, Mister?"

Stern chuckled. "Excuse me. I meant to say, we're going to capture him, aren't we, sir?"

Dtimun's eyes laughed. "After I turn these men loose, yes, I am, and level *Ahkmau* in the process," he added with a glance at the Centaurian princess, who nodded curtly.

"The men will enjoy that," Madeline said.

"So will I," Dtimun replied grimly.

"No official state of war exists between Centauria and the Rojok empire, as I recall," Stern reminded him suddenly. "If you capture the Rojok emperor…"

"You humans are at war with him, Stern," he said. "I'll let you present him to the Council with your own explanations. Ruszel, keep close to Lyceria," he added as they left the cell in the darkness.

"Yes, sir," she replied, managing a smile for the beautiful Centaurian woman, who eyed her with open curiosity and shy friendliness.

Stern watched the two women together, wondering vaguely at the difference between them. Centaurian women had no warrior class as the humans did. Still, they seemed amiable enough. His eyes went to Dtimun, and farther, to Chacon's men confronting the emperor's elite, where loud voices arguing in feverish Rojok echoed through the darkness.

"A benevolent hand guides our path today," Komak said. "The confrontation may give us just enough time to escape."

As they neared the cell closest to the one they'd vacated, the sound of a *chasat* firing echoed in the stillness.

16

As *chasat* fire began to echo around the complex, Dtimun slammed his fist into the magnalock of the next cell in line and popped the hyperglas open.

Before Stern had time to wonder how Dtimun planned to deploy the troops, the problem was already being solved. The cell's occupants, human and Centaurian, poured out into the reddish darkness, acting as if there'd never been a hint of animosity between them.

"Attention!" Dtimun called in a commanding tone. "Who's ranking officer in this group?"

"I am, sir," a thin Strategic Space Command engineer said, moving forward in a salute. "Lieutenant Hugh Jenkins, Terravegan Engineering Corps."

"Jenkins, take Lyceria," he said, leading the princess forward, "and your group through to the *Morcai*. Take the ship. I don't care how, or with what casualties. Get the *Morcai*."

"I'll get it, sir," Jenkins said. "But, the lady, sir…"

"Will be as safe with you as she would with me, Mister," he replied shortly. "And you may find her a help rather than a hindrance if you meet overwhelming opposition. Move out."

"Yes, sir!" The Terravegan engineer whipped a salute and motioned his group into action behind him.

Madeline was saddened to remember, at that moment, the brilliant engineer who'd been part of her now-dead Amazon squad: Tilitha Qua, an Altairian of uncanny mechanical skill. Her squad would have helped level the playing field here. And it might have given this chauvinistic alien commander a few uncomfortable minutes, because her women were the equal of any of his men.

But the moment passed. If she kept looking back, she'd remember Hahnson, and she'd be no good to anyone. This was a dire circumstance, which would require the best they had to give.

With the next cell group, it was the same, and the next and the next, while still the Rojoks returned fire at the entrance of the complex. Dtimun assigned one team the duties of a demolition squad; he sent communications officer Jennings and an ordnance expert to see to the disruption of the complex's massive communications network. But he was careful, Stern noticed, to pick one medic out of each group to stay behind with those who were too weak to travel or fight. And into one separate core group, he gathered the sturdiest looking men of his Holconcom and kept them with the executive officers of both the *Morcai* and the *Bellatrix*.

When the ship's complement was freed, the men quickly scoured the remaining cells in the complex, a task that grew so distasteful that even the nerveless Holconcom began to show signs of nausea. The Jebob nationals among the prison complement were the worst, the most tortured. They had been deprived of solid food for so long that they were unable to sit up without help. They looked like skeletons, their blue skin purplish with lack of protein, their great round eyes so pitiful that they brought tears to Madeline's eyes. There was so little left of their minds after the multisonic torture that they couldn't hear the softest voice without screaming in pain. They simply...sat.

"We have no more time," Dtimun said finally. "We must attack while we have the opportunity, before the confrontation outside is decided and we lose the element of surprise. Leave these people for now. When we have fought free, we will do what we can for them. If we hesitate, we may all remain here forever."

"Yes, sir," Madeline replied sadly. He was right, of course, and her wrist scanner was being put to uses for which it was never designed. She was tired and weak herself.

"Even if we manage to escape," young Crandall said behind them, "how in the seven netherworlds will we ever get all these hundreds, thousands, of prisoners out of here?"

"God knows," Stern said. "The *Morcai* won't hold them."

"The hospital ship *Freespirit* would," Madeline broke in.

"Indeed," Dtimun agreed at once, holding up the remaining three groups of prisoners behind one of the dark guard stations. "But first we must free the camp," he said. "Higgins, take Abemon, Crandall and Mezekar with you and get a message through to the Midmeridian Aid Station on Algomar before Jennings can disable communications here. Tell them the *Freespirit* is desperately needed to assist in evacuation."

"Isn't that taking a hell of a risk?" Stern asked uneasily. "If we don't make it..."

"We'll make it, Mister," Dtimun told him, and the power was there in his eyes, glowing, burning, dark and deadly. "Go, Higgins!"

"Yes, sir!" The *Bellatrix*'s exec threw the Centaurian a smart salute and led his party toward the main command post.

Dtimun pulled eight of the Holconcom out of the group and there was a flurry of discussion, all in Centaurian. He motioned Madeline to him and they all gathered around her. Stern couldn't see what was going on, but it seemed to involve the commander's hair, of all things. Before he had time to wonder, the Holconcom saluted and rushed off into the darkness.

"The rest of you," Dtimun said to the intermingled Centaurians and humans, "we're going to take out as many of the Rojoks as we can on our way to the spaceport. You've all gathered up *chasats* as we freed prisoners from the few remaining guards. You're armed. I know some of you are very weak. But this is our only chance to escape. Let us make the Rojoks pay for what our people have endured here." He looked deliberately at the humans, weak but still standing at attention with determination on their faces. "When I send my Holconcom into battle, it is with but one order—*Malenchar!* I cannot make an exact translation into Standard, but it roughly amounts to this—engage the enemy and give them hell! Your targets are any Rojoks you find in red uniforms. The black-uniformed Rojoks are in as much danger of extermination as we are, so discriminate as carefully as you can when you fire. Questions?"

In the distance was the increasing fire of *chasats,* moving toward the domed complex where the prisoners were still escaping. "I think we've just run out of time," Stern interjected.

"Malenchar!" Dtimun yelled, turning to lead the others toward the source of the disturbance in a dead run.

At the command, the Holconcom began their ritual. The building growls Stern remembered from the *Morcai*'s mess hall echoed through the post with a mind-paralyzing intensity, from threatening growls that lifted into a piercing, blood-freezing scream that was the *decaliphe*—the death cry of the Holconcom. And then, like living shadows, they attacked.

Even to Stern, prepared as he was for it, the sound left a strange knot in the pit of his stomach. But many of the Earthers in the group had never heard it—having missed the fight in the mess hall aboard the *Morcai*—and it froze them in their tracks as they neared the complex entrance.

"*Comcache*," Dtimun said softly to the humans, like the voice of an adult reassuring a frightened child.

Even as he spoke, the Rojoks were standing equally frozen, amid a landscape littered with dead and wounded Rojok bodies, their *chasats* leveled as they started looking wildly around for the source of the screams. Before they could find it, it found them.

The small group of Holconcom pounced on them from all sides, with the grace and speed and ferocity of humanoid cats, their strength as formidable as it had been before the removal of their microcyborgs. Only Madeline knew why, that she'd replaced them with the store she'd secreted under the commander's hair. The Holconcom went for the Rojok throats with a speed and grace that was terrifying to watch.

But it was only the red uniforms they attacked. The black-uniformed faction led by Chacon stood in visible confusion, just watching.

From all sides now, reinforcements were coming up, more *Ahkmau* guards closing with *chasats* firing at anything that moved.

Dtimun hesitated for an instant, fighting the weakness left over from his surgery, but it was only momentary. He straightened. "*Malenchar!*" he called to the remaining groups behind him.

The humans scooped up the fallen Rojok weapons, wading in to fire at the attacking Rojoks. The blue radiation made tiny flames on contact with the red fabric of the Rojok uniforms as it penetrated flesh.

At the same time, Madeline moved behind Stern and touched his scalp with some sort of cold instrument. He gave her a puzzled look. She only grinned.

Seconds later, Stern met the charge of a burly prison guard with taut muscles and a grim smile, his hands chopping at the alien almost simultaneously with the firing of the *chasat* that blasted him. Despite his genetic engineering, the *chasat* blast should have killed him. Incredulously the radiation danced lightly on Stern's chest without penetrating. The Rojok looked as shocked as Stern felt. He threw a *kojo* blow to the alien's neck with the flat of his hand and the Rojok dropped lifelessly to the hypoturf.

Blank-eyed, Stern looked down at himself and glanced at Dtimun, who was watching him with an amusement that Madeline seemed to share.

"Microcyborgs," she mouthed, and grinned.

"Did you...?" he asked Dtimun, for obviously the alien had authorized the removal of one of the units that had been hidden in his own scalp.

Something like a smile touched Dtimun's lips. "You are a member of my crew, are you not?" he asked simply. He turned. "Ruszel, get out of there!" he snapped at the auburn-haired physician, who'd stooped down to try to patch up one of the Holconcom left in her group. She didn't see the four red-uniformed Rojok guards heading straight for her until a *chasat* blast almost severed her ear.

"What the hell do you mean my daughter's lost behind enemy lines?" Colonel Clinton Ruszel yelled at Jeffrye Lawson, his silvered red hair burning against his tanned face in the light of the ceiling panels. "How did she get there in the first place?"

"Will you calm down and listen to me, Clint?" Jeffrye Lawson growled, slamming his fist down on the smooth, glassy surface of his desk.

"How can I calm down? Dammit, I thought she was on a routine rescue hop to Terramer. What happened?"

"Rojoks attacked the rescue party. They killed Holt Stern—you remember him, surely?" Lawson asked sadly, and the Paraguard officer nodded impatiently. "The *Bellatrix* was destroyed in the attack. Afterward, the entire crew of the *Bellatrix* was apparently taken aboard the Holconcom ship *Morcai*…"

"Dtimun's ship," Ruszel said at once and with a sigh of heartfelt relief. He sank down into one of the admiral's rigidly uncomfortable chairs. "Why the hell didn't you say so in the first place? She's all right, then."

"What?" Lawson asked blankly.

"If she's with Dtimun, she's safe, of course. My God, Jeff, I fought with him in the Great Galaxy War. Best damned commanding officer I ever served with. He helped me get Maddie and those Marcopian kids away from the terrorists, too," Ruszel recalled with a grin. "The Rojoks sure as hell couldn't capture him."

"Evidence is to the contrary," Lawson said apologetically. "Our reports indicate there's every chance that they've been taken to *Ahkmau*. It was one reason the Council agreed on a war vote. Old Tnurat practically threatened to declare war on them if they didn't."

"If Dtimun was taken to *Ahkmau*," Ruszel said stubbornly, "it was because he planned it that way. My God, Jeff, he's probably launched an all-out offensive and is liberating the place right now!"

Lawson drew in a weary breath. It was like arguing with a rock. "Clint," he began patiently.

"Admiral!" His adjutant's voice was breathless, his face jubilant as he appeared in the doorway.

"Yes, son?" Jeffrye asked.

"Sir, you're not going to believe this," the young officer said, laughing. "It's the *Freespirit*. She just got a distress call from *Ahkmau* for assistance in evacuating the inmates from the camp. And it was sent by the *Morcai* Battalion!"

"Now, what did I tell you, Jeffrye?" Clinton Ruszel said calmly. "And there you sat, worrying yourself into the grave."

"*Morcai* Battalion?" Jeffrye asked incredulously. "What the hell is that? And evacuating *Ahkmau*? Are you sure you heard right, boy?" he demanded of his adjutant, scowling.

"Yes, sir!" the younger man nodded.

"Well, if that's all you dragged me in here for," Ruszel said impatiently as he adjusted his service cap back on his head, "I'll be getting back to my command. Honest to God, Jeff, scaring the hell out of me, dragging an officer off the front lines with a bunch of garbage about kidnapped crewmen and prison camps…" He was still muttering to himself as he absentmindedly saluted on his way out the door.

Jeffrye Lawson simply stood there, watching him leave, his eyes staring at nothing.

"Do you think they'll get Mangus Lo himself, sir?" the adjutant was asking. "And the Jaakob Spheres? Gee, it would sure throw a monkey wrench into the Rojoks' morale, wouldn't it, sir?"

Lawson didn't hear him. He walked out the door with his hands folded behind him, still incredulous. "I wonder," he mused, "if we traded Tnurat Alamantimichar thirty Malumesser fighters and the design for our cadmium drive battlecruiser…maybe he'd loan us Dtimun?"

Stern started to rush toward Madeline, but Dtimun's steely arm shot out and held him back.

"She is safe, Stern," he said.

"Safe? But…!"

Even as the human protested, a *chasat* blast rocked the four attacking Rojoks, throwing them up into the air, to land in an unconscious heap on the hypoturf.

Madeline caught her breath. She'd been so engrossed in her work that she wasn't even aware of the danger she'd been in.

Chacon moved forward, lowering his *chasat* as he approached the small group. Behind him, there was a fireburst of color in the night sky followed instantly by the thunder of a huge explosion.

"The communications network, I dare say," Chacon said with a tiny smile as he stopped in front of Dtimun. "For a weary, beaten group of outworlders, you accomplish much in little time."

"And just consider that we've barely begun," Madeline agreed, joining them. She smiled self-consciously at the Rojok who'd saved her life. "Thank you, sir."

He nodded solemnly. His eyes studied Dtimun. "Strangely enough, only Mekkar's force was attacked by your men. My bodyguard was not touched. Can you explain this odd method of combat?"

"Black uniforms, sir," Stern said with a straight face. "Very hard to see at night."

"Absolutely," Madeline agreed. "The arrangement of the Terravegan retina, you know. We can hardly see black. Of course, red is easily detected."

"I myself have noticed this abnormality in humans," Komak agreed fervently.

Chacon's slit eyes twinkled. "By all rights," he told them, "I should do everything in my power to put you back in those cells. But the fact is, no state of war yet exists between the Rojok and Centaurian empires—and since these humans seem to belong to you, I must let you go."

"In which case, it might be wise to retire to your flagship, Rojok," Dtimun told him, "because it is my intention to leave bare desert in the place of this abomination."

"And the inmates?" Chacon asked.

"I have sent for the *Freespirit*."

"I understand." He hesitated. "You must know that Mangus Lo is even now at the spaceport in his flagship. He will have troops massing here when he ascertains the communication failure."

"Yes," Dtimun said. "But he will not know of the communications failure until he tries to send for help, and then it will be too late for him to call for reinforcements."

"You understand that I cannot condone your plans for *Ahkmau*, nor assist you."

"As has been said already, it is a pity we find ourselves on opposing sides," Dtimun said quietly. "Good fortune, Rojok."

"And to you," Chacon replied. "My...regards to the Centaurian princess," he added heavily, and without meeting Dtimun's gaze.

Dtimun watched the Rojok walk away proudly, his eyes narrowed in concentration. "By opposing Mekkar's force, he has condemned himself to a public execution. I can almost believe it was intentional, to divert Mekkar while we make our escape."

"With all due respect, Commander," Stern said with solemn, dark eyes, "we'd be dead already if he hadn't intervened. If we took Mangus Lo home with us, there wouldn't be anyone to give the order to execute the Rojok field marshal. Would there?"

Dtimun raised an eyebrow. His eyes twinkled green. "A thought which has also occurred to me," he replied. "Ruszel, arm yourself and stay with Abemon. Komak, Stern, with me."

Madeline glared at him with her hands on her hips. "I will take it personally if you die out there," she muttered. "It wasn't an easy job, putting you back together again. Sir." She glanced at Stern. "That goes double for you."

"Nothing to worry about, Maddie," Stern assured her. "We Centaurians are as formidable as all hell, aren't we, Commander?" He grinned at Dtimun.

A flash of green escaped the alien's control, but was just as quickly erased from his eyes. "We have little time. Can you use that, if you have to?" he asked Madeline as they turned to leave, indicating the captured *chasat* he'd given her.

She gave him an incredulous look. "I commanded an Amazon squad."

He pursed his lips. "I was referring to your knowledge of Rojok technology, not your courage. Of that, I have seen proof."

She cleared her throat. "Sorry, sir." She gave him a snappy salute, raised her eyebrows at Stern and moved out with her group.

With Dtimun in the lead, the three *Morcai* officers swept past the liberation effort, where humans and Holconcom were still opening the huge capsule barracks to free the ragged, cheering inmates. The hypoturf was littered with the bodies of red-uniformed Rojoks, the finest of Mangus Lo's handpicked escort troops. Obviously they'd met their match in Chacon's elite unit.

"What kind of chance have we got of getting through to Mangus Lo?" Stern asked as Dtimun darted through the entrance of the complex into the tube that led to the nearby spaceport.

"A good one," Dtimun replied. "Most of his personal bodyguard was dispatched to eliminate Chacon. There will be only a skeleton crew aboard his flagship."

"Accommodating of Mangus Lo," Stern remarked.

"Indeed," Komak agreed. "Commander, look! Our men have secured the spaceport!"

"Our men" were the humans led by the engineering officer, Jenkins. The Centaurian princess was waiting beside the *Morcai*'s elevator tube, her eyes green with triumphant laughter as she sighted Dtimun.

"You are victorious," she said gently. "I knew you would be."

"*Karamesh,*" Dtimun replied with a flash of green eyes. "Jenkins, was there no resistance?" he asked the human, sweeping the area for signs of Rojoks and finding none.

"Quite a bit, actually, sir," Jenkins replied, scratching his head. "But about time we opened fire on them, the princess moved in front of us and they…well, they ran away, sir," he said feebly. "I'm at a loss to understand it."

Dtimun only smiled. "Leave a crew here to guard the ship," Dtimun told him. "And assist Dr. Ruszel in getting the Terramer survivors back aboard. The *Freespirit* has been sent for. If it arrives before the three of us return, take the *Morcai* back to Trimerius. You understand?" he added deliberately. "Tell Higgins."

Jenkins swallowed, hard. He knew what the commander meant. The three of them might not come back. "Yes, sir," he said quietly.

Dtimun led his two companions toward a sleek sandskimmer and slammed into the pilot's seat, leaving Stern and Komak to jump in as he activated the engine and it began to whine.

"Insanity," Dtimun muttered. "Komak, you, at least, should stay behind."

"Unnecessary," Komak said smugly.

The older alien gave him a glare. "I distrust this perception of yours. You might at least give the impression that you are not reliving history."

Komak cleared his throat. "There is Mangus Lo's flagship," he said quickly, indicating a ship from which a few red-uniformed Rojoks were exiting.

"We're going to storm his flagship, aren't we?" Stern asked with a cold smile. "I'm looking forward to that."

"Keep your hands away from Mangus Lo, Mister," Dtimun cautioned as the skimmer lifted and shot ahead toward the distant Rojok ship.

Stern said nothing, but his thoughts were dark. Because of the Rojok tyrant, he would go through life as a carbon copy of a dead man, with fewer rights in Terravegan society than a block of wood. He would never command a ship again. He would never know the pleasure of comrade-ship with his mates. He would never forget the sound of Hahnson's screams. And for the sum total of his living nightmares, he owed Mangus Lo a debt he fully intended to pay. And if the Centaurian killed him for it, that was all right, too. After all, he was already dead.

Dtimun landed the skimmer a short distance from the ship. It was a Rojok skimmer, and it attracted no attention from the two bored guards at the lift.

As they exited the skimmer, a Rojok voice cried, *"Cleemaah!"* and a *chasat* fired at the three uniformed humanoids he hadn't even seen until he ran right into them.

Stern automatically threw the alien's arm aside and darted a sharp thrust of his fingers up under the Rojok's rib cage, dropping him instantly.

"Mangus Lo should have the Jaakob Spheres on his ship, along with the captive scientists. His paranoia would not have allowed him to leave them on Enmehkmehk," Dtimun told them as they moved closer to the lift. "He does not even trust his own guards in matters of security. But the ship will be well guarded. We must expect resistance."

"I hope we get it," Stern said coldly. "Nothing would please me more. Lead on, sir."

17

Dtimun led the way through minor resistance. Rojok guards were quickly and quietly disposed of along the way. They arrived at the entrance to Mangus Lo's portable throne room in a matter of minutes.

The door, gleaming with color, was reminiscent of carnival colors in its gaudiness. "The throne room," he told the others quietly. "I memorized textdiscs of the Rojok flagship many years ago."

That didn't surprise Stern. "How many bodyguards will he have, do you think?"

Dtimun closed his eyes. He opened them almost immediately. "Twelve. Two to the left of the entrance, four at either side of the entrance to the tyrant's throne room, six near the throne itself. Let's go!"

Stern didn't have time to wonder how he knew that. The instant the bulkhead entrance was opened up, red-uniformed Rojoks swarmed the incoming threat.

Pulse racing, throat dry, Stern ducked a *chasat* blast and attacked, knocking down one of the Rojok guards and finishing him in one smooth motion. He grabbed up the fallen *chasat* and leveled it at the next enemy soldier who came into range, firing instantly. Oblivious to the sounds of the *decaliphe* that burst from the throats of his companions behind him, he moved quickly down the corridor that led directly to the throne room.

The six remaining Rojoks were massed at the entrance to the throne room, *chasats* leveled and ready. Stern would have rushed them, even so, but just as he crouched for a burst of speed, two red blurs went past him with a grace and speed that left him breathless.

The horror of *Ahkmau,* the sacrificed comrades, the sadistic jeering of the guards while they tortured Hahnson—all of it added to the flame of his hatred as he waded into the fray. All he could see were shocks of blond hair and blurs of reddish bronzed skin and red uniforms. Blindly he shouldered his way through the Rojoks while Komak and Dtimun attacked. Mangus Lo. Mangus Lo. He was going to kill the madman. Nobody in the world was going to stop him. There was no other thought in his mind as he made his way into the imperial chamber. Something hit his arm with a staggering blow, and for a moment it burned with pain. He didn't spare it a glance. As long as the muscles still worked, he didn't care if the flesh was stripped down to the bone. He remembered vaguely that the bone was almost indestructible anyway. He kept moving.

As he reached the door, *chasating* one last Rojok guard to the floor, he rammed the handle of the weapon into the magnalock housing. The sound of tinkling glass accompanied the sudden release of the door to the imperial throne. It slipped up like a tightly wound spring suddenly released.

And there he was. The scourge of Enmehkmehk. The terror of

Ahkmau. The source of the Tri-Galaxy Council's nightmares. The emperor of the Rojoks. Majesty in red robes that looked two sizes too big for him. Authority with one dead leg that dragged behind his squat body. Arrogance with bowed legs and a face like a wrinkled red prune.

"Who are you?" Mangus Lo screamed.

"Death on two legs," Stern replied quietly, raising the *chasat.*

Eyes dial-round in fear, Mangus Lo backed against his trophy case. If Stern had any idea of sparing his life, it was abruptly gone. There, within the oval confines of the huge, glassy showcase, was the head of a beautiful young Altairian boy, staring ahead with sightless spherical eyes, the blue skin pale in death.

"You sadist," Stern breathed venomously, remembering what had been done to Hahnson. "You bloody, inhuman…!"

Throwing the *chasat* down, his hands went to the alien's neck and he shook him violently, ignoring the pleas and threats, the cries that grew strangled in the Rojok's thick throat. Hahnson's head might have been in that case, or Madeline's, if Chacon hadn't arrived when he did.

Somewhere in the back of his mind he heard a voice shouting at him. He ignored it. His hands tightened. Blind, deaf, dumb, he smiled down at the terrified little alien with bloodlust burning in his mind as the fear in Mangus Lo's eyes fed his satisfaction.

But suddenly the neck of his dirty, ragged uniform contracted like a tourniquet, jerking him clear of the floor to hang some two feet off the ground, as if suspended by a coathook. His hold on the little dictator only tightened.

"Drop him," a cold, familiar voice commanded.

He knew Dtimun's voice, but it didn't register. He wasn't letting go.

"Drop him!" The hand contracted.

Stern reluctantly let the emperor slide out of his grasp onto the floor.

He slumped. He was suddenly very tired. Sadly, it seemed that the Holconcom commander wasn't going to allow him to kill Mangus Lo. Pity.

"Spoilsport," he muttered as he rearranged his collar.

"Dtimun!" Mangus Lo whispered through his tortured windpipe, his slit eyes widening. "I have you now! With you as my prisoner, I can conquer the galaxies! No Centaurian would dare stand against me...!"

Dtimun's eyes burned black. His hand shot out and grasped the Rojok's fat neck, lifting him completely off the deck. And for an instant, Mangus Lo wavered between life and death.

"No fair, Commander!" Stern grumbled. "If I can't kill him, neither can you."

Dtimun met the human's eyes levelly. He drew in a long breath. His eyes, calmer, went back to the Rojok emperor. "The Jaakob Spheres. Where are they?"

"Here!" Komak said from the rear of the throne room, his green eyes laughing as he held up a glowing amber globe with the hope of the free galaxies inside. In the center was a cluster of tiny globes, each containing DNA from a racial type, with documentation written in a dead language. He smiled. "Evidently the Rojok scientists could not decipher them," he added. "They are recorded in Old High Martian."

"Where are the scientists?" Dtimun demanded of Mangus Lo.

The old emperor glared at him. "They refused to translate them. They were expendable."

"As was the Centaurian prince?" Dtimun added in a voice so soft and dangerous that Stern felt uncomfortable.

Mangus Lo looked at him blankly. "He would not tell me where you were," he said, as if it should have been perfectly clear why the boy was tortured. "I have had this plan in mind for some time, to attack Terramer and kidnap the Centaurian elite, so that you would be forced to come and rescue them." The Rojok smiled coldly. "What are a few thousand lives, if I have you at my side? The greatest of the alien commanders—without you, the Tri-Galaxy Fleet could not menace us…!"

Dtimun glared at him. "You are completely mad," he pronounced.

The old Rojok blinked. "You will decipher the Spheres for me," he said quickly. "Then you may take Chacon's place at my side. I will give you a planet to rule, servants, women! Chacon must die," he added, his mind obviously far removed from the reality of his capture. "He disobeyed me and came here. My guards say that he actually saved the Centaurian princess. I sent her here to die, because your men would not give you to my guards…" He frowned and stared at Dtimun. "How did you escape?"

"You will have a brief time to ponder that before your execution," Dtimun told him, still furious.

The emperor smiled. "You will never get out of here alive, with or without me."

Dtimun smiled back. "We will all get out of here alive," he countered. "You will face justice."

"I am a sovereign ruler. You cannot try me in a court."

Dtimun didn't grace the remark with a reply.

Stern straightened. "I hear marching feet," he said. "Reinforcements?"

"I have many troops in other ships," Mangus Lo said pleasantly. "You are mine now, Dtimun."

"Do you think so?" Dtimun's eyes flashed green, just as the door burst open behind him.

Madeline Ruszel could have kissed every medic aboard the *Freespirit* as she watched them gently go to work on the survivors of *Ahkmau* who could be saved. So quietly, so efficiently, they consoled the broken-spirited, the half-dead, the mentally torn. Medics of all races were represented in that crew, and possessed of a dedication rare for the time. Most of them were retired from high-pressure work. They were too old for conventional medicine, so they formed this fraternity of healers, bought a space-going vessel, and became the most famous rescue ship in the three galaxies. Madeline admired them with all her heart.

"How many of them can we save, do you think?" she asked the head surgeon, Lindsey Bagnacdor of Terravega.

The dark-skinned, dark-eyed surgeon shrugged. "There are several hundred who are starved already beyond salvation, despite our sophistication. Another two hundred have minds so completely destroyed that we will never be able to identify them. In forty years of medical practice, I have never seen the likes of this place. Never!"

Madeline nodded. "A nightmare," she agreed. Her eyes went to the spaceport where the *Morcai* was filled with her crew and waiting to be boarded. Most of the camp's inmates had been teleported aboard the *Freespirit* while the battle still raged between Chacon and Mangus Lo's warring forces, and the survivors of the Holconcom. It was impossible to tell who was winning, but the diversion gave the *Freespirit* time to land and evacuate the camp. In the meantime, the rest of the *Morcai* complement found its way aboard, including a grinning Lieutenant Jennings, the communications officer, who had mined the rest of the base's communications network after disabling the primary unit.

Dtimun and Stern and Komak were still missing, however. Jenkins and Higgins were adamant about waiting. Dtimun had commanded them to lift if he wasn't back when the *Freespirit* was ready to depart. It was a direct order, and they meant to obey it.

"We can't risk waiting, Dr. Ruszel," Higgins said apologetically. "By now, Mangus Lo's ship will have realized that primary base communications are out, and he'll have ordered reinforcements here from his ship. If we don't get out now, we could all be recaptured."

"I know, Higgins, but…" she argued sadly.

"We have to get out while we can," he said.

He was only doing what he was told. In all honesty, she couldn't even blame him. But she still procrastinated, even now, hoping to buy just a little more time for Stern and Komak and the commander…

"Dr. Ruszel, we have to go now!" Higgins insisted.

At his side, Jennings listened to the microchip receiver in his ear and grimaced. "It's Abemon," he called to Higgins. "The *kelekoms* are registering an entire fleet of Rojok fighters on the way here!"

Which raised the question of how the *kelekoms* had been hidden from the Rojoks all this time, but she didn't have time to ask, and she could no longer argue her position.

"Okay. I'm on my way," she called. She extended her hand to Bagnacdor. "Thank you for responding so promptly. You must leave now."

"I'm only glad we could be of assistance," he said, smiling. "Our size is our greatest asset in rescue missions like this. Of course, that bulk makes us sluggish, and we can't run very fast. But very few warring cultures try to shoot at us. We have a good reputation."

"The best. If ever I can be of service…"

"When you get too old to be a combat medic, come and see me," he offered. "You'd be an asset. *Bon chance.*"

"And you."

She moved slowly back toward the *Morcai* even as the *Freespirit* signaled to her medics that they had five minutes to teleport the remainder of the survivors aboard. Damn, Higgins, she thought as her eyes scanned the crowded spaceport where battles were still raging, they wouldn't leave you!

"Aren't we even going to blow up the place before we leave?" she asked the young first officer as she paused reluctantly at the hatch to the elevator tube of the mammoth ship. Its coppery hull gleamed like Vegan honey in the first rays of the sunrise.

"Already taken care of, Doc," he said, smiling. "The demolition teams have been busy while you and the rescue medics evacuated the survivors. Everything goes up in atoms when we lift."

She glanced behind her and winced. "Higgins, couldn't we...?"

"Doc, I don't want to leave them, either," he told her gently. "But the C.O. said to lift, and I've got to. You haven't heard yet, but we received a lasergram from HQ. The Centaurian dectat just forced a war vote through the Council and announced its own. We're now officially at war with the Rojok empire, and that includes the entire Centaurian fleet, as well as Tri-Galaxy Fleet forces. That means Chacon will soon be ordered by the Rojok Military Command to stop us from escaping. Maybe he hasn't heard about the war vote of the Tri-Galaxy Council yet, but he will, any minute. I'm sorry. We have to go. Now!"

"Karamesh," she murmured with a weary, sad smile. The thought of the cloned Stern sitting out the war in a prison camp like this was wounding, not to mention the treatment that Dtimun and Komak would receive. It had been a hard day. First, preparing Hahnson's scarred body for urning. Now, giving up what was left of Holt Stern, abandoning him to fate. It had been a very hard day. She turned slowly and made her way to the elevator tube, her heart sagging around her ankles.

"Maddie!" a familiar voice called from nearby. "Wait for us!"

That voice! She whirled, her eyes alight with joy as she saw the three missing officers running toward her. There was someone being carried like a sack of *chovamecks* over Dtimun's broad shoulder.

"Talk about timing!" she exclaimed. "Where were you?"

"In Mangus Lo's flagship," Stern grinned, sweating and gritty faced.

"The sandskimmer would not start, so we had to make our way here on foot," Komak explained with a flash of green eyes.

Madeline glanced at the unconscious form over the Centaurian's shoulder. Her eyes widened as she recognized the dumpy little form in Royal robes. "Mangus Lo?" she exclaimed, disbelieving. "You've got Mangus Lo?"

Dtimun nodded. "Stern and I reluctantly decided to leave him alive to face justice at the hands of the Council."

"An unfortunate set of circumstances force me to contest that decision," came a commanding voice from behind them.

Chacon and six of his men, armed with *chasats,* stood suddenly between the small group and the *Morcai's* elevator tube.

"The war vote from the Council just came over our communications network," Madeline told Dtimun sadly.

"A pity it did not come one day later," Chacon said. "Put Mangus Lo down."

Madeline stepped forward, right in front of the Rojok field marshal's *chasat.* "Before you go any farther, Commander," she told the tall Rojok, "look around you, please. Over there."

Where she pointed, the *Freespirit* medics were loading over a hundred children onto the teleportation mat. Some had limbs missing. Others were so thin, their bones stuck through the flesh. All races were represented in that sad, young group. And the sight of it was enough to turn even a combat medic's stomach.

"Multiply that by several million," she persisted, her eyes steady on the Rojok's face, "and see if your conscience can bear it. Even our own worst races don't target children."

The Rojok's expression was rigid, expressionless. For one long minute, he hesitated. Wavered. Relaxed. He drew in a short breath.

"In exactly five solar minutes," he told Dtimun, "I will hear of the war vote for the first time." He glanced at Madeline with an odd twinkle in his slit eyes. "If I were you, I would run...very fast."

She grinned at him, turned and rushed toward the ship, where the last of her patients was being brought up into the belly of the giant copper-hulled ship.

"I will remember what you have risked for the sake of these wretched survivors," Dtimun told the Rojok field marshal. "As will they."

"Would you have done less, Dtimun of Centauria?" Chacon asked with a knowing smile. "*T'cleemech.*"

"*T'cleemech,* Chacon."

Dtimun turned and carried the unconscious Rojok emperor into the elevator tube. Chacon's men watched with unreadable expressions. It went without saying that they, his personal bodyguards, would have followed him straight into hell if he'd asked them to. They wouldn't betray him to whatever authority replaced the tyrant Mangus Lo in the Rojok government.

Stern paused as he and Komak followed Dtimun. "Commander, if I were you, I'd get my ship the hell out of here," he told Chacon. "In less than two standard minutes, there's going to be a lot of noise and dust where *Ahkmau* once stood."

"An improvement, I would think," Chacon replied, eyeing the mounds of dead inmates that still lay in the red dust.

He turned, commanding and regal, as he led his men quickly toward the Rojok flagship that Mangus Lo had just, unwillingly, vacated.

The *Freespirit* lifted as the vator tubes locked shut on the *Morcai.*

Within seconds, the *Morcai* was airborne. Below it, a chain reaction of explosions sounded on the red desert, sending earth-shattering tremors to the distant chain of mountains beyond.

"Nice of the Rojok field marshal to let us go," Stern commented when they were on the bridge.

"Do not be deceived," Dtimun said from his command chair. "Chacon is first and foremost a soldier. He will honor the plight of the survivors and not, I think, attack the *Freespirit*. We, however, are fair game now. I do not expect the Rojok commander to hold anything back."

"If we can outrun them," Stern said, "we've got a fighting chance."

"That depends on the results of Abemon's survey on the ship's condition. They cannot equal our normal speed, but they have firepower that we lack," Dtimun said quietly. "Abemon, how are we?" he called to the Centaurian engineer.

Abemon looked up from his panel. "It's a miracle that we even made orbit, sir," he replied. "Some of the circuitry is fried. Weaponry's still out." He shook his head wearily. It had been a long day for the engineering and communication officers. "Sir, we lost five engineers and ten techs taking the ship back. I'm that many understrength—and it's a big ship."

"By *Simalichar,* why did you not say so earlier?" Dtimun demanded. His fist hit the intership comm switch on his console. "Personnel!"

"Sir!" came the instant reply.

"Run a check through your database and find me the name of every crewman, human or Centaurian, who has advanced training in ship engineering, regardless of his current assignment aboard ship."

"Yes, sir. It will only take a moment."

"How long do you estimate the repairs will take?" he asked Abemon.

"Impossible to say, sir," Abemon replied apologetically. "These replacement parts we removed from the Rojok ships are inferior at best. We have to adjust them to make them fit, and that takes precious time. I can give you half power now, but that's pushing it."

"I'll want two-thirds in fifteen minutes, engineer, and don't tell me it's impossible," he added when Abemon opened his mouth to protest. "For me, the word does not exist. Weaponry section, report your progress," he called to the Centaurian officer on his right.

The weaponry officer turned from his console. "We're separating the main unit now, Commander. By the time engineering completes its repairs, we can give you one-third firepower," he said proudly.

Dtimun cursed quietly in Centaurian, mumbling something about five soldiers with novapens being able to climb onto the hull and do better than that.

Stern felt the sensors pulse under his fingers at the helmsman's console he was occupying, replacing the Holconcom helmsman who had died on Enmehkmehk, and he scowled as his eyes briefly touched the starmaps. "Rojoks!" he muttered.

Before he could comment further, one of the ship's four *kelekom* operators walked onto the bridge, his *kelekom* transported by clinging to the front of his uniform and glowing a soft green color.

"Commander," the operator said with a salute, "we have detected a wing of Rojok fighters coming after us."

Dtimun's eyes colored a solemn blue as he studied the *kelekom*. He closed his eyes for an instant. When they opened, they were a darker shade. He nodded, and as if he and the *kelekom* had communicated somehow.

"There is another matter," the operator added sadly. "We have lost Koras, and with him the youngest of our *kelekoms*. It is dormant. I think it may not survive."

Dtimun only nodded. "His courage will be noted. Do what you can for the unit."

"Yes, sir." The operator left the bridge.

"As I expected, the truce dissolved only seconds ago, and Chacon's ships are in full pursuit." He glanced at Stern curiously. "How can you read starmaps so well when part of our power is drained and you have no direct link to the charts?"

Stern shrugged. "I learned to fly by instinct. I rarely look at a sensor screen or a starmap. I follow paths I can see in my mind. I suppose I sensed the ships—" He broke off, embarrassed.

Dtimun smiled. "It is how we ourselves navigate, Stern," he replied, "with the help of the *kelekoms*. Cut your speed to sublight and come about to 234 Brichtlar Scale. Let's try evasion first."

"Aye, sir," he said, feeling the surge of power under his hands as he made the adjustments on the console. It was a dream of a ship, he thought, the excitement making his dark eyes shimmer as he felt the mammoth ship respond to his fingers. Pilots spent their lives and careers praying for one fling at the controls of such a precision piece of equipment. It would, most likely, be the last time he ever sat at the controls of a ship, he thought bitterly. Clones weren't admitted to the pilot rolls. The thought took some of the pleasure out of his maneuvers, but he managed to ignore it. Like Komak said, better to flow with the current than to fight against it and go under.

He made the correction quickly, neatly, and the great ship reduced speed. But the engines were sluggish, and the process took much longer than would have been normal.

His eyes went to the sensors. He grinned. "They flew right over us," he laughed.

Dtimun's eyes gave a soft green smile. "Abemon, I've bought you a few more seconds. I expect results."

The young Centaurian nodded. "You'll get them, sir."

Komak came up the access ladder and joined his commander by the main console. "The casualties are managing well, although Madelineruszel is using some very strange words in connection with the Rojok prison guards."

"No doubt. And Lyceria?" Dtimun asked, standing up.

Komak lifted his shoulders in a facsimile of a shrug. "She remains in her compartment. I think she mourns for her brother, Marcon."

"And more, perhaps," the *Morcai*'s commander said quietly, moving to the side of his spool chair.

"Commander!" Stern called. "I'm picking up six Rojok starfighters on my sensors, coming at us sublight on intercept!"

Dtimun whirled. "Abemon?"

"No chance, sir," the engineering officer said in a grim tone. "We've got to have another five minutes, minimum."

"Weaponry!" Dtimun called. "Status?"

"We've got your one-third firepower, sir," the officer replied. "It won't cut through the Rojok force shields, but it might be enough to hold them off until we can do better."

Dtimun sat down in the command chair, deep in thought. "Stern," he said quickly, "cut power to zero."

"Sir?"

"I don't repeat orders on this bridge, Mister!"

"Yes, sir!" Stern said sharply, and complied.

"Divert all unnecessary power to the weaponry units and defensive shields," Dtimun added, his fingers going simultaneously to the intership switch.

"Security!"

"Yes, Commander," came the reply.

"Send two of the Holconcom to the brig. Should the ship be taken, their orders are to kill Mangus Lo."

"They are on the way, Commander."

Dtimun broke the connection with a glance at Stern. "They may recapture this ship, by some miracle," the alien said. "But, by *Simali-char,* Mangus Lo won't live to see it!"

Stern nodded agreement, his eyes going to the starmaps as he tried to unravel the Centaurian's flurry of orders. It was an old strategist's trick, playing helpless to draw an enemy into firing range.

But the *Morcai* didn't have that kind of firepower now. Could Dtimun be trying to buy more time for repairs? But speed wouldn't help, either. They couldn't outrun the Rojoks from a standing start, even with two-thirds engine capability.

"They're coming on the screen," Stern said quietly, his eyes following the colored spheres on his sensor net.

Dtimun's eyes began to smile greenly as the six Rojok fighters moved into position, facing the *Morcai.*

"Sir, there's a message coming in from the Rojok lead ship," Jennings, the communications officer, said.

"Ignore it."

"But, sir, they say we have one minute to..."

Dtimun gave the young human communications officer a single look, silencing him instantly.

Seconds wobbled by like centuries. The bridge was utterly quiet, except for the audible breathing of the crew. Stern kept his eyes locked on his sensors. If only they had enough power to blow those blasted Rojoks out of space! What the devil was Dtimun up to, anyway?

A movement of lights on the screen alerted him. "Commander, they're throwing magnabeams on us!" he said quickly.

"How many?"

"Just the three lead ships."

Dtimun nodded. "Stern, give me half power. Abemon, match the Rojok magnabeams and exert one-third again as much pull against them."

Abemon looked puzzled, but he switched the power on. "Done, sir."

"They're hitting us with three more magnabeams," Stern remarked. "We can't pull away, now."

"I've no intention of trying," Dtimun replied, his elongated eyes still laughing in his golden-skinned face. He leaned back comfortably in his chair. "Weaponry, lock in on all magnabeams, wide scan."

"Locked in, units primed, sir."

"Fire!"

A spreading green light burst from the *Morcai*'s hull, pushing against some invisible force that the eye couldn't see. Stern watched the viewscreen with tensed muscles. Perhaps it was wiser to lose the ship, and Mangus Lo, than be recaptured, he rationalized. His hands gripped the armrests of his chair. He'd expected the alien to put up a fight. This, he reasoned, was suicide. He bit his lip and tried to think of the afterlife as a place of joy...

18

Just as the Rojok ships stopped in space, their green magnabeams barely visible against the black of space, Stern suddenly realized what Dtimun was doing. Even as he watched, the green of the *emerillium* scatterbeams pressed closer and closer to the Rojok vessels.

"They're fighting it, sir," the weaponry officer said.

"Let them," Dtimun replied confidently. "If they release their magnabeams now, they're still finished. Maintain fire."

"Now they're trying to back away. They're doing it!" Jennings said excitedly.

"I'm not deaf, Jennings," Dtimun said with a laughing glance at the young officer. "Abemon, reverse polarity on our scatterbeams."

"Yes, sir. Here goes!"

As Abemon threw the switch, the green light overtook the Rojok ships like a blinding blur of gaseous emeralds. Closer, closer and closer, and Stern held his breath as the Rojoks tried to back away.

Suddenly the viewscreen on his console became a wild sparkle of emerald patterns growing brighter by the second. Then, with a gigantic, silent explosion that hit his eyes like a green sun going nova, the Rojok starfighters...disappeared. There was no sound, except for the faint metallic noises in the *Morcai*'s pressurized interior as pieces of the starfighters flew against the *Morcai*'s hull and scattered off into space.

The ship began to move. Slowly at first, rocking and turning, then picking up speed like a comet and rocketing forward, driving Stern back against his couch.

"Sir, the engines aren't even engaged," Abemon burst out. "I can't hold her back!"

"Neither can I," Stern added over his shoulder. His fingers coaxed the cyberbionic units, but they wouldn't respond. It was as if they felt the dread of the crew and were frozen by it. "She won't respond!"

"Brace for hyperlighting," Dtimun barked into the intercom. "Close crash bulkheads, all personnel maintain crash positions! *Kelekom* units, stand by!"

Stern held on to his chair for all he was worth. On the sensor screen before him, the stars and distant galaxies became a bright, sparkling blur in the center of the screen. His ribs pushed against his lungs with a gravity force that seemed about to crush the life out of him. It was all he could do to breathe, and for an instant he thought he was going to suffocate.

Then, suddenly, he felt lighter than air. The process of living seemed to have slowed to zero. The beating of his heart took hours. His hands moved like they had steel weights attached to them. The breath he drew took forever to inflate his lungs. And, on the sensor screen, space was black except for a pinpoint of light.

Time crawled, with the ship moving in unbelievable velocity under him. Silence. Dead silence on the bridge. The only audible sound now was the high-pitched whine of the ship. A sound not like engines at all, but like infinity. Infinity that was a circle of life and death and life again. Awesome, inevitable, inescapable. It had all happened before. It would all happen again. He closed his eyes.

A harsh, grinding jerk sent him flying to the deck. His eyes opened. Around him, personnel were lying in tangled masses on the deck, just beginning to pick themselves up. Stern shook his head, absently wondering how long he'd been out.

Dtimun caught his arm and pulled him easily to his feet. "Check with all sectors," he called to Komak, "and see what damage we've sustained."

"At once," Komak replied. "But it will be minor," he added with a flash of green eyes.

Dtimun sent him a warning, dark glance and he turned and rushed to his chore.

Stern shook his head as if to clear it. "That, sir, was a close call," he said, shaken.

"The *Morcai* was never built to withstand such forces," Dtimun replied. "It is miraculous, as your race would say, that any of us survived."

"I don't know how fast we were going," Stern said, "but I'd sure as hell like to know what caused it."

"We couldn't have outrun the Rojok fighters," Dtimun told him. "Nor could we have won a battle with our firepower understrength. So I turned the Rojok magnabeams back on their own ships, reversing polarity at the same time. The combination of the explosion and the disrupted magnetic force threw us from one point in space to another—although we did not actually travel through the entire distance. Rather, we rode through a fold of space."

"Our scientists said several hundred years ago that what we just did was impossible," Stern remarked.

The alien's eyes made a green laugh. "Did they not also say that colonization of solar systems beyond your own was impossible?"

Stern frowned. "That strategy you just used is one I've never read about in textdiscs."

"It was never recorded," Dtimun explained. "It was used only once, two centuries ago, by an old-style Centaurian warship."

Stern's eyes narrowed curiously. "What happened to that old-style Centaurian warship, if I might ask?"

Dtimun actually grinned at him. "It blew up."

Before Stern could react, the Holconcom commander returned to his command chair. "All right, Stern, plot our position while the *kelekoms* determine where we are." Even as he spoke, he shot a garble of Centaurian into his ship intercom and received an instant reply. "I've had the *kelekoms* input their data into your terminal," he added, turning to Stern. "Where are we?"

Stern sat down and studied the charts. The breath rushed out of him. "My God," he breathed. "We're less than two parsecs from Trimerius! That's halfway across the galaxy from where we were!"

Dtimun's eyes smiled. "Indeed it is. Take us to Trimerius, Stern. Since your Tri-Galaxy Council had the fortitude to declare war on the Rojok dynasty, perhaps they might even have the stomach to prosecute the prize we bring them in our brig."

"They just might," Stern agreed, understanding that the commander meant Mangus Lo.

But as he considered the landing, he also was faced with the apprehension of facing Lawson with his own story, that he was only a clone of the original Captain Holt Stern. He put it aside firmly. It had been a fascinating ride. It was worth the cost. At least, he'd saved Madeline...

"For the record," he told Dtimun with a smile, "I'd rather have gone to glory in the *Morcai* than go back to Mangus Lo's sandy playpen. But there's just one comment I'd like to make about your strategy, sir."

"Yes?"

"I think you're crazier than an Altairian *kibbit,*" he said. "Sir," he added respectfully.

"So Komak has told me, many times," the Centaurian admitted. "Plot your course and leave over when ready."

"Yes, sir!"

Trimerius was dark except for the diamond sparkle of the spaceport when the *Morcai* penetrated the continent-wide force dome that contained the Tri-Galaxy Fleet's headquarters. The arrival of the Holconcom flagship went unnoticed except by the communication tower and the regular SP night patrol around the sprawling spaceport, where smaller vessels lifted and landed in profusion and much haste, as if an offensive was being mounted.

Mangus Lo, groggy and disguised in a borrowed SSC uniform, was taken from the ship by a full squad of Dtimun's Holconcom under the concealing cover of semidarkness.

Stern watched him exit the ship down on deck three with bitter eyes. It all flashed back in his mind. His capture on the Peace Planet while he was scouting alone. The cloning. The conditioning. The infiltration of the *Bellatrix*'s crew. The destruction of the *Bellatrix* and the transfer to the *Morcai*. The capture by the Rojoks. The confinement. His own betrayal of his men, his flag, his military heritage, his citizenship. Living with what he was now was going to be hard enough, without having to live with what he'd done. His betrayal had killed not only many men, human and Centaurian alike, but it had led to Hahnson's horrible torture and death.

His career was over the minute he stepped off this ship onto Trimerian soil. His stars of rank would be stripped away. If he managed to get off with thirty years in the rimscouts as punishment, he'd still be a clone when he came out. And the military opportunities available to clones, especially those convicted of crimes such as his, were nil.

His heart hanging around his knees, he managed a smile for Madeline Ruszel as she and Komak joined him near the elevator tube.

"Rocky ride, wasn't it?" she asked with a wan smile. "We had our hands full down below. I expect you did, too."

"Abundantly," he agreed. "Did we lose anybody else?"

She shook her head. She drew in a slow breath and flexed her tired shoulders. "Home feels good, doesn't it?"

"Do you really want me to answer that?" he asked with a trace of bitterness that he couldn't conceal. "Never mind. Yes, Ladybones, it's great to be back. For them, especially," he added fervently, watching the medics move the ambutubes out the hatch near the elevator tubes and in a line to the base medical relief station.

Madeline touched his sleeve gently. "I'll stand by you, for what it's worth. That goes without saying, I hope."

He smiled warmly down at her. "Thanks." He drew in a long breath. "I wish Strick were here."

She ground her teeth together. She mustn't cry, she told herself. "Yes," she said in a choked tone. "So do I."

"So this is the Tri-Fleet home planet," Komak said enthusiastically as he joined them. He looked through the transparent skin of the ship to the facilities beyond, domed and glowing in the distance. "I have only seen it in history discs..."

"History discs?" Madeline asked, aghast.

He frowned. "This is not the word? In data discs, then," he said quickly, clearing his throat. "I seem to remember that there is a place of many intoxicants on the base where our men once had glorious disagreements with another set of Holconcom in years past. It is still here?"

"Of course!" Madeline said, laughing. "But I thought you people were forbidden to fight, Komak."

"Only with physically inferior outworlders," he corrected. He sighed. "Sadly that is now going to be the case, with our microcyborgs in place once more." He brightened. "But among ourselves we may do what we like as long as the commander does not see us." His eyes sparkled green as he looked at the humans. "When we have finished at the debriefing, perhaps we three might seek refreshments together?"

A spasm of dark pain washed over Stern's swarthy face. Clones weren't allowed in the base bar. And he, Hahnson and Madeline had always headed straight for it after missions away...

"*Maliche,* why are you still here?" Dtimun growled from behind them. "The crew was dismissed for debriefing five of your minutes ago. Come! Lawson is almost as impatient as I am, and we report directly to him."

"To Lawson?" Madeline burst out as she followed the men into the elevator tube. "But we've never reported to the admiral!"

"Have you had a reply from Tnurat Alamantimichar?" Komak asked quickly.

"From the president of the dectat," Dtimun corrected irritably. "You are surely aware that the emperor and I do not speak. An envoy is being sent to escort Lyceria back to Memcache. I offered her the freedom of the consulate here, but she prefers to wait in the privacy of her quarters aboard the *Morcai.*"

Madeline sighed as they walked toward the waiting military skimmers. "How soon do I go before the Military Tribunal?" she asked Dtimun.

"That was my question, too," Stern added solemnly.

"That is something I intend to discuss with Lawson," the commander said, without looking at them.

They exchanged puzzled glances. But nobody spoke until the skimmers had deposited them outside the towering liquid crystal walls of the Tri-Galaxy Fleet Headquarters building.

All four of them were transported by quick lift to Lawson's airy office, where they stood at rigid attention while the admiral studied them.

Lawson, his white hair gleaming in the light of the glowing walls, stared at Stern blankly for a long time, just shaking his head. "I still can't believe it," he said gruffly. "I saw your body on the discs the rescue mission recorded. The injuries were such that you couldn't have survived!"

Stern took a deep breath. Now was the time. He couldn't put it off any longer. "Sir," he began respectfully, "that body was…"

"A clone," Dtimun said for him, his eyes narrowed as they met Stern's, daring him to say another word. He hesitated. "You are aware that the Rojoks have refined the process of cloning to the point that memories and personality are transferred instantaneously into the reconstructed subject? They cloned Stern, but had the misfortune to shoot the wrong man. Their mistake. The body they left on Terramer was the cloned Stern."

Lawson was confused. "But you were taken prisoner?"

"Yes," Dtimun said easily. "Chacon arrived with his personal bodyguard and suspended the torture of Dr. Hahnson. In the subsequent confusion, we liberated ourselves and retook the *Morcai*. In the process, we apprehended Mangus Lo. He is in the stockade as we speak."

Lawson just stared at him, dumbfounded. That wasn't the story he'd heard from one of the ambassadors.

Madeline and Stern looked as if they'd just been thrown headfirst into ice water. They shared an incredulous glance.

Lawson frowned. "I understood that *Ahkmau* was destroyed," he began.

"Indeed it was," Dtimun added confidently. "The *Freespirit* liberated the bulk of the inmates, we accommodated those of our crewmen who could be saved. We also lifted the survivors from Terramer, and the Jaakob Spheres." He raised his chin. "Chacon made the rescue possible, although once the war vote was known to him, he pursued us diligently."

"A gentleman, is Chacon," Lawson pronounced. "A true gentleman. But a formidable enemy and the war has only just begun."

"We have Mangus Lo," Dtimun said. "Perhaps a truce may be constructed."

Lawson shook his head. "Mangus Lo has a nephew," he said irritably. "Han Cho. He assumed power the instant Mangus Lo's capture made it back to Enmehkmehk. He announced his intentions over a broad laserband width. He says the Rojoks still need room to expand their starving billions and they aren't going to agree to any peace treaty that doesn't guarantee them ownership of the Binarius System." He glanced at them. "It goes without saying that the Binarius System is the ancestral home of the Altairian Triumvirate, and she isn't willing to donate it to the Rojoks."

"They also claim the Tupari biosphere," Dtimun added.

"Yes. Without it, the Tri-Fleet would be forced to barter with the Rojoks for *emerillium* deposits. We'll never agree to that. So. It's still war. And I remind you Chacon will fight no less fiercely for Han Cho than he did, in the beginning, for Mangus Lo."

"Tnurat Alamantimichar led the war vote, we understand," Dtimun queried.

"Yes, he did. He and his government are in mourning for the death of his only son," Lawson replied, curiously aware that Dtimun avoided meeting his eyes. "But the knowledge that his daughter is safe has brought a little peace to him. He's agreed to attach the Holconcom to my command," he added, watching the alien commander closely.

Dtimun raised both eyebrows. "Attach? I interpret the act to mean that you may request our assistance," he said with pure arrogance.

Lawson glared at him. "I knew it was going to be a fight to the death. Listen here, young man…!"

"It is you who are the young man, Jeffrye, being some five years my junior," Dtimun said with a flash of green eyes.

"Yes, I heard from your medics that you went into the *dylete* and the whole unit protected you while Ruszel operated, before they killed Hahnson. Hell of a shame about Hahnson. But at least we still have Ruszel and Stern. Now about a new ship," he began.

"That will not be necessary," Dtimun said easily. "I intend to add Stern and Ruszel, as well as the rest of the surviving *Bellatrix* crew, to the Holconcom."

Madeline stiffened. She was in line for the position of medical chief of staff. It was just beginning to occur to her that her career was in the process of being blown to hell by this Centaurian headhunter.

"Now just a damned minute here," she flashed, her auburn hair glowing in the light.

"Bataashe!" Dtimun snapped at her, his eyes fighting both hers and Stern's. "Remember to whom you speak, Madam!"

She looked as if she'd tried to swallow a *Gresham* whole, even as she stiffened into a military posture. Her green eyes made threats that Dtimun simply ignored. Komak's eyes were glittering green, as if he was enjoying the whole episode.

"Yes, just a damned minute here," Lawson appropriated Madeline's opening. "You can't transfer my personnel across military lines, even if you are Tri-Fleet allies!"

"Oh, but I can," Dtimun replied. "The combination of humans and Centaurians in my *Morcai* Battalion will make a statement about the adaptability of command. If the other governments see that our races can successfully merge on a warship, it will inspire others to work harder at getting along together."

"But the emperor," Lawson protested.

Dtimun's eyes flashed green. "It will make him furious," he said smugly. "Especially when he hears of the addition of a human female to my crew. In the history of the Holconcom, there has never been a female aboard a Centaurian warship."

"He'll have you killed!" Lawson protested. "Court-martialed! Banished!"

"He cannot. I command the Holconcom. He has no authority over it, or me."

"I hope you know what you're doing." Lawson sighed as he turned to Dtimun, a grimace tugging at his mouth. He shook his head. "All right. I'll approve the transfers. But if the emperor comes in here looking for blood, I'm sending him right over to collect yours!"

Stern and Madeline stood like statues as what the alien was saying finally got through to them.

"We're…being attached to the Holconcom," Stern said. "Both of us?"

"Of course," Dtimun said, scowling impatiently. "And immediately. In case the two of you have forgotten, we are still at war against an empire with Chacon at the head of its armies. We destroyed *Ahkmau,* but some facsimile will certainly replace it. We also captured Mangus Lo, but not the bureaucracy that supported his empire. The war will be long, and each part of the Tri-Galaxy must fight to win it." He turned to Lawson. "I need those orders cut now, Jeffrye, giving me possession of the *Bellatrix*'s surviving crew."

"I'll whip them out," Lawson agreed, moving back to his desk. He paused, pulling out a tiny cube of personal effects. "Stern, these are yours, I believe. Would you like to have them?"

Stern reached out and took the cube. In it was, among other effects, a piece of blue velvet ribbon. As he took it out and held it in his hand, he remembered a promise he'd made to his crew and vowed to fulfill it as soon as possible—at the same time he informed them that they'd been shanghaied by this alien tyrant here, and appropriated into the Holconcom. He doubted there would be any fuss, however.

Then it dawned on him that Dtimun was sparing his career by the move. He would still have his old status. But he would command even more respect, as a member of the galaxy's most notorious and feared military authority. Incredulously, he gaped at the alien, whose eyes smiled at him.

"Blame yourself, Mister," Dtimun told him. "The idea of a *Morcai* Battalion had never crossed my mind."

Stern tried to speak, with Lawson's voice on the interbase communications band deep and slow in the office around them. But he couldn't manage the words. His eyes met Madeline's as if in apology, but she was still glaring at Dtimun with venom in her whole look.

Dtimun glanced at her and smiled. "There will be compensations, Madam."

"Sir?" she asked curtly.

But Lawson was off the band, smiling. "Their transfers are in Operations now and being lasered to your ship. What have you got planned, can I just ask that before you rush off and disrupt my whole battle plan?" he added, glaring at Dtimun.

"Your battle plan will self-destruct at the beginning of every encounter," Dtimun replied calmly.

"Don't change the subject. There's something else, too," he added worriedly. "We've had a complaint already from the Terravegan senators. There was a spacing before your ship was captured, an SSC noncom named Declan Muldoon…"

Dtimun's eyes twinkled. "Komak?" he said.

Komak went to the sliding door, peered out it and motioned.

"Declan Muldoon, reporting as ordered, sir!" the Irishman saluted with a grin, while Stern and Madeline gasped. "The commander here had me disguised as a Centaurian and put in a stasis tube. When we were captured, I hid the *kelekoms* and stashed myself in a, well we could call it a crawlspace, where the Rojoks' scans couldn't detect me."

Dtimun shrugged. "An example was required to keep the humans in line," he told Lawson. "I had one of my men and one of Stern's stage a confrontation, so that I could deal with the problem before it cost lives. My officer was given a drug, which allowed him to feign death, after which he was sent back on duty in another sector. Muldoon was 'spaced' but in a transparent survival suit that was not apparent to the spectators. Jeffrye, no one yet has been advised of Muldoon's survival, or my officer's. I have transferred them both to the engineering depot on Altair to keep the secret—at least until the two units are more comfortably united."

Lawson just shook his head, laughing.

Declan was sent to debriefing, winking at Madeline and Stern as he exited the office. "We dead men will do our best to keep the Tri-Fleet ships flying, sir," he added cheekily to Dtimun on the way out. "Even if we have to do it on Altair!"

"Humans," Dtimun said. "They are a fascinating race," he added.

"Which brings me back to my former question, about your plans,"

Lawson began again. "I know you don't have the first idea of how to belong to a fleet and coordinate battle strategies, and I don't have any real authority over the Holconcom, but since you're stealing two of my best officers and some talented SSC techs, I do feel that I have some rights!"

Dtimun's eyes gave a green laugh. "I will consider the request," he told the irritated old soldier.

"While you're considering it, you might give me some suggestions on how to break this to Clinton Ruszel," he added heavily. "He's already been in here once, assuring me that nobody could capture you unless it was part of your strategy…" He stopped. "How the hell were you captured, anyway? And what's this I hear about a spy infiltrating your crew?"

"Goodbye, Jeffrye," Dtimun said quickly, motioning his officers out the door. It closed on Jeffrye Lawson's last question.

"Outside, double stride," Dtimun called to them, leading the way, "before he can ask any more embarrassing questions."

They were outside, under the semidark cover of night, where two moons drifted lazily above the planet, one red and one glowing white. Moga trees made sinister shadows over the hypoturf as the officers made their way toward the base recreation hall.

"I was in line to be base medical chief of staff! I'll never forgive you," Madeline growled furiously. "Not if I live to be two hundred!"

"Madam, we have just survived one battle, must we fight another now?" Dtimun asked in mock weariness as he held them up just outside the officer's club.

"Sorry, Maddie," Stern said. "I'll forgive you, sir, on the spot. I'm more grateful than I can tell you. But, why?"

Dtimun pondered that question silently, as the din from inside the club reached outside with the lure of music and gamevids and laughter. "Why," he asked finally, "do you carry a piece of blue velvet ribbon?"

"I promised never to tell," he began.

"You promised to tell the men," Madeline argued.

"I promised to tell them *about* it," he corrected with a grin. "It's blue, made of velvet, 5.2 centimeters long and six years old."

"The woman who wore it in her hair was a physician," Dtimun said quietly, "who threw herself in front of a *chasat* to save two children. A medal was awarded to her posthumously, and received by you as her commanding officer," Dtimun replied, folding his arms across his broad chest. "You buried the medal with her. Now you and Ruszel— and Hahnson, when he was alive—pass the ribbon back and forth among you as an accolade."

"How did you know that?" Stern asked huskily.

Dtimun only smiled mysteriously. "I have attached you and your crew to the Holconcom as a measure of respect for your courage. You would have been discarded by your insane society because you were a clone. I wanted the entire complement, which seems to me the most capable of your entire military. Lawson will believe that your clone died on Terramer. And so will everyone else in the Tri-Fleet."

"That still doesn't explain why I got transferred to the *Morcai* Battalion, too," Madeline grumbled. "You didn't even ask!"

He raised an eyebrow. "I didn't have to," he said meaningfully and with a look that made her cheeks flush.

"My career in the SSC is gone forever," she muttered. "I was in line for medical chief of staff, I had plans, I had—"

"Madam, will you cease and desist for just one moment?" Dtimun interrupted as he glanced toward the door of the officer's club, where Komak had just entered and was now nodding in a conspiratorial manner. He looked down at her. "I have something for you. In recompense."

"Something, for me?" she stammered, surprised.

"For both of you," he replied solemnly. He glanced at Komak and motioned to him. And then, he moved aside as a second figure stepped out onto the hypoturf. First in shadow, then into the light of the two moons. The husky figure was suddenly outlined in light. It was smiling.

"Oh, my God!" Madeline whispered brokenly.

"This is...a hell of a way—" Stern broke off, choking on emotion.

They moved, all three at once, together. Arms opening, then closing. Heads touching. Bodies closing together. Tears rolling down cheeks that were forbidden to know tears. Voices husky with emotion that all the tortures of *Ahkmau* hadn't been able to drag out of them, suddenly loosened unashamedly, while the two Centaurians stood quietly, watching.

"Strick! Oh, Strick!" Madeline sobbed against the physician's broad shoulder.

"You son of a...!" Stern growled affectionately.

Dr. Strick Hahnson's clone chuckled as his big arms clasped his two friends to his side. "God, it's good to see you two reprobates again!" he said. "Komak brought me back from a couple of cells while the rest of you were liberating the camp. The C.O. hid me out with Muldoon in the hold on the way back. He said he was going to need a surprise to keep Maddie from landing in the brig. I guess I see what he meant, now." He smiled at her. "And I thought I was going to end up alone with the Holconcom and the rest of our crew. It just wouldn't have been the same, without you two!"

Madeline turned a red-eyed, tear-streaked face up to Dtimun's, and everything she felt was there, naked, in her mind for him to read. She was the only one of the three who knew about his psychic abilities, a secret she would gladly carry to her grave after this joyful reunion.

He read that, all of it, in her eyes. And he smiled. "Come," he said to the three humans. "We have just enough time for an intoxicating beverage before we lift."

Komak came to join them. "Am I not the best keeper of secrets in the three galaxies?" he bragged. "And I said nothing!"

"You're a prince," Stern told him.

Komak looked warily at Dtimun, whose raised eyebrows and hard glare made him shake himself mentally.

"It's a human expression," Madeline told Komak. "You'll get used to them."

"You know, I think I will," Komak agreed.

"Now, about Muldoon," Madeline began.

Dtimun held up his hand. "I refuse to divulge any more command secrets in an unsecured location," he said. "I must try to find a new *kelekom* operator before we lift."

"That will take skill," Komak remarked. "They are rare, minds that can endure the joining."

The three humans burst ahead of them into the officer's club, to be greeted with waves and cheers and, then, catcalls. Nobody knew that Stern and Hahnson were clones. Madeline was certain that nobody would ever know, except Dtimun, Komak and Stern and herself. It would be the best-kept secret of the war. And, she had to admit, getting Strick back in any form was worth the sacrifice of her career advancement. She wouldn't admit that serving aboard Dtimun's ship was going to be invigorating, dangerous and exciting. But he probably knew, just the same.

"Ruszel, you fractured my wrist last time. Now it's my turn!" an SSC pilot from another unit was yelling.

"Oh, yeah?" she replied. "Come here, you second-cousin to a space fungus, and I'll fracture the other one for you!"

Dtimun glanced past Komak at the humans and smiled softly. "It will be a challenge, combining these crews."

Komak chuckled. "She is everything I expected her to be," he began.

Dtimun held up a hand and his eyes darkened. "Careful!"

"Very well. But she may sustain a fracture. I should assist her," Komak remarked.

Dtimun's eyes narrowed. "You have twice the strength of the humans," he pointed out.

Komak took a small device, lifted it through his jet-black hair and handed it to the Holconcom commander. "There. All my microcyborgs are in your keeping. Madelineruszel, I will save you!" he yelled as he darted through the open sliding door into the officer's club.

Dtimun stared down at the glowing microcyborgs in his golden palm, looked around him, sighed and walked into the building. The humans weren't the only problem he was going to face in the months ahead, he considered, watching Komak bound above and into a group of spacers from a rival SSC ship.

But then, he assured himself, the *Morcai* Battalion was going to be the pride of the fleet one day. He glanced at the communidisc in his hand and scowled. This was something he didn't want to have to share with his officers just yet. After their ordeal, they did deserve a night of fun. This new problem could wait, at least until the next day.

He walked through the open door into the boisterous club, looking for his officers, his eyes twinkling with green lights as he spotted them.

"Hey, Commander," Stern yelled happily. "Catch!"

A tall, thin crewman from the rival ship came flying through the air, directly at Dtimun's nose.

The startled crewman was hanging from one large golden hand as the sliding door closed.

GLOSSARY

Ahkmau: The Rojok prison complex to which enemy soldiers are transported. It is located on one of the moons of the Rojok home world, Enmehkmehk, and features some of the most diabolical tortures known to sentient beings. No one who enters its gates ever leaves. It is the pet project of the Rojok emperor, Mangus Lo, a madman who uses terror to control the populace and advance his conquest of new planetal resources for his overpopulated home world.

Altairian: A blue-skinned race noted for its stoicism, allied to the Tri-Galaxy Federation.

Ambutubes: Cylinders in which wounded and dead are placed for transport; operates on zero-point energy and can be floated to a ship through remote control.

AVBD: Audio visual bio detectors, placed in corridors and individual units aboard the *Morcai* to monitor the interior of the ship against sabotage.

The *Bellatrix*: One ship of a fleet of SSC ships, this one captained by Holt Stern, a Terravegan national. The ship's medical chief of staff is Lieutenant. Commander Madeline Ruszel, who specializes in Cularian medicine. Her colleague, Dr. Strick Hahnson, is a specialist in human physiology and pharmacology. Both Ruszel and Hahnson, like Stern, are Terravegans, born on far-flung colonies whose settlers originated hundreds of years ago in the Sol system, on planet Earth. A planetal catastrophe reduced the human population to less than ten thousand souls; but just before it occurred, the colony ships had embarked from the international space station in orbit above Earth and were weeks away by the time the disaster occurred.

Benaski Port: The only neutral port in the vicinity of the Tri-Galaxy Fleet headquarters planet, Trimerius; listed on star charts as a favorite haunt of renegades, outcasts and deserters, with many pleasure domes, bars, gambling emporiums and a small unit of ship outfitters who can make minor repairs on space-going vessels. Notorious for trafficking in Dacerian women and various hallucinogenic substances. No extradition treaties with any outworlders, thus a haven for those fleeing law enforcement.

Berdache: A third sex of Terravegans who prefer their own gender as mates. They may marry at the pleasure of the state. They are also permitted to serve in the military. The term berdache is reportedly rooted in Native American language on ancient Earth.

Breeders: The Terravegan state has evolved into two classes of citizens. One class is assigned to the military, another is assigned to breeding camps. Breeders are males and females considered ineffectual for military service. They are allowed to marry. They are placed on farms, where they are given every comfort and luxury so long as they produce eggs and sperm for artificial breeding. They are not allowed to know their children or have contact with them. They are not permitted to have children in the natural manner, but can cohabit and bond for life. Other than the duty of aiding procreation, they are permitted to work in factories or agricultural communities or in support industries. They may also opt for political service. Another class of citizens allied to breeders is charged with the training and education of the children up until age nine, at which time they are given over to their military units. Children are taught to bear allegiance only to the state, and that military service is the greatest honor available to a Terravegan. They are not clones, but they are discouraged from any fraternization with other children, especially children who will be selected as breeders. Their education begins at birth, with implanted technology and physical conditioning a daily chore.

Centaurian: A misnomer deriving from first contact between humans and people of the Cehn-Tahr system near the Eridani solar system. They were at first believed to be natives of the Centauri system 4.3 light-years from earth. A fleet of colony ships from ancient Earth went off course due to a glitch in the programming that went undiscovered since the crew and complement were in cryosleep. The ships entered an unstable area of space, which "folded" into a system many parsecs from the Sol system. When they woke, it was to the sight of an alien vessel approaching them. The Cehn-Tahr boarded the lead colony ship and the captain assumed that they had reached their destination of the

Centauri system. By the time the mistake was discovered, humans were used to calling these natives Centaurians and the name stuck. The Centaurians guided them to a planet in a nearby system that had the basic necessities of life—light, heat, water, breathable air—and introduced them to the natives who lived on the planet. They were accepted easily and blended into the existing human colony, all of whom were vegetarians, since there were no animals on the planet. They intermarried with the locals. In time, they colonized other systems, and the race as a whole became known as Terravegan.

The Centaurians are humanoid, but their race traces its evolutionary roots to a species of giant cat, the galot, which was found on Memcache, the home planet of the Cehn-Tahr. They are one race only, and their features include golden skin, jet-black hair and elongated cat's eyes that change color to mirror mood. Their ears, nose, mouth, etcetera are exactly like any human's, and they do not have either tails or fur. There is a narrow ribbon of fur that lies along the length of the spinal cord, a vestigial racial trait that is not visible, and that is never shown to outworlders.

Cehn-Tahr have two system-wide military units: the regular space navy and the elite Holconcom, which is the commando force, feared by other races. Women do not serve in their military, preferring to use their talents in the political and social arenas. Each Centaurian comes from a specific Clan, which is part of the individual's social status. The commander of the Holconcom, Dtimun, has never given the name of his Clan. He is the only member of the Holconcom who is not a clone. Among the Cehn-Tahr, clones have the same status as any normally born member of the society.

Chacon: Field Marshal and commander of the Rojok military, and one of the most famous of warriors in his own right. Unlike his emperor, he is an honorable and compassionate being, respected even by his enemies. He will have no part of terrorism and is openly critical of the death camp *Ahkmau*. He believes in the war, because the Rojoks are so overpopulated that they have no more room in their dynasty to search for natural resources. Tri-Galaxy politics made it impossible for them to petition for the right to colonize in the New Territory, so war was the only recourse. But he hates Mangus Lo's policies and refuses to send prisoners to the death camps. He is so popular with the Rojok population that the Rojok tyrant is afraid to openly oppose or criticize him.

Clones: They can be created in less than a solar day among the Rojok. The process takes longer for Terravegans and Centaurians. However, in the human colonies, clones have no official status and are used for spare parts. They are treated as subhuman. Not so among Centaurians, where they are given full official status.

Cularian medicine: A specialty of exobiology that deals with Centaurian and Rojok physiology and pharmacology. Until Ruszel began serving with the Holconcom, it was largely theoretical, because few humans had ever seen either a Centaurian or a Rojok, since the Terravegan forces were headquartered on Trimerius, in the human colonies. Not until the Rojoks invaded neutral planetary systems and then destroyed a trial colony did the Rojoks and Centaurians come into contact with humans.

Dacerius: A desert planet famous for its yomuth races, silver work and exotic women, many of whom are captured and sold by slavers. Famous, also, for its bureaucracy, which deals in doublespeak and exasperation. Many nomadic tribes, most of whom have no affiliation with the central government. Tribal leaders are still chosen by combat.

Dtimun: Commander in Chief of the Holconcom, the galaxy's most elite commando unit. Except for its leader, the entire unit is made up of clones. The commander has led the unit for many years and is greatly respected not only by his own men, but by allied commands, as well. He and the Centaurian emperor, Tnurat Alamantimichar, are enemies; no one knows why. He has never revealed to which Clan his family claimed kinship, in a world where Clan affiliation was honor itself. He does not like humans, especially the Terravegan doctor Ruszel, who thinks of him as a barbarian because he objects to having a woman in a combat unit. Ruszel was once the captain of an elite SSC Amazon squad, the Amazons (all female) being one of the most respected and courageous of the combat elite.

Dylete: Centaurians have two hearts. There is only one heart at birth. Over a period of years approaching middle age, a new heart begins to form in concert with the original organ. At the time of half-life, approximately eighty-four to eighty-eight years of age, the first heart stops functioning and the new heart accepts the burden from the old one. The old heart is then reabsorbed into the body. Sometimes this process of changeover fails, and the patient dies. A Centaurian in his eighties is comparable to a thirty-four-year-old human male.

Emerillium: A crystal that, in its refined form, has electrical and magnetic properties, first used as a power source by the Cehn-Tahr, the technology was subsequently shared with the human military under treaty.

Enmehkmehk: The home planet of the Rojok dynasty. One of its moons contains the notorious prison complex *Ahkmau,* which translates as "place of tortures."

Galot: A huge feral cat found originally on Memcache. Reports of them have been noted on a few colony planets, probably from kittens illegally transported as pets.

Great Galaxy War: Decades ago, a group of arms smugglers, tech producers and anarchists formed an alliance and secretly induced various governments to attack other governments after "incidents of terror" provoked public opinion against former allies. The Centaurians and the Terravegans joined forces, along with the Altairians and Jebobs, to combat the growing totalitarian states that were replacing republics. Eventually, alliances would be formed with governments throughout the galaxy and, when the war inevitably spread to two adjacent galaxies through the time-warp technological advances, other races joined the proponents of freedom and formed the Tri-Galaxy Federation and the Tri-Galaxy Fleet. A good portion of the original aggressors were captured and their ships confiscated. The rest fled into exile. The political wing of the Federation is the Tri-Galaxy Council, headquartered on Trimerius.

Gresham: A weapon powered by *emerillium* technology that uses a cartridge to shoot a cutting beam of high-intensity modulated energy at an enemy. Standard issue in the SSC.

Holconcom: The most elite, and feared, commando force in the three civilized galaxies. Created by the Centaurian emperor, Tnurat Alamantimichar, and strengthened by secret nanotechnology called mi-crocyborgs, the Holconcom is the vanguard in any battle. It is under the sole command of its leader—at present, Dtimun—and even the emperor himself may not command it. The Centaurians who serve in the unit are all clones, except for the commander, and their strength and method of combat are legendary. Few humans have ever seen them fight. They sport high-collared red uniforms. They can be attached to an ally military only with the consent of their leader, and they are difficult to command. Their leader's contempt for protocol and chain of command is well-known, as well as his refusal to follow orders. The Holconcom operate behind enemy lines, creating havoc and cutting lines of communication, as well as seeking out supply and communications networks, which are then targeted for attack. They are allowed forbidden technology that enhances speed and weaponry and is unknown to outworlders.

Hyperglas: A synthetic material that resembles glass but has the strength of steel, widely used in terraforming projects and architecture.

Jaakob Spheres: An orb containing many smaller orbs that preserve in stasis the DNA of all member Tri-Galaxy Federation races, as well as cellular specifications for exotic weaponry native to those cultures. A true prize for the Rojoks who capture them, except that the orbs are transcribed in Old High Martian, an ancient human tongue, of which the Rojoks know nothing. The orbs were in transit on a diplomatic observation tour to the Peace Planet, Terramer, just before the Rojoks attacked the planet, killed many of the colonists and one of the Centaurian observers (a young son of the Centaurian emperor) and kidnapped both the diplomatic observers and the Spheres. Among their captives is Lyceria, daughter of the Centaurian emperor.

Jebob: A member race of the Tri-Galaxy Federation. Offshoots of the Altairian race, they are also blue-skinned.

Kelekoms: A sentient race of energy beings who can attach themselves to host bodies and share information psychically. Through an ancient treaty with the Cehn-Tahr, they send emissaries to the Holconcom and host Centaurian diplomats on their home world. Only four emissaries are allowed to serve with the Holconcom. They bond with their hosts until death. Usually, due to their longevity, the hosts die long before they do—so a new host is offered in place of one who is killed in combat or dies of natural causes. The *kelekoms* are extremely susceptible to alien bacteria and have to be kept in sterile fields aboard the Holconcom ship, *Morcai*.

Komak: Dtimun's second in command of the Holconcom, an enigmatic and charming Centaurian who is overly curious and has a howling sense of humor that frequently exasperates his commanding officer. But on the front lines, he is brave and formidable. He is also very mysterious and enigmatic, and is fascinated with humans.

Lawson, Admiral Jeffrye: Leader of the Tri-Galaxy Fleet, composed of Terravegan, Altairian and Jebob military, but also the authority over any ally military seconded to the fleet in time of war. An old battle horse who is known for his bad temper and his soft heart. Winner of the Legion of Honor, the fleet's highest award, in the Great Galaxy War thirty years ago.

Lightsteds: Secret Centaurian technology that controls the rate of flow of *emerillium* power banks, much like control rods in a nuclear reactor.

Mangus Lo: Leader of the Rojok dynasty, a small misshapen Rojok who poisoned his uncle and proclaimed himself emperor, supported by a group of bloodthirsty militants who rushed in to silence any detractors. He imposes terror to control the Rojok population. It was he who constructed *Ahkmau,* first used to house political prisoners and then to house enemy aliens.

Memcache: Home planet of the Centaurian Empire.

Mental Neutering: The Terravegan military is mentally neutered for service, so that males, females and berdache may shower, sleep and fight together with no sexual distraction. The process is chemical and irreversible. Cadets are chosen from children in the breeder colonies for traits that enhance combat abilities. Most cadets are initiated into military school at the age of nine. Type of service and specialties are chosen for them. They serve until they are of retirement age, at which time they may specify a vocation they wish to pursue. This is usually at the age of sixty, although many officers are allowed to continue to serve if their abilities are considered necessary to the state. Military may not marry. In the event that the neutering does not "take" completely, there is a statute that requires the death penalty for any fraternization between members of the military. The Centaurian government also invokes the death penalty for any fraternization between their soldiers and other races.

Microcyborgs: Implants, nanotechnology, which greatly enhance strength and endurance. Secret Centaurian technology. Usually implanted in the hair.

Milish Cone: A pocket-size water synthesizer.

Morcai: A legendary group of alien warriors who in ages past warred with a vastly superior force, and through tactics, strategy and sheer ferocity won a resounding victory. The flagship of the Holconcom is named for them: The *Morcai*.

Rigellians: A race of small humanoids descended from reptiles, with pale yellow skin and slit pupils. They are distant cousins of the Rojoks (who also have traces of reptilian DNA but deny any link to reptilian ancestors).

Rojok: An alien species in the Cularian classification of humanoids. Rojoks are one race, with reddish skin, thin mouths, slit eyes that are usually yellow or brown, and blond hair. Only officers are allowed to wear their hair long. The Rojok were a peaceful race until the Great Galaxy War, when they suffered at the hands of the renegades and were forced to study combat techniques and remake their military. They are now a military culture, having forsaken the arts in their determination never to be occupied by an alien force again. They have scientists, but are known to use spies to steal innovative technology from their enemies. They are led by an emperor, Mangus Lo, a Rojok who took power during the Great Galaxy War when he and his corps of terror troops protected the capital from being captured by the enemy. Now he rules with terror, using fear of imprisonment to keep the public in line. Every Rojok must give ten years to military service, although women are not permitted to serve; they are considered property, and the former royalty among the Rojoks are confined in camps. The system is supposed to be egalitarian, but Mangus Lo lives a life of incredible luxury and decadence, as do his ministers and bodyguards. The economy is based on military production, and property is owned by the state alone. Few dissidents are ever lucky enough to escape the military spies.

Spacing: A fatal walk in space without a space suit.

SSC: Strategic Space Command, an elite combat unit under the auspices of the Terravegan government, seconded to the Tri-Galaxy Fleet based on the planet Trimerius. Holt Stern's ship, the *Bellatrix,* was part of the SSC Fleet.

Terravega: The first and only human colony from Earth established outside the Sol solar system. Now established in many other colonies on far-flung planets. The original colony site is referred to as Terra-vega, and the systems that it populated are known, collectively, as the Terravegan Colonies.

Trimerius: A planet in the Alpha Trimeri system. It is the headquarters of the Tri-Galaxy Fleet and home planet of the exobiological and human life sciences complex, which also boasts one of the finest medical centers in existence. The spaceport covers several square acres of land and is bordered by barracks for the military personnel stationed on the base. Not conducive to human life in its original state, the planet has been terraformed by the addition of many city-size hyperglas domes. The weather is controlled. The vegetation is very alien.

Vegan: The Meg-Vegan colonies are near the New Territory. Vegans are very tall and have light green skin. They are notorious pacifists.

Wimbat: A small, winged mammal found on Celeb IV that hibernates for two-year periods.

Wrist Scanner: Dr. Madeline Ruszel's medical kit is embedded in her left forearm, in such a way that it is wired to her own nervous system and uses it as a power source. It contains a minibank of electronically linked instruments, along with a modem, and a minisynthesizer that can produce a limited amount of drugs in the field. With it, she can read vital signs, do surgery, contact any linked medical facility for assistance and even transfer patient information across the galaxy. The unit has a cover that mimics human flesh, so when it is not in use, it is not noticeable.

Yomuth: A giant rodent, found on Dacerius. They can go for two weeks without water in the deep deserts and they can run like the wind. If attacked, they fight standing on their hind legs, using their thick, sharp claws as weapons. They also bite. Many Dacerians race them at meets held throughout the year among nomadic tribesmen.